This volume contains INU-YASHA PART 6 #8 through
INU-YASHA PART 6 #12 in their entirety.

STORY AND ART BY
RUMIKO TAKAHASHI

ENGLISH ADAPTATION BY
GERARD JONES

Translation/Mari Morimoto
Touch-Up Art & Lettering/Wayne Truman
Cover Design/Hidemi Sahara
Layout/Sean Lee

Editor/Julie Davis
Editor-in-Chief/Hyoe Narita
Publisher/Seiji Horibuchi
VP of Sales and Marketing/Rick Bauer

Printed in Canada

Published by Viz Communications, Inc.
P.O. Box 77010 • San Francisco, CA 94107
www.viz.com • store.viz.com • www.animerica-mag.com

10 9 8 7 6 5 4 3 2 1
First printing, September 2002

INU-YASHA GRAPHIC NOVELS TO DATE:

INU-YASHA VOL. 1
INU-YASHA VOL. 2
INU-YASHA VOL. 3
INU-YASHA VOL. 4
INU-YASHA VOL. 5
INU-YASHA VOL. 6
INU-YASHA VOL. 7
INU-YASHA VOL. 8
INU-YASHA VOL. 9
INU-YASHA VOL. 10
INU-YASHA VOL. 11
INU-YASHA VOL. 12

VIZ GRAPHIC NOVEL

INU-YASHA
A FEUDAL FAIRY TALE™

VOL. 12

STORY AND ART BY

RUMIKO TAKAHASHI

CONTENTS

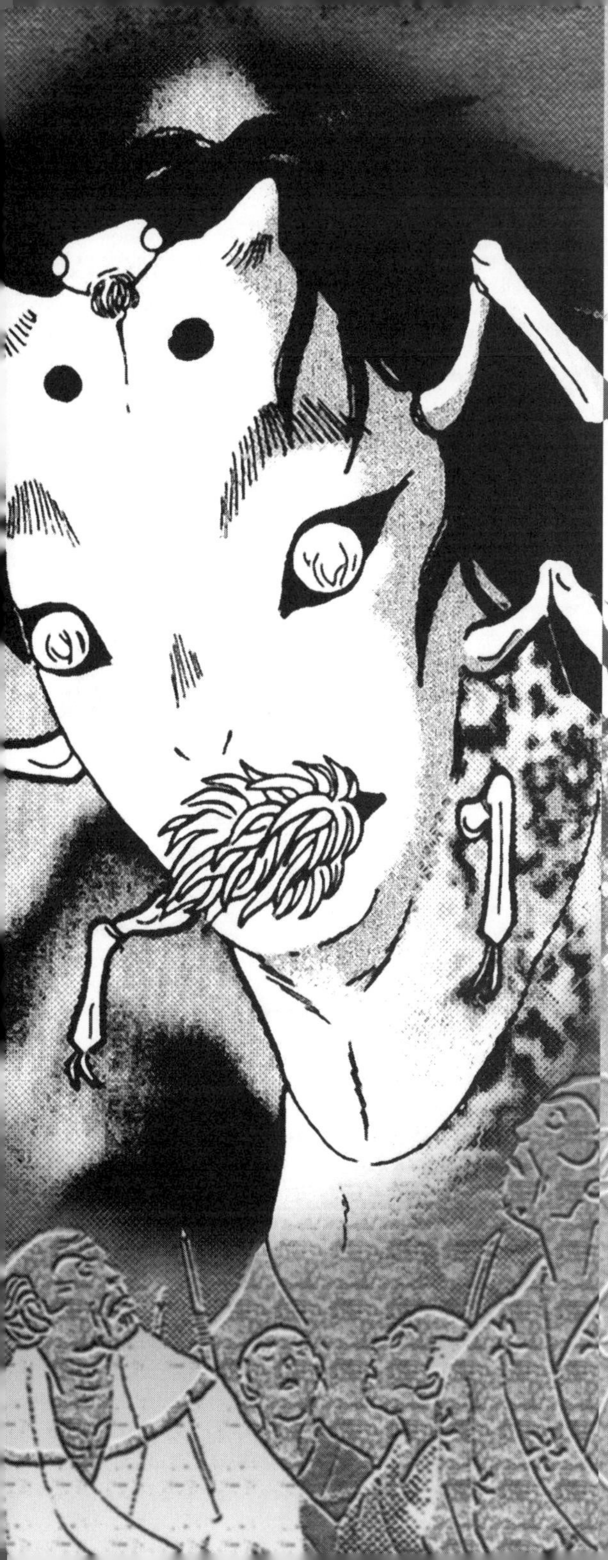

THE STORY THUS FAR

Long ago, in the "Warring States" era of Japan's Muromachi period (*Sengoku-jidai*, approximately 1467-1568 CE), a legendary doglike half-demon called "Inu-Yasha" attempted to steal the Shikon Jewel, or "Jewel of Four Souls," from a village, but was stopped by the enchanted arrow of the village priestess, Kikyo. Inu-Yasha fell into a deep sleep, pinned to a tree by Kikyo's arrow, while the mortally wounded Kikyo took the Shikon Jewel with her into the fires of her funeral pyre. Years passed.

Fast forward to the present day. Kagome, a Japanese high school girl, is pulled into a well one day by a mysterious centipede monster, and finds herself transported into the past, only to come face to face with the trapped Inu-Yasha. She frees him, and Inu-Yasha easily defeats the centipede monster.

The residents of the village, now fifty years older, readily accept Kagome as the reincarnation of their deceased priestess Kikyo, a claim supported by the fact that the Shikon Jewel emerges from a cut on Kagome's body. Unfortunately, the jewel's rediscovery means that the village is soon under attack by a variety of demons in search of this treasure. Then, the jewel is accidentally shattered into many shards, each of which may have the fearsome power of the entire jewel.

Although Inu-Yasha says he hates Kagome because of her resemblance to Kikyo, the woman who "killed" him, he is forced to team up with her when Kaede, the village leader, binds him to Kagome with a powerful spell. Now the two grudging companions must fight to reclaim and reassemble the shattered shards of the Shikon Jewel before they fall into the wrong hands.

THIS VOLUME

Sango is forced to deal directly with the demon Naraku in a battle for the life of her younger brother, even if it means betraying her comrades. Then, Inu-Yasha comes face to face with his own past in the form of another half-breed demon.

INU-YASHA
A half-human, half-demon hybrid son of a human mother and a demon father, Inu-Yasha resembles a human but has the claws of a demon, a thick mane of white hair, and ears rather like a dog's. The necklace he wears carries a powerful spell which allows Kagome to control him with a single word. Because of his human half, Inu-Yasha's powers are different from those of full-blooded monsters—a fact that the Shikon Jewel has the power to change.

KIKYO
A powerful priestess, Kikyo was charged with the awesome responsibility of protecting the Shikon Jewel from demons and humans who coveted its power. She died after firing the enchanted arrow that kept Inu-Yasha imprisoned for fifty years.

KAGOME
Working with Inu-Yasha to recover the shattered shards of the Shikon Jewel, Kagome routinely travels into Japan's past through an old, magical well on her family's property. All this time travel means she's stuck with living two separate lives in two separate centuries, and she's beginning to worry that she'll *never* be able to catch up to her schoolwork.

NARAKU
An enigmatic demon, Naraku is the one responsible for both Miroku's curse and for turning Kikyo and Inu-Yasha against one another for reasons that are as yet unknown.

SHIPPÔ
A young fox-demon, orphaned by two other demons whose powers had been boosted by the Shikon Jewel, the mischievous Shippô enjoys goading Inu-Yasha and playing tricks with his shape-changing abilities.

KOHAKU
Sango's little brother. Possessed by Naraku, he killed his own father and died in battle

MIROKU
An easygoing Buddhist priest with questionable morals, Miroku is the carrier of a curse passed down from his grandfather. He is searching for the demon Naraku, who first inflicted the curse.

SANGO
A "Demon Exterminator" from the village where the Shikon Jewel was first born, Sango lost her father and little brother to an ambush by a demon using a shard of the Jewel…a demon summoned by none other than the mysterious Naraku.

SCROLL ONE
NARAKU'S CASTLE

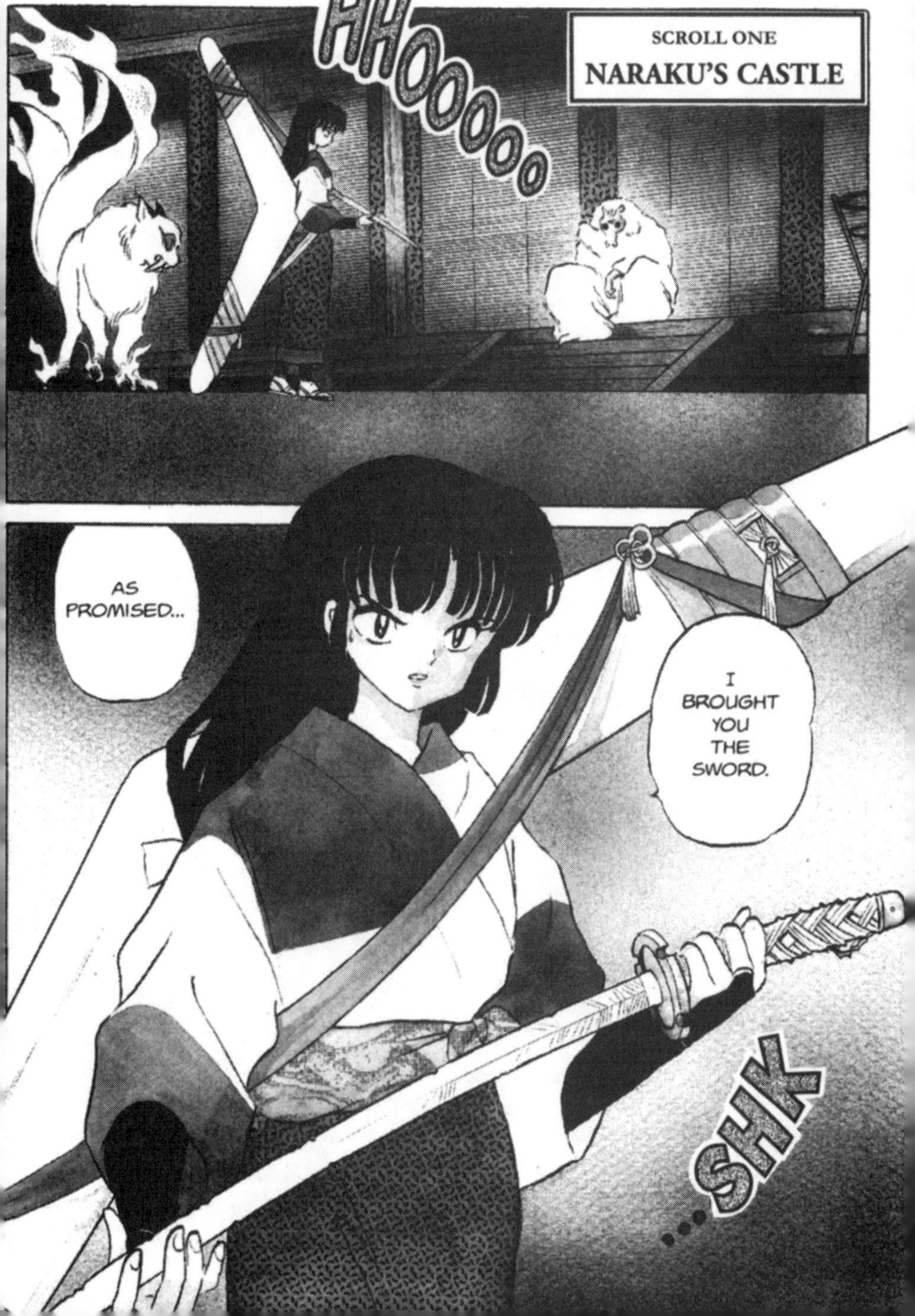
HHOOOOO
AS PROMISED...
I BROUGHT YOU THE SWORD.
SHK...

SCROLL ONE
NARAKU'S CASTLE

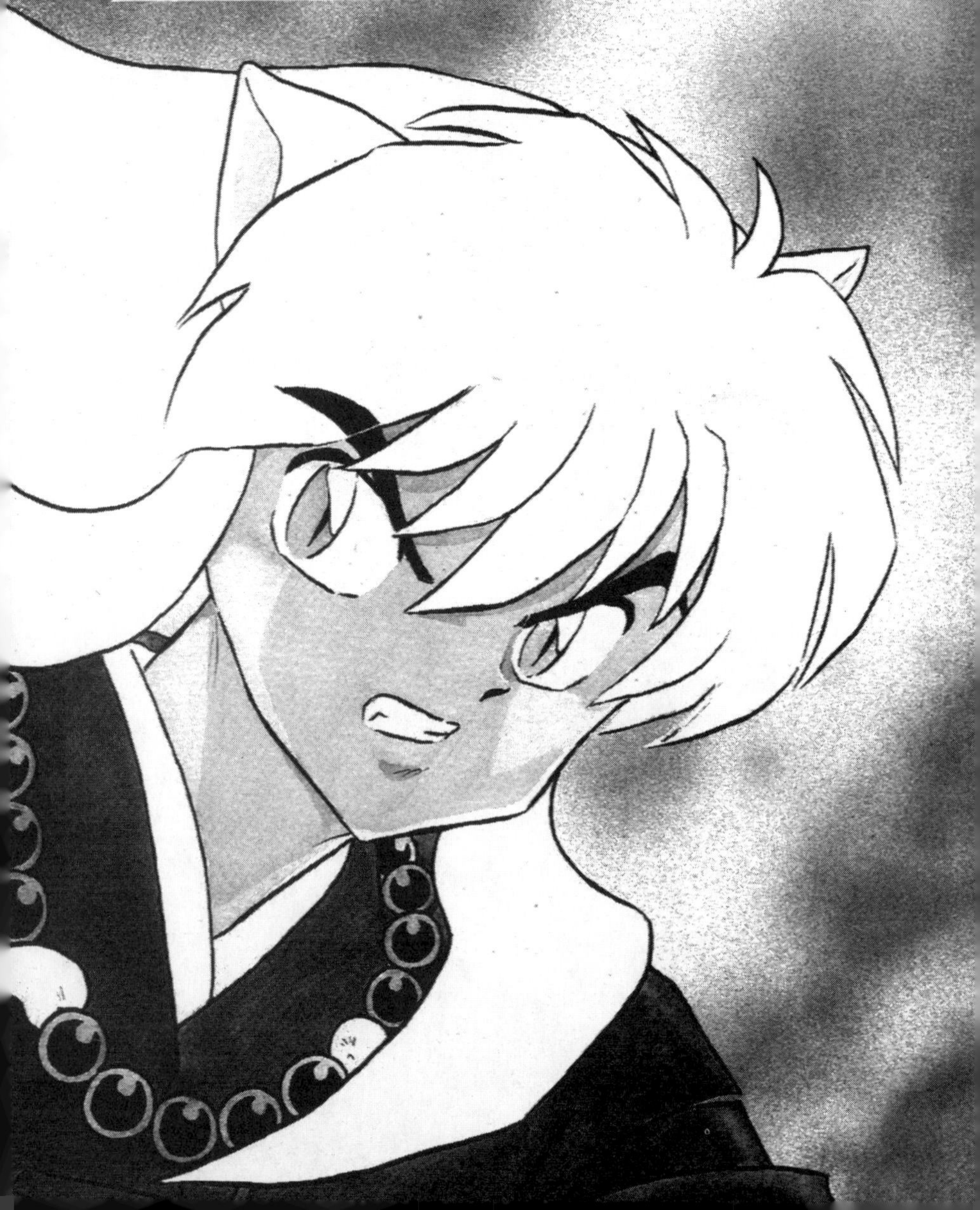

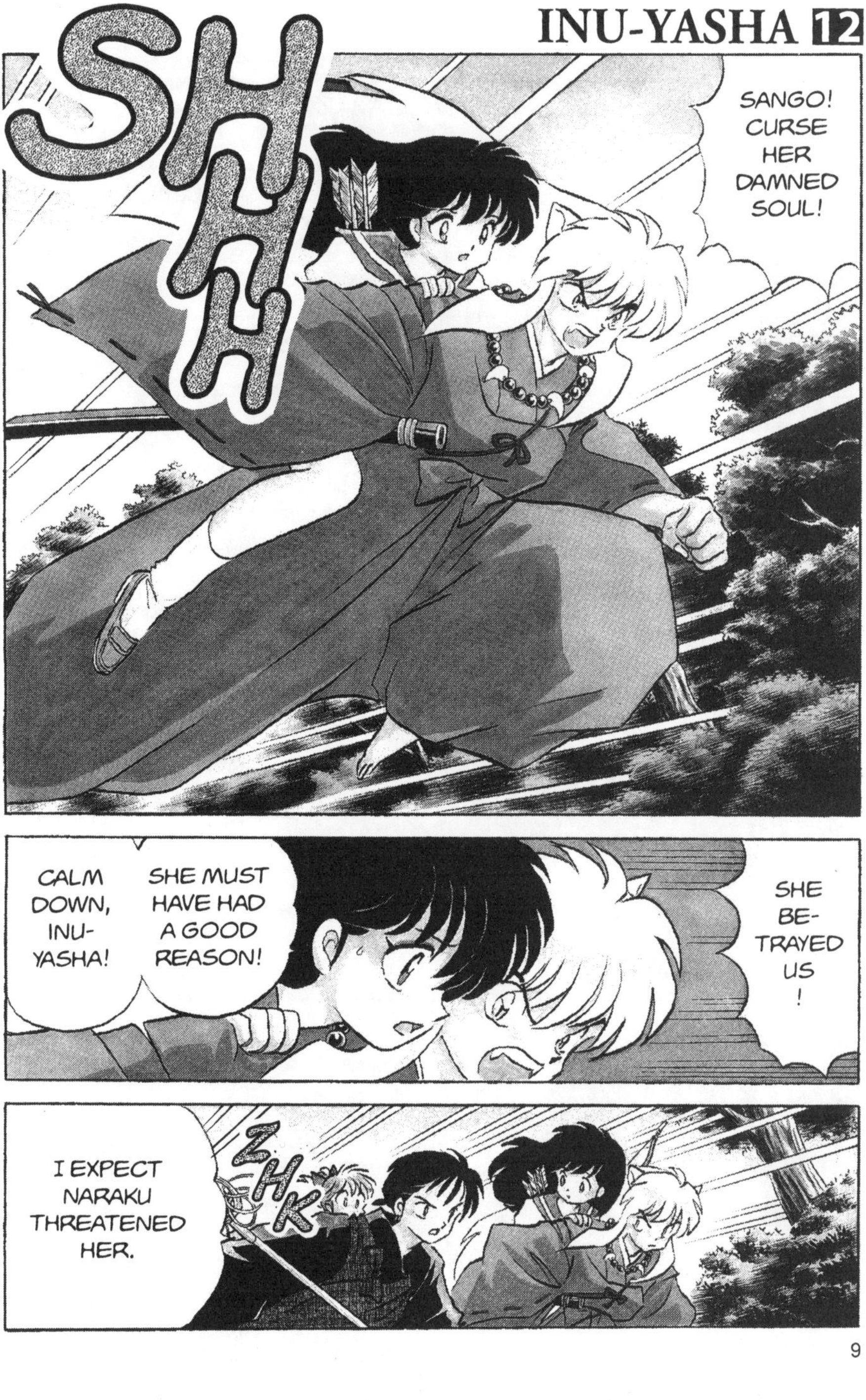
SHHH
SANGO! CURSE HER DAMNED SOUL!
CALM DOWN, INU-YASHA!
SHE MUST HAVE HAD A GOOD REASON!
SHE BETRAYED US!
I EXPECT NARAKU THREATENED HER.
ZHK

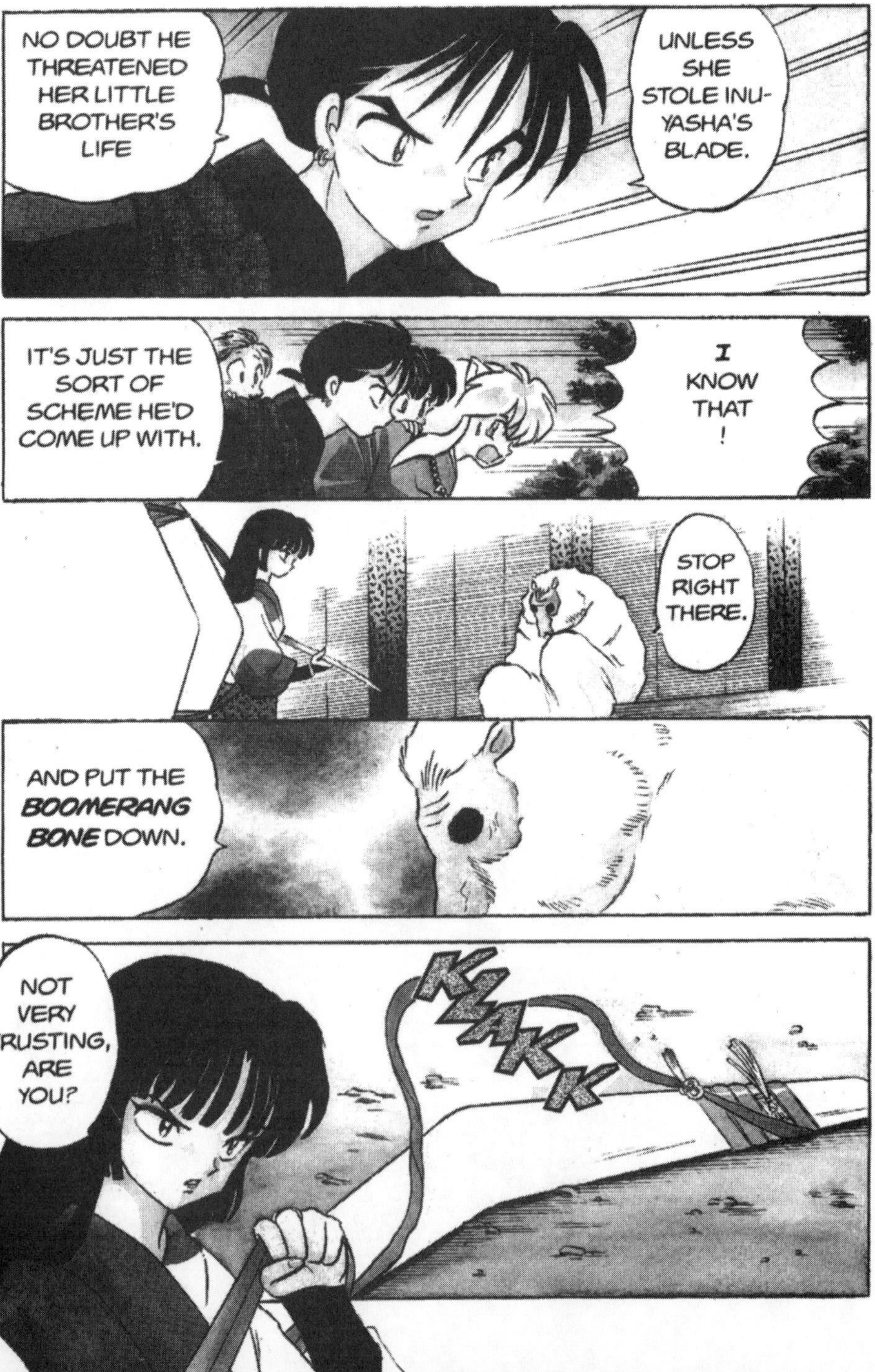
NO DOUBT HE THREATENED HER LITTLE BROTHER'S LIFE
UNLESS SHE STOLE INU-YASHA'S BLADE.
IT'S JUST THE SORT OF SCHEME HE'D COME UP WITH.
I KNOW THAT!
STOP RIGHT THERE.
AND PUT THE *BOOMERANG BONE* DOWN.
NOT VERY TRUSTING, ARE YOU?
KLAKK

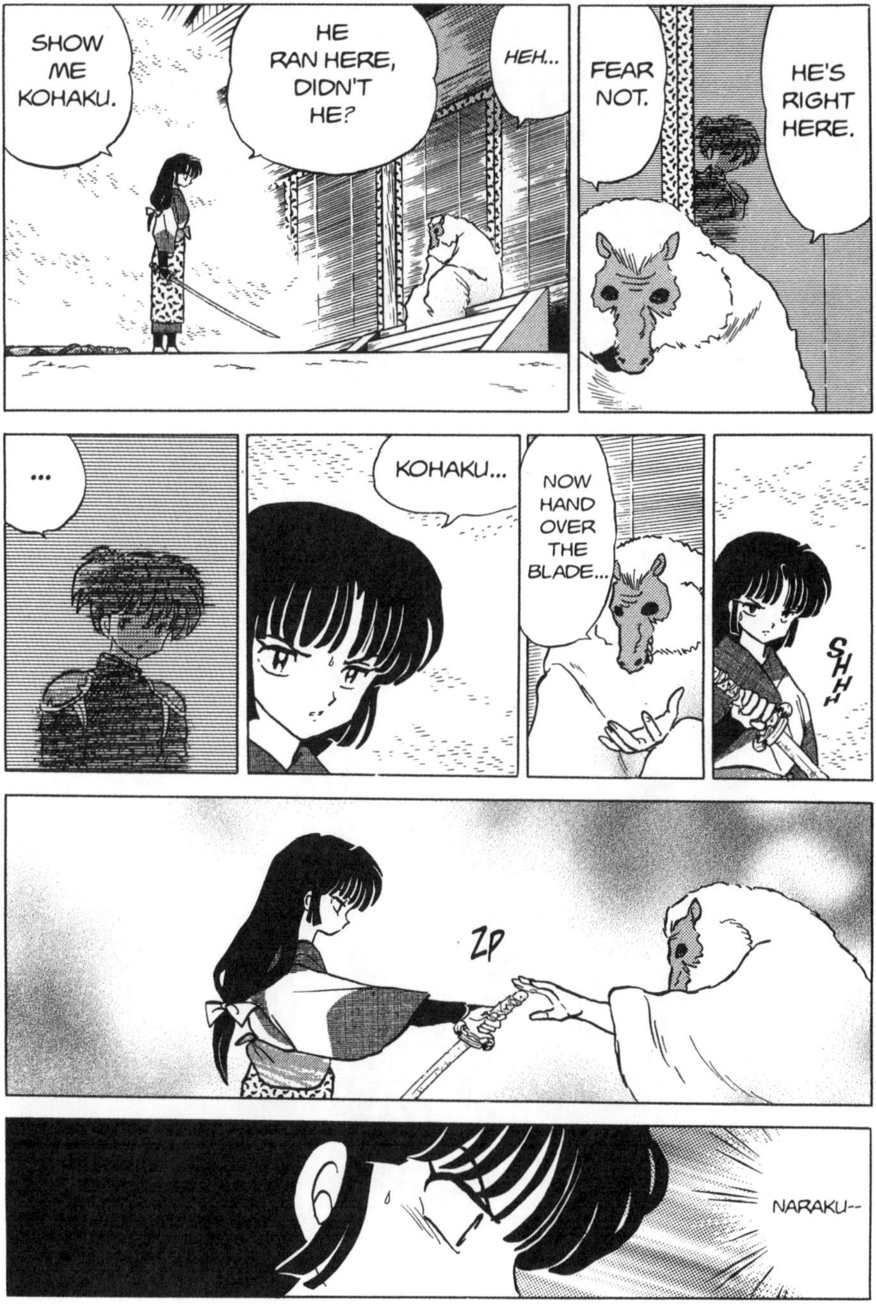
SHOW ME KOHAKU.
HE RAN HERE, DIDN'T HE?
HEH...
FEAR NOT.
HE'S RIGHT HERE.
...
KOHAKU...
NOW HAND OVER THE BLADE...
SHHH
ZP
NARAKU--

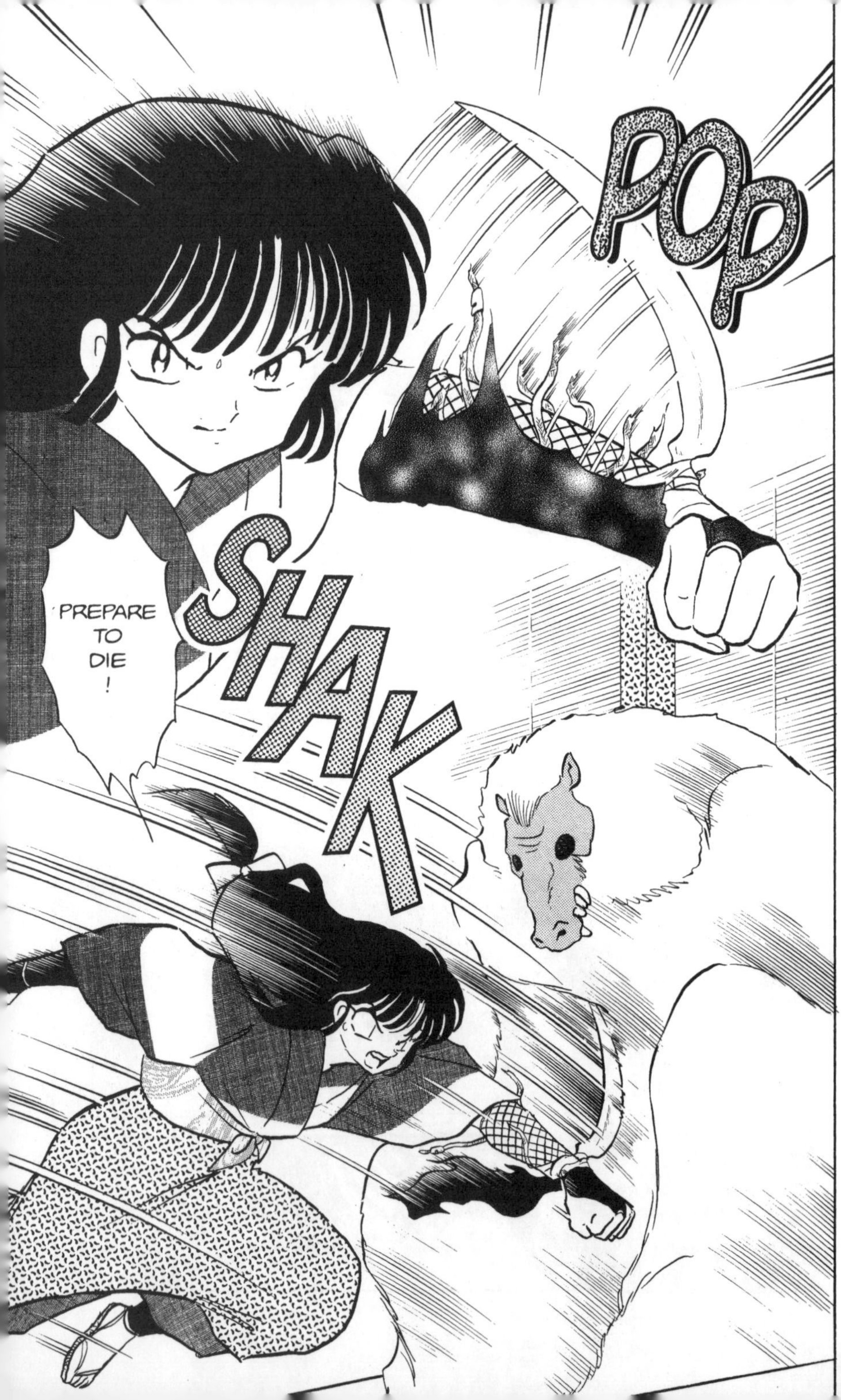
POP
SHAK
PREPARE TO DIE!

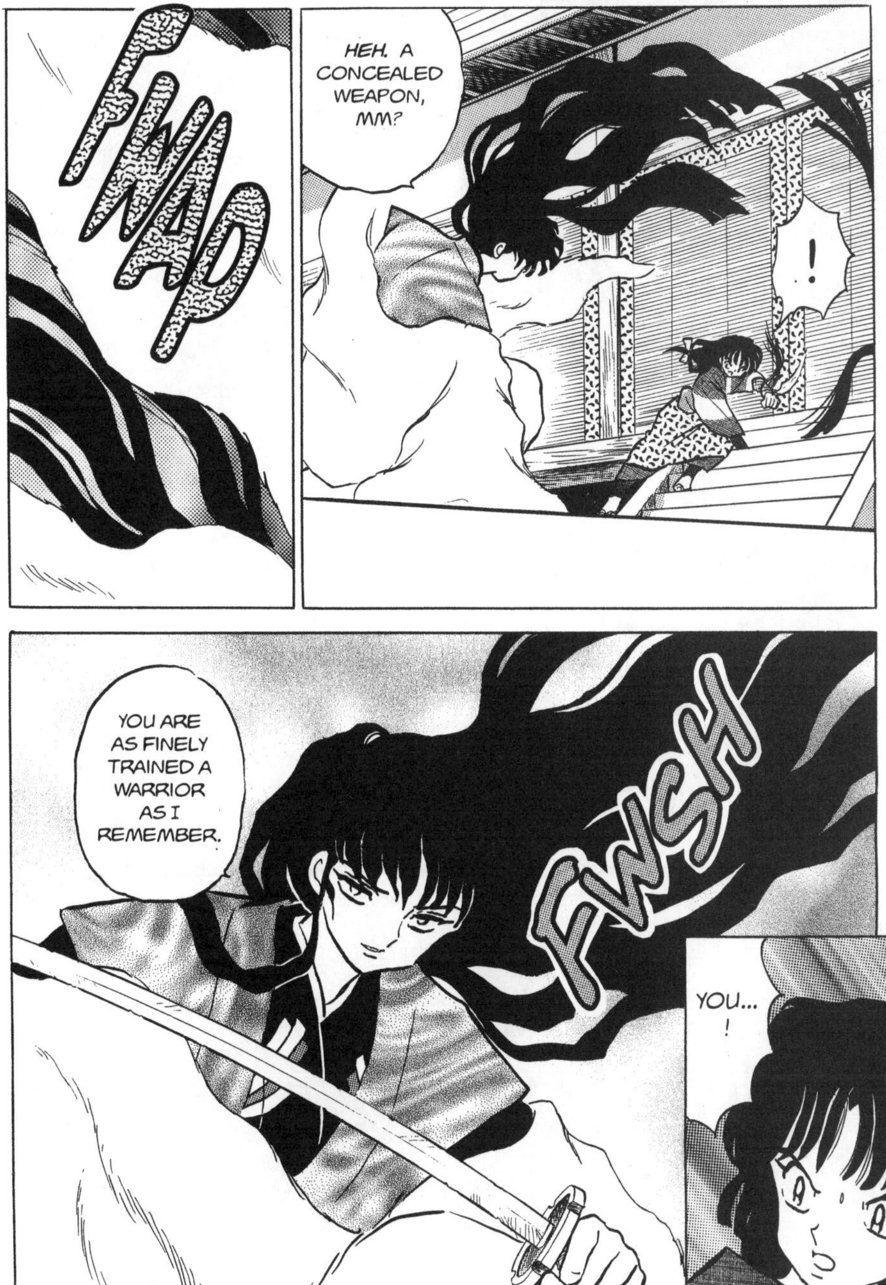
FWAP
HEH. A CONCEALED WEAPON, MM?
!
YOU ARE AS FINELY TRAINED A WARRIOR AS I REMEMBER.
FWSH
YOU... !

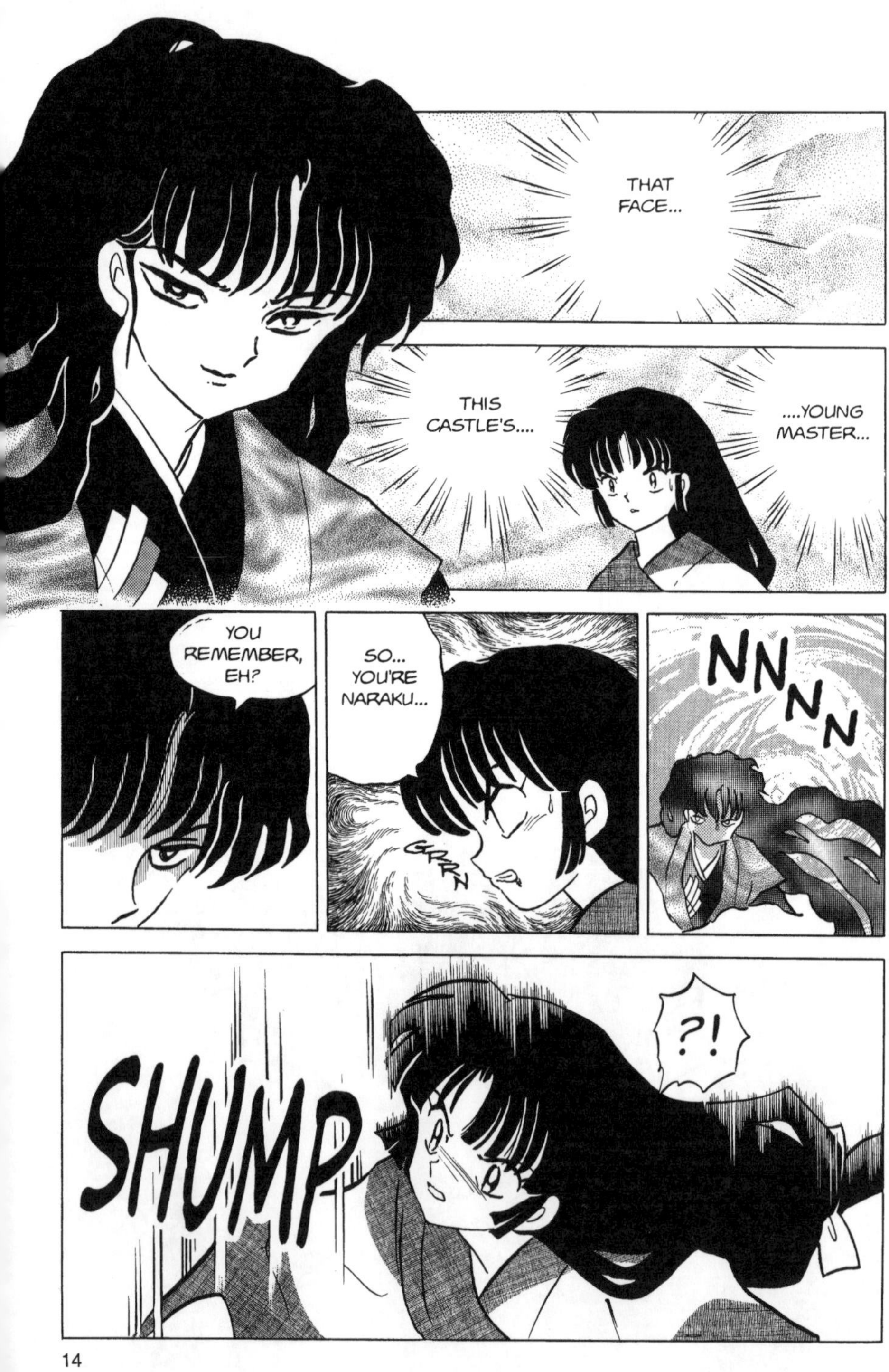
THAT FACE...
THIS CASTLE'S....
....YOUNG MASTER...
YOU REMEMBER, EH?
SO... YOU'RE NARAKU...
GRRRN
NNNNN
SHUMP
?!

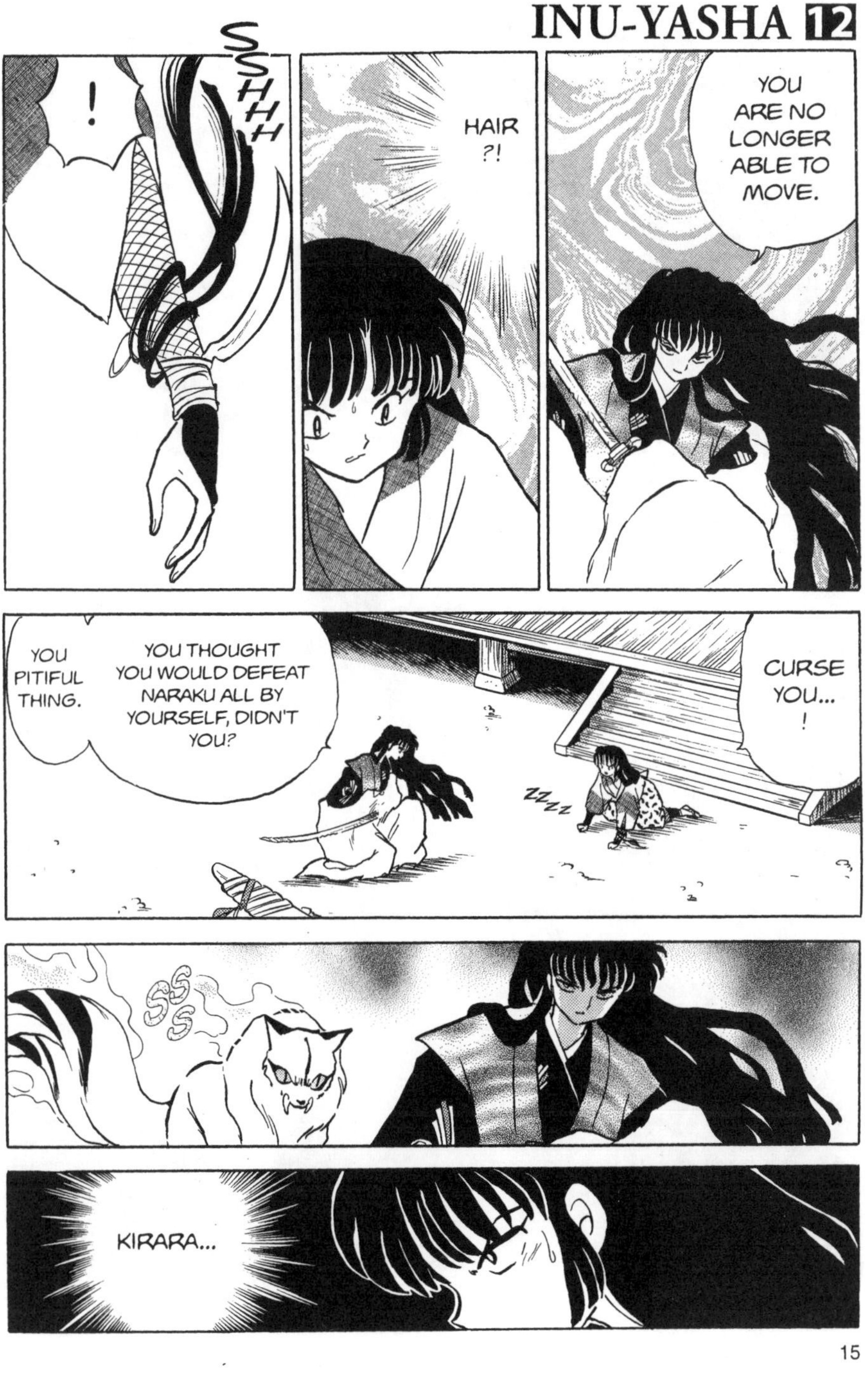
!
SSHHH
HAIR ?!
YOU ARE NO LONGER ABLE TO MOVE.
YOU PITIFUL THING.
YOU THOUGHT YOU WOULD DEFEAT NARAKU ALL BY YOURSELF, DIDN'T YOU?
ZZZZ
CURSE YOU... !
SSS
KIRARA...

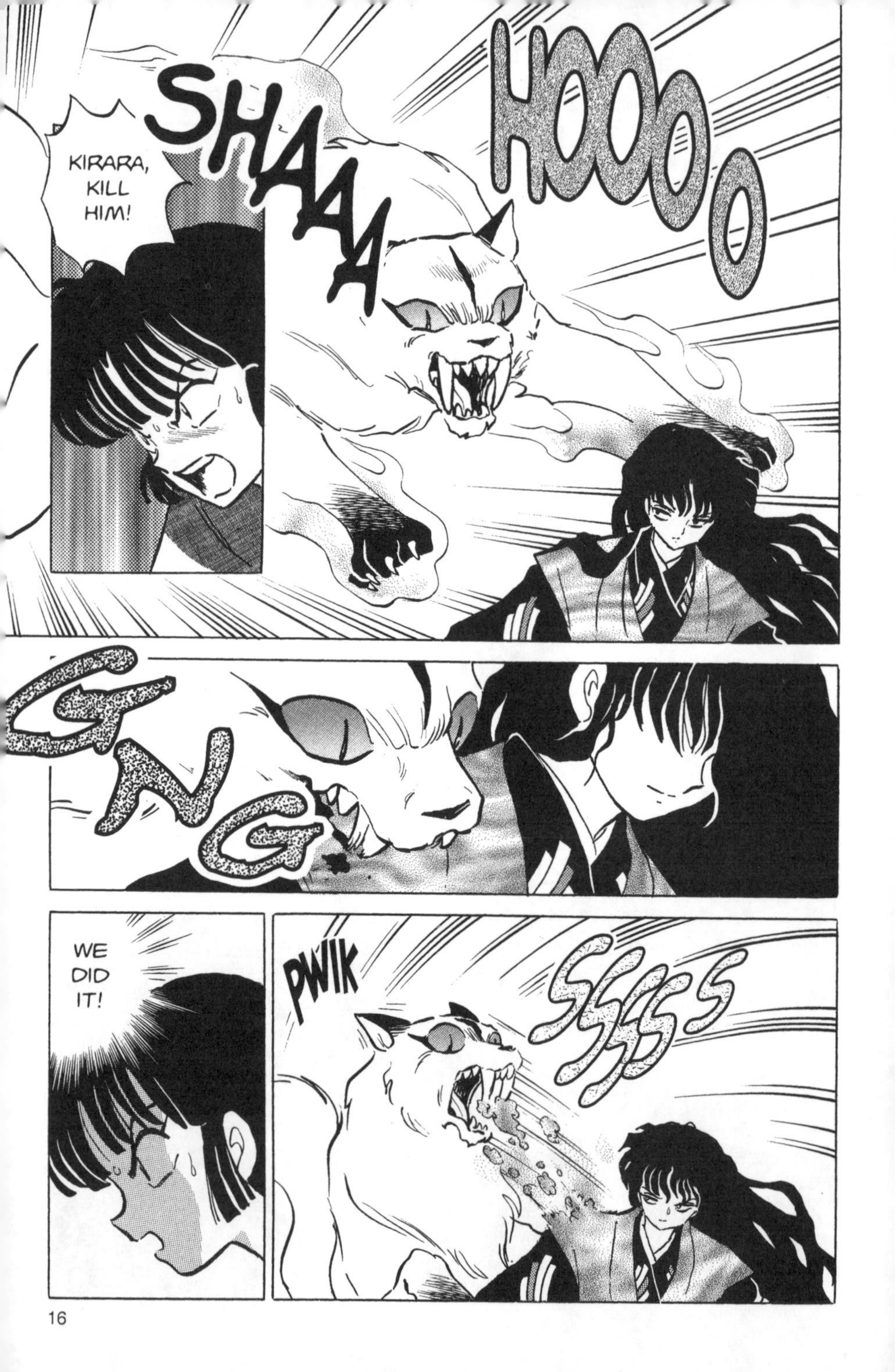
KIRARA, KILL HIM!
SHAAAA
HOOOOO
GNG
WE DID IT!
PWIK
SSSSSS

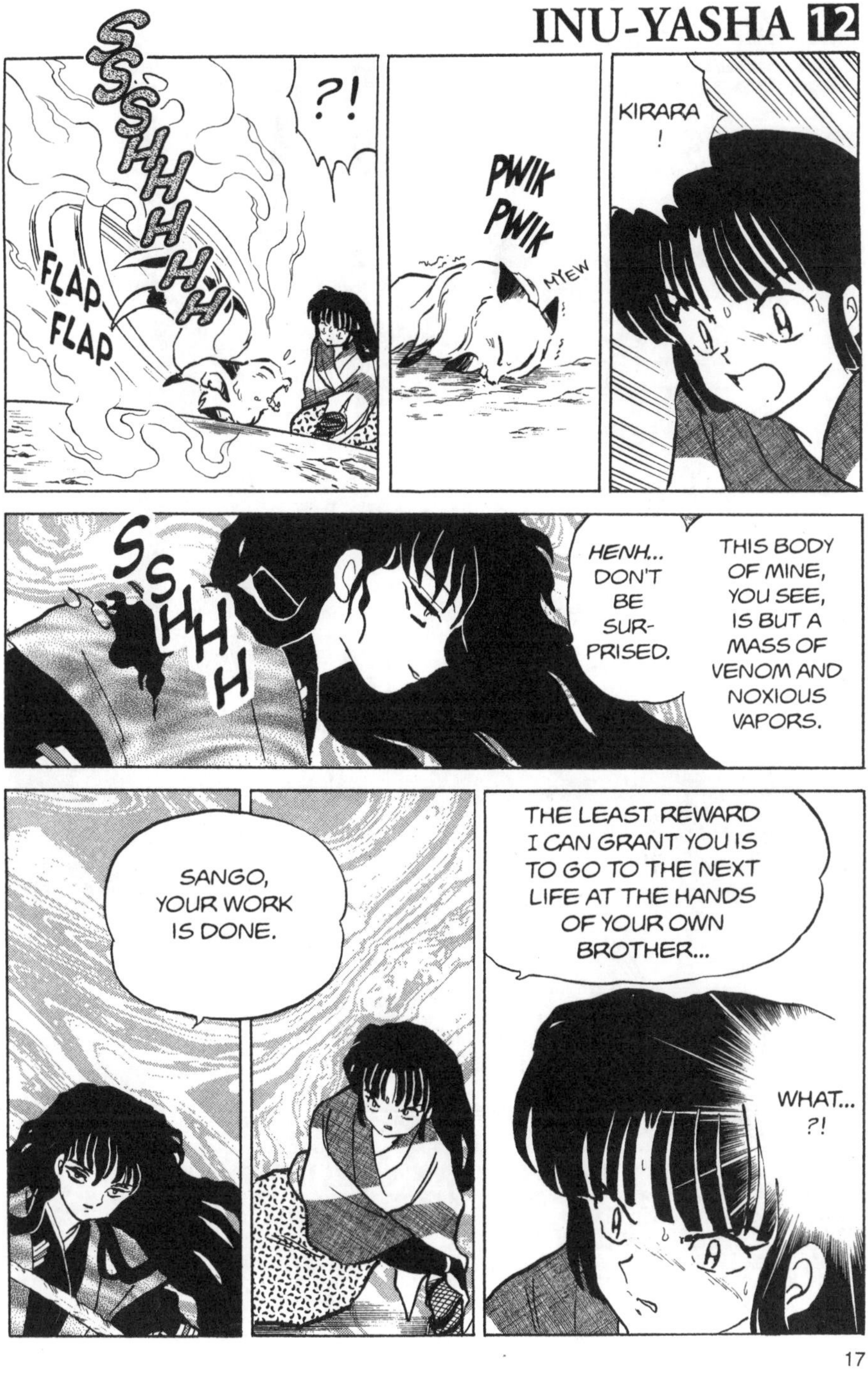
SSSHHHHH
FLAP FLAP
?!
PWIK PWIK
MYEW
KIRARA !
SSHHH
HENH... DON'T BE SUR-PRISED.
THIS BODY OF MINE, YOU SEE, IS BUT A MASS OF VENOM AND NOXIOUS VAPORS.
SANGO, YOUR WORK IS DONE.
THE LEAST REWARD I CAN GRANT YOU IS TO GO TO THE NEXT LIFE AT THE HANDS OF YOUR OWN BROTHER...
WHAT... ?!

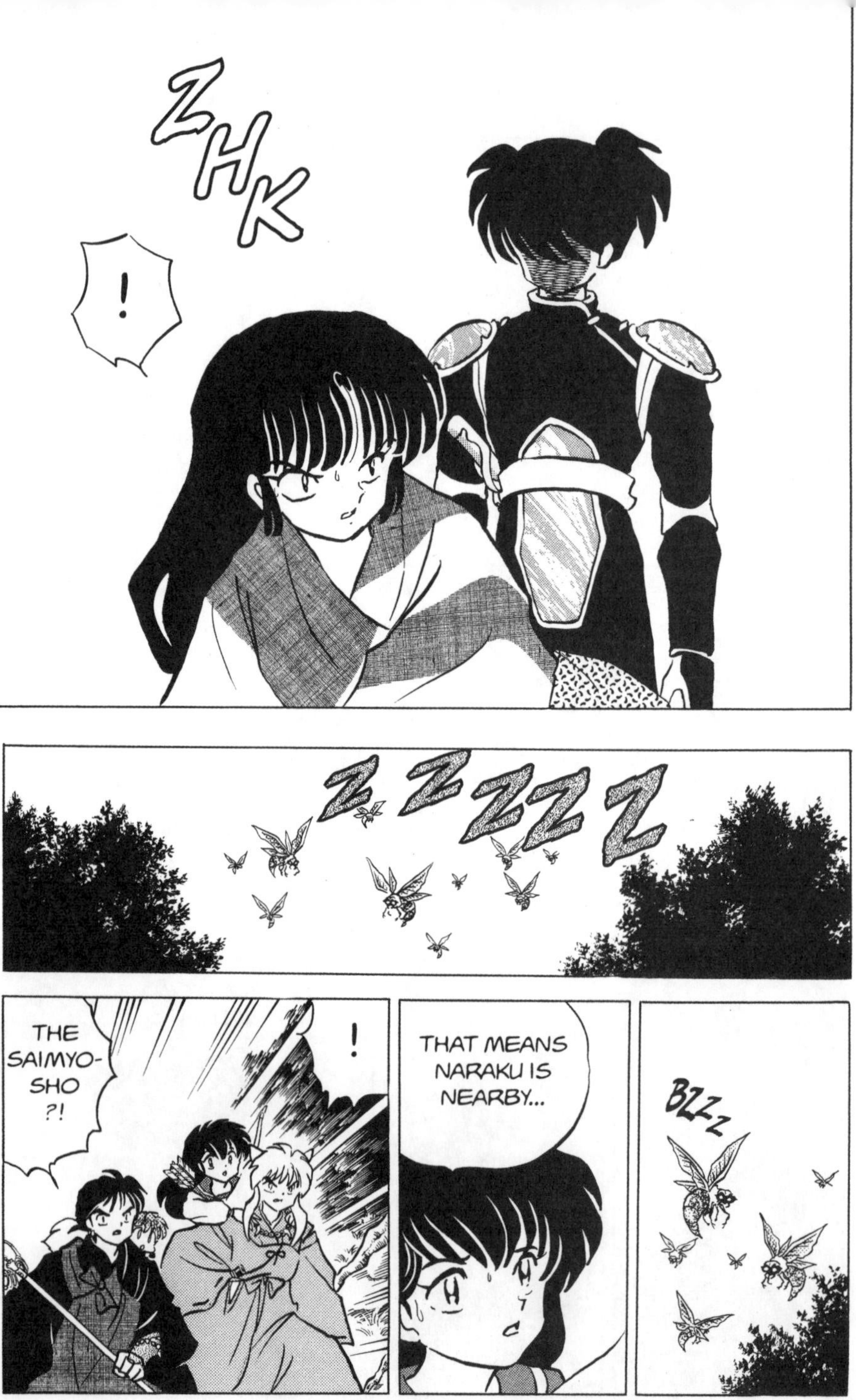
ZHK
!
ZZZZZZ
THE SAIMYO-SHO ?!
!
THAT MEANS NARAKU IS NEARBY...
BZZZ

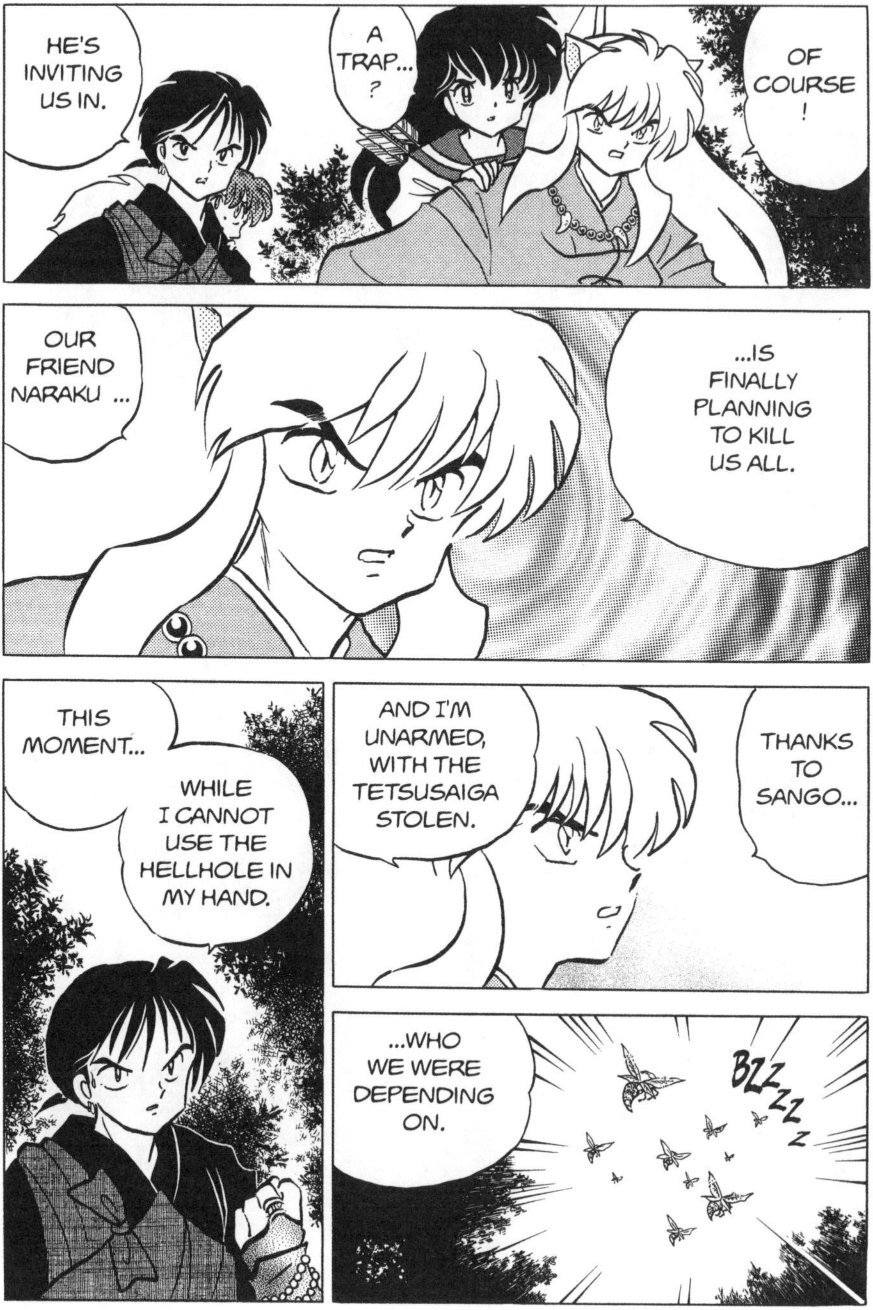
HE'S INVITING US IN.
A TRAP... ?
OF COURSE !
OUR FRIEND NARAKU ...
...IS FINALLY PLANNING TO KILL US ALL.
THIS MOMENT...
WHILE I CANNOT USE THE HELLHOLE IN MY HAND.
AND I'M UNARMED, WITH THE TETSUSAIGA STOLEN.
THANKS TO SANGO...
...WHO WE WERE DEPENDING ON.
BZZZZZ

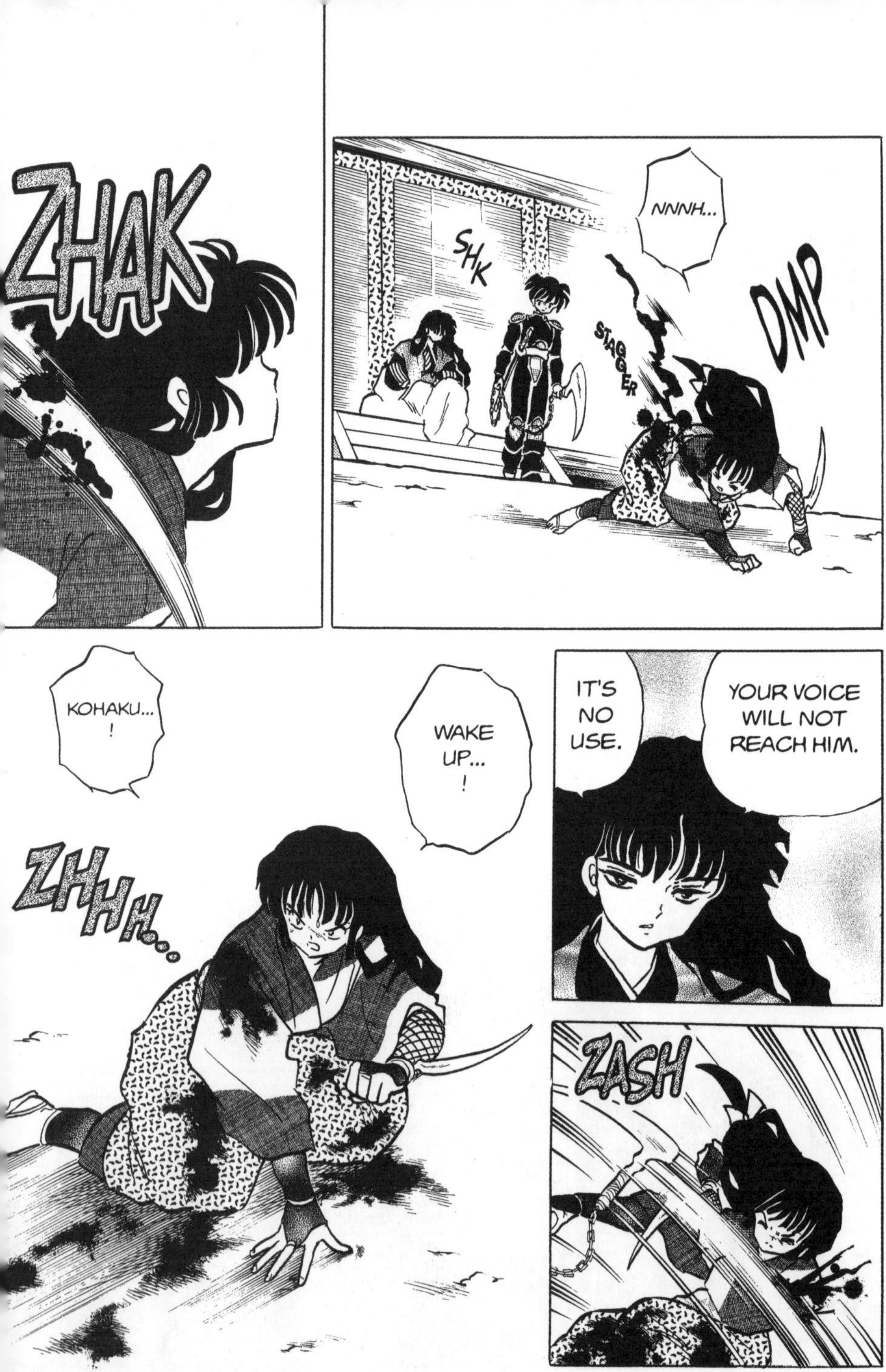
ZHAK
SHK
NNNH...
STAGGER
DMP
KOHAKU... !
WAKE UP... !
ZHHHH...
IT'S NO USE.
YOUR VOICE WILL NOT REACH HIM.
ZASH

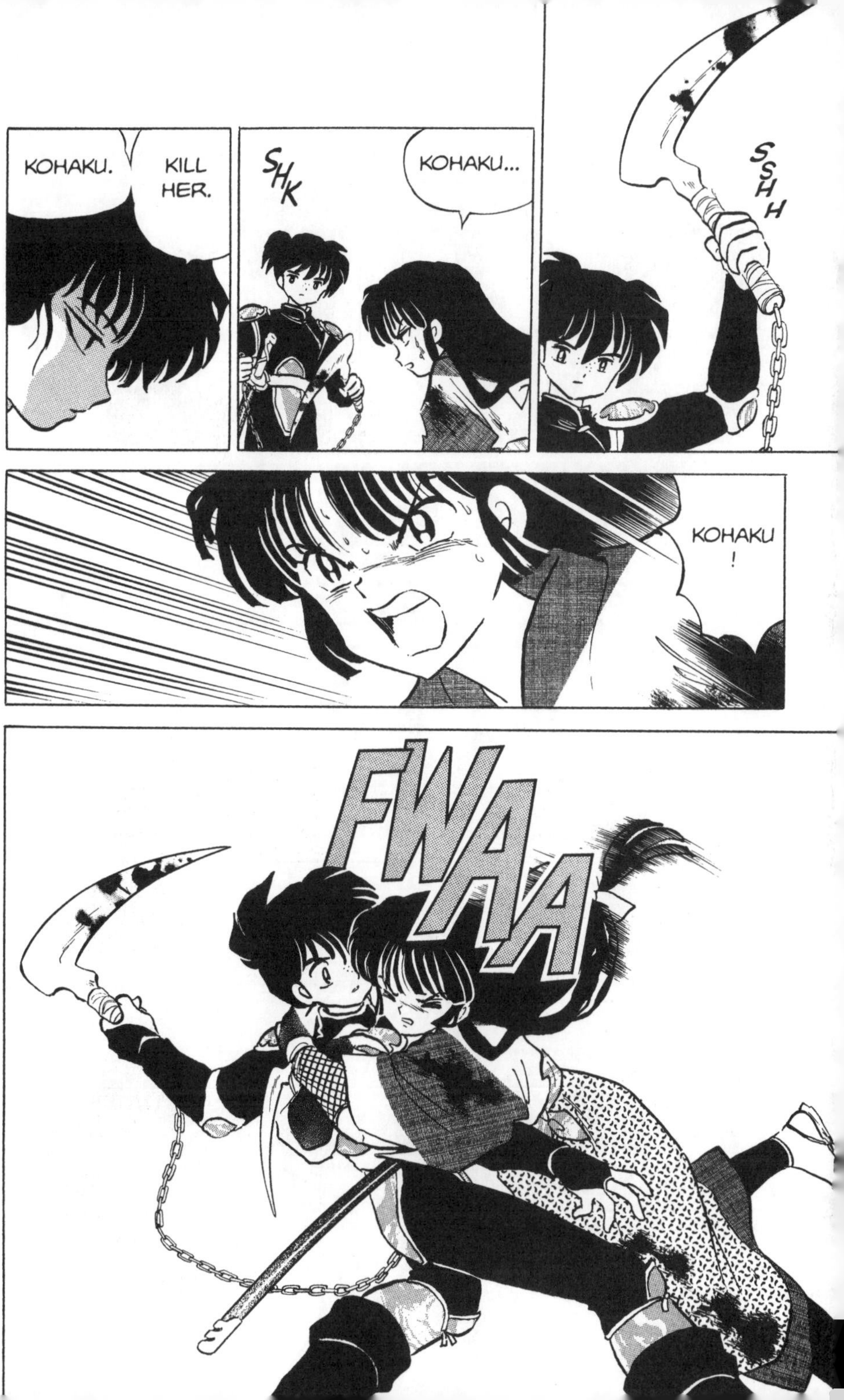
KOHAKU.
KILL HER.
SHK
KOHAKU...
SSHH
KOHAKU !
FWAAA

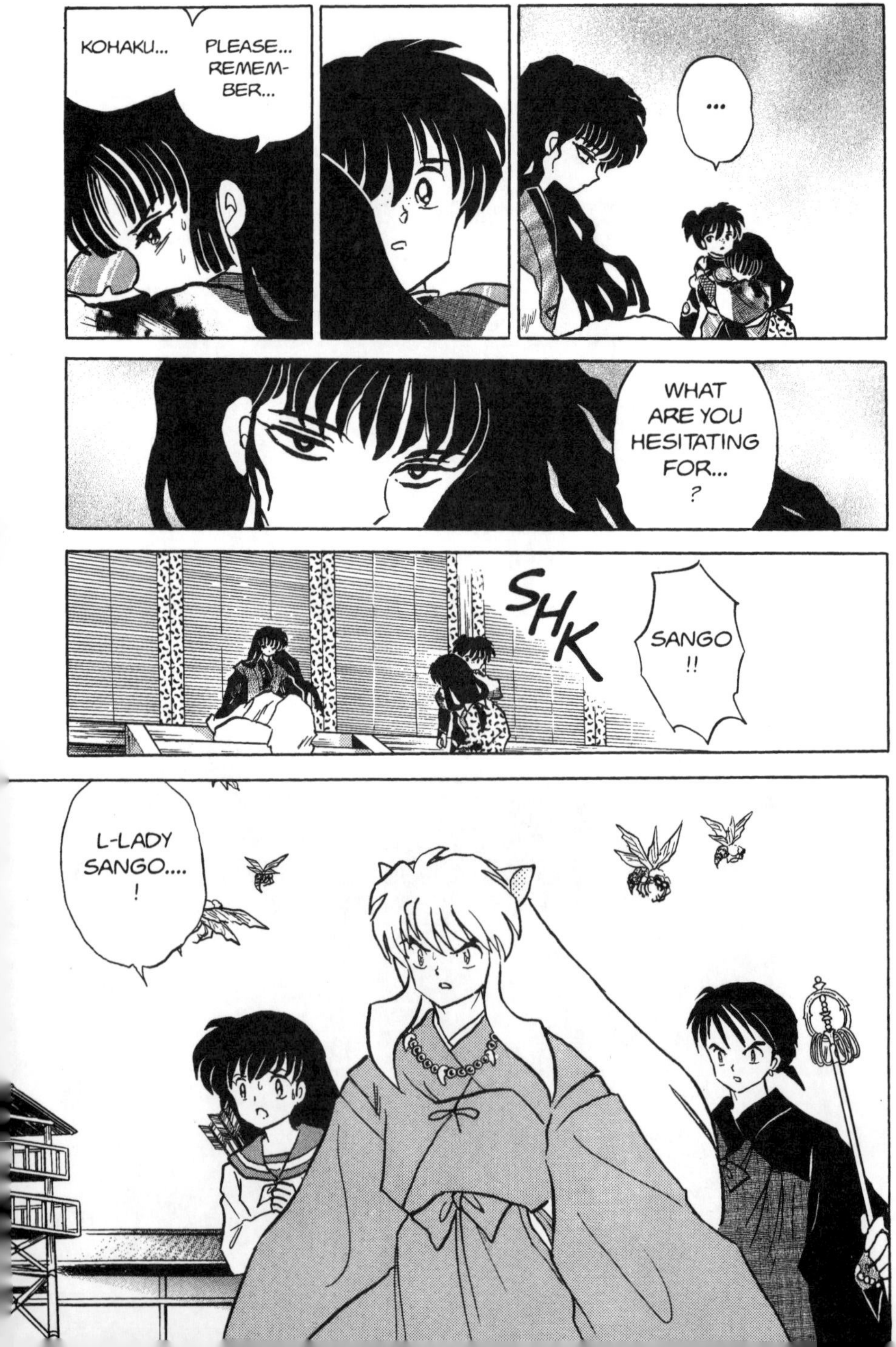
KOHAKU... PLEASE... REMEMBER...
...
WHAT ARE YOU HESITATING FOR...?
SHK
SANGO!!
L-LADY SANGO....!

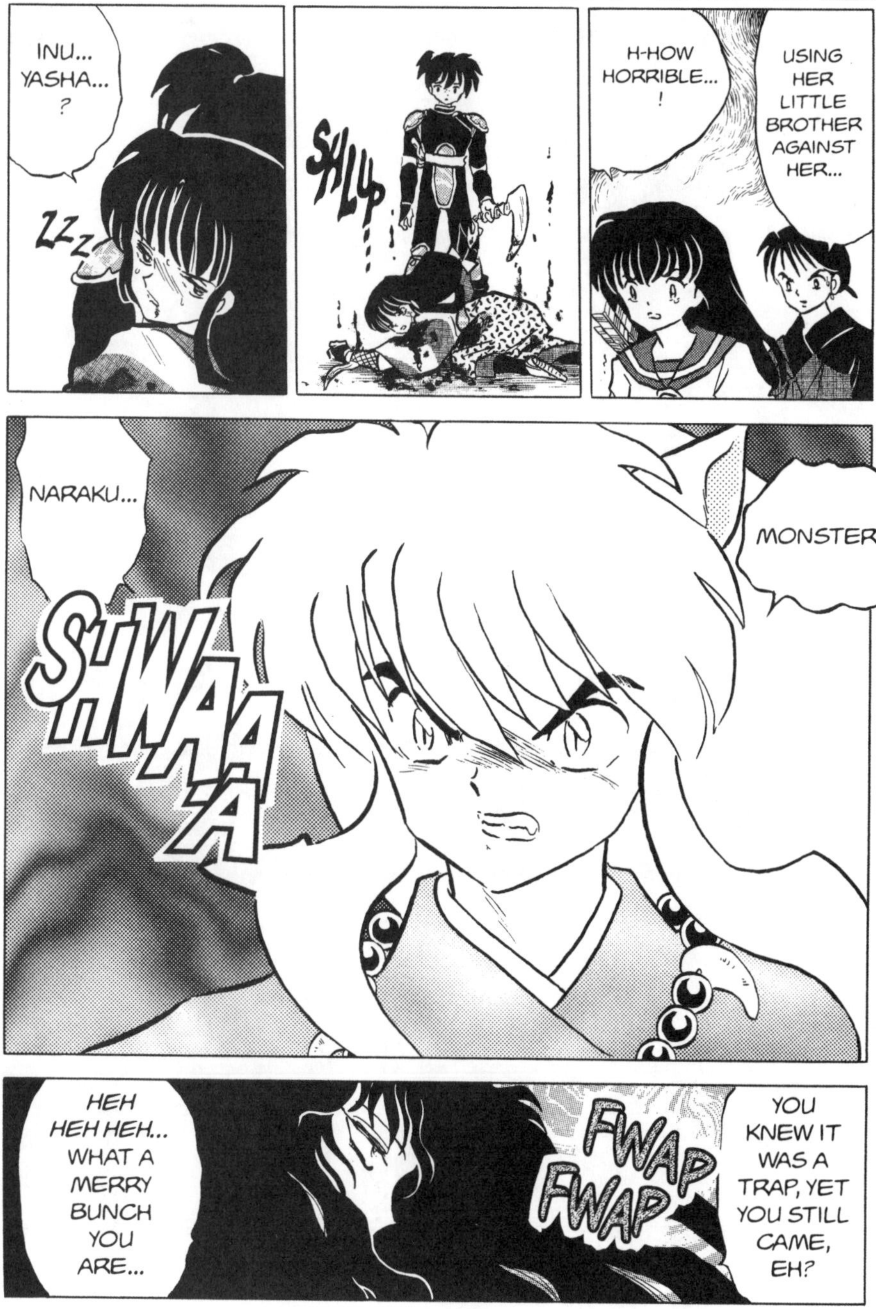
INU... YASHA... ?
ZZZ
SHLUP
H-HOW HORRIBLE... !
USING HER LITTLE BROTHER AGAINST HER...
NARAKU...
SHWAAA
MONSTER...
HEH HEH HEH... WHAT A MERRY BUNCH YOU ARE...
FWAP FWAP
YOU KNEW IT WAS A TRAP, YET YOU STILL CAME, EH?

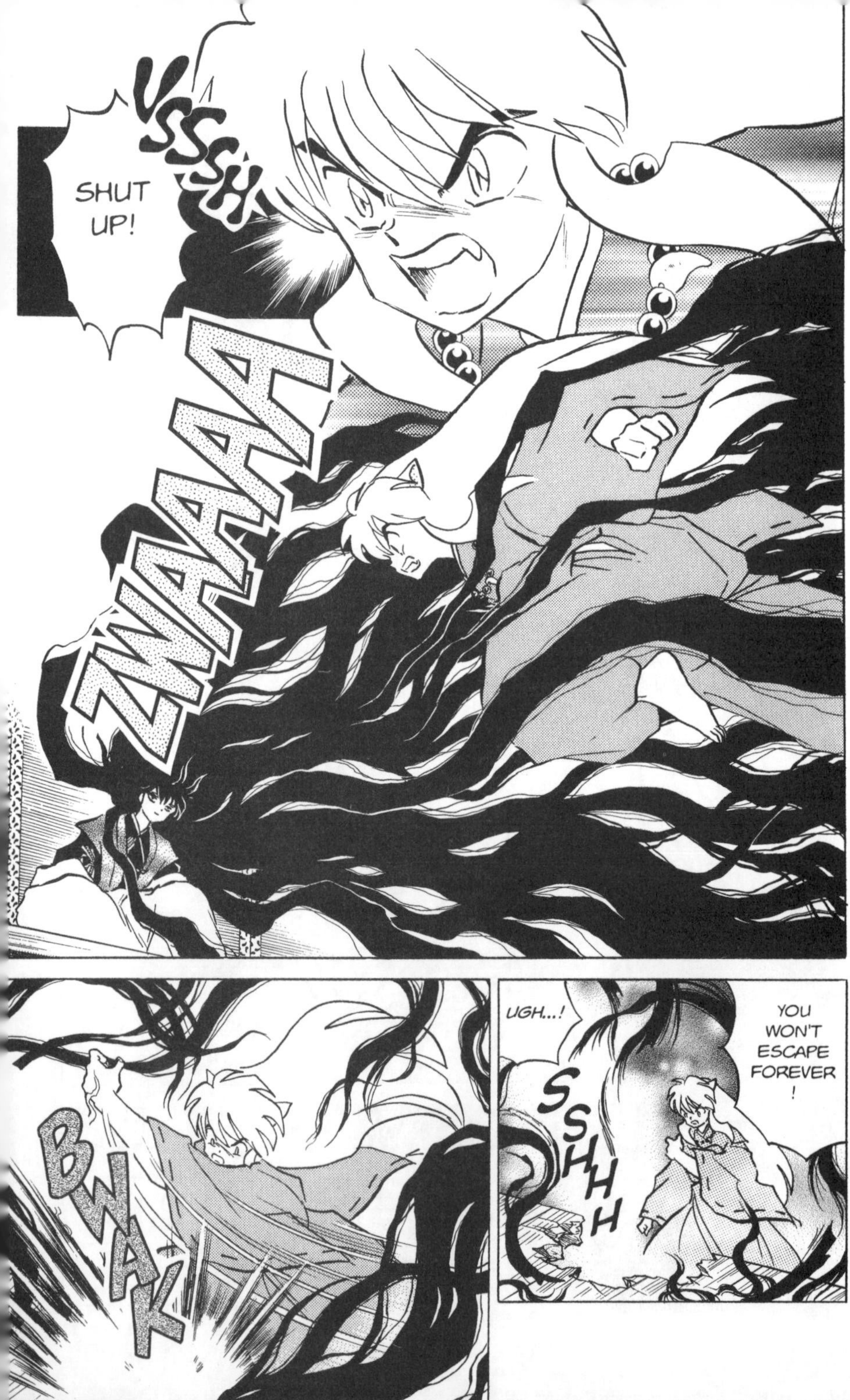
SHUT UP!
VSSSH
ZWAAAH
BWAK
UGH...!
SSHHHH
YOU WON'T ESCAPE FOREVER!

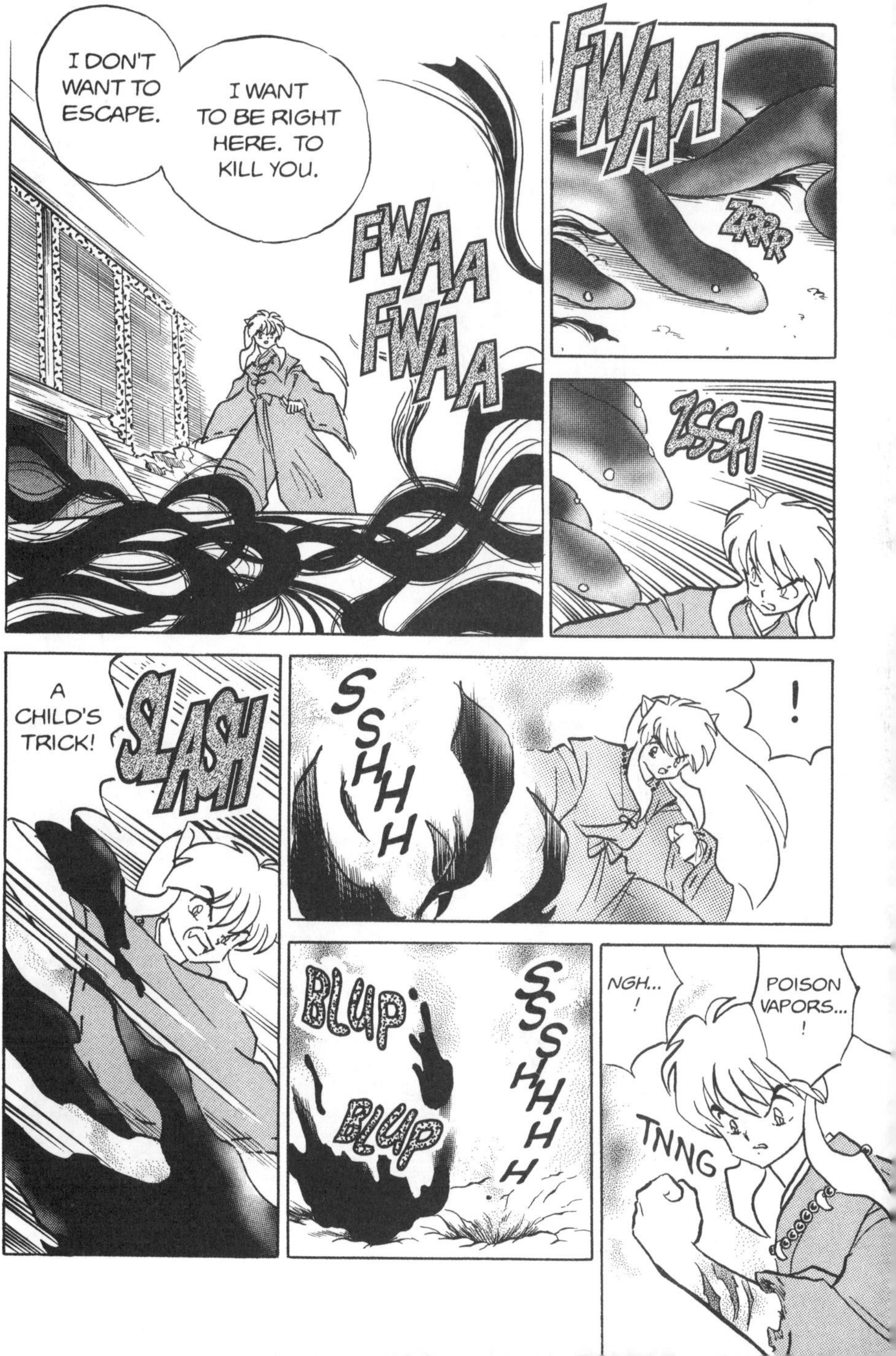
I DON'T WANT TO ESCAPE.
I WANT TO BE RIGHT HERE. TO KILL YOU.
FWAA
FWAA
FWAA
ZRRR
ZSSH
A CHILD'S TRICK!
SLASH
SSHHHH
!
BLUP
BLUP
SSSHHHH
NGH... !
POISON VAPORS... !
TNNG

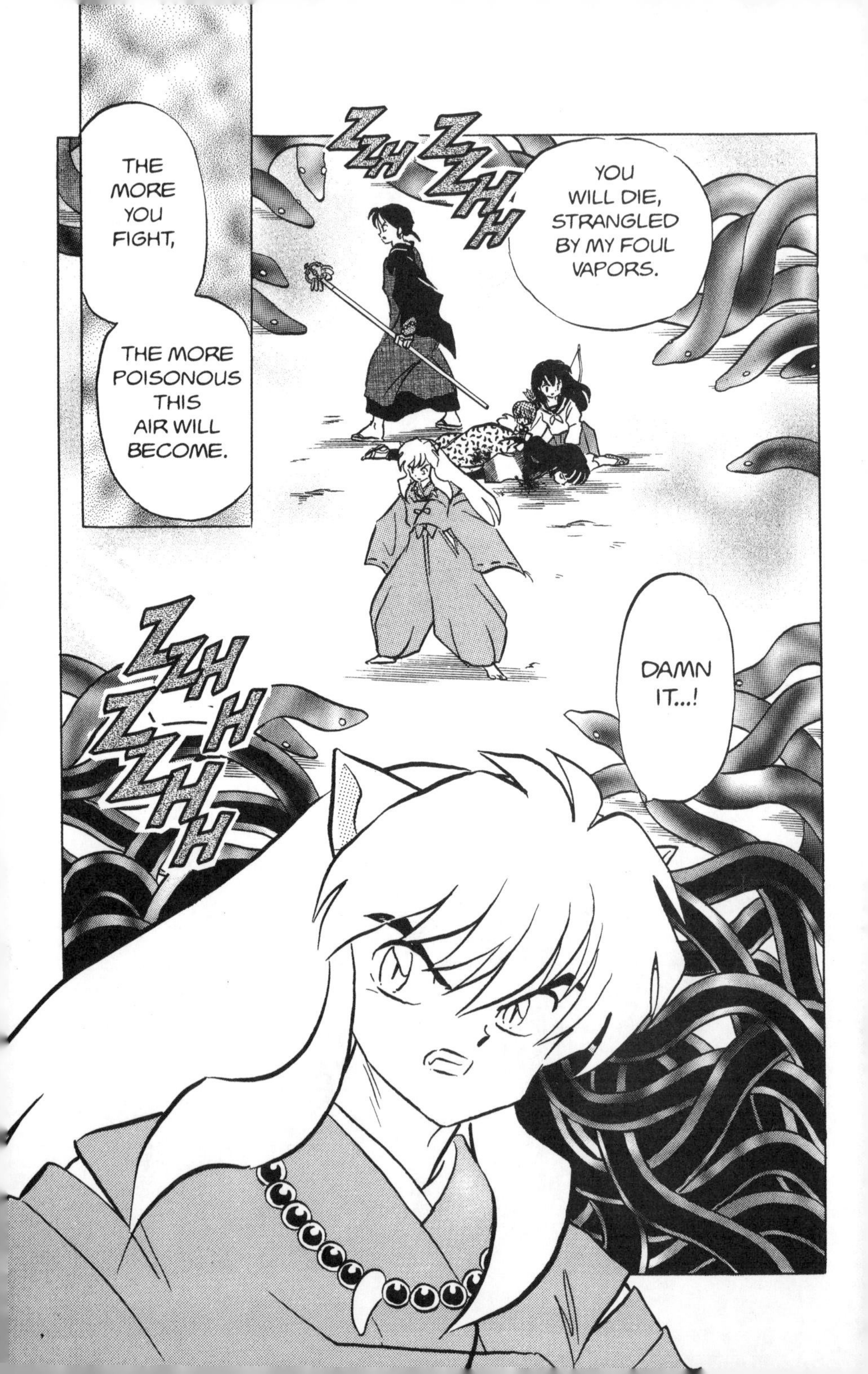
THE MORE YOU FIGHT,
THE MORE POISONOUS THIS AIR WILL BECOME.
ZZH ZZHH
YOU WILL DIE, STRANGLED BY MY FOUL VAPORS.
ZZH ZZH ZZHH
DAMN IT...!

SCROLL TWO

THE VAPORS

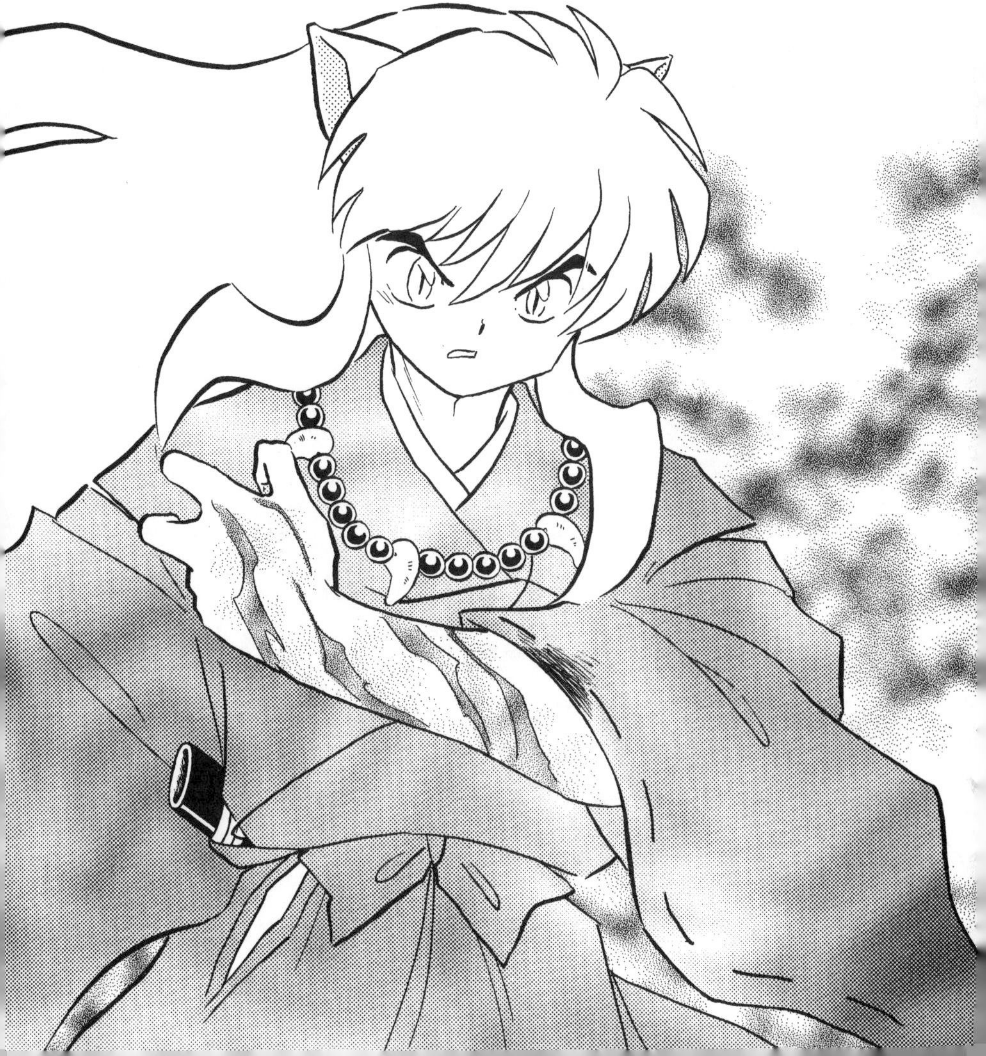

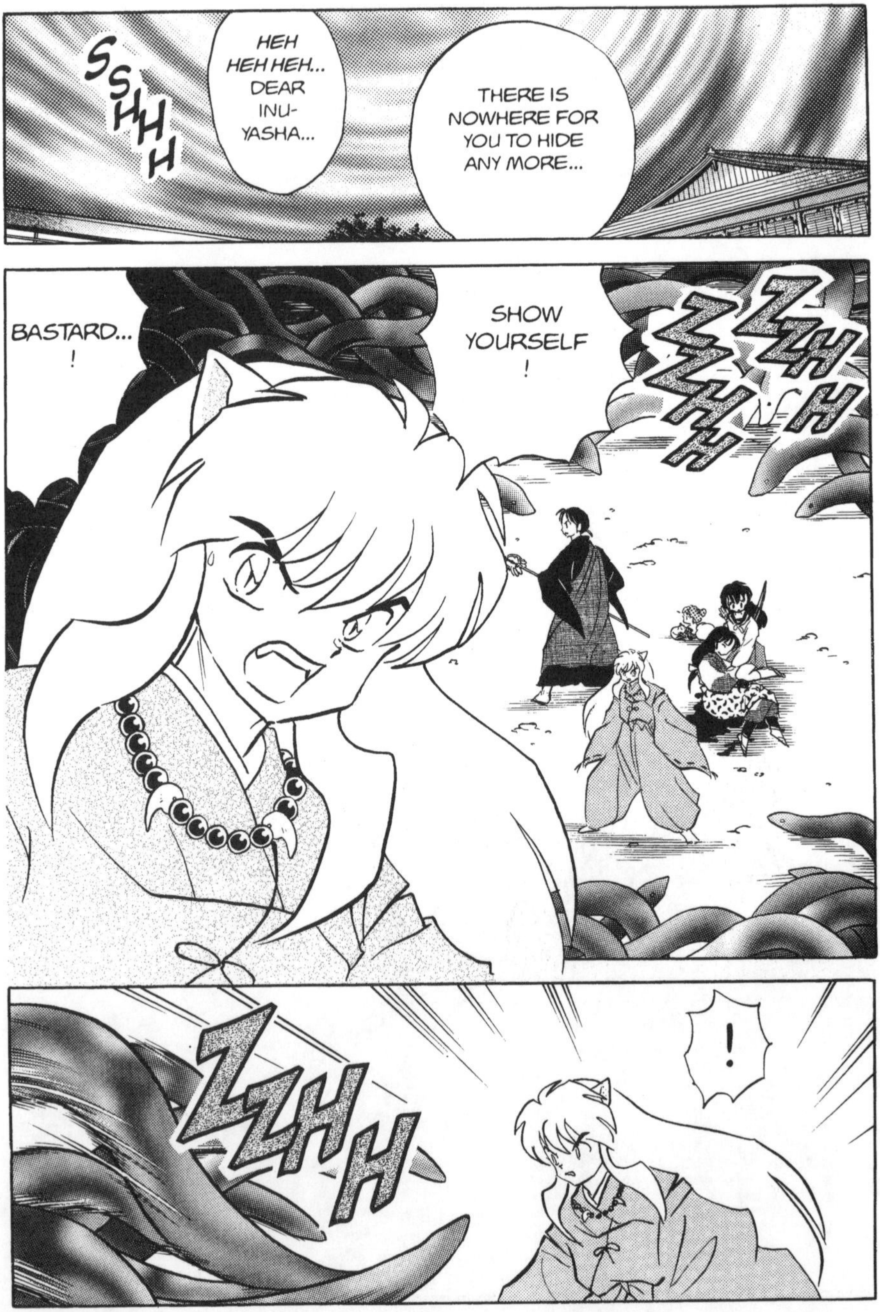
SSHHH
HEH HEH HEH... DEAR INU-YASHA...
THERE IS NOWHERE FOR YOU TO HIDE ANY MORE...
BASTARD...!
SHOW YOURSELF!
ZZHHH
ZZHHH
ZZHHH
!

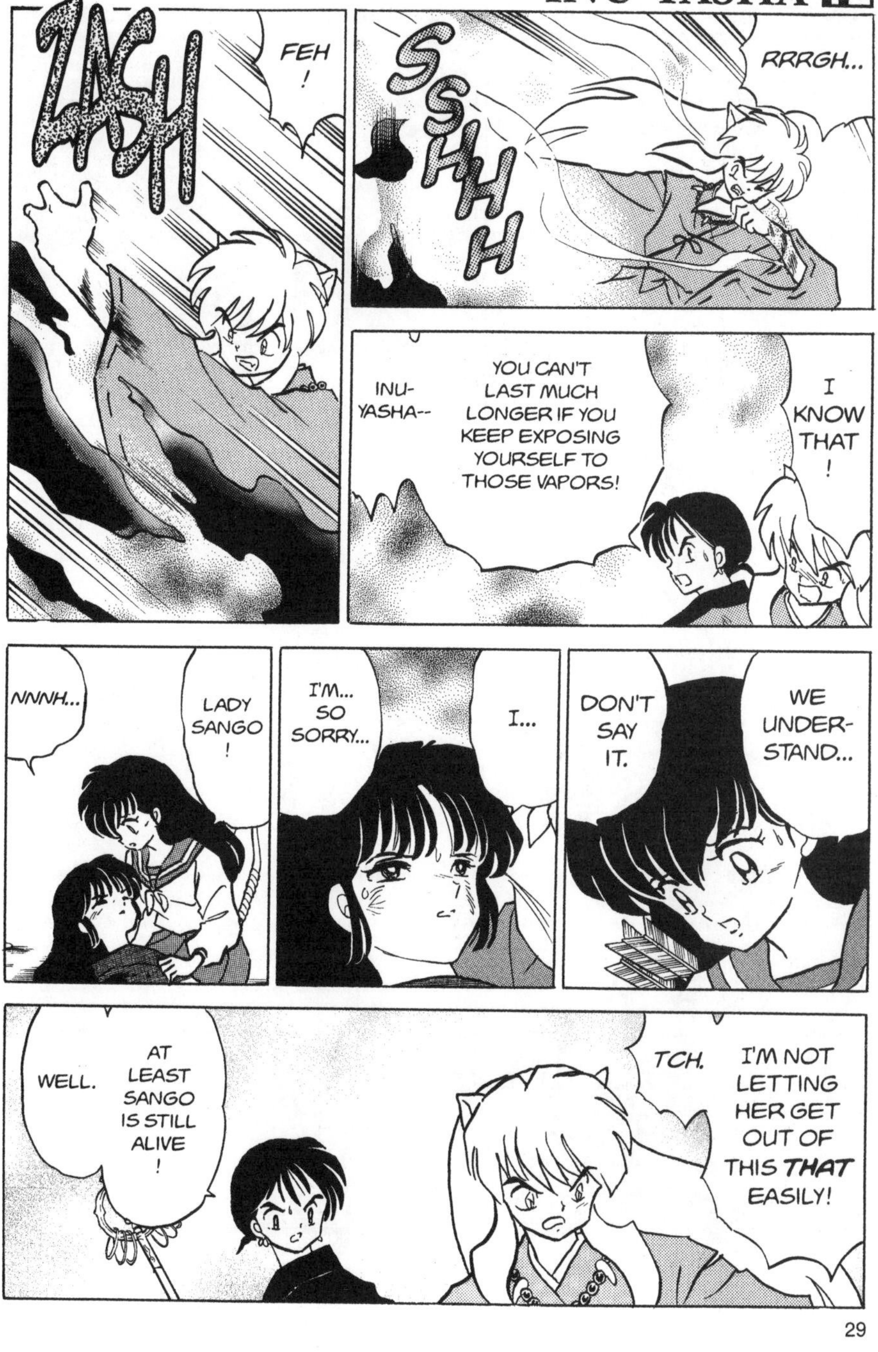
ZASH
FEH!
SSHHHH
RRRGH...
INU-YASHA--
YOU CAN'T LAST MUCH LONGER IF YOU KEEP EXPOSING YOURSELF TO THOSE VAPORS!
I KNOW THAT!
NNNH...
LADY SANGO!
I'M... SO SORRY...
I...
DON'T SAY IT.
WE UNDERSTAND...
WELL.
AT LEAST SANGO IS STILL ALIVE!
TCH.
I'M NOT LETTING HER GET OUT OF THIS *THAT* EASILY!

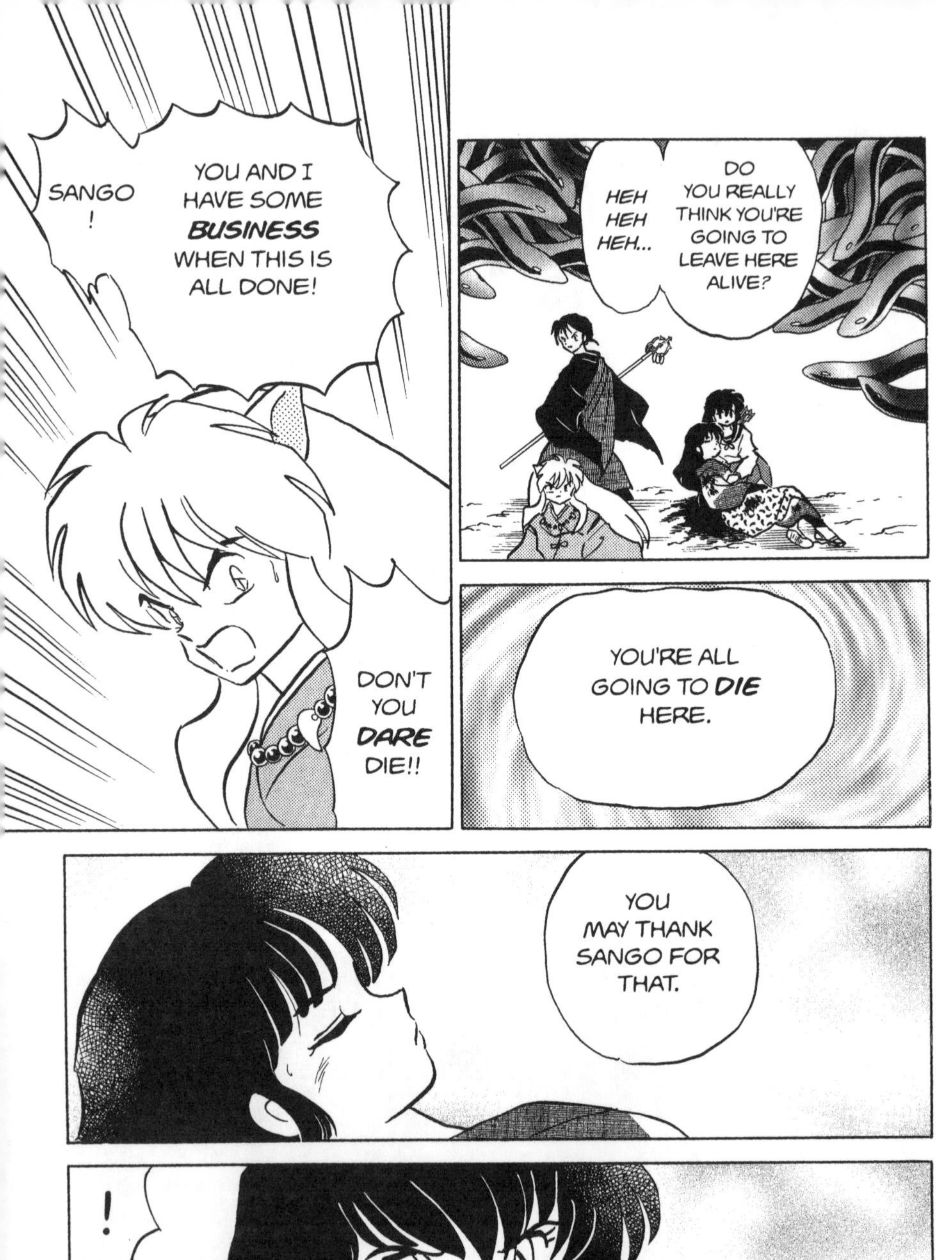
SANGO!
YOU AND I HAVE SOME BUSINESS WHEN THIS IS ALL DONE!
DON'T YOU DARE DIE!!
HEH HEH HEH...
DO YOU REALLY THINK YOU'RE GOING TO LEAVE HERE ALIVE?
YOU'RE ALL GOING TO DIE HERE.
YOU MAY THANK SANGO FOR THAT.
!

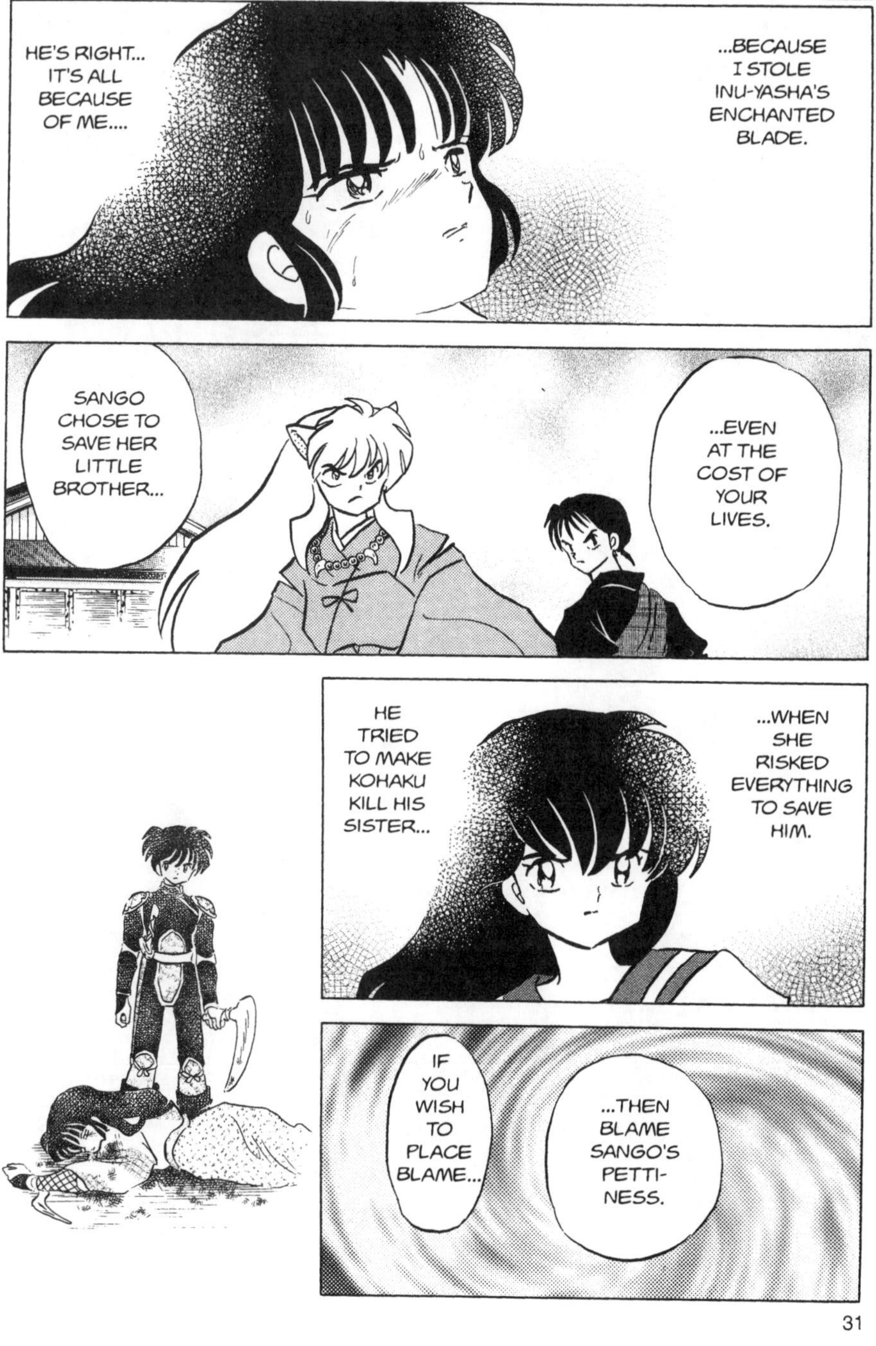
HE'S RIGHT... IT'S ALL BECAUSE OF ME....
...BECAUSE I STOLE INU-YASHA'S ENCHANTED BLADE.
SANGO CHOSE TO SAVE HER LITTLE BROTHER...
...EVEN AT THE COST OF YOUR LIVES.
HE TRIED TO MAKE KOHAKU KILL HIS SISTER...
...WHEN SHE RISKED EVERYTHING TO SAVE HIM.
IF YOU WISH TO PLACE BLAME...
...THEN BLAME SANGO'S PETTI-NESS.

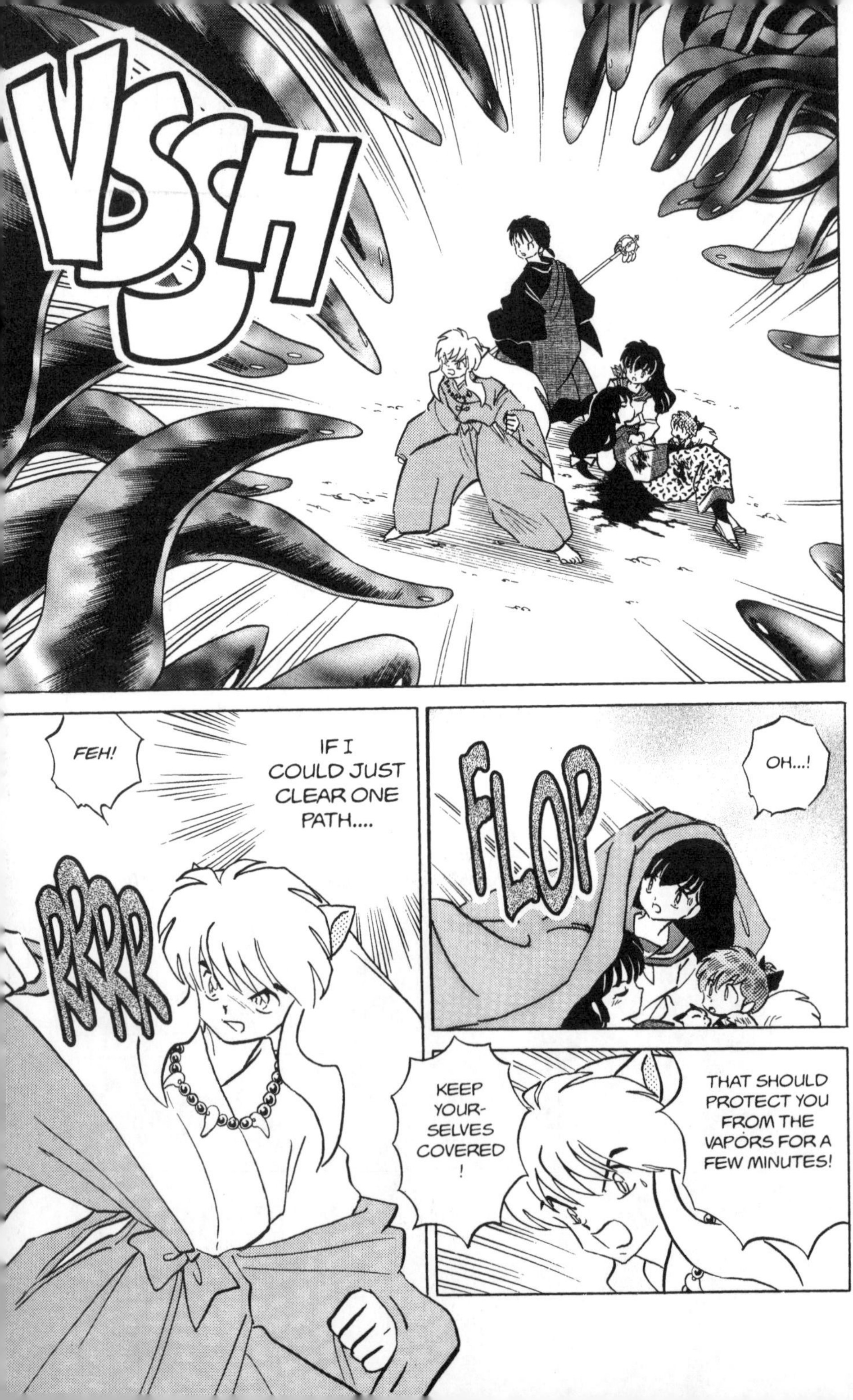
VSSH
FEH!
IF I COULD JUST CLEAR ONE PATH....
RRRR
FLOP
OH...!
KEEP YOURSELVES COVERED!
THAT SHOULD PROTECT YOU FROM THE VAPORS FOR A FEW MINUTES!

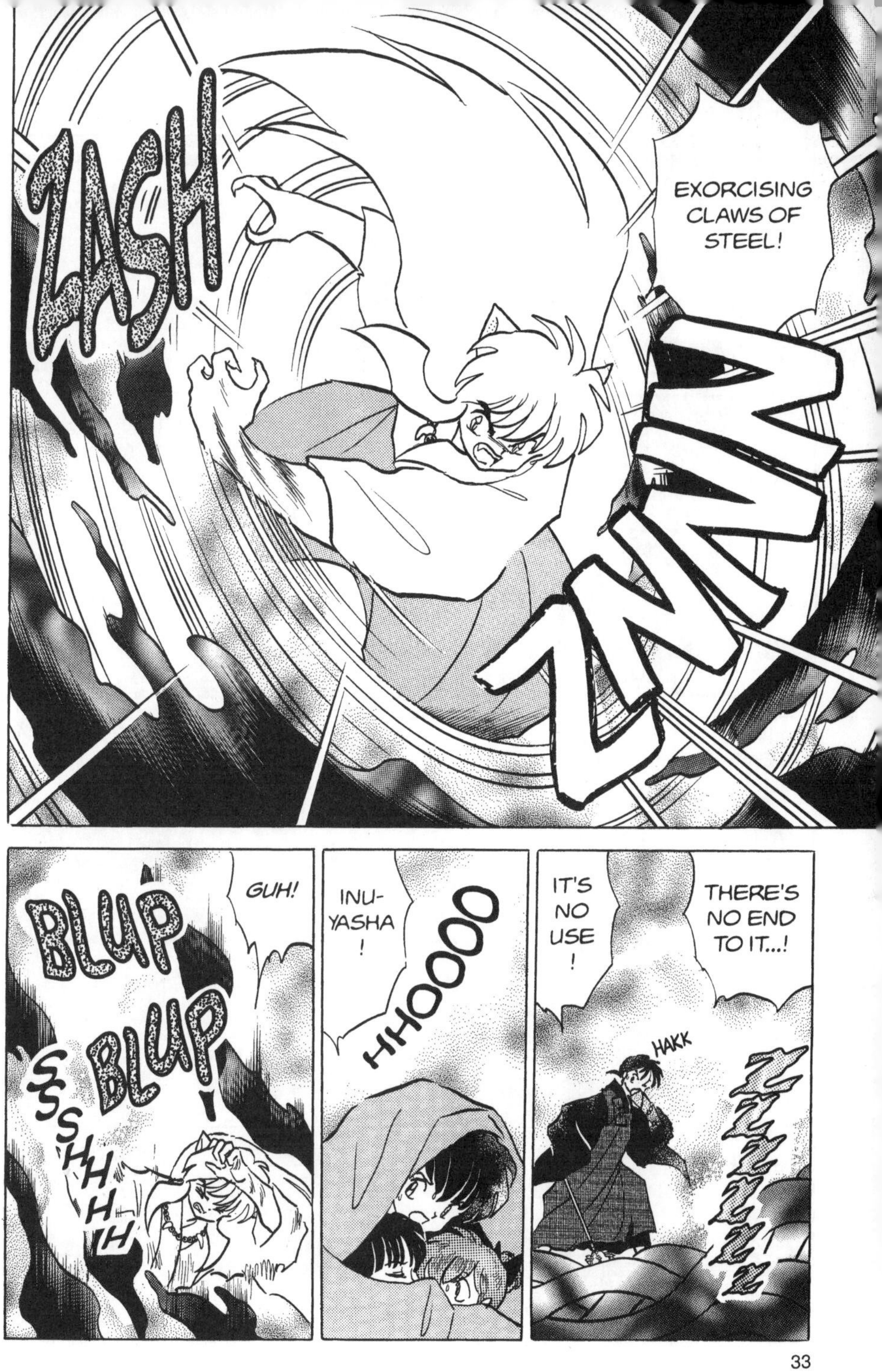
ZASH
EXORCISING CLAWS OF STEEL!
ZWANN
BLUP BLUP
SSHHHH
GUH!
INU-YASHA!
HHOOOOO
IT'S NO USE!
THERE'S NO END TO IT...!
HAKK
ZZZZZZZ

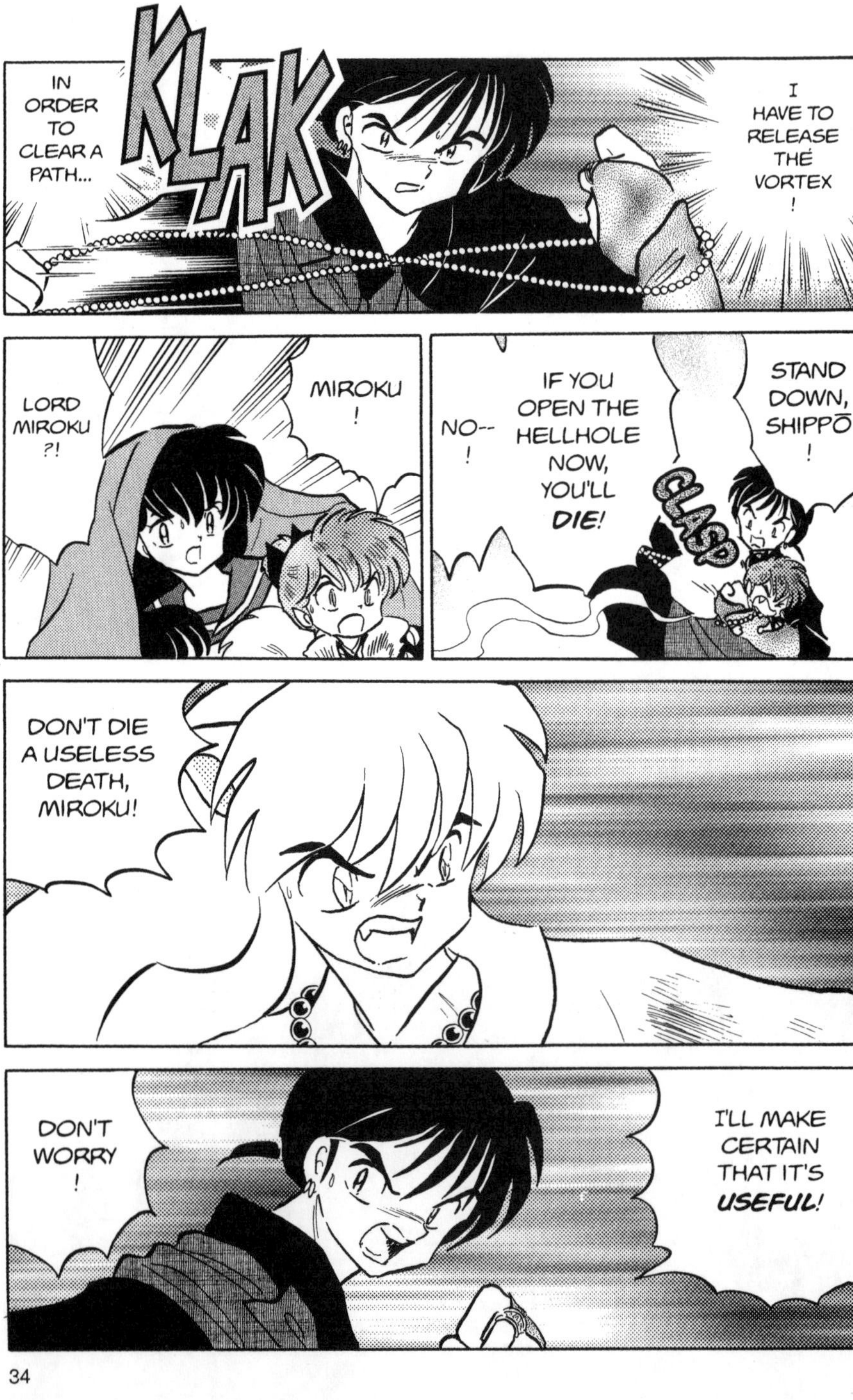
KLAK
IN ORDER TO CLEAR A PATH...
I HAVE TO RELEASE THE VORTEX!
LORD MIROKU ?!
MIROKU!
NO--!
IF YOU OPEN THE HELLHOLE NOW, YOU'LL DIE!
STAND DOWN, SHIPPŌ!
CLASP
DON'T DIE A USELESS DEATH, MIROKU!
DON'T WORRY!
I'LL MAKE CERTAIN THAT IT'S USEFUL!

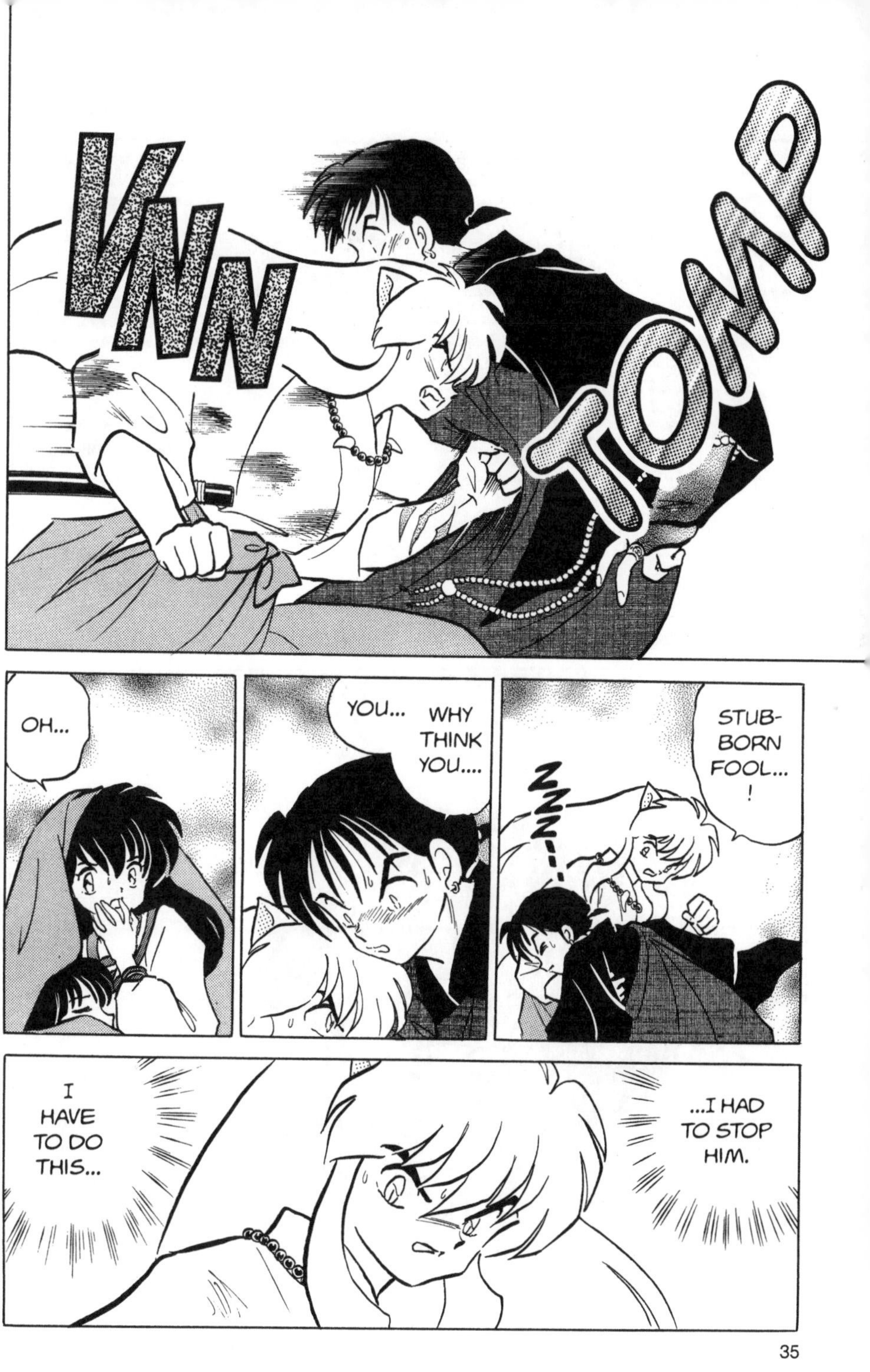
VNN
TOMP
OH...
YOU... WHY THINK YOU....
STUB-BORN FOOL...!
ZZZ...
I HAVE TO DO THIS...
...I HAD TO STOP HIM.

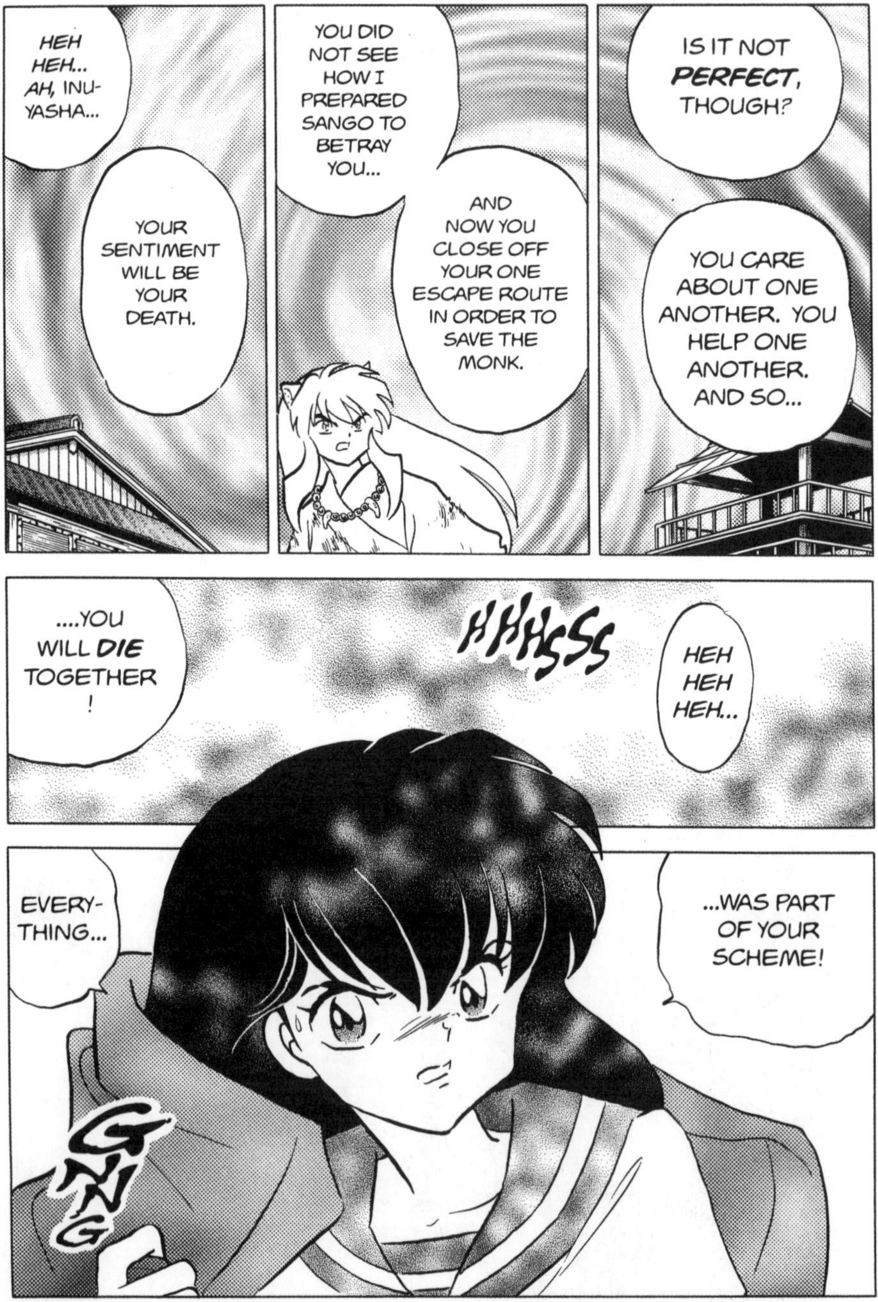
HEH HEH... AH, INU-YASHA...
YOUR SENTIMENT WILL BE YOUR DEATH.
YOU DID NOT SEE HOW I PREPARED SANGO TO BETRAY YOU...
AND NOW YOU CLOSE OFF YOUR ONE ESCAPE ROUTE IN ORDER TO SAVE THE MONK.
IS IT NOT PERFECT, THOUGH?
YOU CARE ABOUT ONE ANOTHER. YOU HELP ONE ANOTHER. AND SO...
....YOU WILL DIE TOGETHER !
HHHSSS
HEH HEH HEH...
EVERY-THING...
...WAS PART OF YOUR SCHEME!
GNG

NARAKU...

WHERE ARE YOU?!

YOU'VE GOT TO BE NEARBY...

WE'RE GOING TO STOP YOU!

SSHH!

ZZZ
ZZZ

THE POISON VAPORS...!

SSHH

I'VE GOT TO HURRY!

OH...!

GLINT...

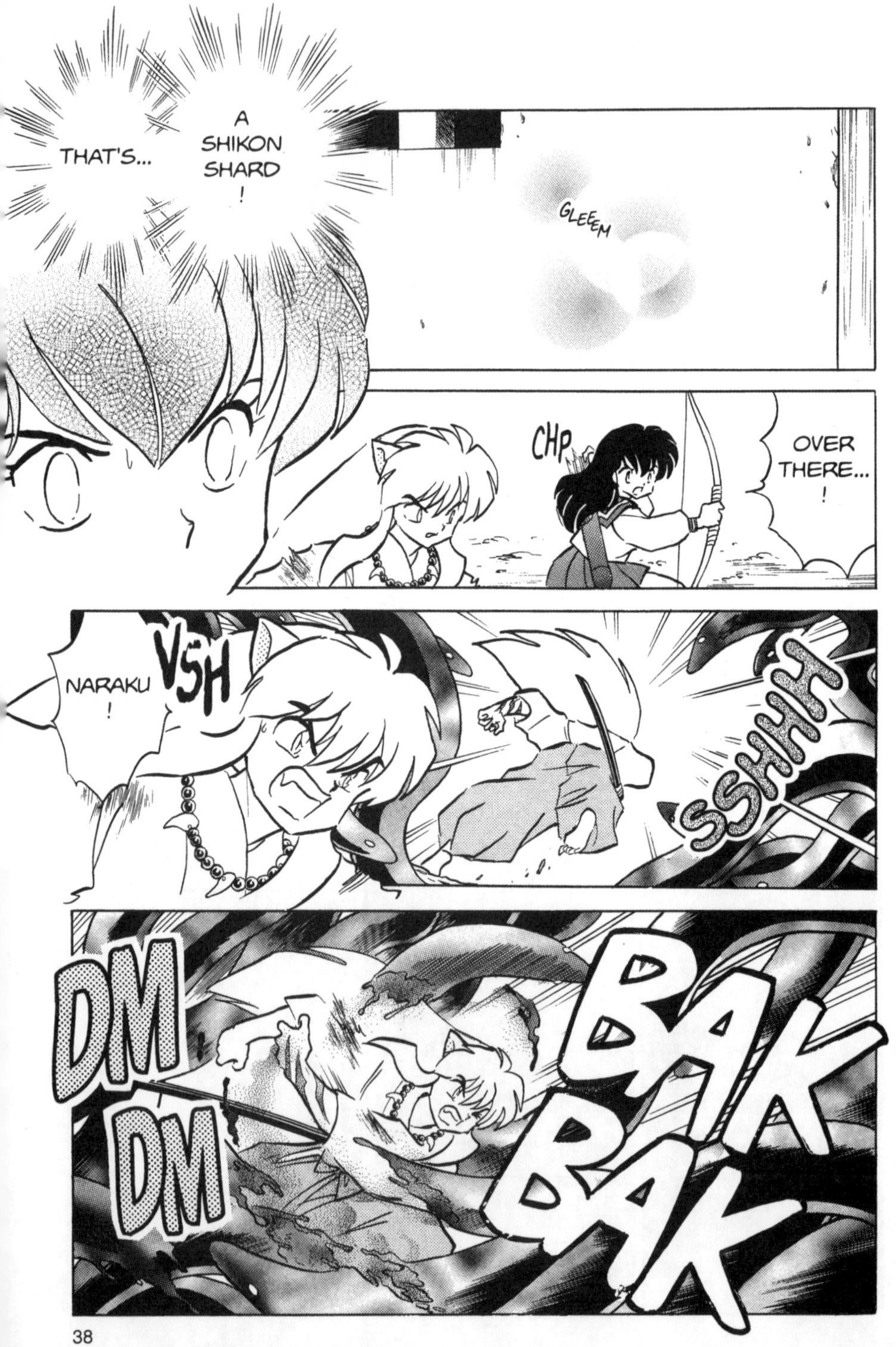
THAT'S...
A SHIKON SHARD !
GLEEEM
CHP
OVER THERE... !
NARAKU !
VSH
SSHHH
DM DM
BAK BAK

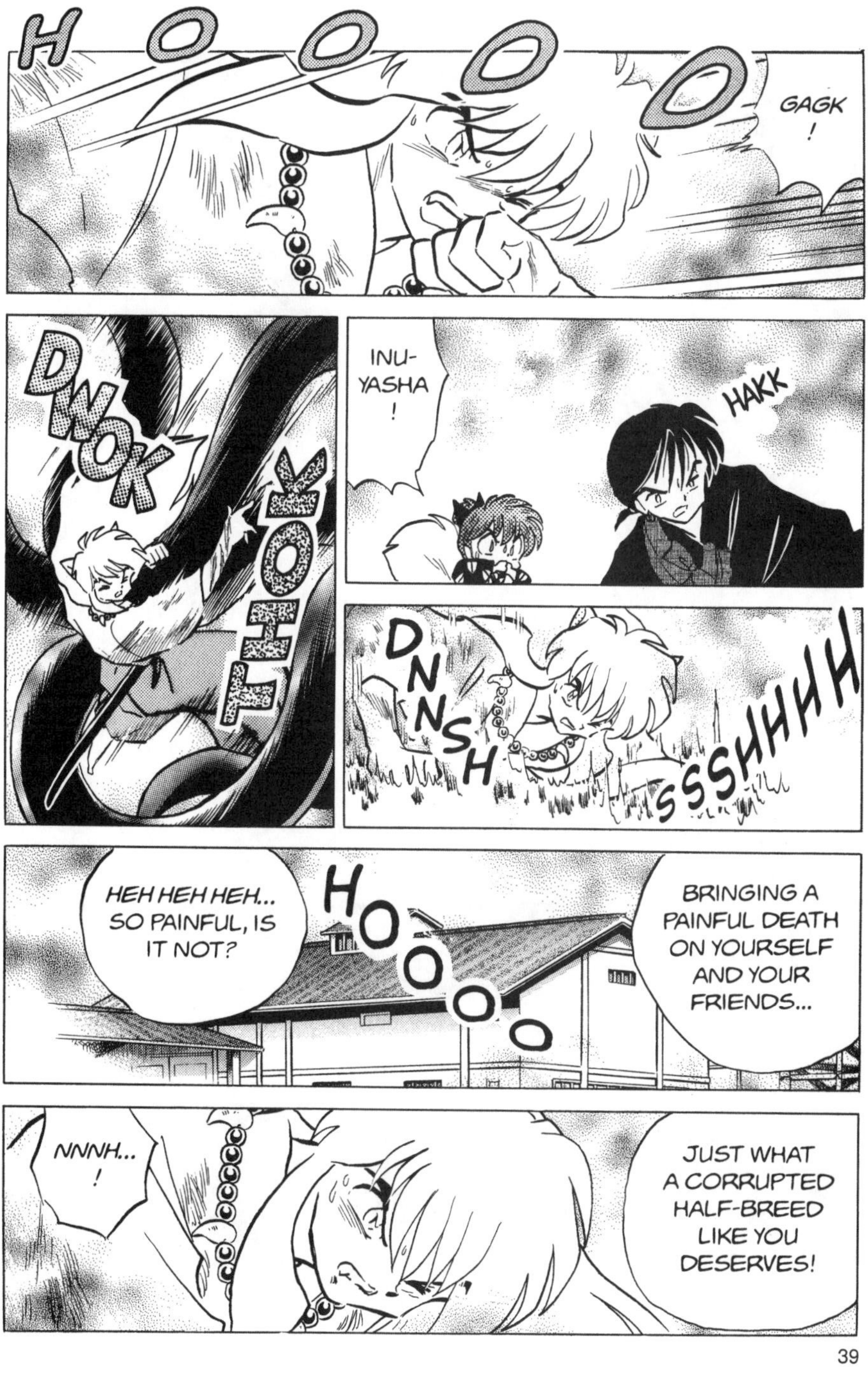
HOOOOO
GAGK!
DWOK
THOOK
INU-YASHA!
HAKK
DNNSH
SSSHHHH
HEH HEH HEH... SO PAINFUL, IS IT NOT?
HOOOOO
BRINGING A PAINFUL DEATH ON YOURSELF AND YOUR FRIENDS...
NNNH...!
JUST WHAT A CORRUPTED HALF-BREED LIKE YOU DESERVES!

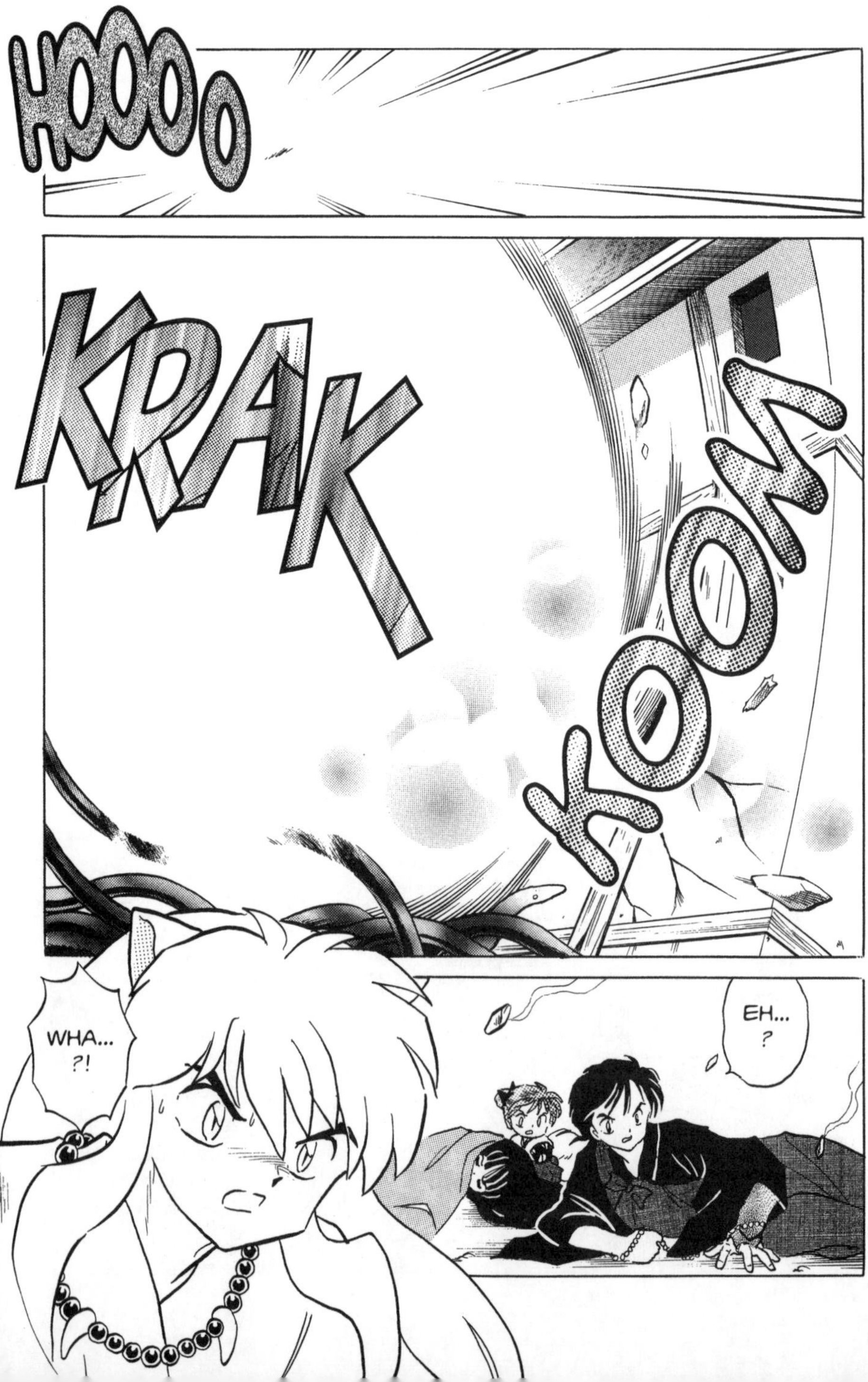
HOOOO
KRAK
KOOOM
WHA... ?!
EH... ?

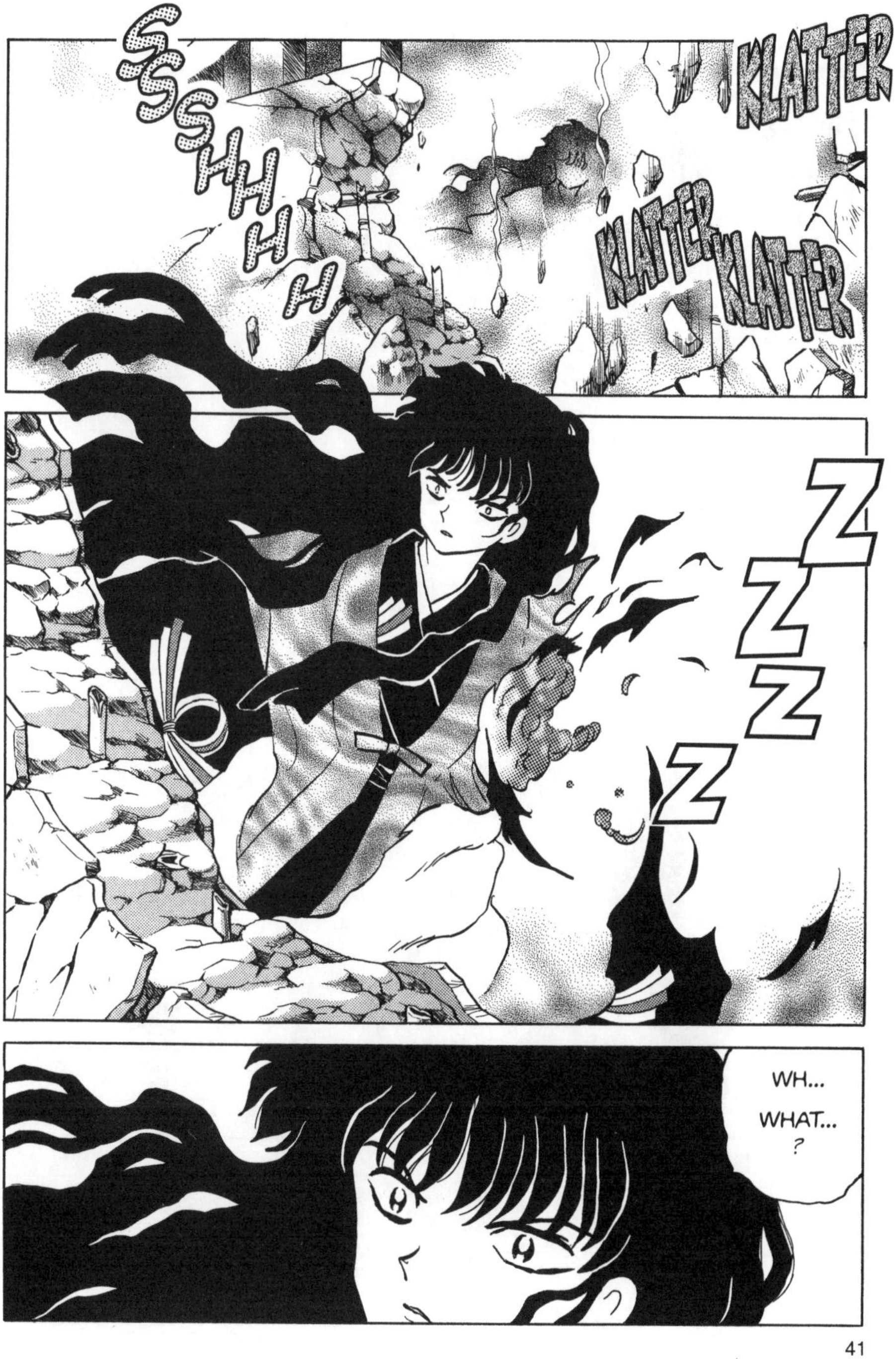
SSSHHHHH
KLATTER
KLATTER KLATTER
ZZZZ
WH... WHAT... ?

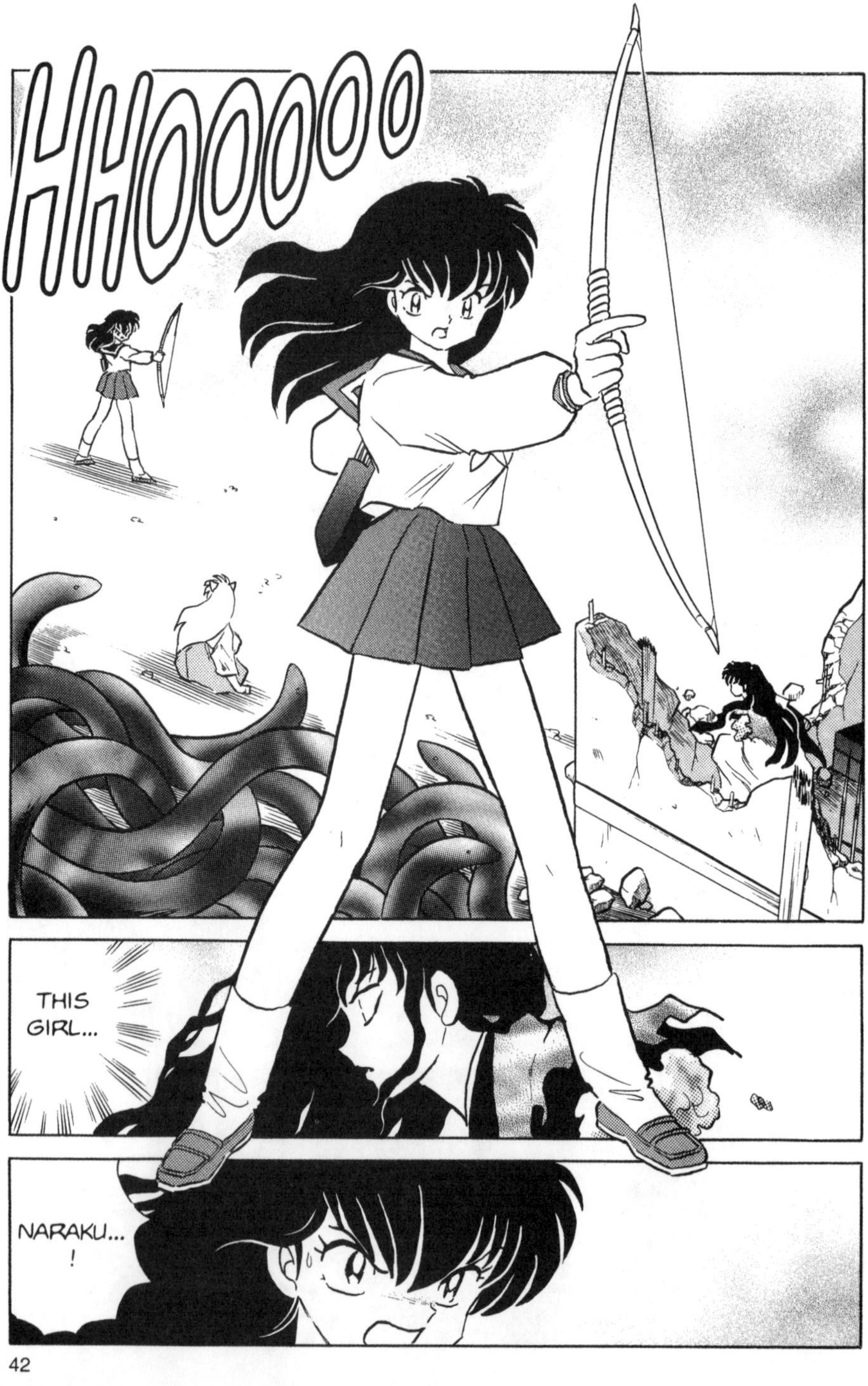
HHOOOOO
THIS GIRL...
NARAKU... !

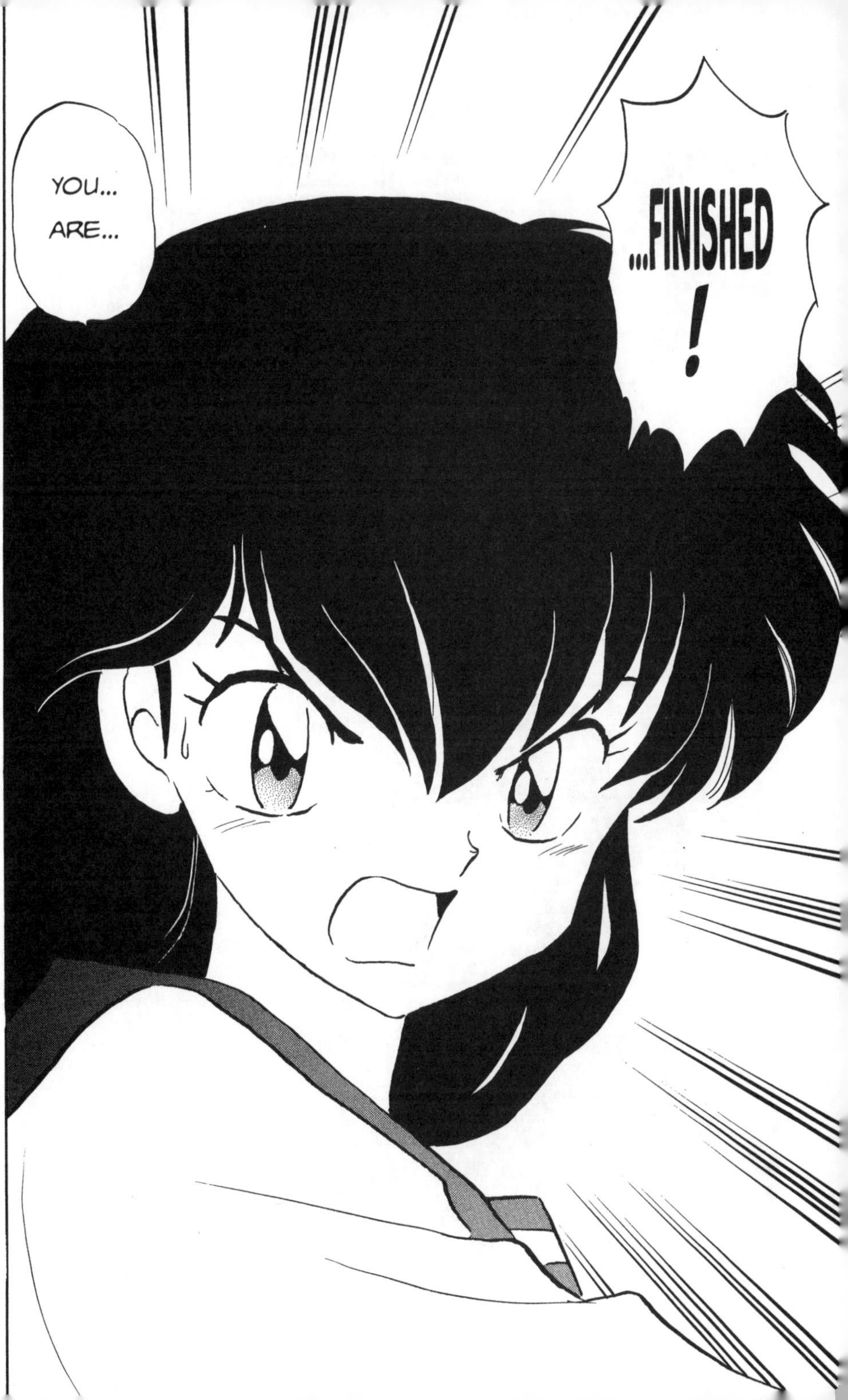
YOU... ARE...
...FINISHED!

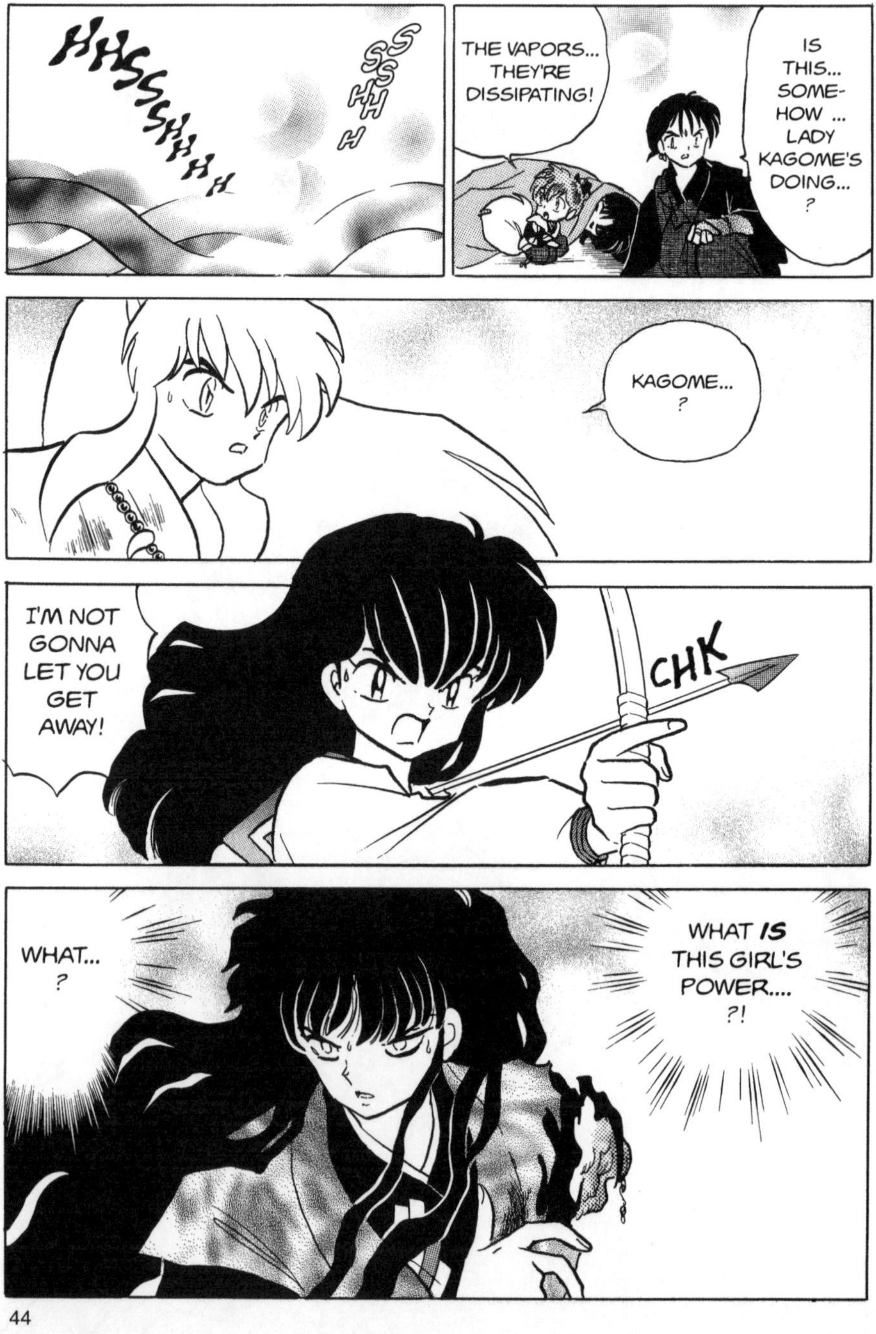
HHSSSHHHH
SSHHH
THE VAPORS... THEY'RE DISSIPATING!
IS THIS... SOMEHOW ... LADY KAGOME'S DOING... ?
KAGOME... ?
I'M NOT GONNA LET YOU GET AWAY!
CHK
WHAT... ?
WHAT IS THIS GIRL'S POWER.... ?!

SCROLL THREE

PURIFICATION

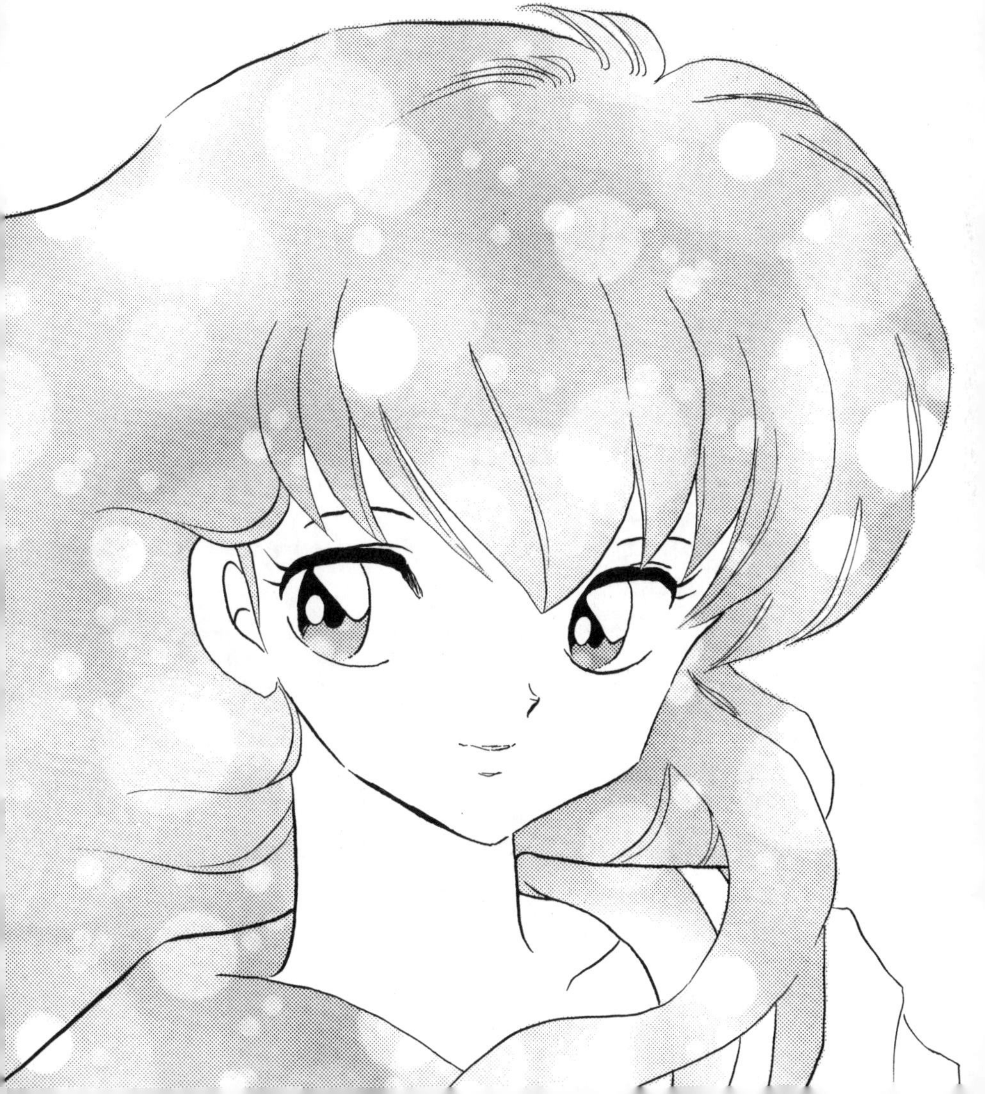

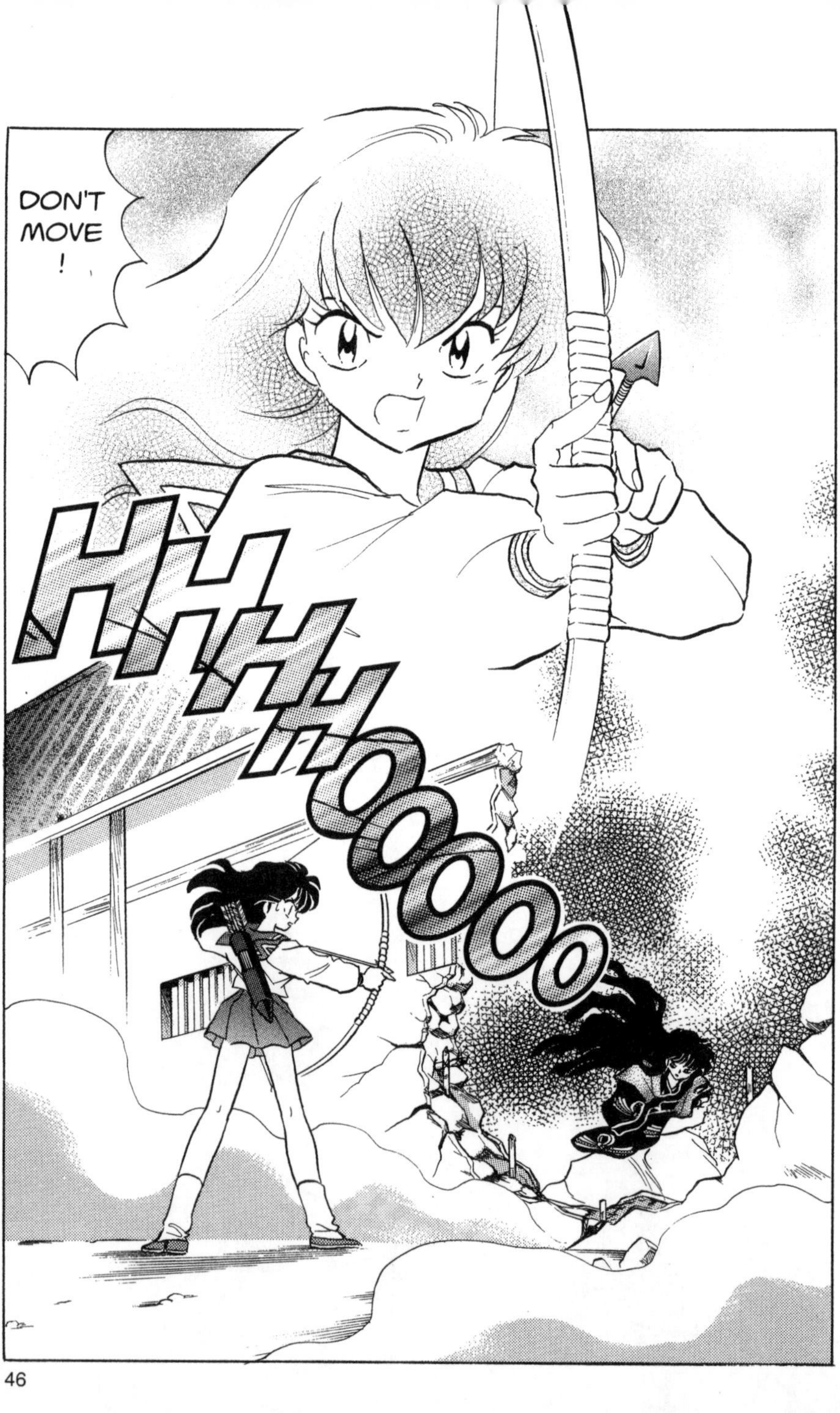
DON'T MOVE !
HHHHOOOOOOO

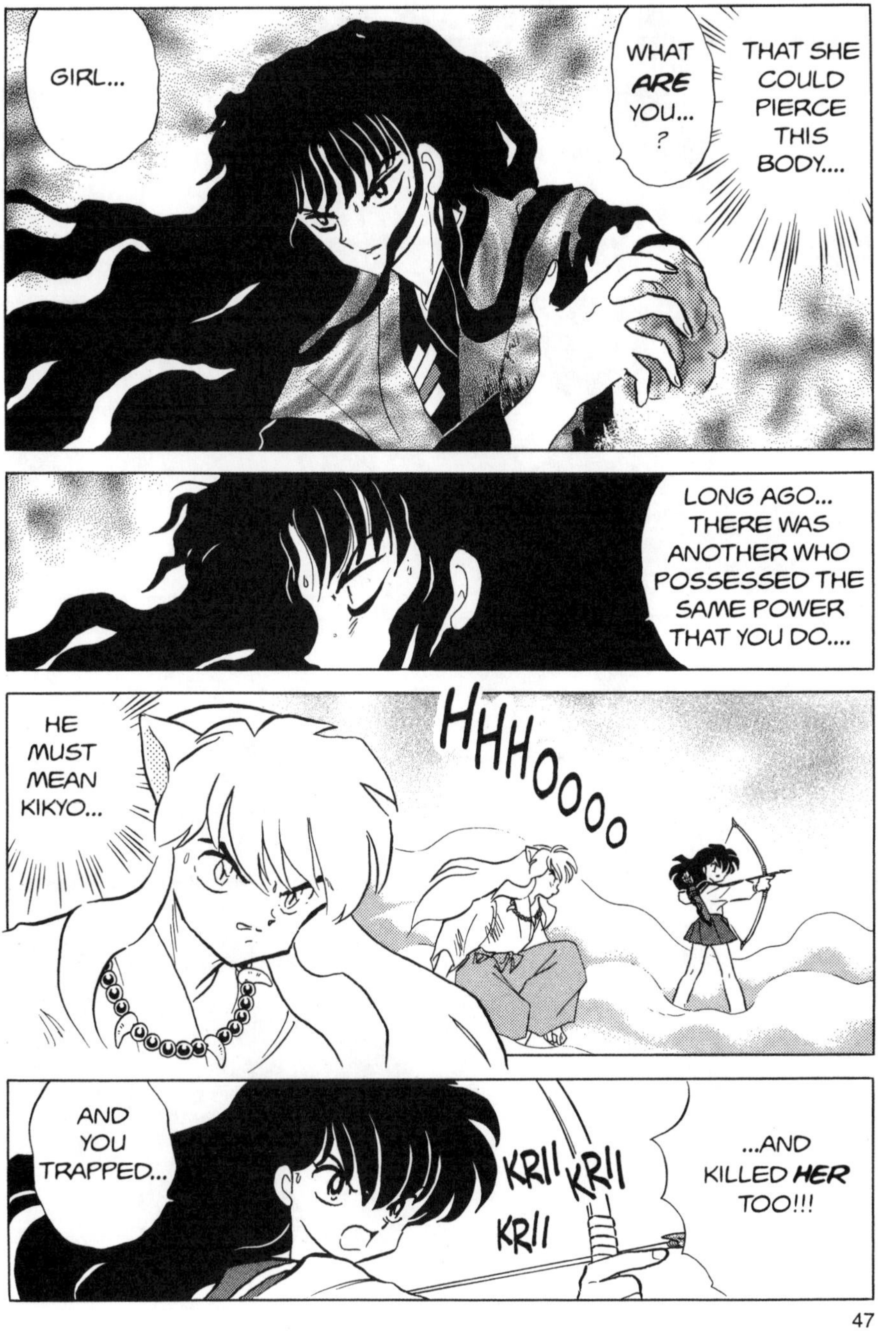
GIRL...
WHAT **ARE** YOU...?
THAT SHE COULD PIERCE THIS BODY....
LONG AGO... THERE WAS ANOTHER WHO POSSESSED THE SAME POWER THAT YOU DO....
HE MUST MEAN KIKYO...
HHHOOOOO
AND YOU TRAPPED...
KRII KRII
KRII
...AND KILLED **HER** TOO!!!

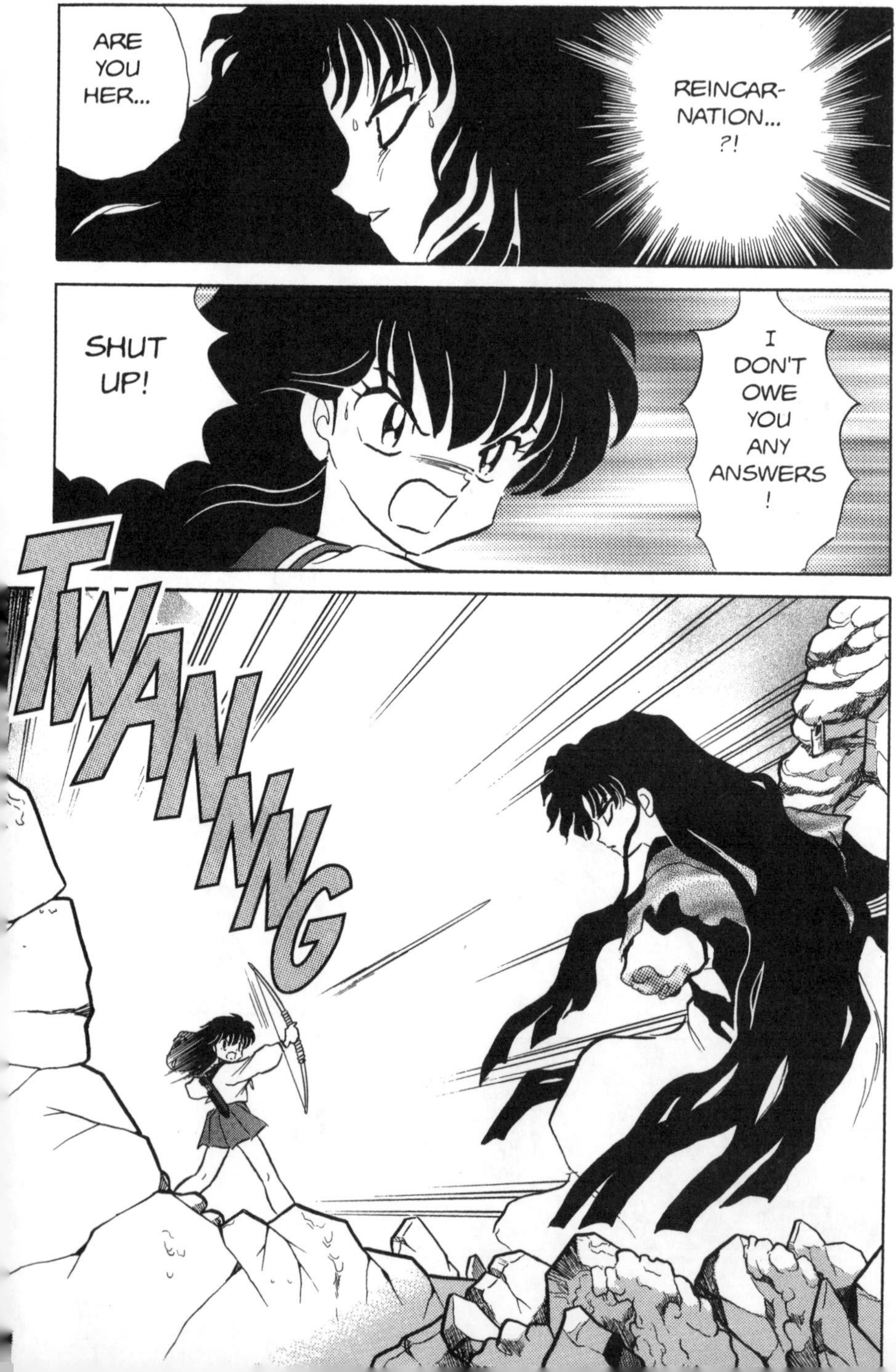
ARE YOU HER...
REINCAR-NATION... ?!
SHUT UP!
I DON'T OWE YOU ANY ANSWERS !
TWANNNG

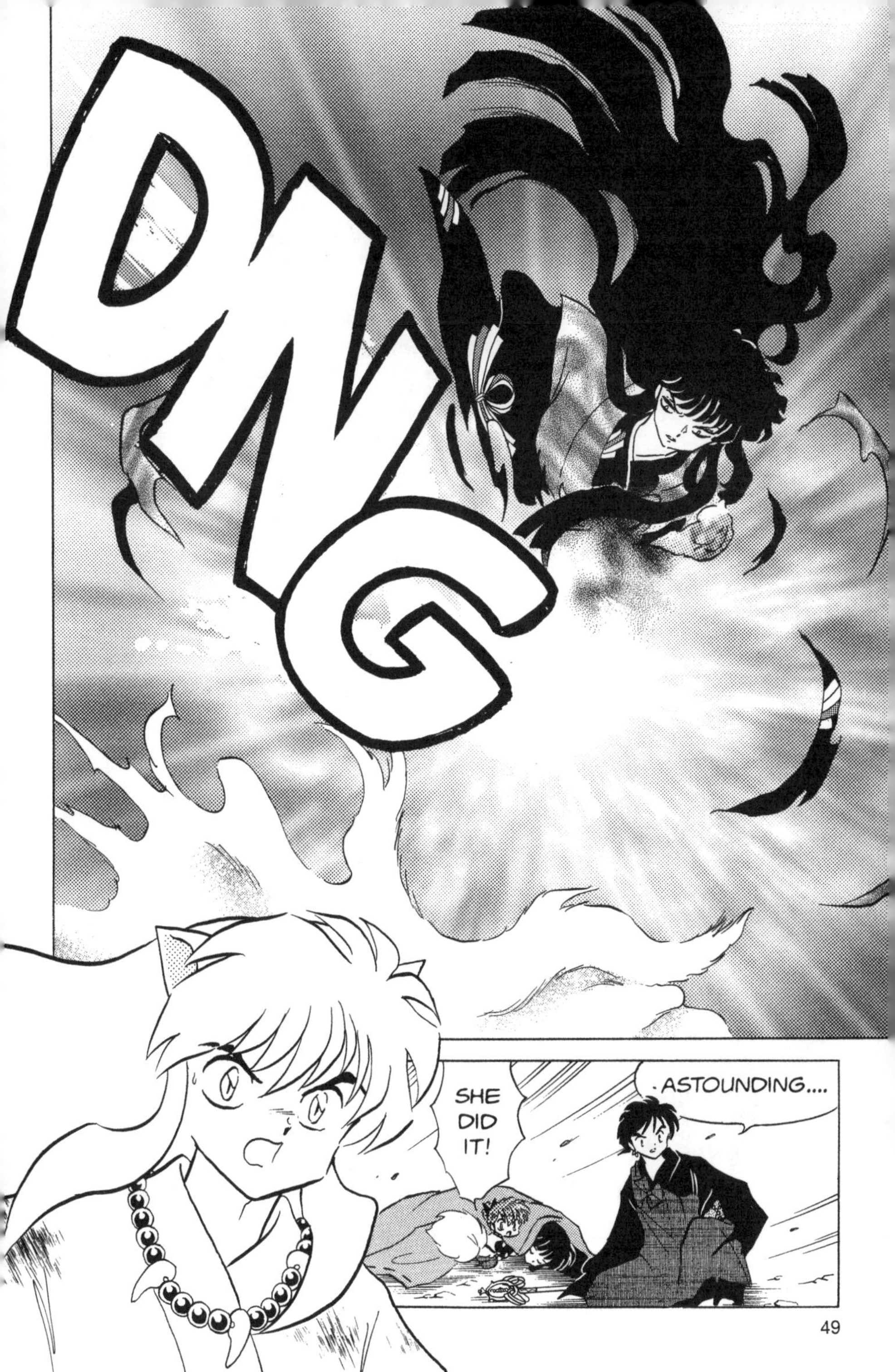
DNG
SHE DID IT!
...ASTOUNDING....

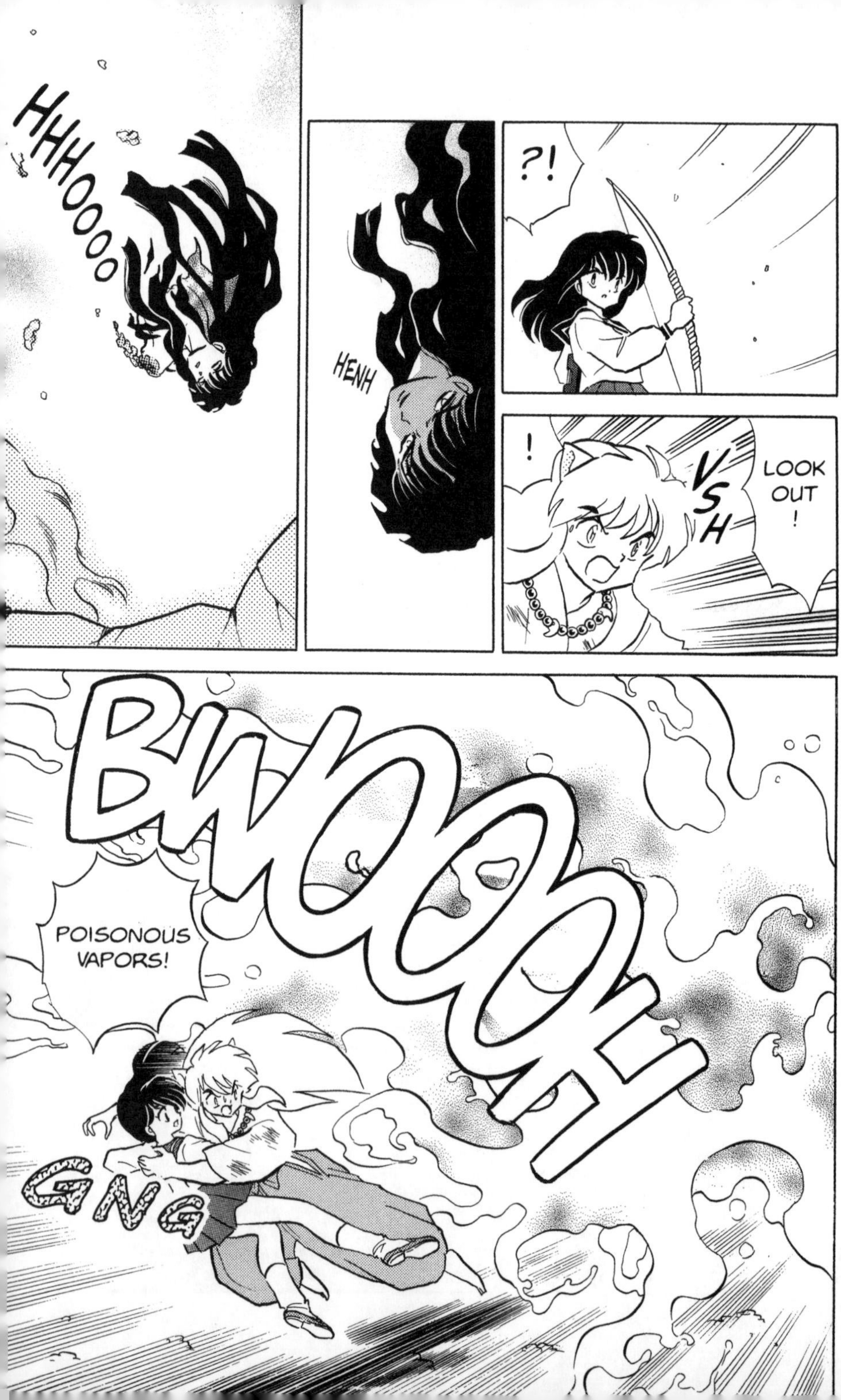
HHHOOOO
HENH
?!
!
VSH
LOOK OUT !
BWOOOOH
POISONOUS VAPORS!
GNG

ZZZSH
SSSZZZLLL
HWOOOO
UGH... !
SSSZZZLLL
BLK BLLK
HHHSSS
BLK BLK BLK
HHOOORR

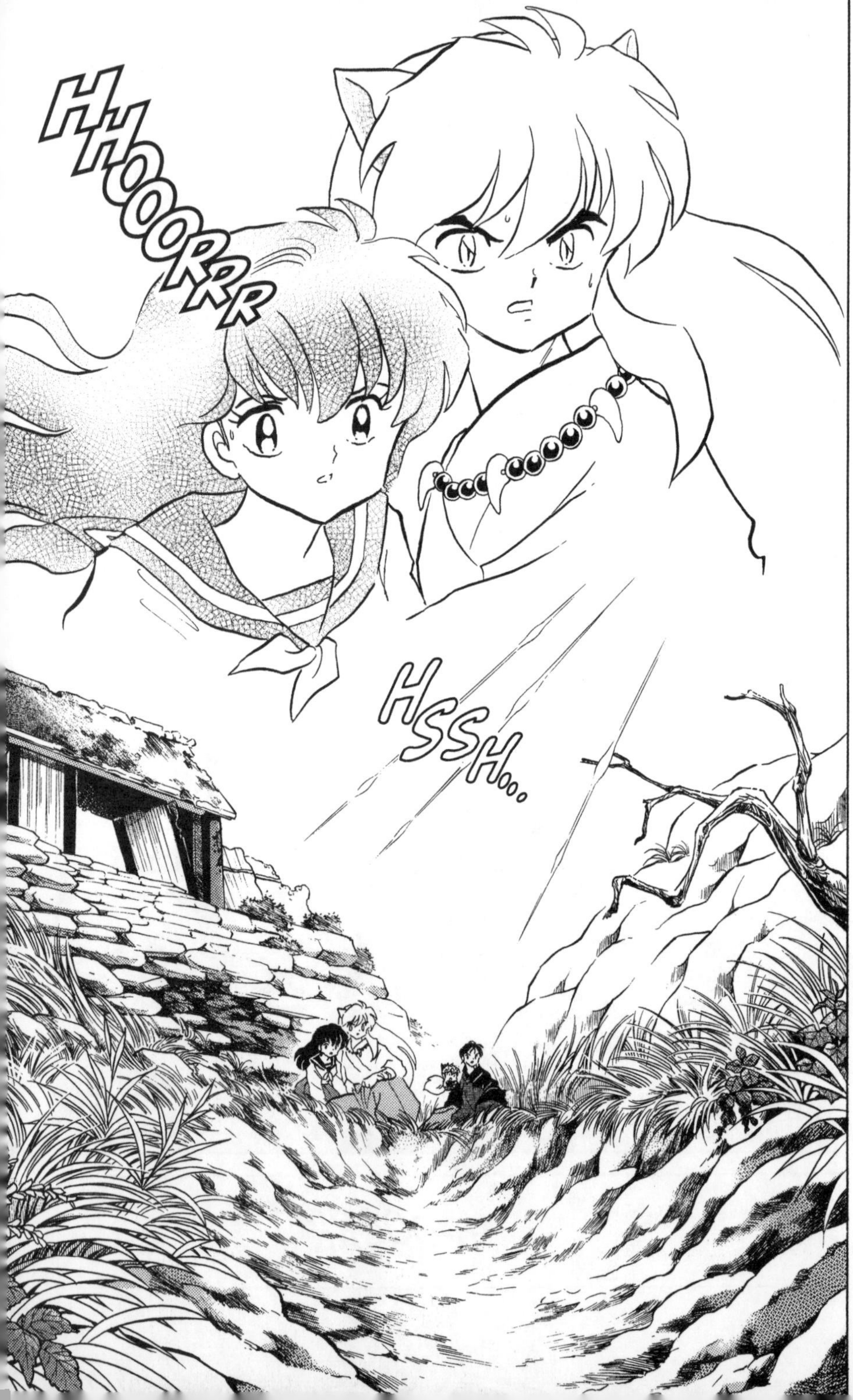
HHOOORRR
HSSH...

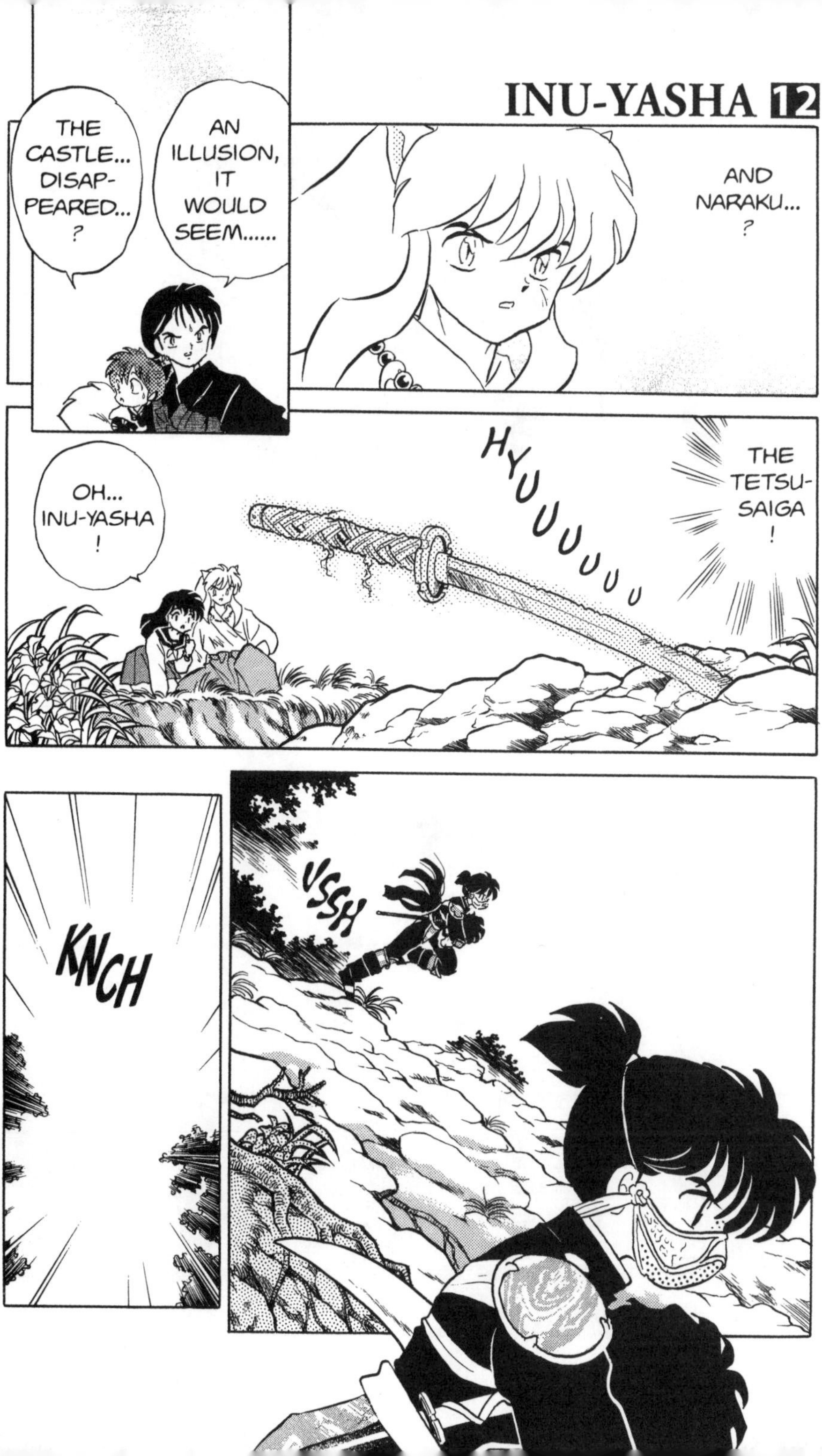
THE CASTLE... DISAPPEARED...?
AN ILLUSION, IT WOULD SEEM......
AND NARAKU...?
OH... INU-YASHA!
HYUUUUUUU
THE TETSU-SAIGA!
KNCH
VSSH

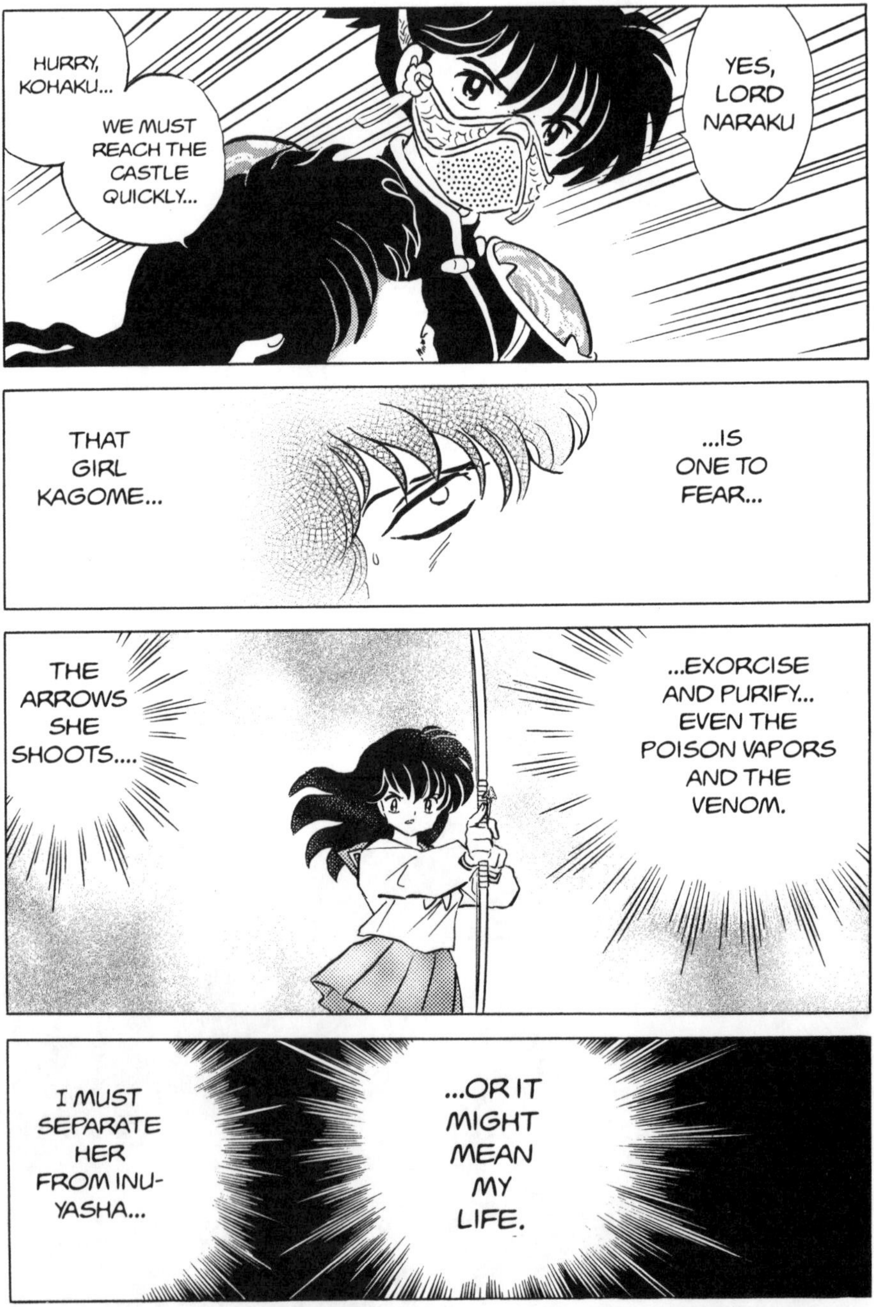
HURRY, KOHAKU...
WE MUST REACH THE CASTLE QUICKLY...
YES, LORD NARAKU
THAT GIRL KAGOME...
...IS ONE TO FEAR...
THE ARROWS SHE SHOOTS....
...EXORCISE AND PURIFY... EVEN THE POISON VAPORS AND THE VENOM.
I MUST SEPARATE HER FROM INU-YASHA...
...OR IT MIGHT MEAN MY LIFE.

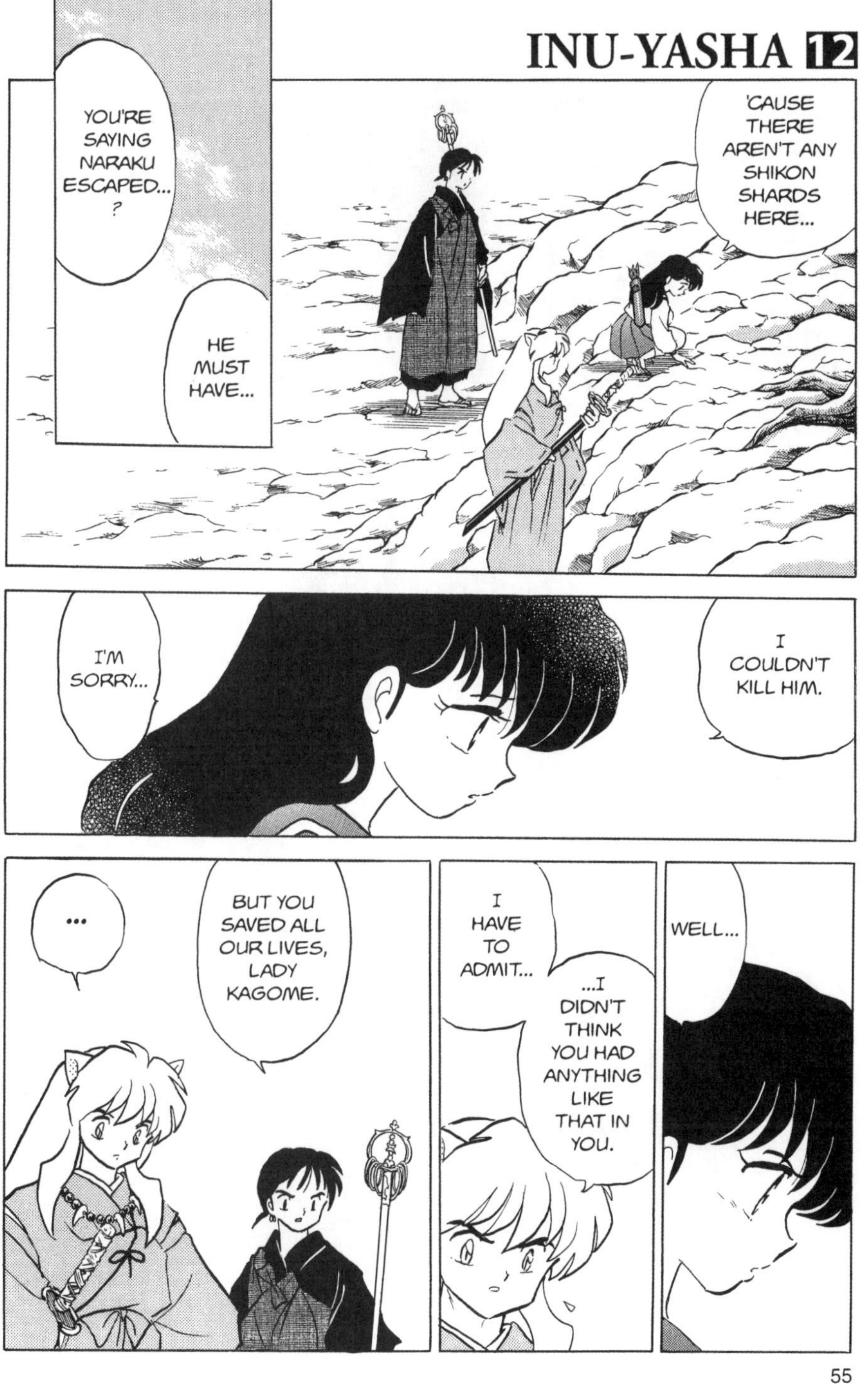
YOU'RE SAYING NARAKU ESCAPED...?
HE MUST HAVE...
'CAUSE THERE AREN'T ANY SHIKON SHARDS HERE...
I'M SORRY...
I COULDN'T KILL HIM.
...
BUT YOU SAVED ALL OUR LIVES, LADY KAGOME.
I HAVE TO ADMIT...
...I DIDN'T THINK YOU HAD ANYTHING LIKE THAT IN YOU.
WELL...

HE WAS... MAKING SUCH A FOOL OF YOU...
...I COULDN'T TAKE IT ANY MORE!
...
YOU MEAN...
ALL THAT RAGE... WAS OVER JUST *THAT*?!
WH-WHAT DO YOU MEAN, "JUST THAT"?!
INDEED...
NO, SANGO...YOU MUSTN'T TRY TO MOVE YET.

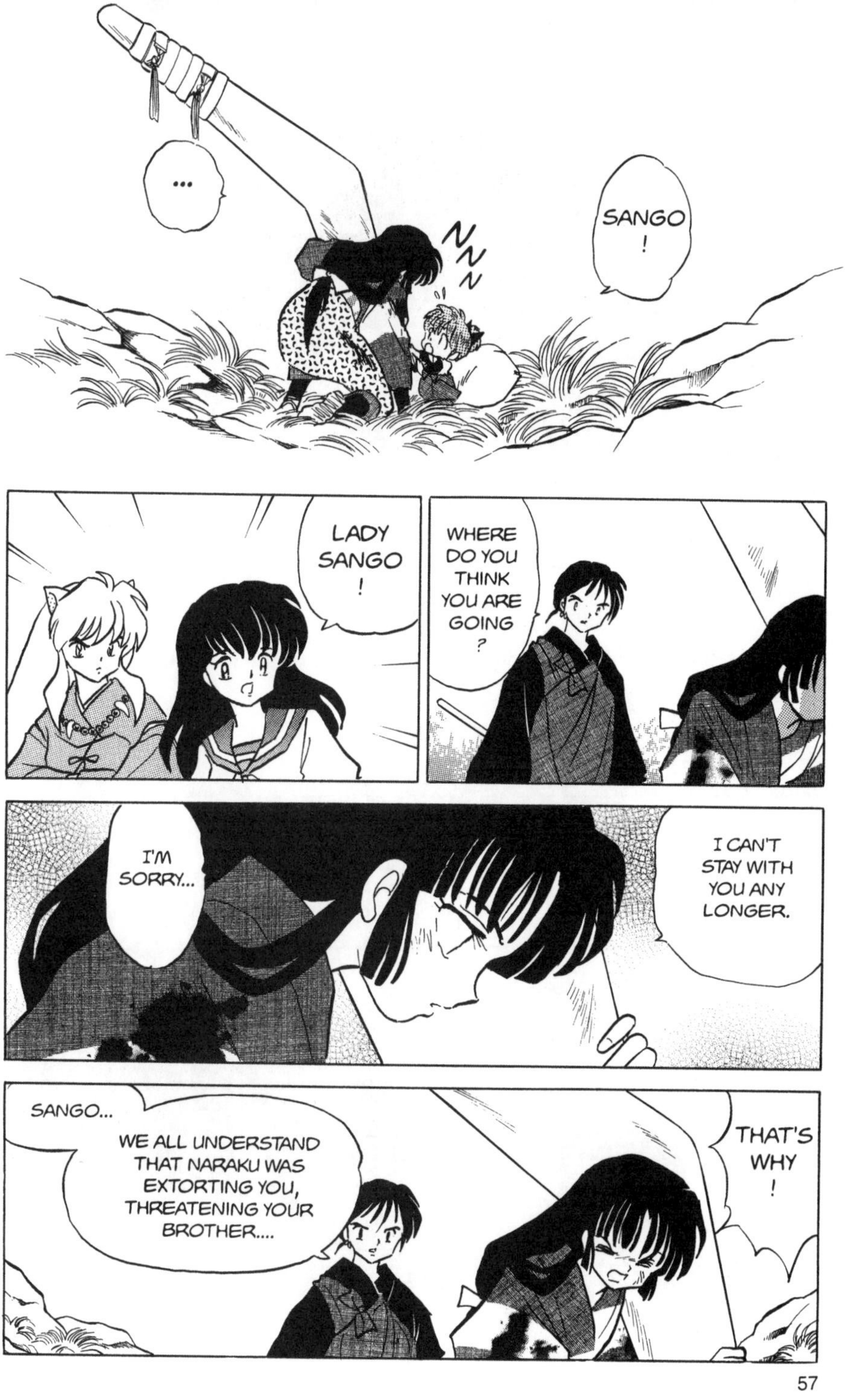
...
NNN
SANGO !
LADY SANGO !
WHERE DO YOU THINK YOU ARE GOING ?
I'M SORRY...
I CAN'T STAY WITH YOU ANY LONGER.
SANGO...
WE ALL UNDERSTAND THAT NARAKU WAS EXTORTING YOU, THREATENING YOUR BROTHER....
THAT'S WHY !

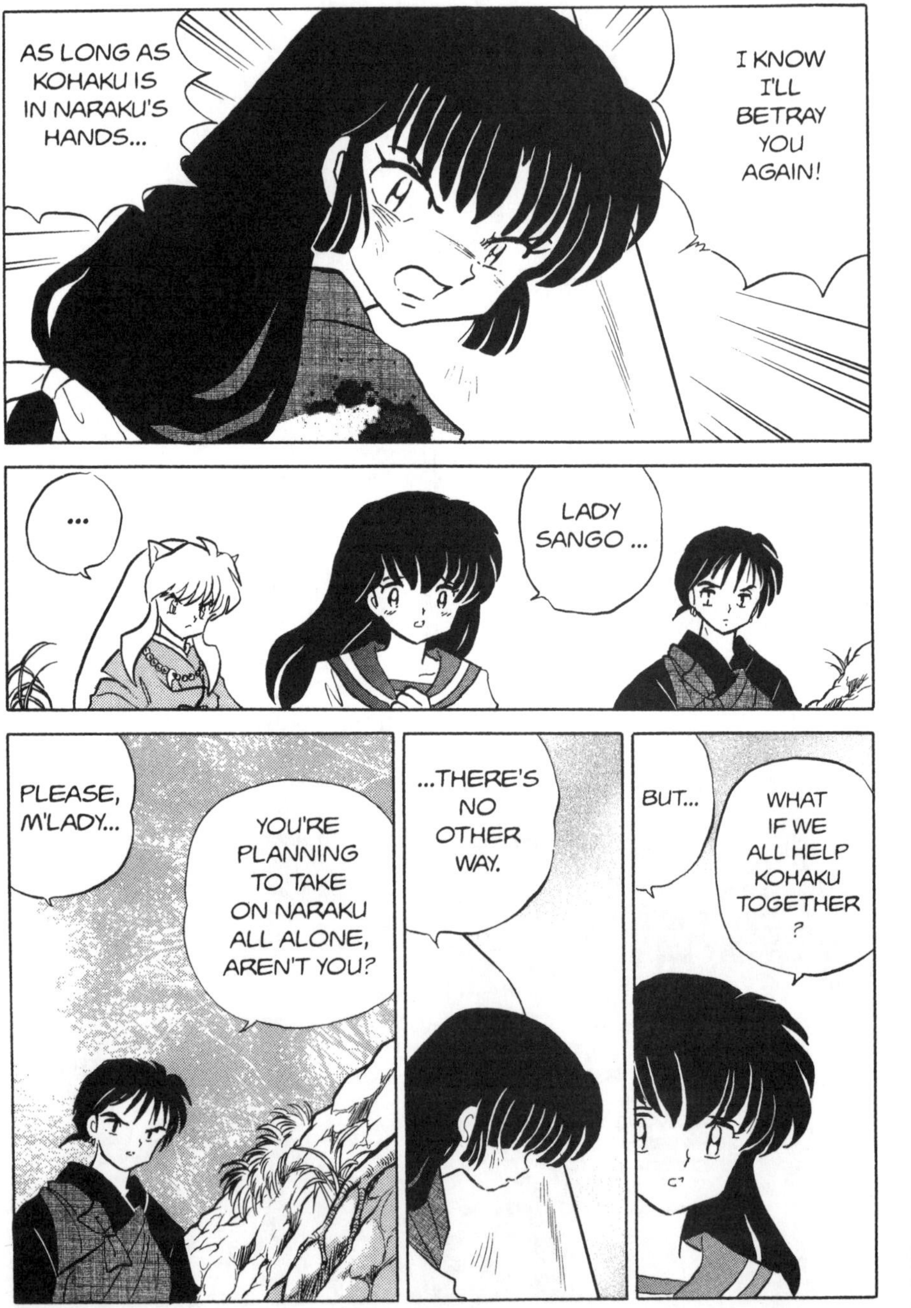
AS LONG AS KOHAKU IS IN NARAKU'S HANDS...
I KNOW I'LL BETRAY YOU AGAIN!
...
LADY SANGO ...
PLEASE, M'LADY...
YOU'RE PLANNING TO TAKE ON NARAKU ALL ALONE, AREN'T YOU?
...THERE'S NO OTHER WAY.
BUT...
WHAT IF WE ALL HELP KOHAKU TOGETHER?

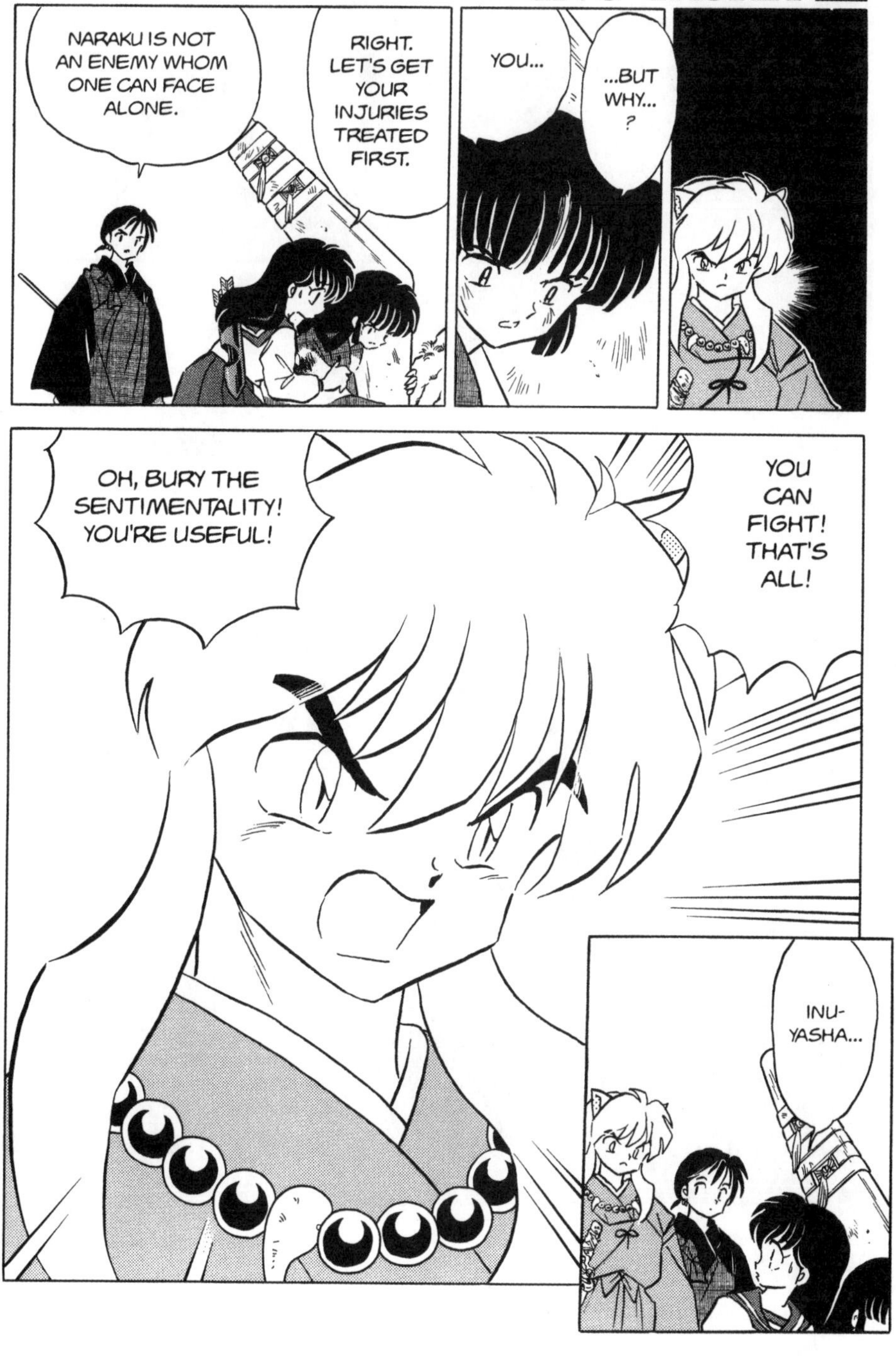
NARAKU IS NOT AN ENEMY WHOM ONE CAN FACE ALONE.
RIGHT. LET'S GET YOUR INJURIES TREATED FIRST.
YOU...
...BUT WHY... ?
OH, BURY THE SENTIMENTALITY! YOU'RE USEFUL!
YOU CAN FIGHT! THAT'S ALL!
INU-YASHA...

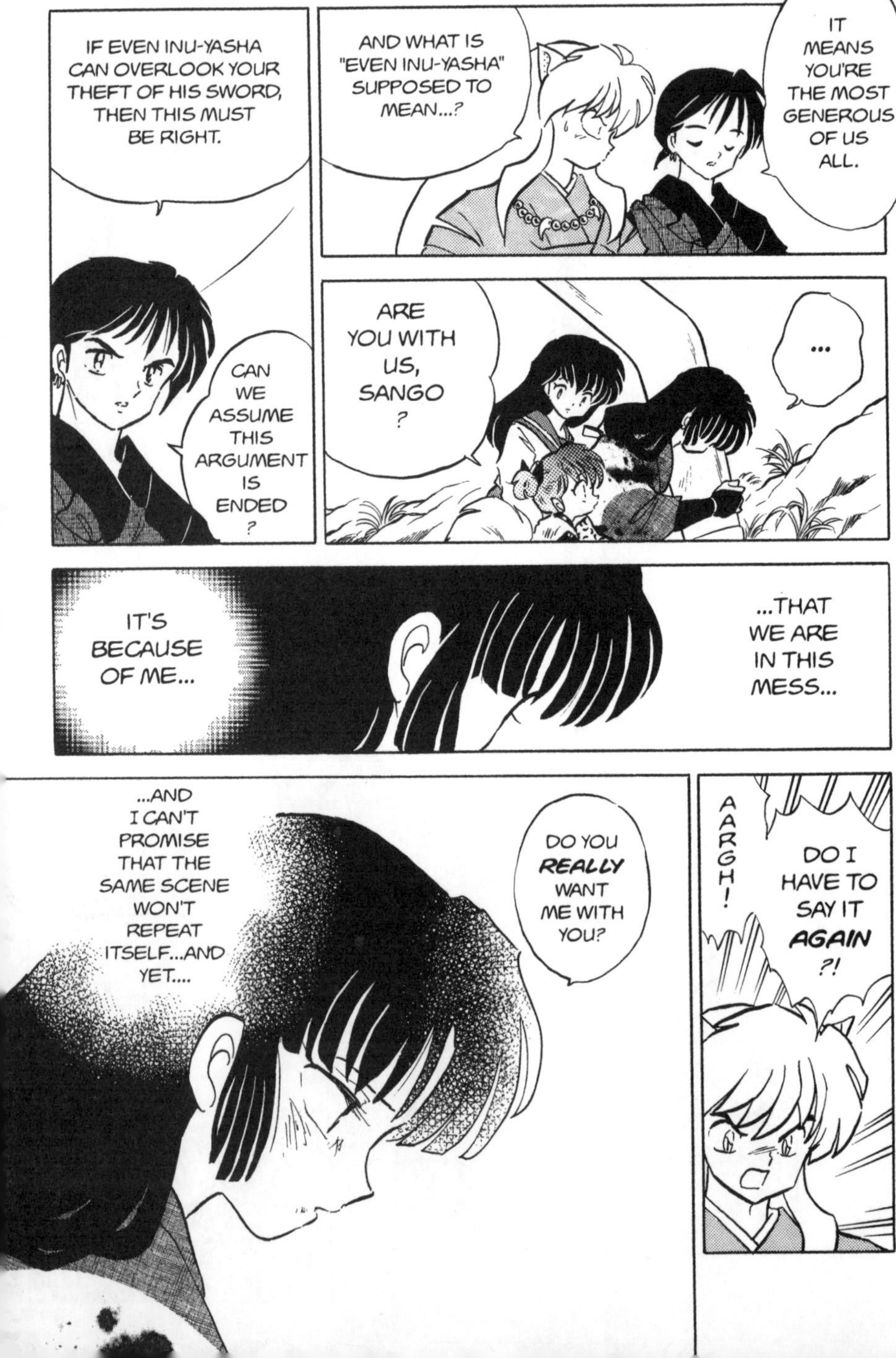
IF EVEN INU-YASHA CAN OVERLOOK YOUR THEFT OF HIS SWORD, THEN THIS MUST BE RIGHT.
CAN WE ASSUME THIS ARGUMENT IS ENDED?
AND WHAT IS "EVEN INU-YASHA" SUPPOSED TO MEAN...?
IT MEANS YOU'RE THE MOST GENEROUS OF US ALL.
ARE YOU WITH US, SANGO?
...
IT'S BECAUSE OF ME...
...THAT WE ARE IN THIS MESS...
...AND I CAN'T PROMISE THAT THE SAME SCENE WON'T REPEAT ITSELF...AND YET....
DO YOU **REALLY** WANT ME WITH YOU?
AARGH!
DO I HAVE TO SAY IT **AGAIN**?!

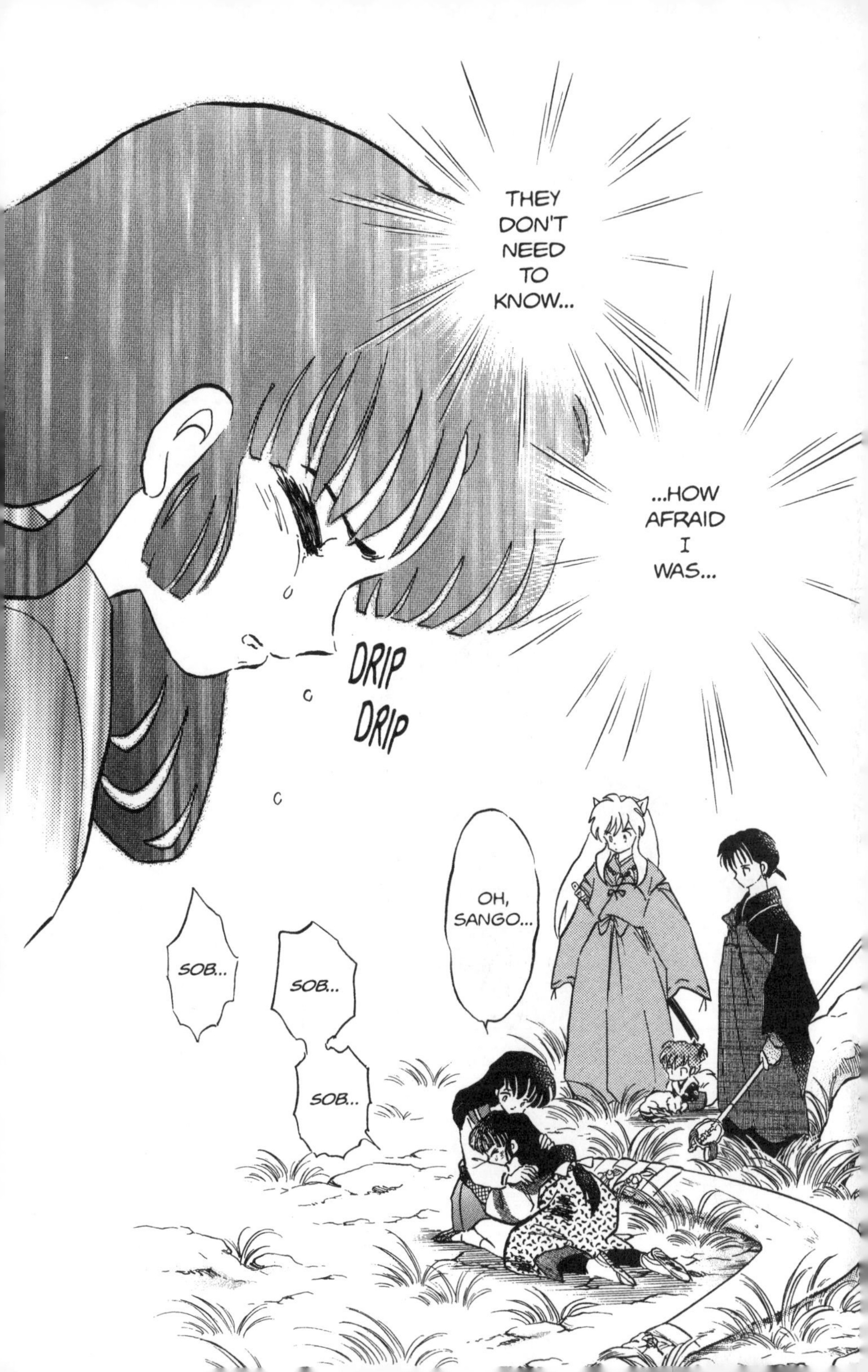
THEY DON'T NEED TO KNOW...
...HOW AFRAID I WAS...
DRIP DRIP
OH, SANGO...
SOB...
SOB...
SOB...

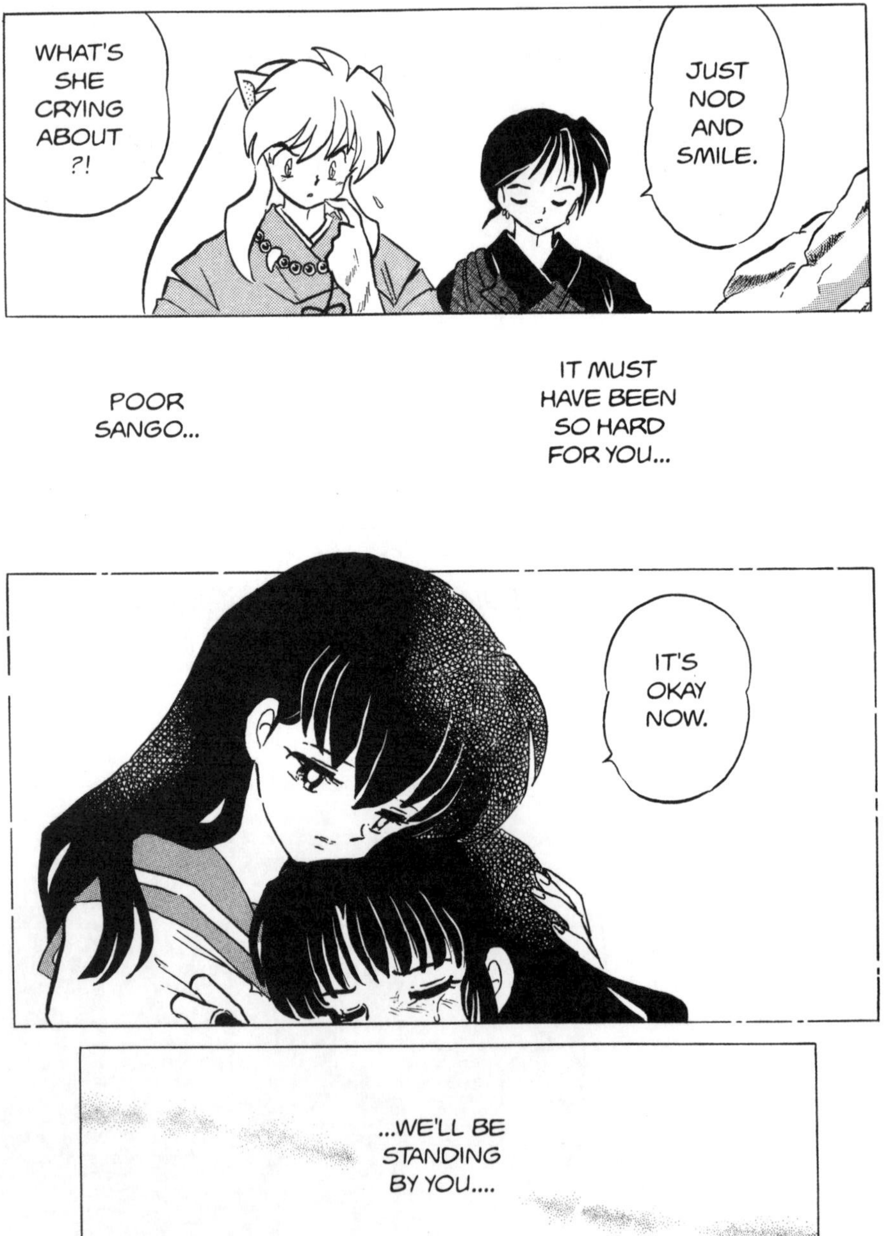
WHAT'S SHE CRYING ABOUT ?!
JUST NOD AND SMILE.
POOR SANGO...
IT MUST HAVE BEEN SO HARD FOR YOU...
IT'S OKAY NOW.
...WE'LL BE STANDING BY YOU....

SCROLL FOUR

THE EARTH BOY

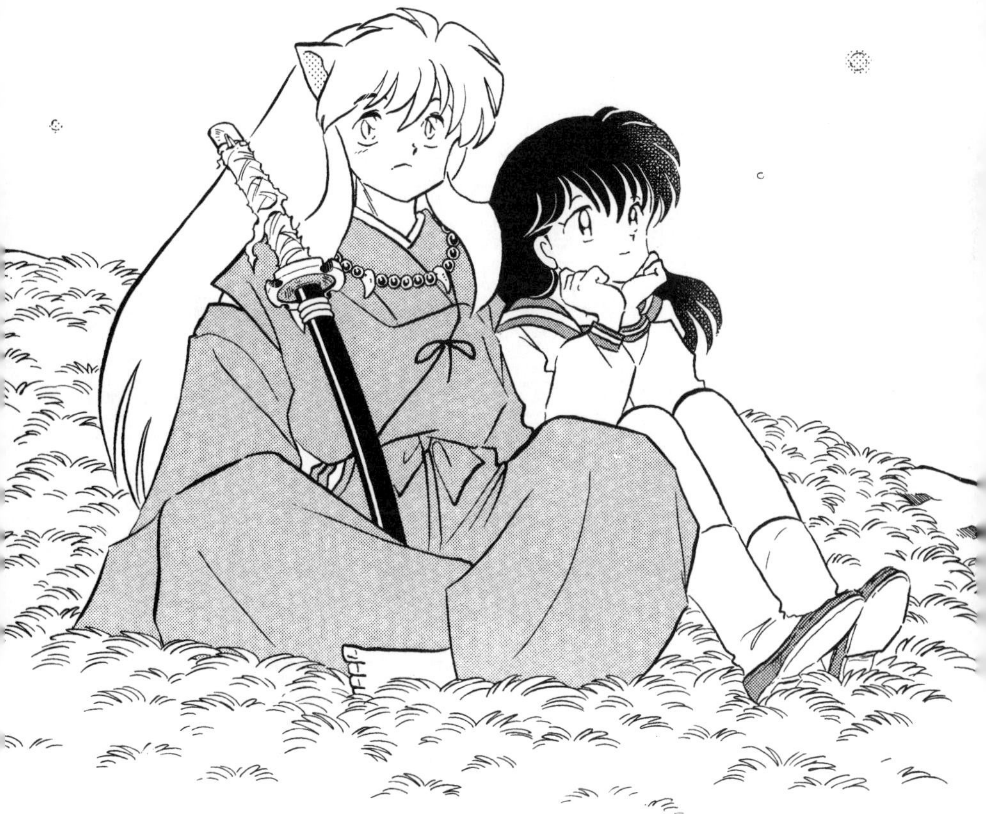

KIRARA... ARE YOU HURTING?

NARAKU'S VENOM MUST NOT HAVE BEEN FLUSHED COMPLETELY FROM HER BODY YET...

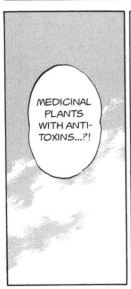

MEDICINAL PLANTS WITH ANTI-TOXINS...?!

SO YOU'RE SAYING THEY'LL HEAL THE CAT, MYŌGA?!

MM-HM.

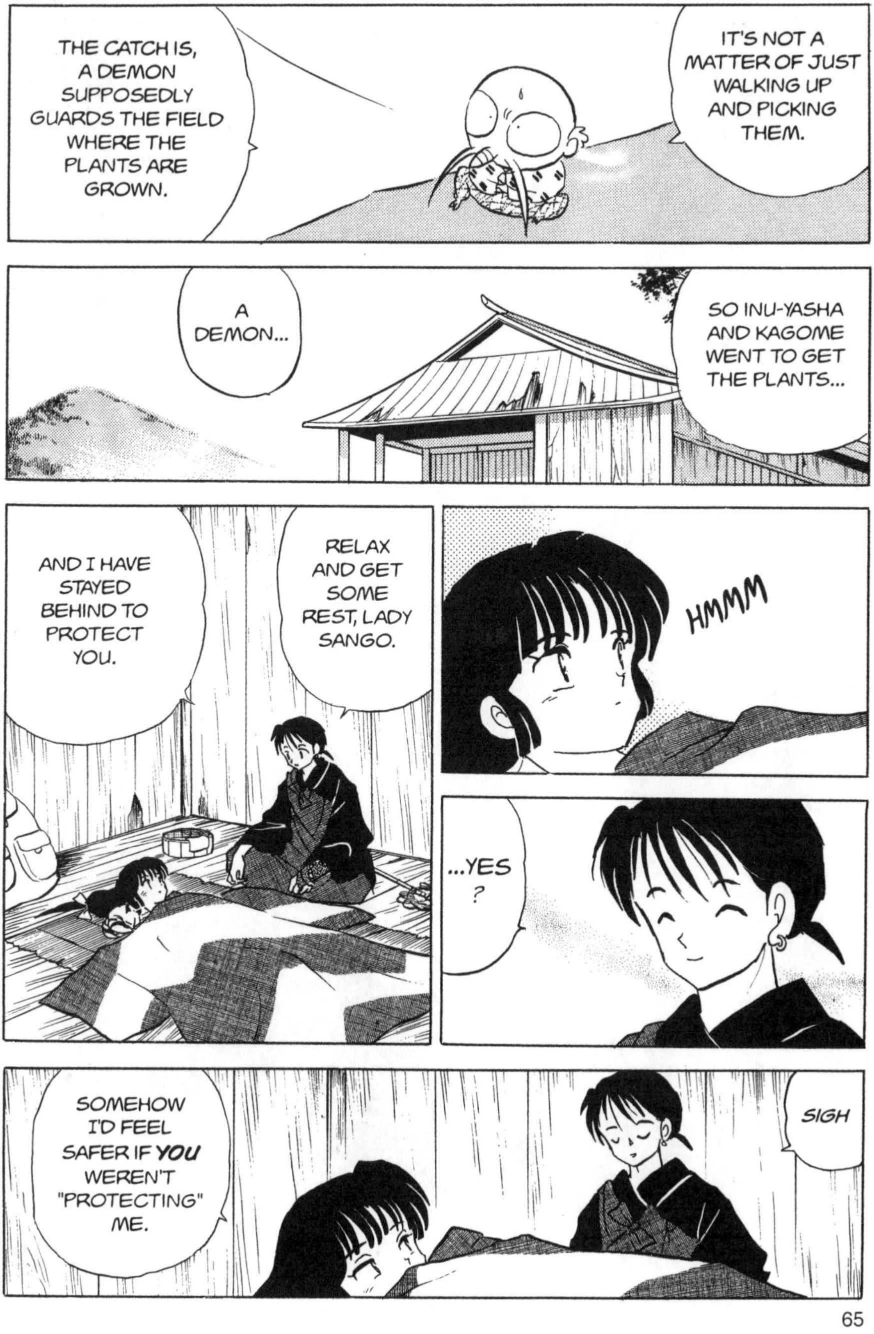
THE CATCH IS, A DEMON SUPPOSEDLY GUARDS THE FIELD WHERE THE PLANTS ARE GROWN.
IT'S NOT A MATTER OF JUST WALKING UP AND PICKING THEM.
A DEMON...
SO INU-YASHA AND KAGOME WENT TO GET THE PLANTS...
AND I HAVE STAYED BEHIND TO PROTECT YOU.
RELAX AND GET SOME REST, LADY SANGO.
HMMM
...YES ?
SOMEHOW I'D FEEL SAFER IF **YOU** WEREN'T "PROTECTING" ME.
SIGH

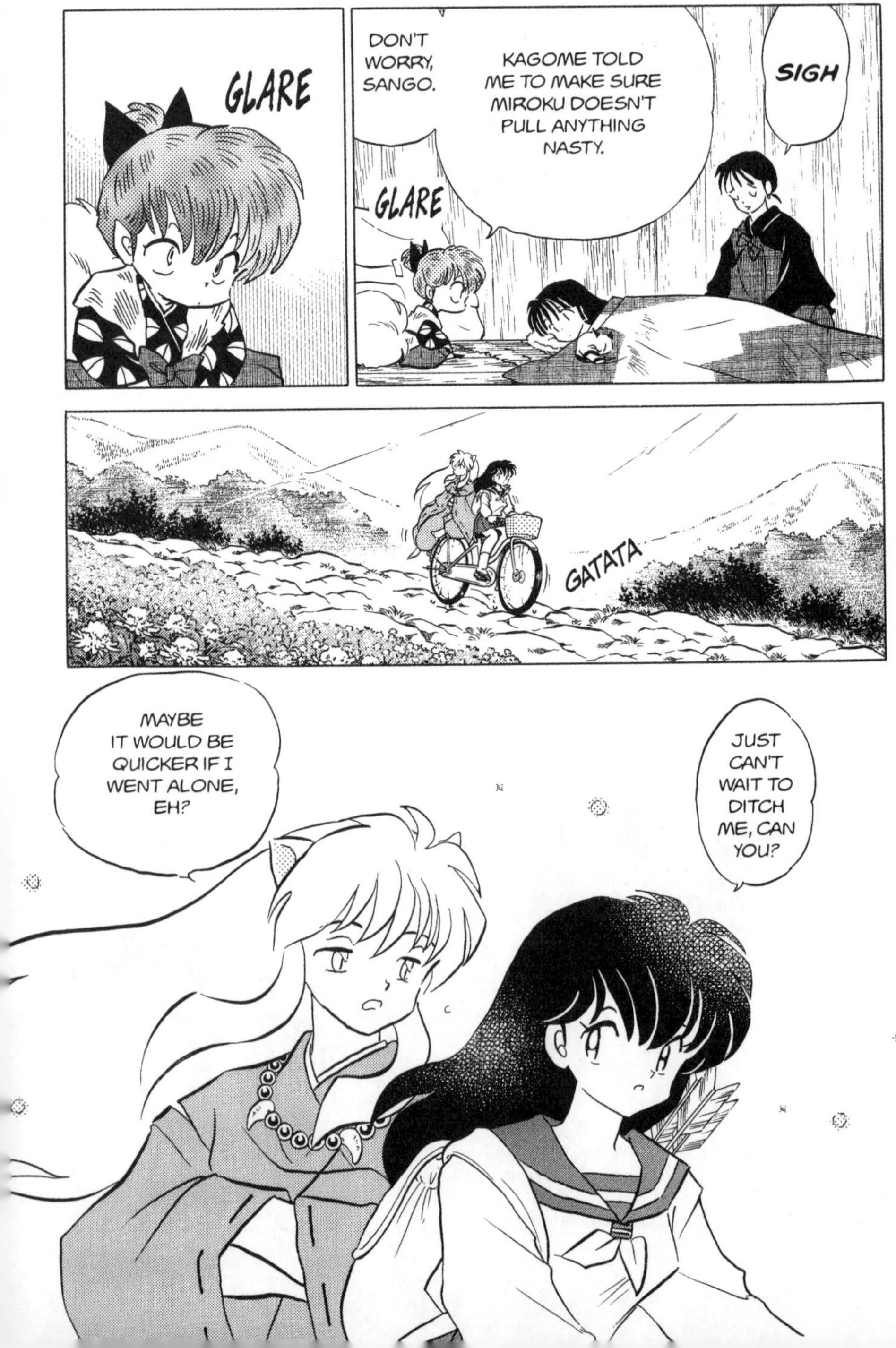
SIGH
DON'T WORRY, SANGO.
KAGOME TOLD ME TO MAKE SURE MIROKU DOESN'T PULL ANYTHING NASTY.
GLARE
GLARE
GATATA
MAYBE IT WOULD BE QUICKER IF I WENT ALONE, EH?
JUST CAN'T WAIT TO DITCH ME, CAN YOU?

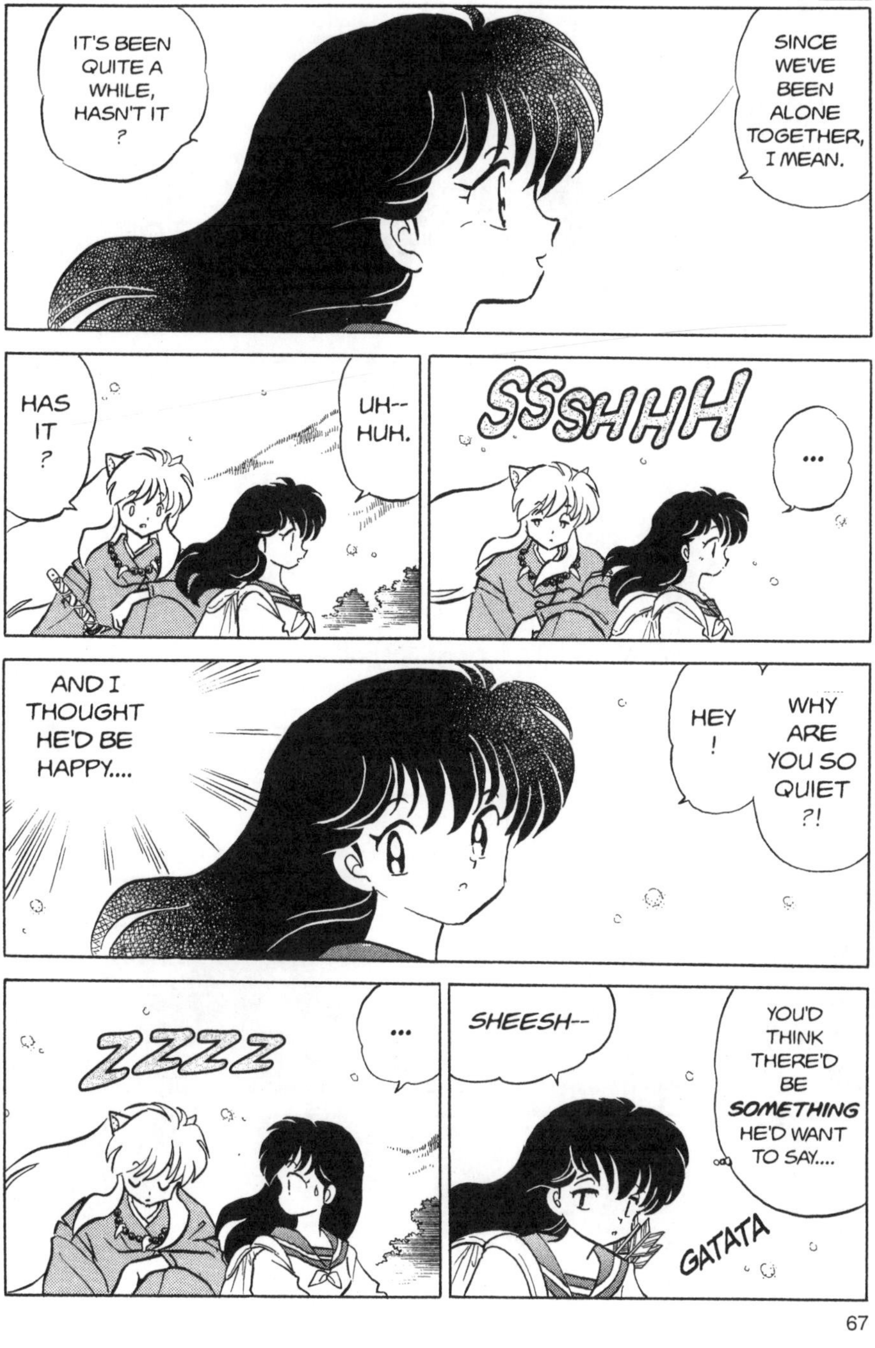
IT'S BEEN QUITE A WHILE, HASN'T IT?
SINCE WE'VE BEEN ALONE TOGETHER, I MEAN.
HAS IT?
UH--HUH.
SSSHHH
...
AND I THOUGHT HE'D BE HAPPY....
HEY!
WHY ARE YOU SO QUIET?!
ZZZZ
...
SHEESH--
YOU'D THINK THERE'D BE SOMETHING HE'D WANT TO SAY....
GATATA

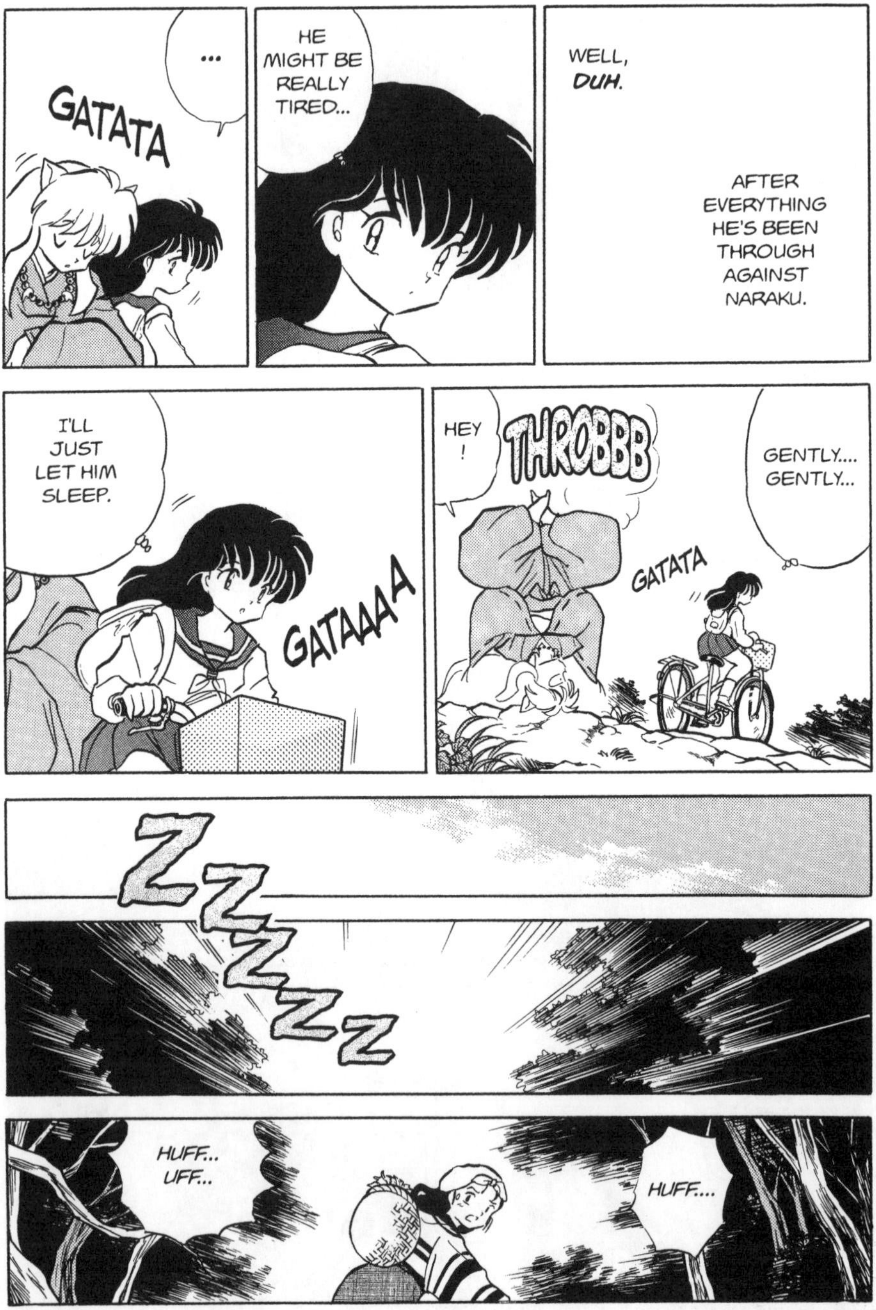
...
GATATA
HE MIGHT BE REALLY TIRED...
WELL, *DUH*.
AFTER EVERYTHING HE'S BEEN THROUGH AGAINST NARAKU.
I'LL JUST LET HIM SLEEP.
GATAAAA
HEY!
THROBBB
GATATA
GENTLY.... GENTLY...
ZZZZZZ
HUFF... UFF...
HUFF....

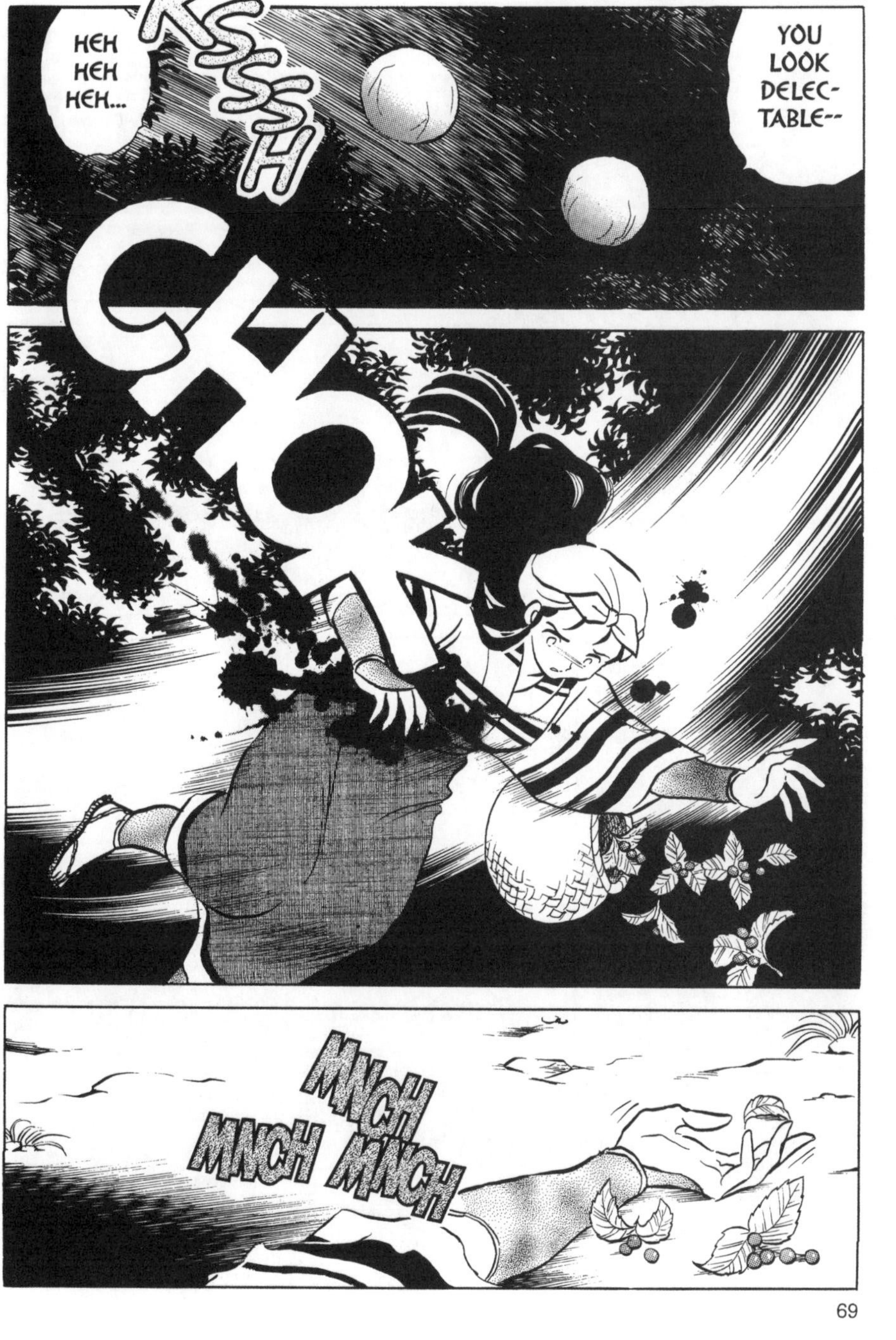
HEH HEH HEH...
KSSSH
YOU LOOK DELEC-TABLE--
CHOK
MNCH MNCH MNCH

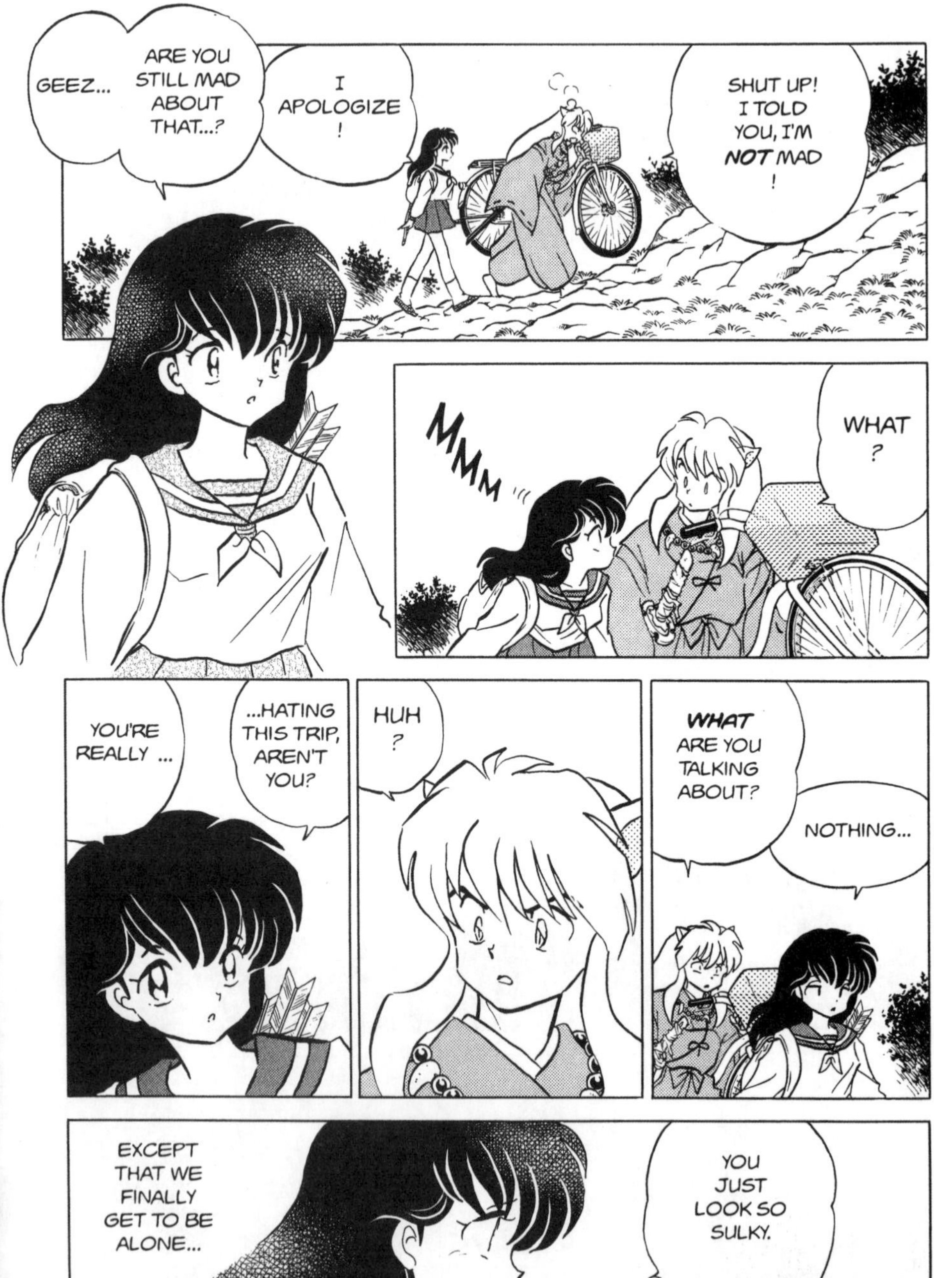
GEEZ...
ARE YOU STILL MAD ABOUT THAT...?
I APOLOGIZE!
SHUT UP! I TOLD YOU, I'M NOT MAD!
MMM
WHAT?
YOU'RE REALLY ...
...HATING THIS TRIP, AREN'T YOU?
HUH?
WHAT ARE YOU TALKING ABOUT?
NOTHING...
EXCEPT THAT WE FINALLY GET TO BE ALONE...
YOU JUST LOOK SO SULKY.

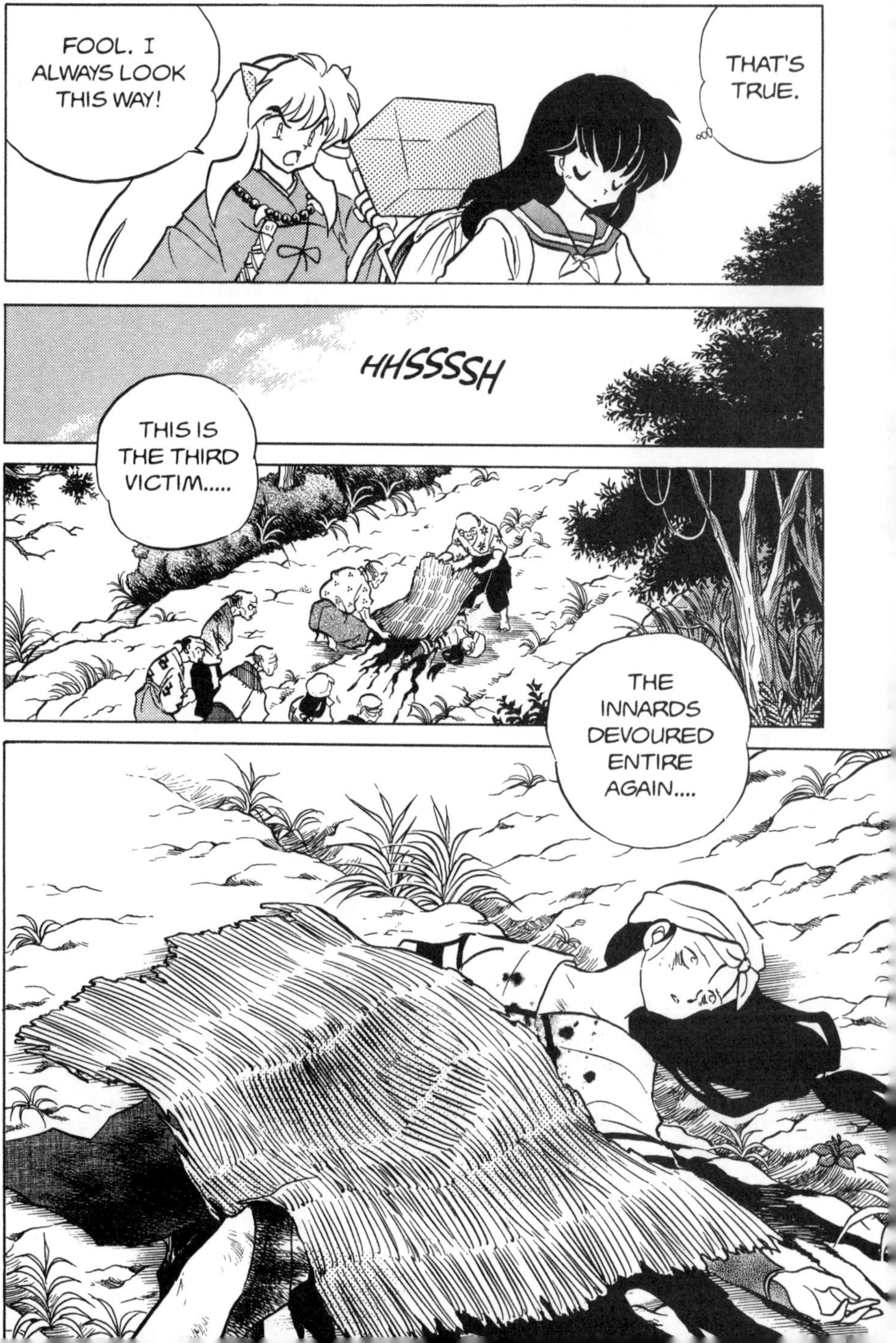
FOOL. I ALWAYS LOOK THIS WAY!
THAT'S TRUE.
HHSSSSH
THIS IS THE THIRD VICTIM.....
THE INNARDS DEVOURED ENTIRE AGAIN....

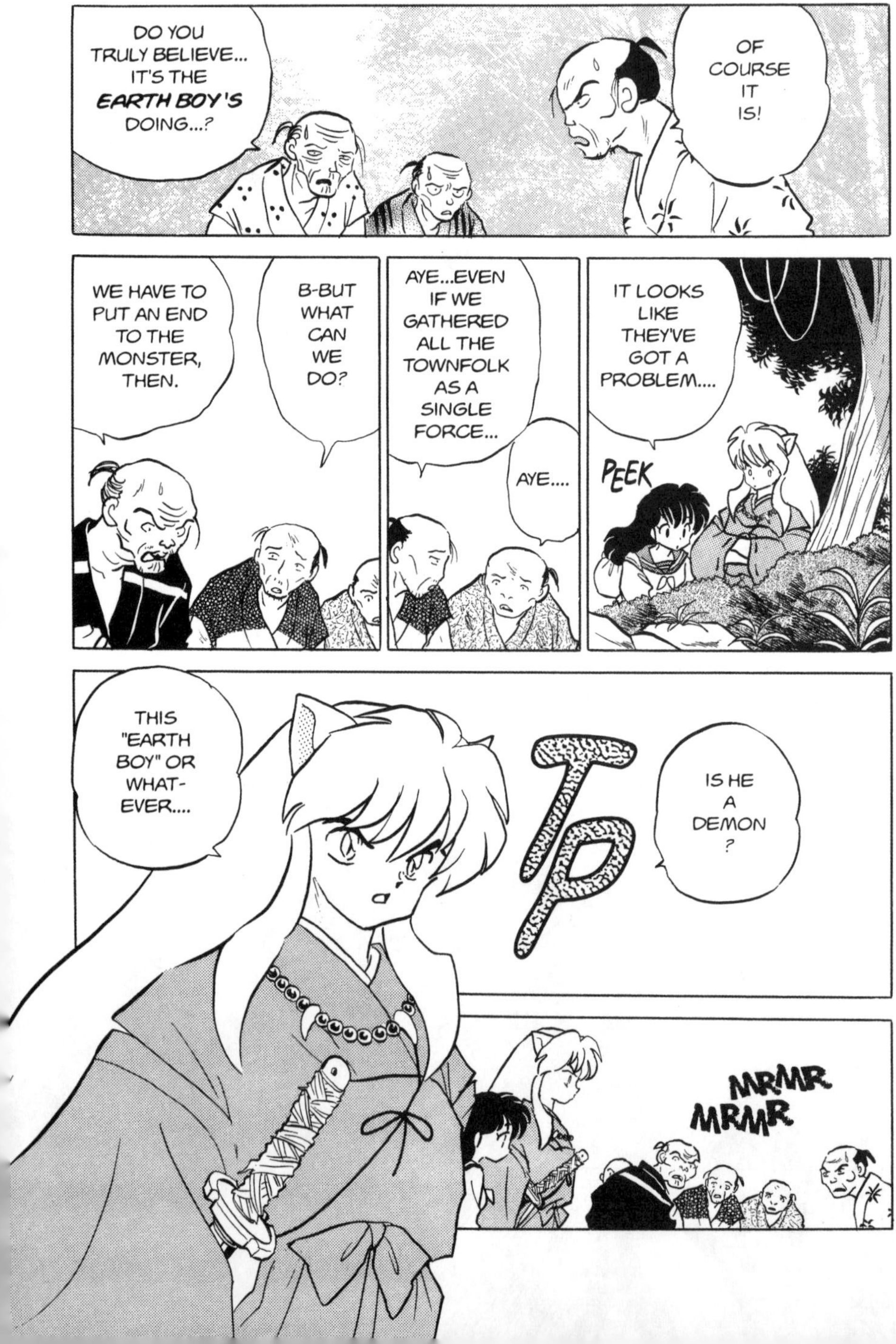
DO YOU TRULY BELIEVE... IT'S THE ***EARTH BOY'S*** DOING...?
OF COURSE IT IS!
WE HAVE TO PUT AN END TO THE MONSTER, THEN.
B-BUT WHAT CAN WE DO?
AYE...EVEN IF WE GATHERED ALL THE TOWNFOLK AS A SINGLE FORCE...
AYE....
IT LOOKS LIKE THEY'VE GOT A PROBLEM....
PEEK
THIS "EARTH BOY" OR WHAT-EVER....
TP
IS HE A DEMON ?
MRMR MRMR

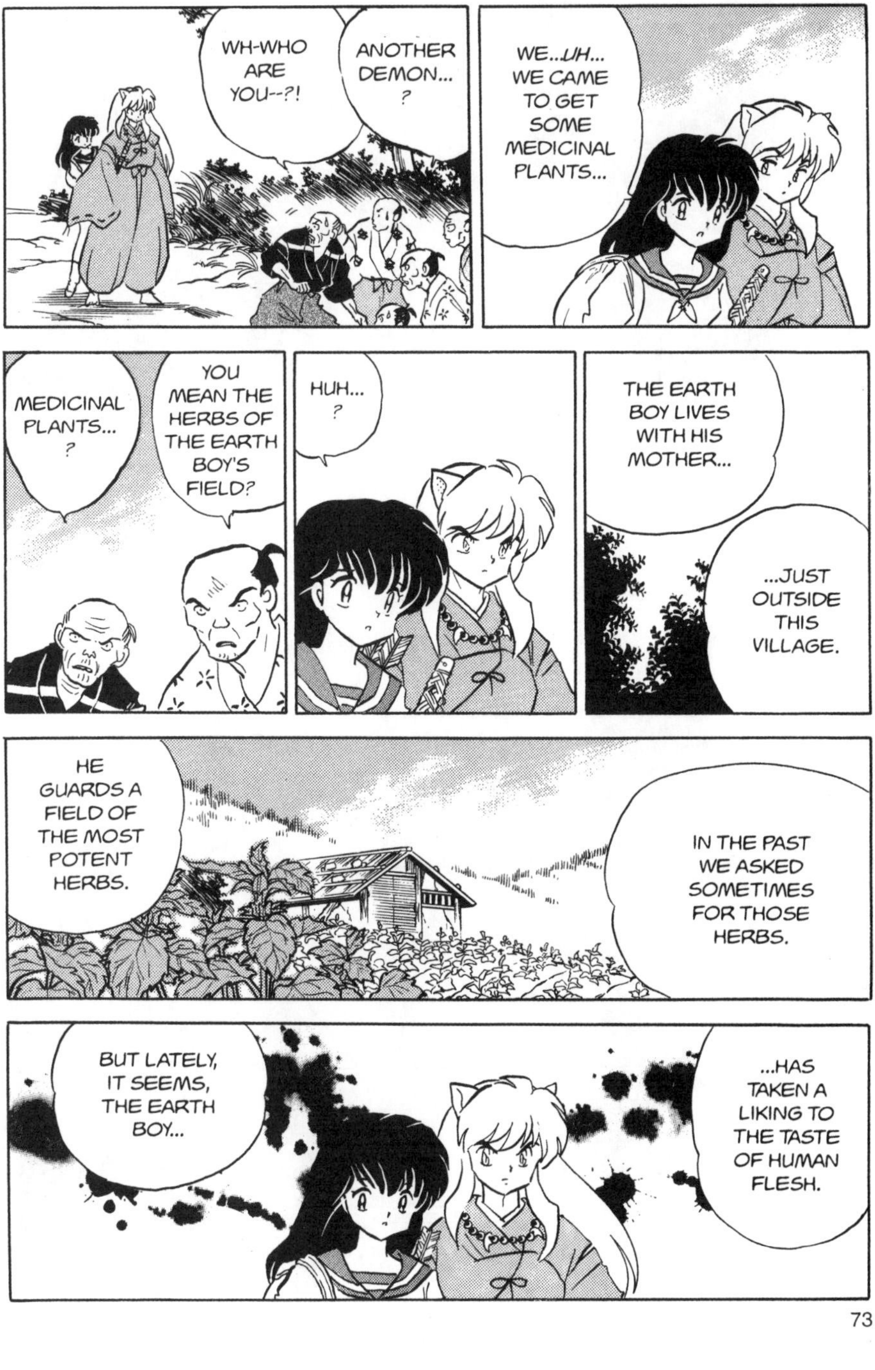
WH-WHO ARE YOU--?!
ANOTHER DEMON... ?
WE...*UH*... WE CAME TO GET SOME MEDICINAL PLANTS...
MEDICINAL PLANTS... ?
YOU MEAN THE HERBS OF THE EARTH BOY'S FIELD?
HUH... ?
THE EARTH BOY LIVES WITH HIS MOTHER...
...JUST OUTSIDE THIS VILLAGE.
HE GUARDS A FIELD OF THE MOST POTENT HERBS.
IN THE PAST WE ASKED SOMETIMES FOR THOSE HERBS.
BUT LATELY, IT SEEMS, THE EARTH BOY...
...HAS TAKEN A LIKING TO THE TASTE OF HUMAN FLESH.

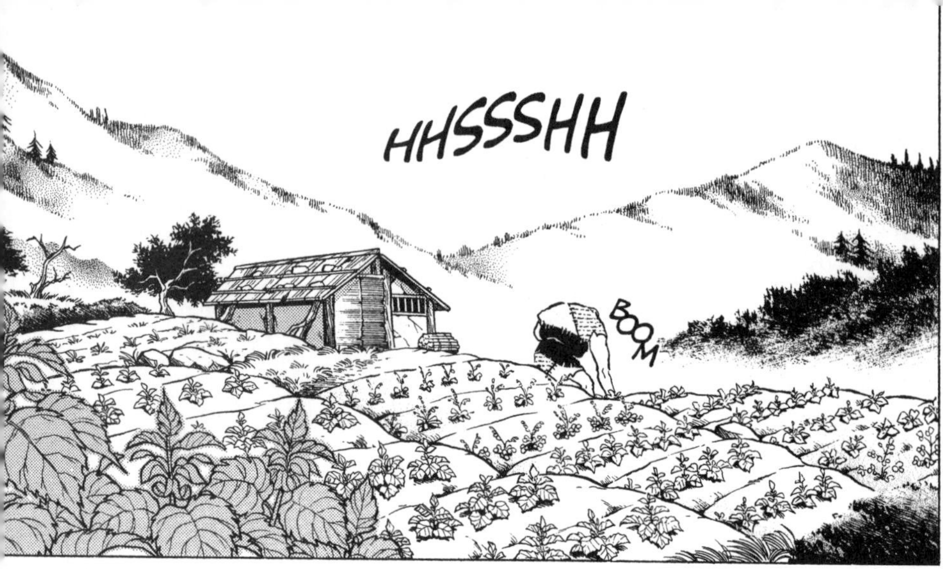
HHSSSHH
BOOM
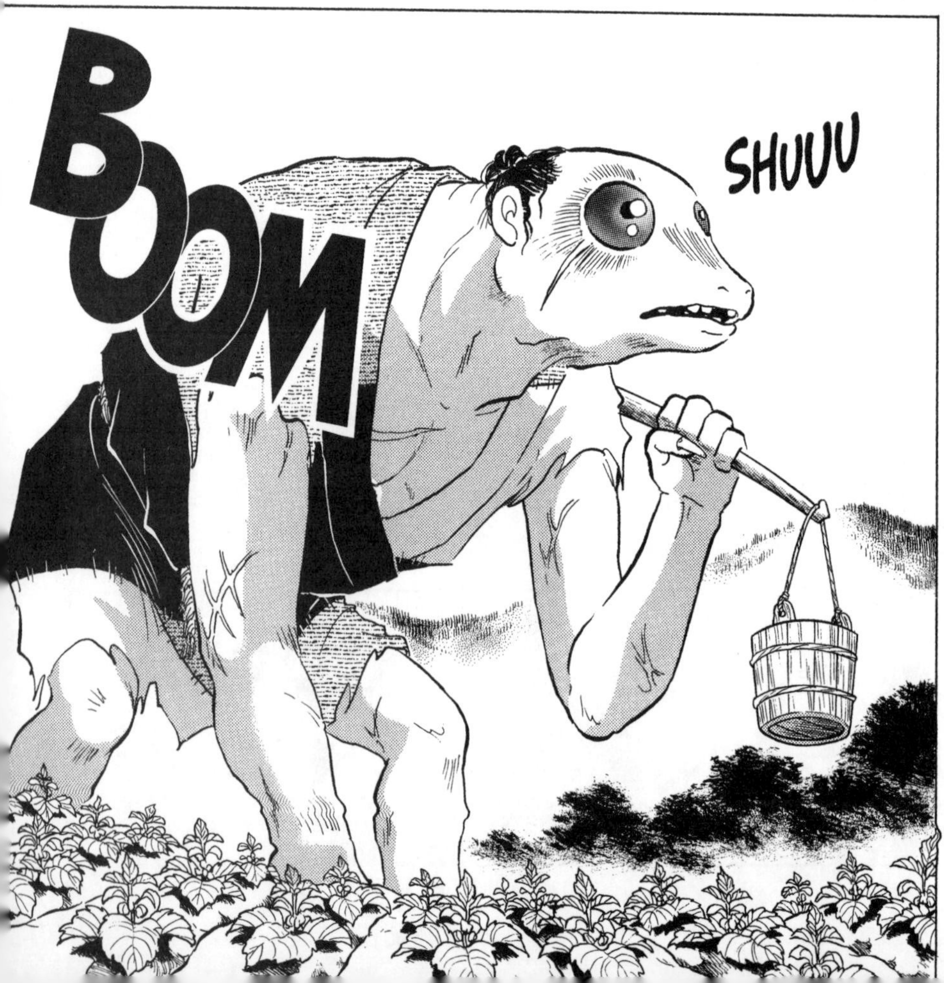
BOOM
SHUUU

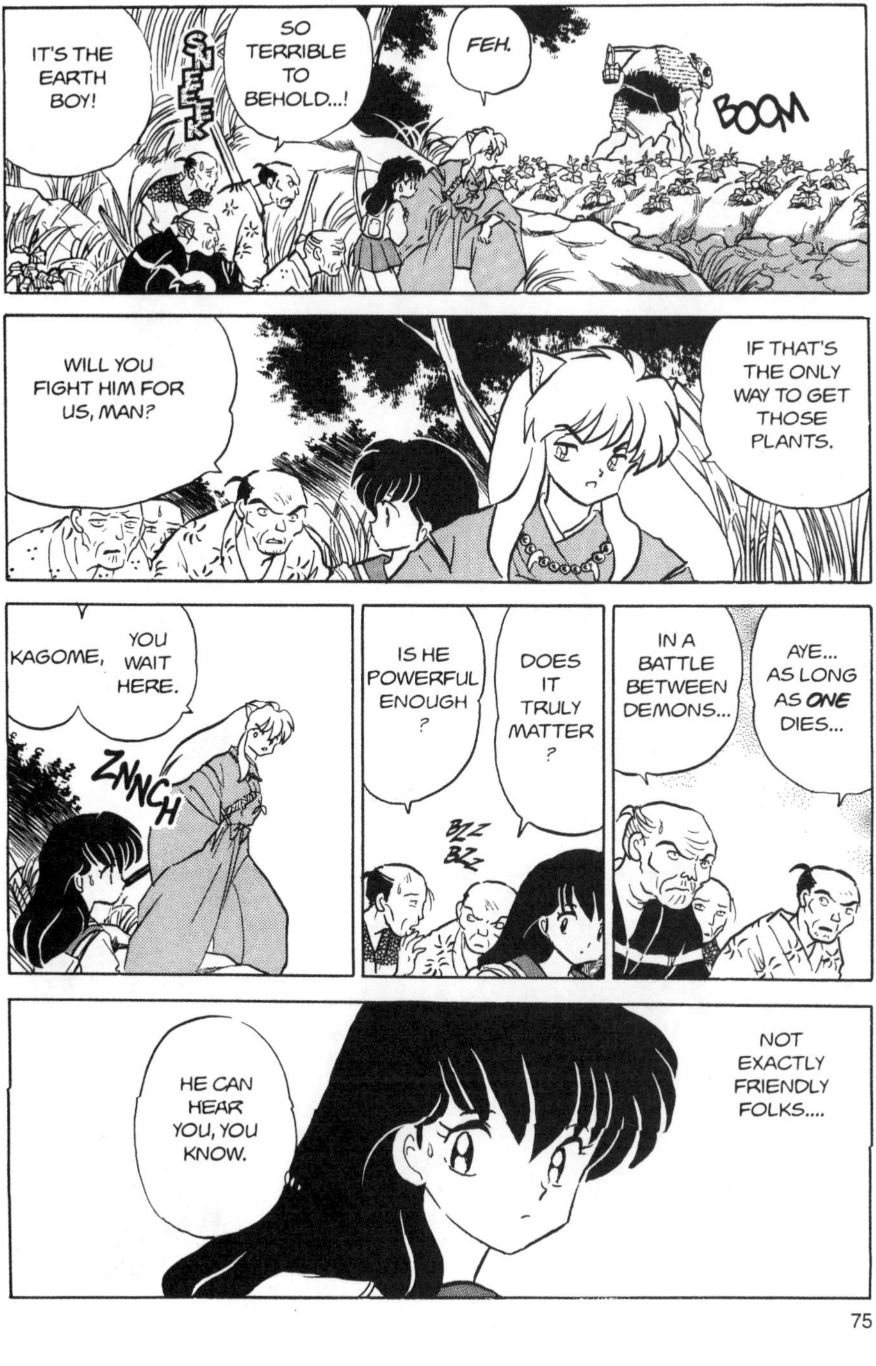
IT'S THE EARTH BOY!
SNEEK
SO TERRIBLE TO BEHOLD...!
FEH.
BOOM
WILL YOU FIGHT HIM FOR US, MAN?
IF THAT'S THE ONLY WAY TO GET THOSE PLANTS.
KAGOME, YOU WAIT HERE.
ZNNCH
IS HE POWERFUL ENOUGH?
DOES IT TRULY MATTER?
BZZ BZZ
IN A BATTLE BETWEEN DEMONS...
AYE... AS LONG AS ONE DIES...
HE CAN HEAR YOU, YOU KNOW.
NOT EXACTLY FRIENDLY FOLKS....

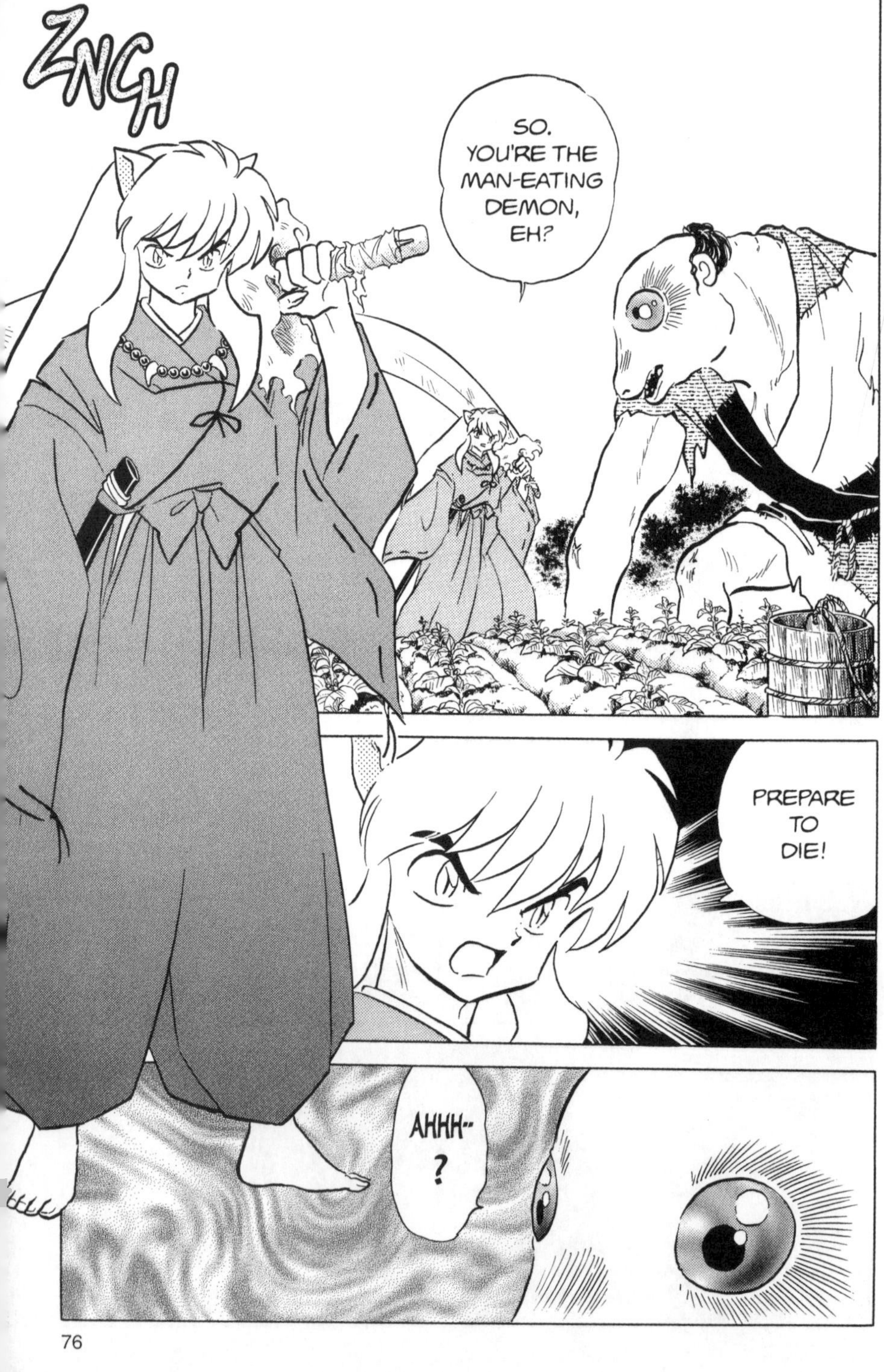
ZNCH
SO. YOU'RE THE MAN-EATING DEMON, EH?
PREPARE TO DIE!
AHHH-- ?

HUH... ? THIS GUY...

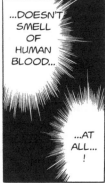

...DOESN'T SMELL OF HUMAN BLOOD...

...AT ALL...!

FSSH

KLOK

HEY, HEY! EARTH BOY, PREPARE TO DIE!

KILL HIM! HURRY!

SSSHH

BRRR BRRR BRRR

!

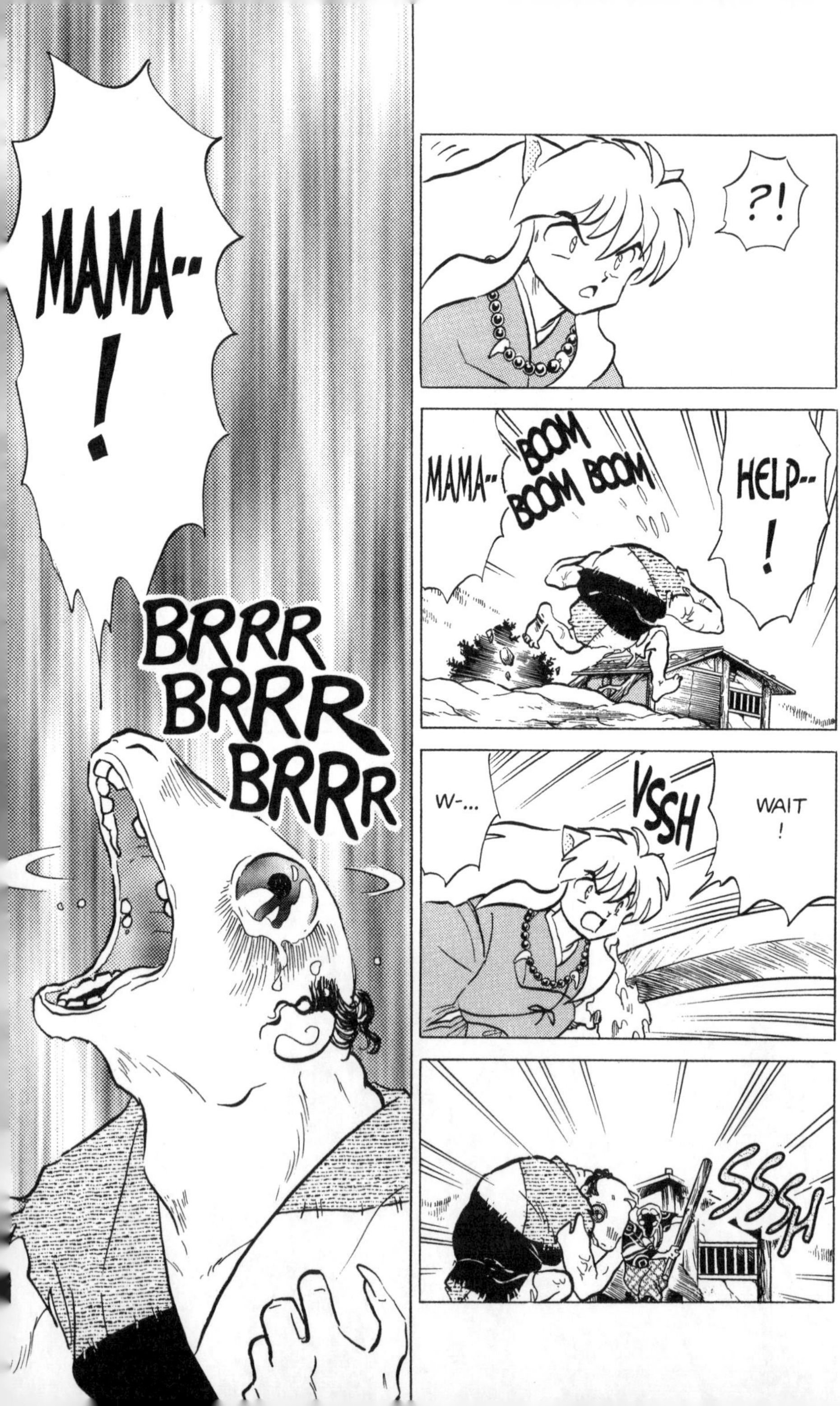
MAMA-- !
BRRR BRRR BRRR
?!
MAMA--
BOOM BOOM BOOM
HELP-- !
W-...
VSSH
WAIT !
SSSH

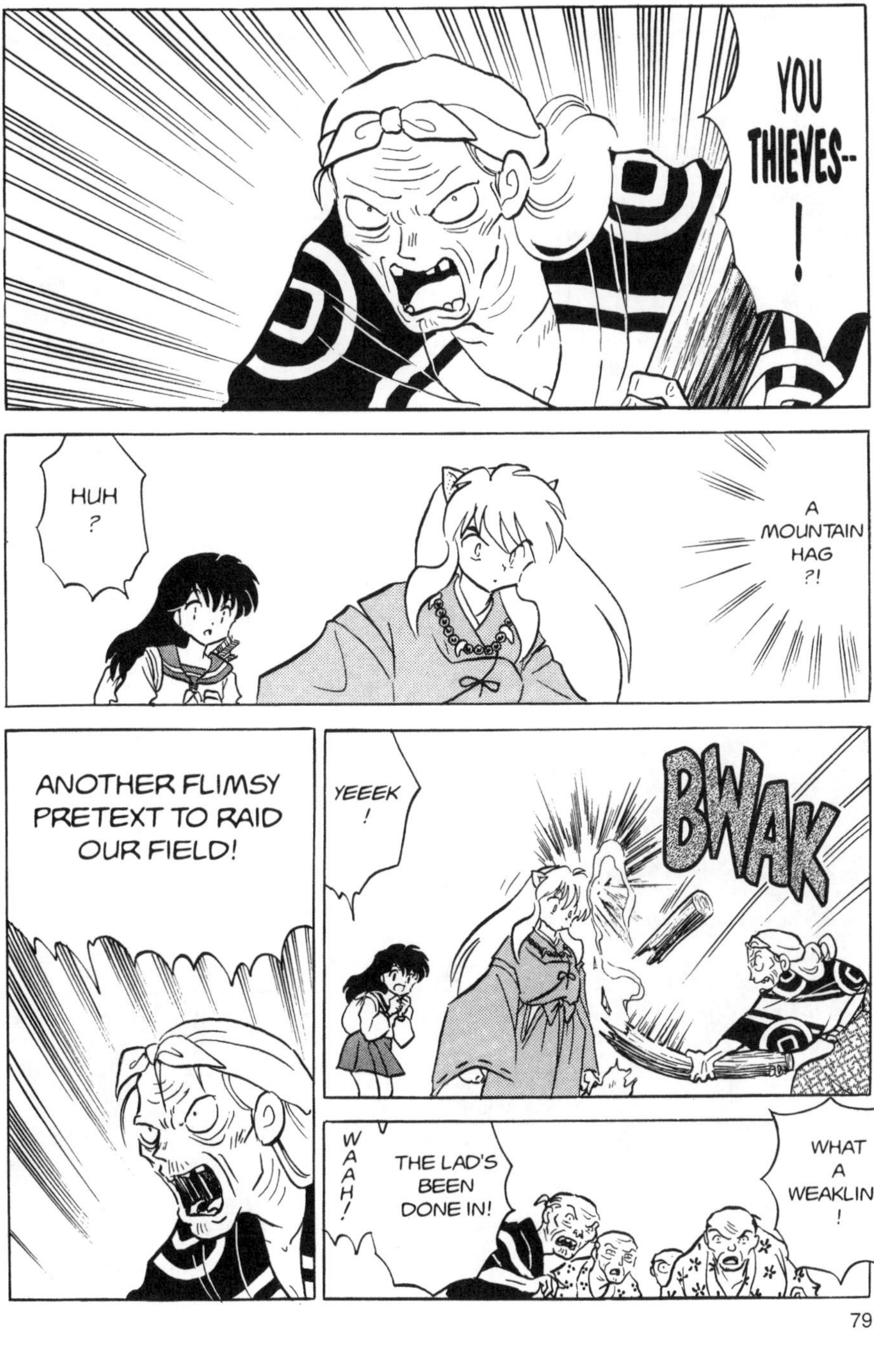
YOU THIEVES--!
HUH?
A MOUNTAIN HAG?!
ANOTHER FLIMSY PRETEXT TO RAID OUR FIELD!
YEEEK!
BWAK
WAAAH!
THE LAD'S BEEN DONE IN!
WHAT A WEAKLING!

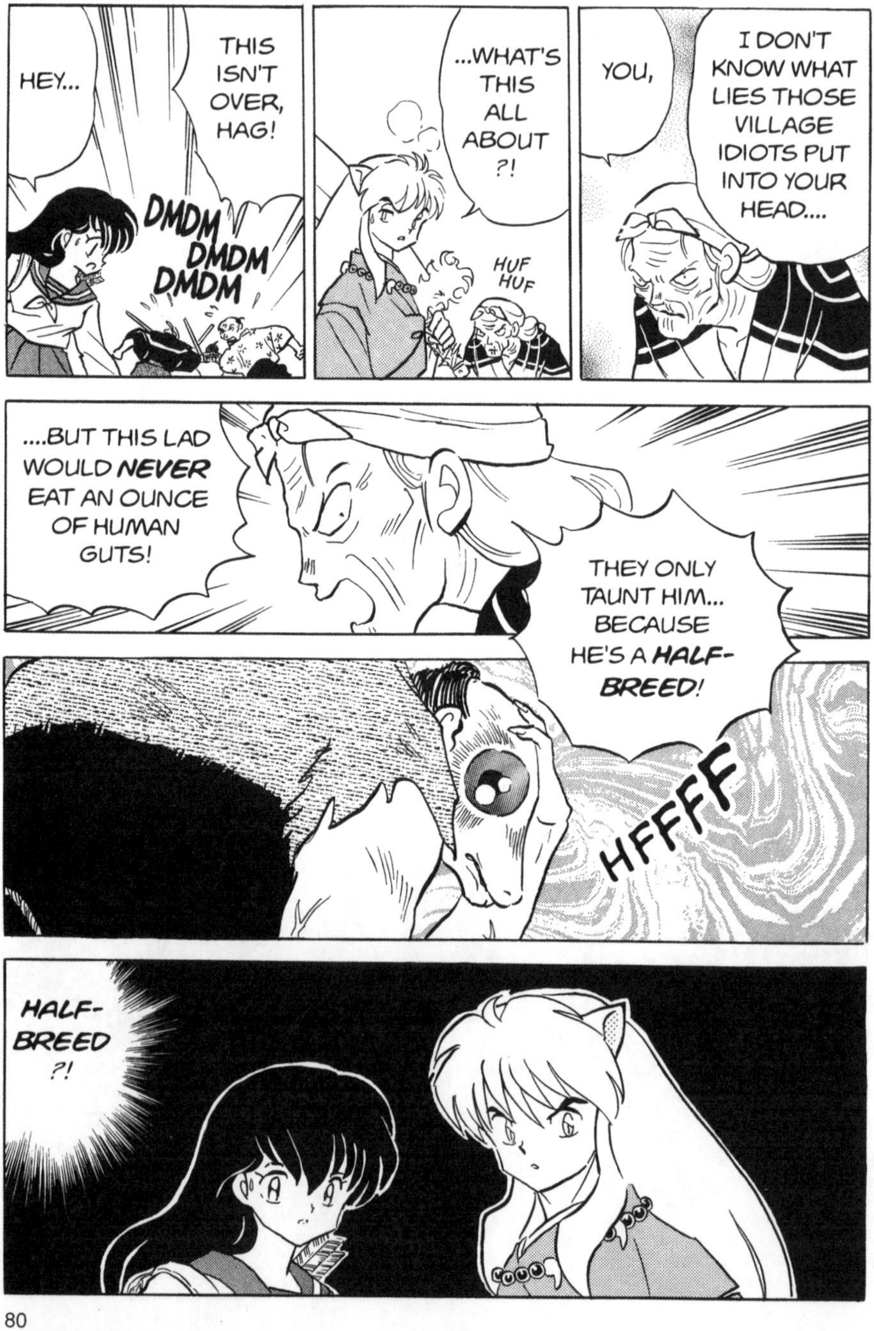
HEY...
THIS ISN'T OVER, HAG!
DMDM DMDM DMDM
...WHAT'S THIS ALL ABOUT ?!
HUF HUF
YOU,
I DON'T KNOW WHAT LIES THOSE VILLAGE IDIOTS PUT INTO YOUR HEAD....
....BUT THIS LAD WOULD **NEVER** EAT AN OUNCE OF HUMAN GUTS!
THEY ONLY TAUNT HIM... BECAUSE HE'S A **HALF-BREED**!
HFFFF
HALF-BREED ?!

SCROLL FIVE

THE RAID

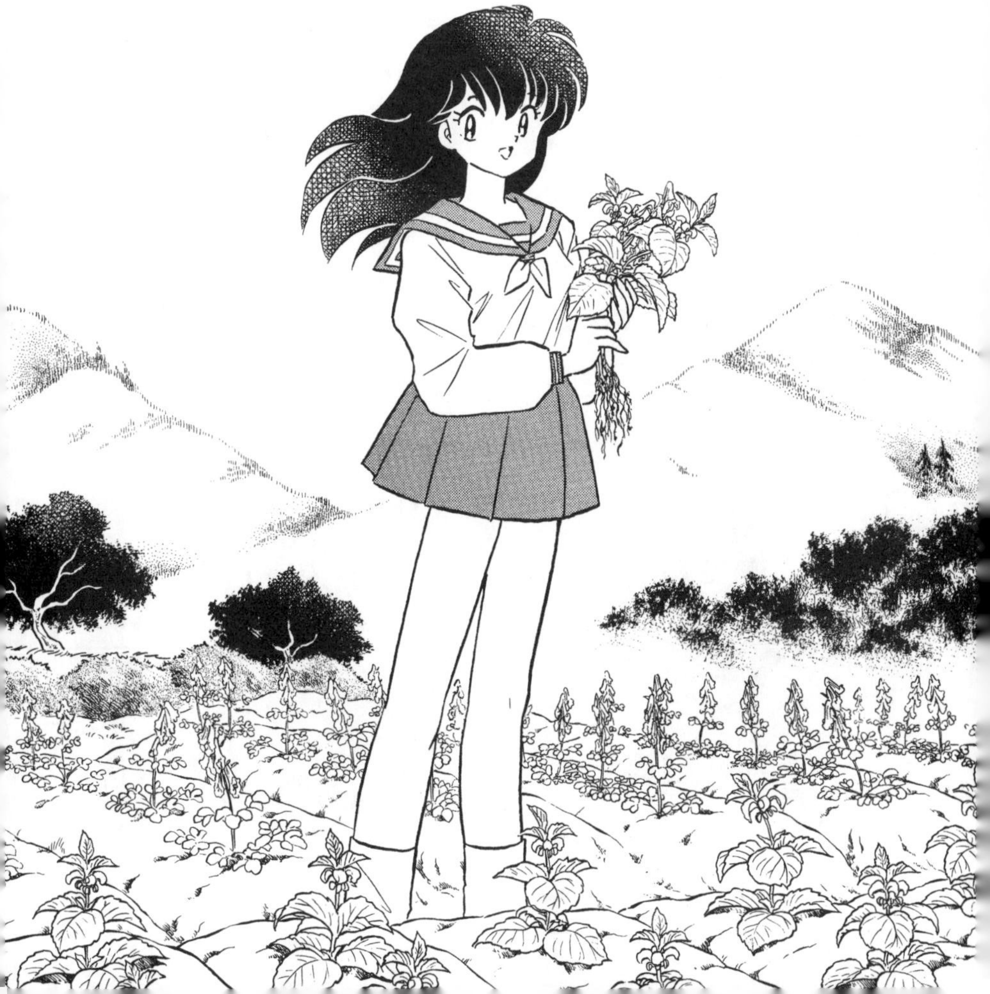

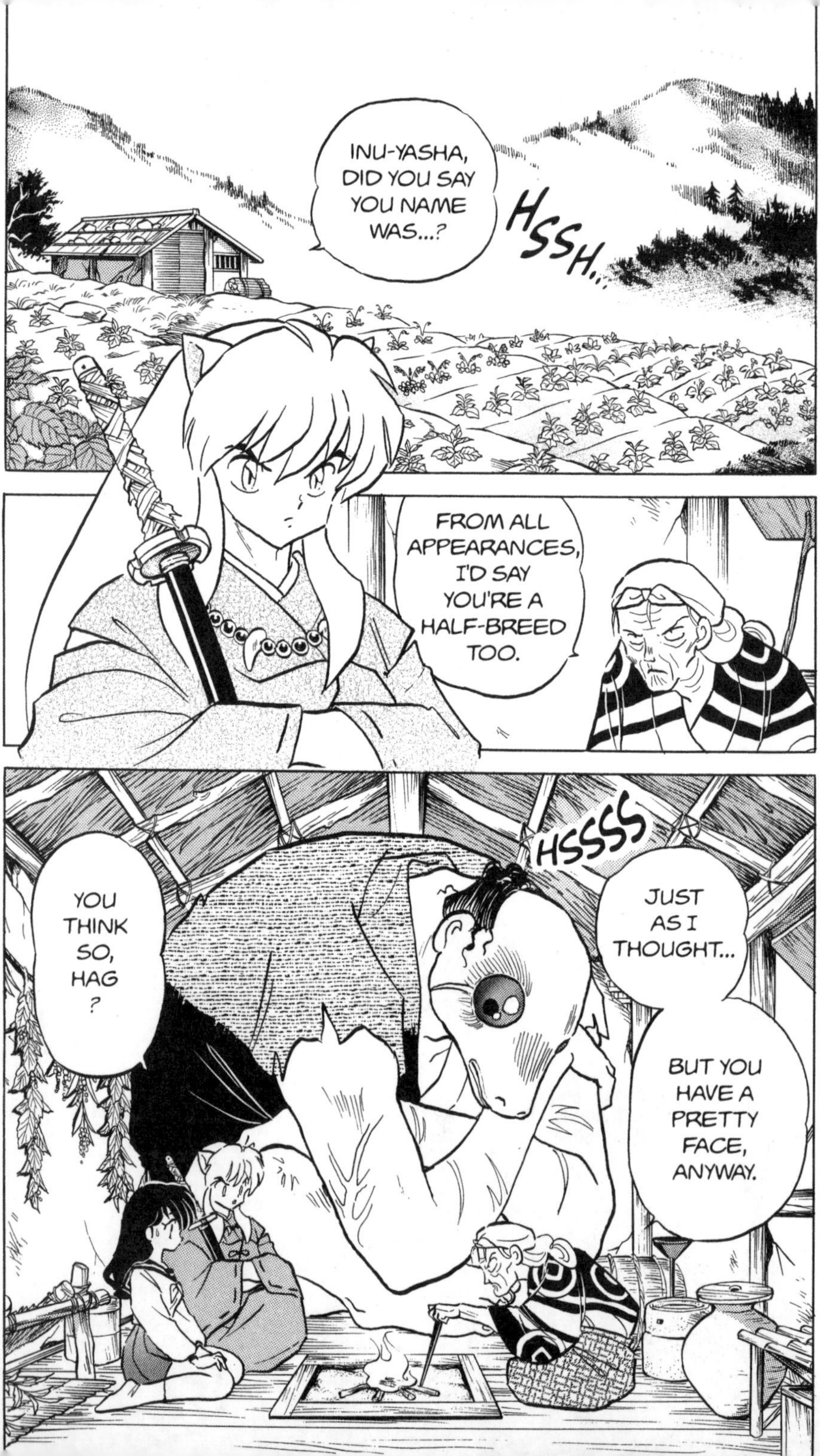
INU-YASHA, DID YOU SAY YOU NAME WAS...?
HSSH...
FROM ALL APPEARANCES, I'D SAY YOU'RE A HALF-BREED TOO.
HSSSS
JUST AS I THOUGHT...
BUT YOU HAVE A PRETTY FACE, ANYWAY.
YOU THINK SO, HAG?

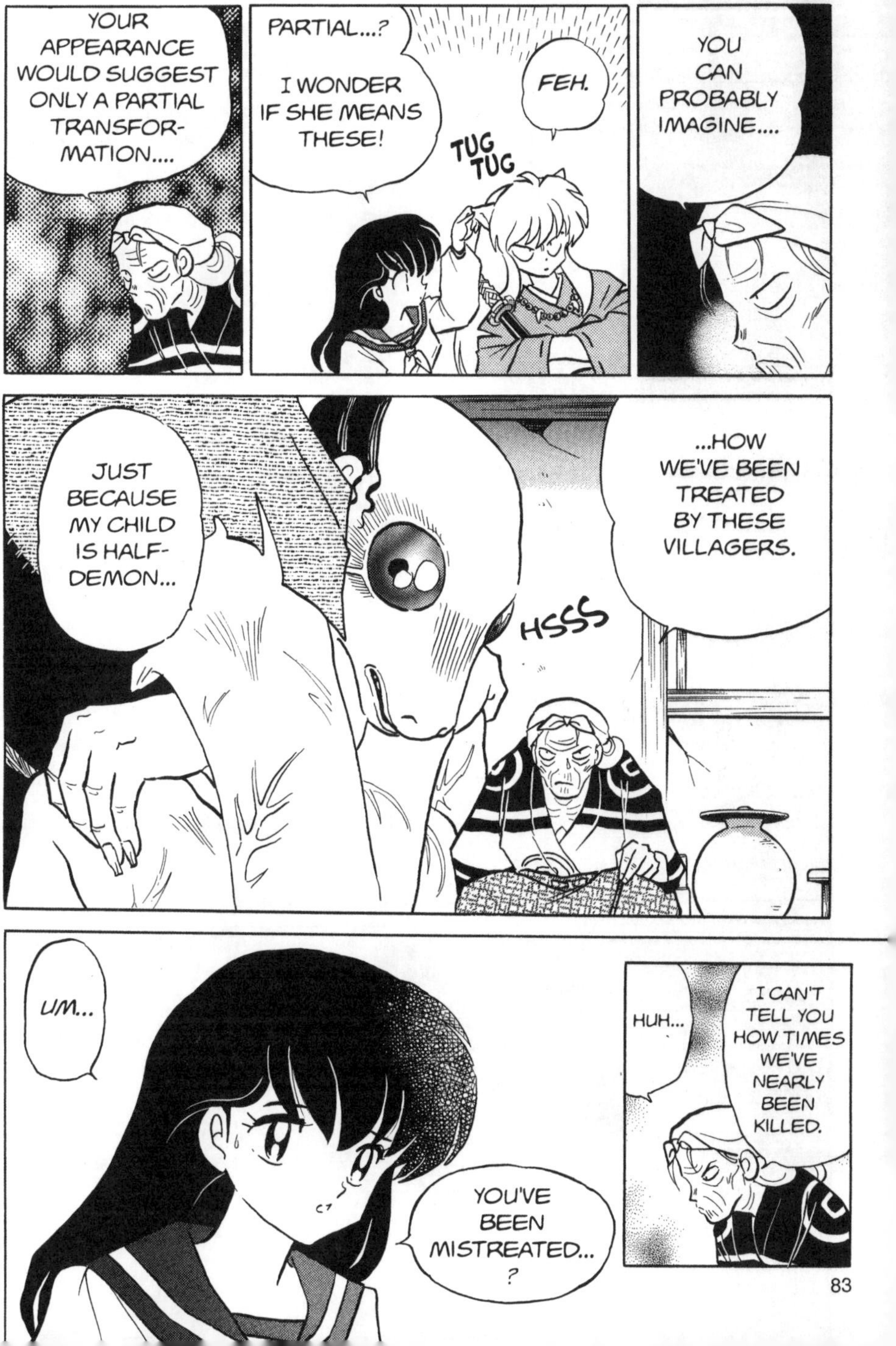
YOUR APPEARANCE WOULD SUGGEST ONLY A PARTIAL TRANSFOR-MATION....
PARTIAL...?
I WONDER IF SHE MEANS THESE!
FEH.
TUG TUG
YOU CAN PROBABLY IMAGINE....
JUST BECAUSE MY CHILD IS HALF-DEMON...
...HOW WE'VE BEEN TREATED BY THESE VILLAGERS.
HSSS
UM...
YOU'VE BEEN MISTREATED...?
HUH...
I CAN'T TELL YOU HOW TIMES WE'VE NEARLY BEEN KILLED.

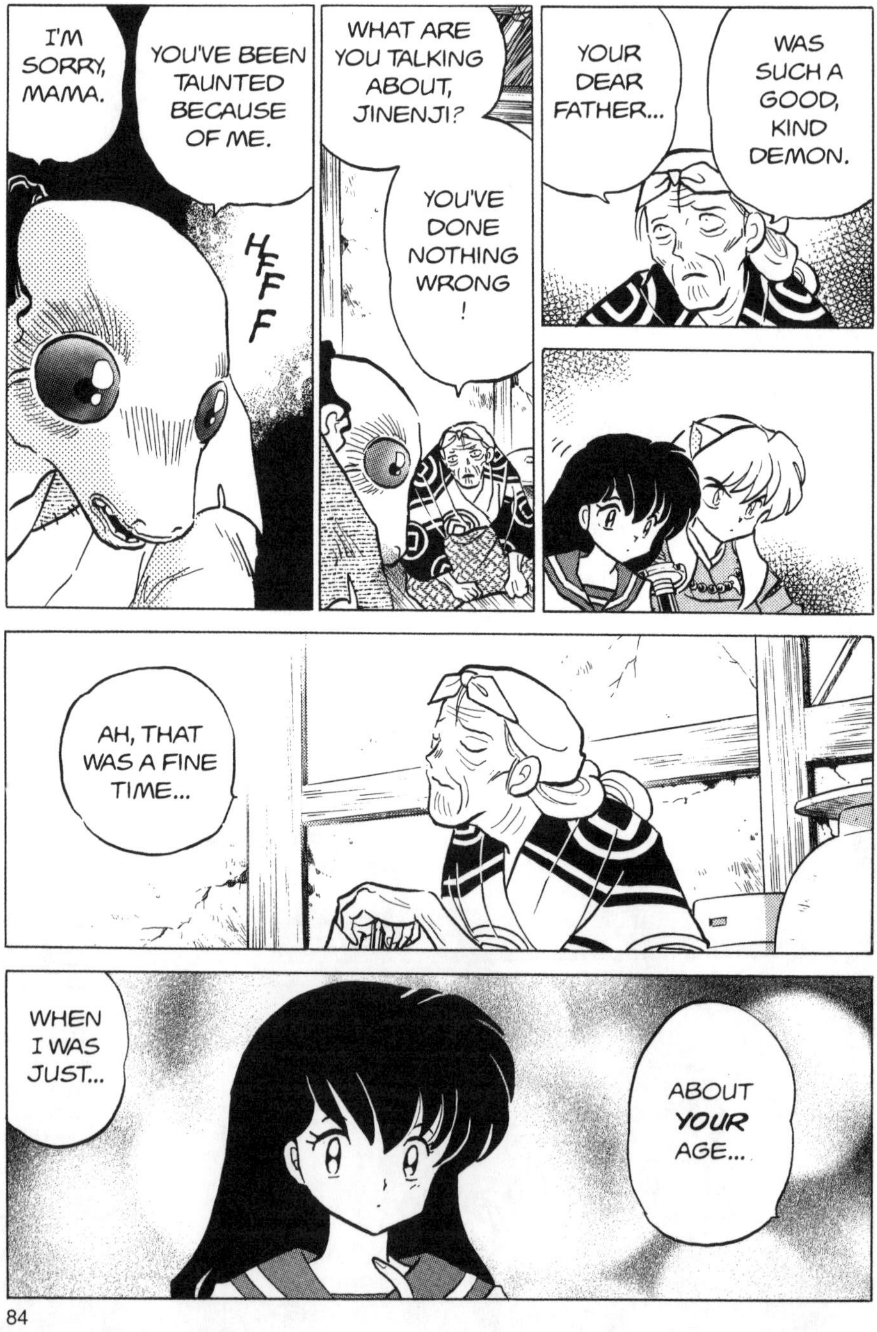
I'M SORRY, MAMA.
YOU'VE BEEN TAUNTED BECAUSE OF ME.
HFFF
WHAT ARE YOU TALKING ABOUT, JINENJI?
YOU'VE DONE NOTHING WRONG!
YOUR DEAR FATHER...
WAS SUCH A GOOD, KIND DEMON.
AH, THAT WAS A FINE TIME...
WHEN I WAS JUST...
ABOUT **YOUR** AGE...

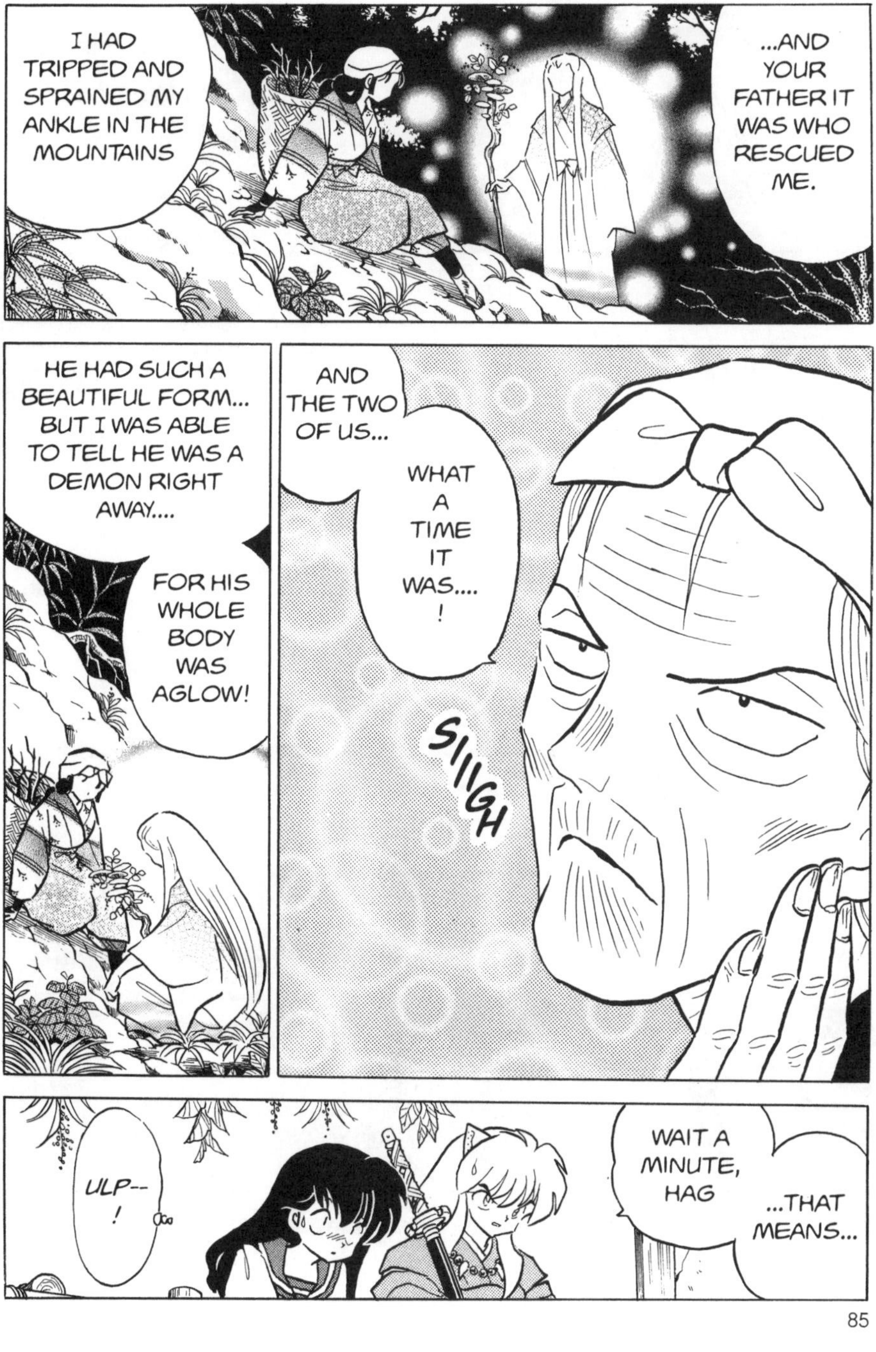
I HAD TRIPPED AND SPRAINED MY ANKLE IN THE MOUNTAINS
...AND YOUR FATHER IT WAS WHO RESCUED ME.
HE HAD SUCH A BEAUTIFUL FORM... BUT I WAS ABLE TO TELL HE WAS A DEMON RIGHT AWAY....
FOR HIS WHOLE BODY WAS AGLOW!
AND THE TWO OF US...
WHAT A TIME IT WAS....!
SIIIGH
ULP--!
WAIT A MINUTE, HAG
...THAT MEANS...

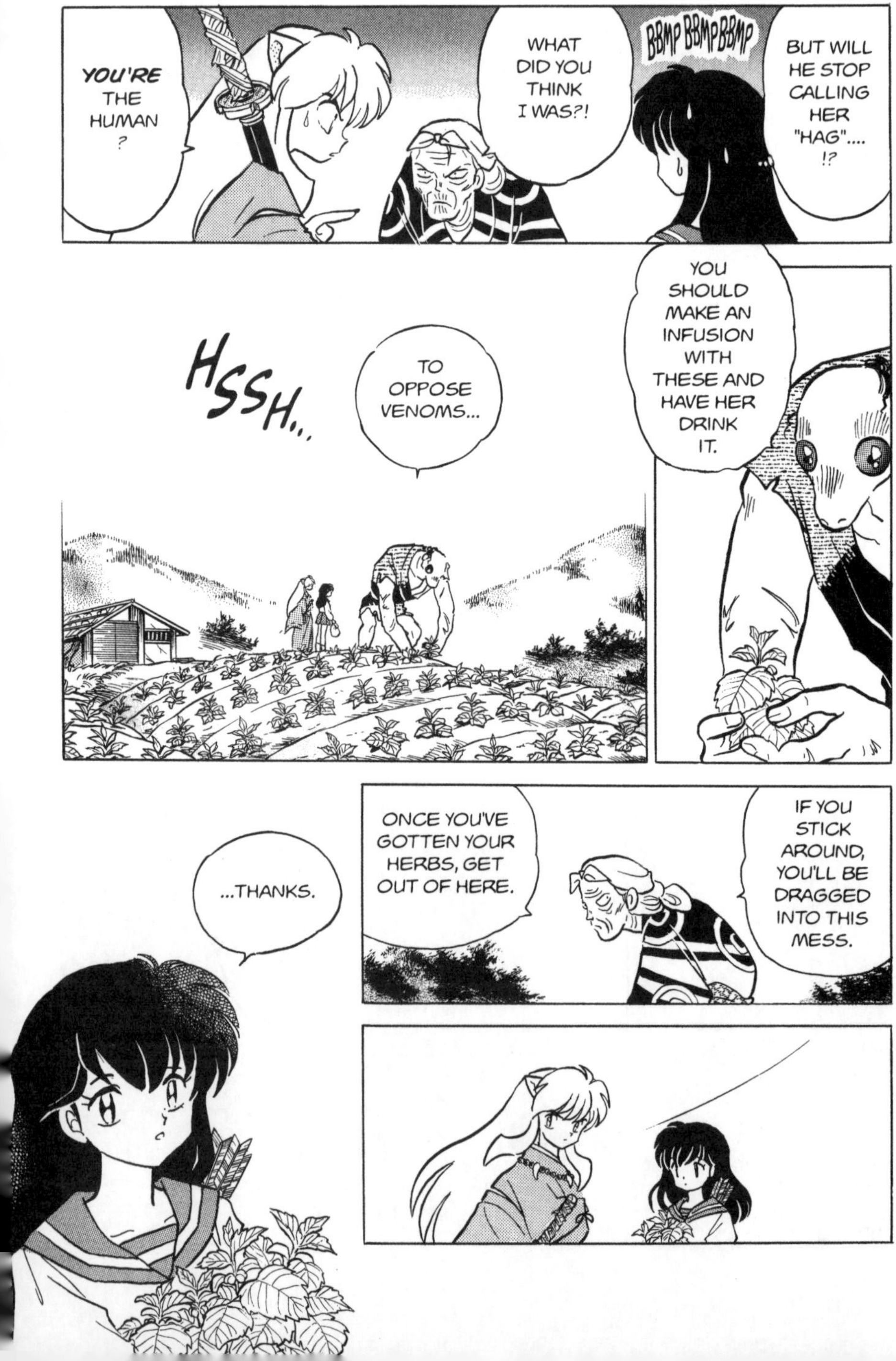
YOU'RE THE HUMAN?
WHAT DID YOU THINK I WAS?!
B-BMP B-BMP B-BMP
BUT WILL HE STOP CALLING HER "HAG"....!?
HSSH...
TO OPPOSE VENOMS...
YOU SHOULD MAKE AN INFUSION WITH THESE AND HAVE HER DRINK IT.
...THANKS.
ONCE YOU'VE GOTTEN YOUR HERBS, GET OUT OF HERE.
IF YOU STICK AROUND, YOU'LL BE DRAGGED INTO THIS MESS.

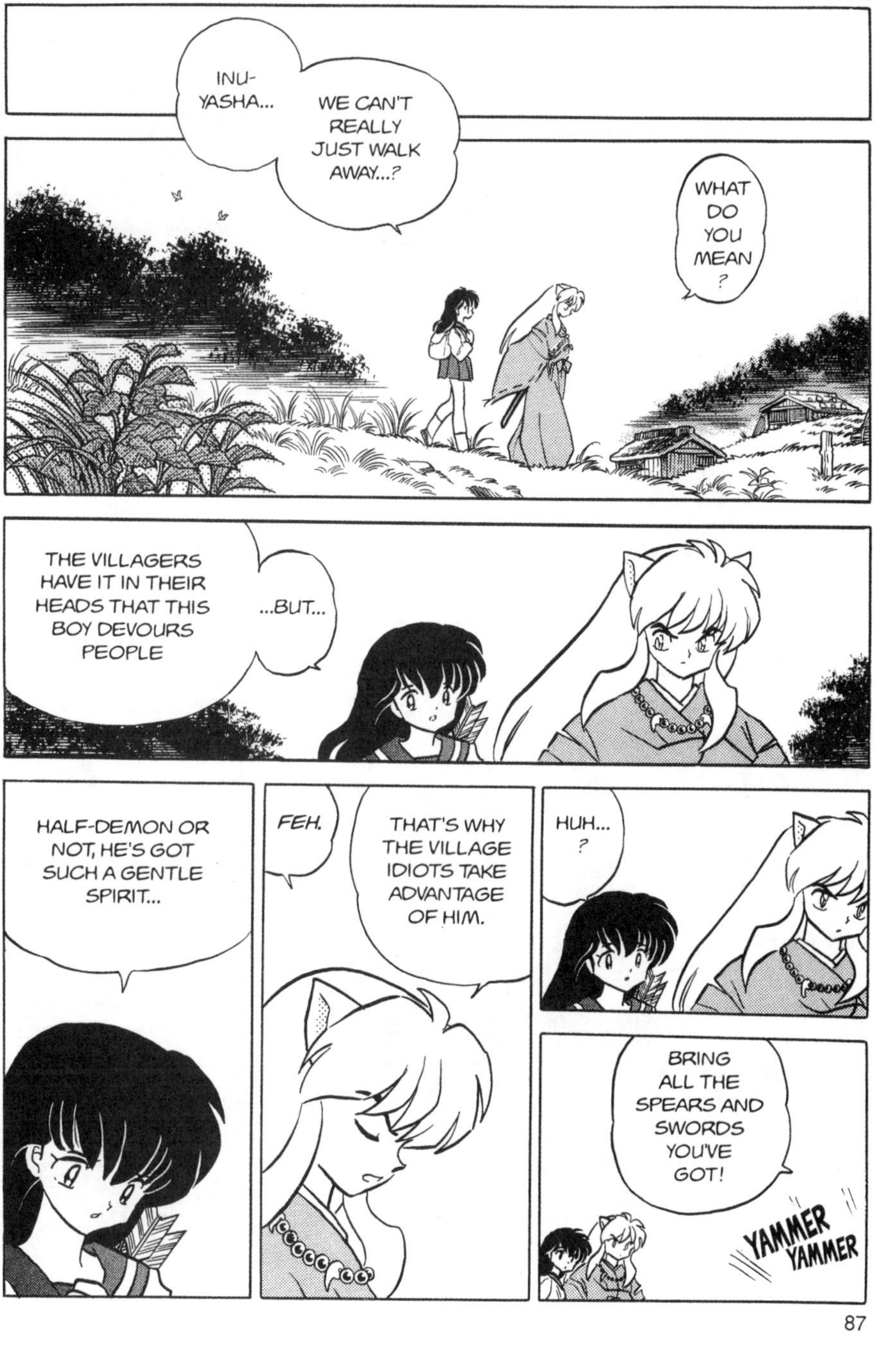
INU-YASHA...
WE CAN'T REALLY JUST WALK AWAY...?
WHAT DO YOU MEAN?
THE VILLAGERS HAVE IT IN THEIR HEADS THAT THIS BOY DEVOURS PEOPLE
...BUT...
HALF-DEMON OR NOT, HE'S GOT SUCH A GENTLE SPIRIT...
FEH.
THAT'S WHY THE VILLAGE IDIOTS TAKE ADVANTAGE OF HIM.
HUH...?
BRING ALL THE SPEARS AND SWORDS YOU'VE GOT!
YAMMER YAMMER

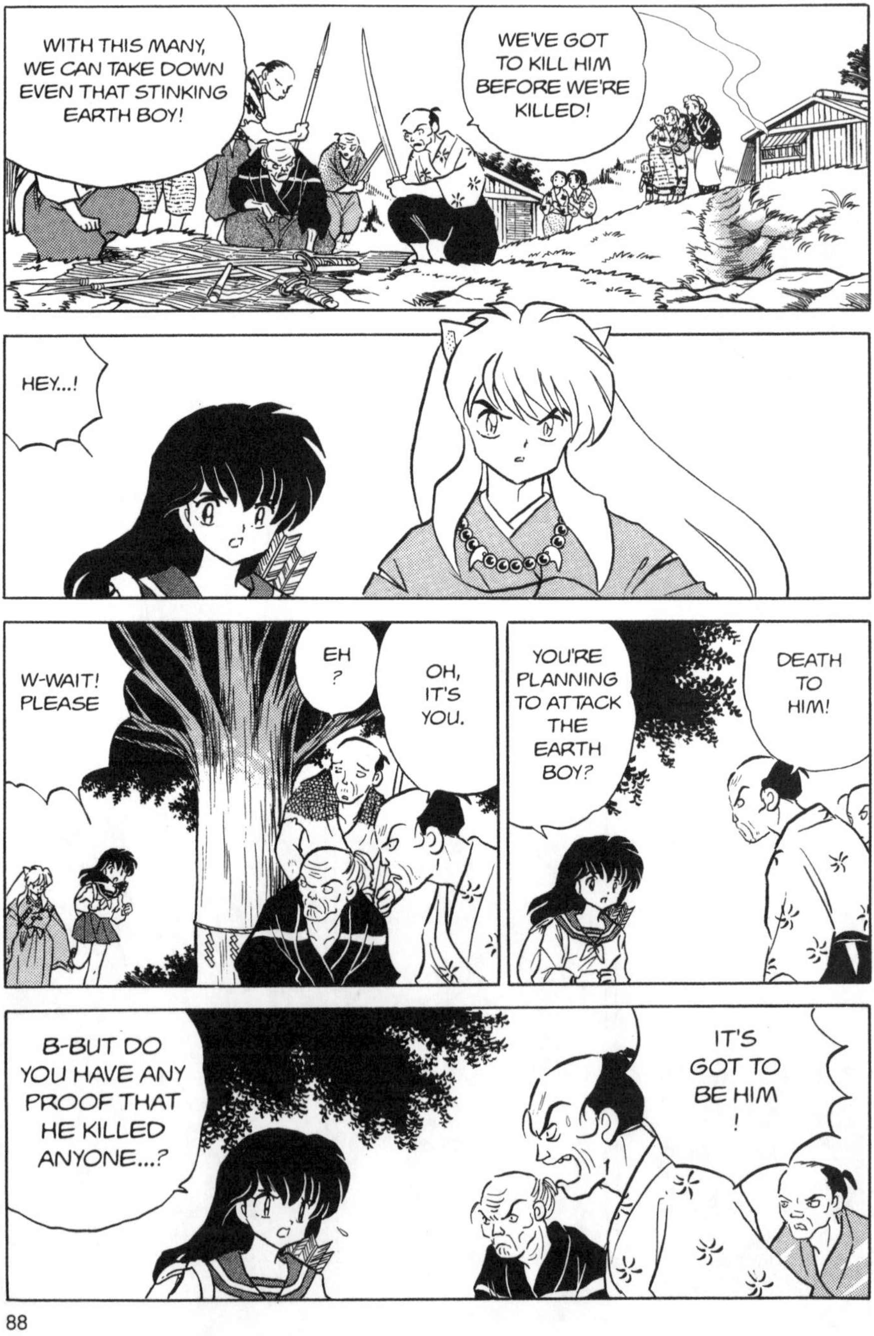
WITH THIS MANY, WE CAN TAKE DOWN EVEN THAT STINKING EARTH BOY!
WE'VE GOT TO KILL HIM BEFORE WE'RE KILLED!
HEY...!
W-WAIT! PLEASE
EH ?
OH, IT'S YOU.
YOU'RE PLANNING TO ATTACK THE EARTH BOY?
DEATH TO HIM!
B-BUT DO YOU HAVE ANY PROOF THAT HE KILLED ANYONE...?
IT'S GOT TO BE HIM !

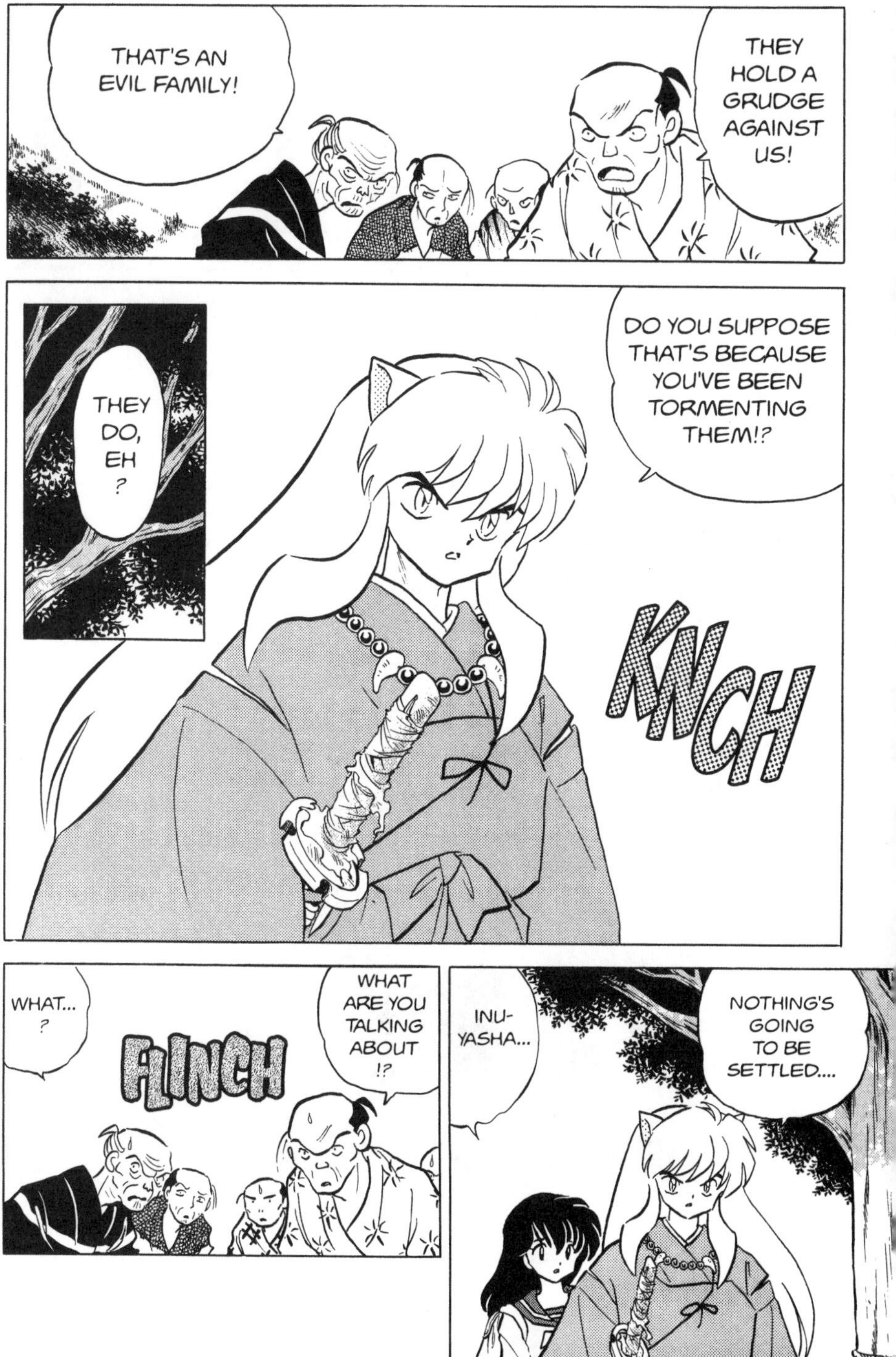
THAT'S AN EVIL FAMILY!
THEY HOLD A GRUDGE AGAINST US!
THEY DO, EH?
DO YOU SUPPOSE THAT'S BECAUSE YOU'VE BEEN TORMENTING THEM!?
KNCH
WHAT...?
FLINCH
WHAT ARE YOU TALKING ABOUT!?
INU-YASHA...
NOTHING'S GOING TO BE SETTLED....

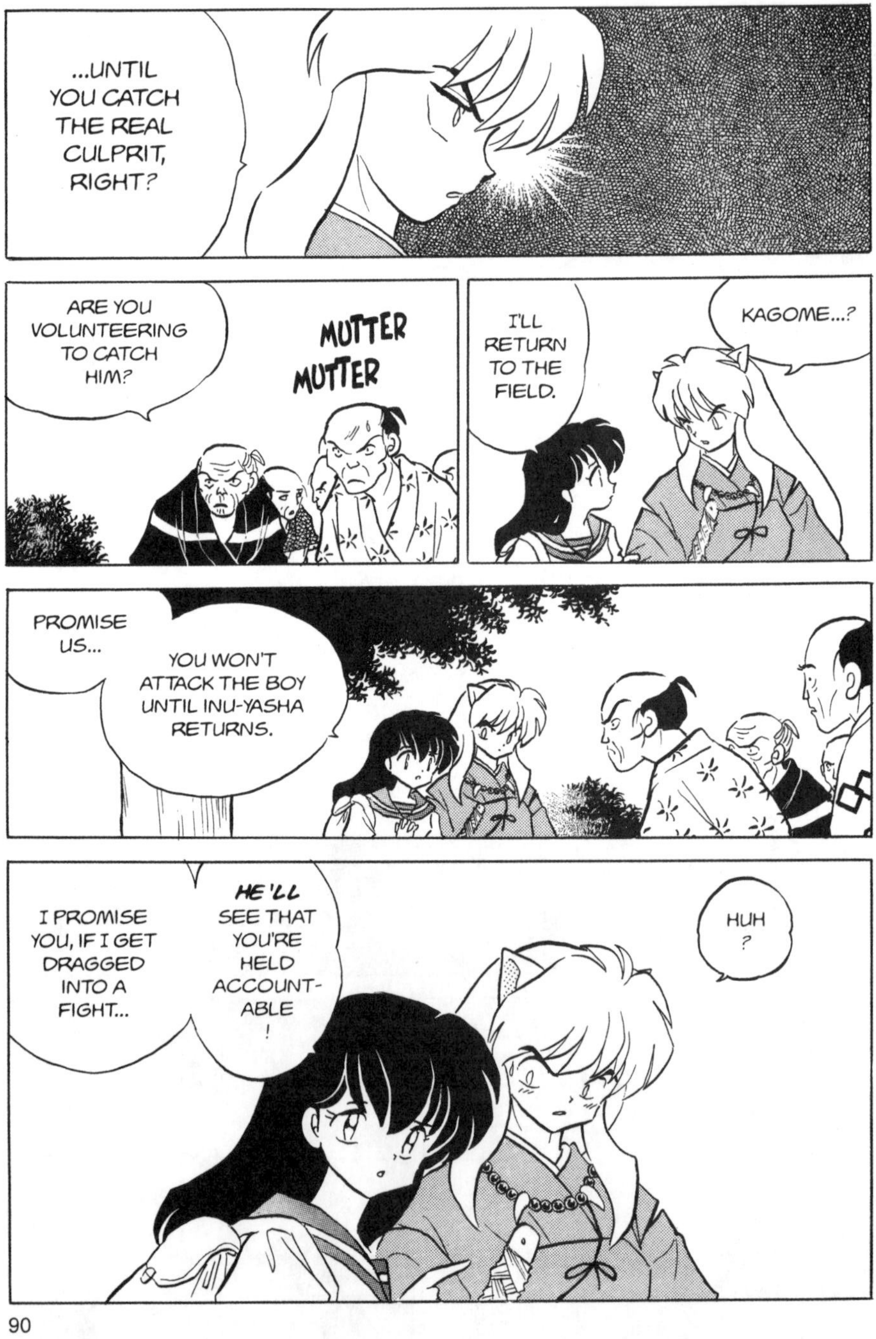
...UNTIL YOU CATCH THE REAL CULPRIT, RIGHT?
ARE YOU VOLUNTEERING TO CATCH HIM?
MUTTER MUTTER
I'LL RETURN TO THE FIELD.
KAGOME...?
PROMISE US...
YOU WON'T ATTACK THE BOY UNTIL INU-YASHA RETURNS.
I PROMISE YOU, IF I GET DRAGGED INTO A FIGHT...
HE'LL SEE THAT YOU'RE HELD ACCOUNTABLE!
HUH?

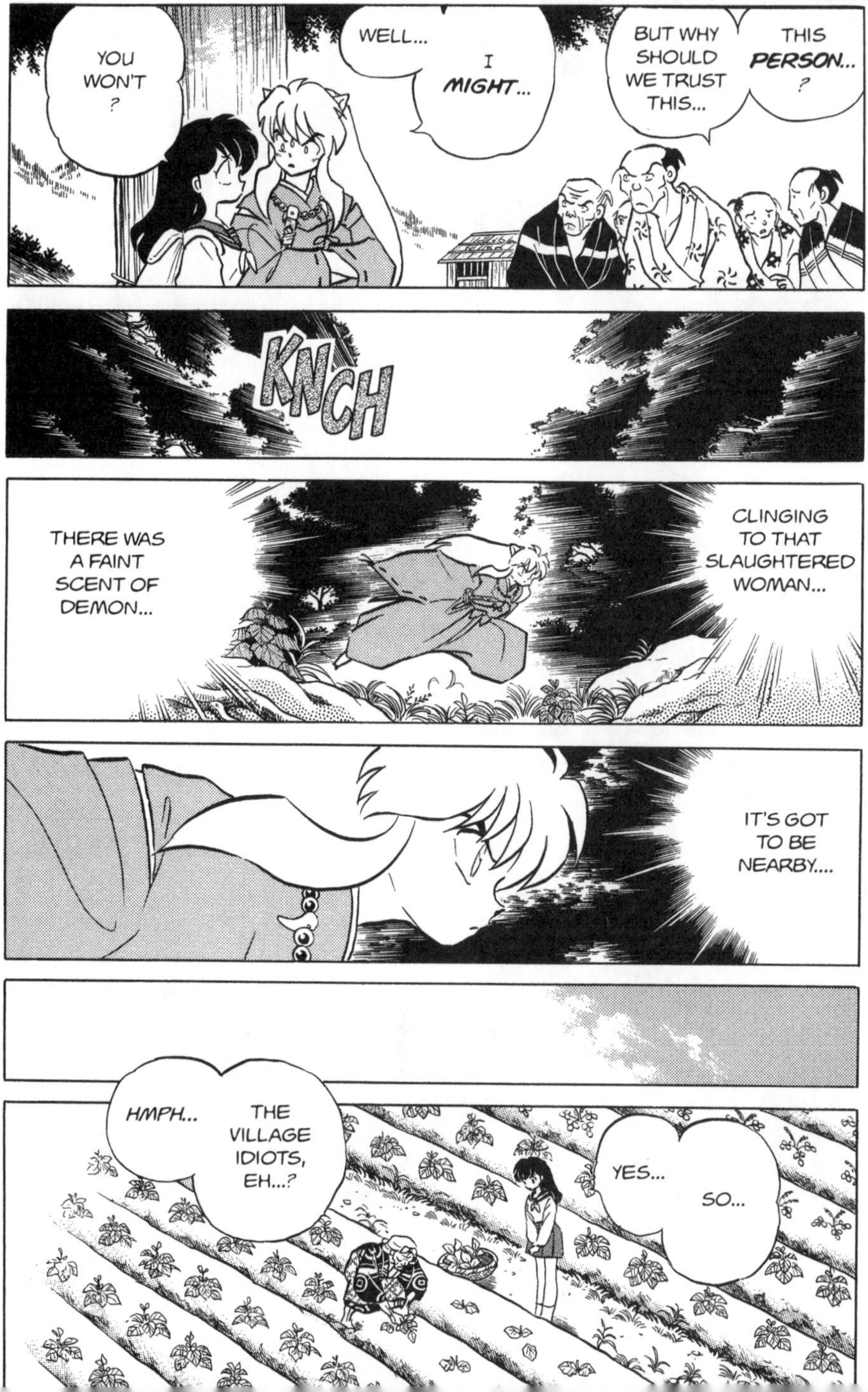
YOU WON'T ?
WELL... I *MIGHT*...
BUT WHY SHOULD WE TRUST THIS...
THIS *PERSON*... ?
KNCH
THERE WAS A FAINT SCENT OF DEMON...
CLINGING TO THAT SLAUGHTERED WOMAN...
IT'S GOT TO BE NEARBY....
HMPH... THE VILLAGE IDIOTS, EH...?
YES... SO...

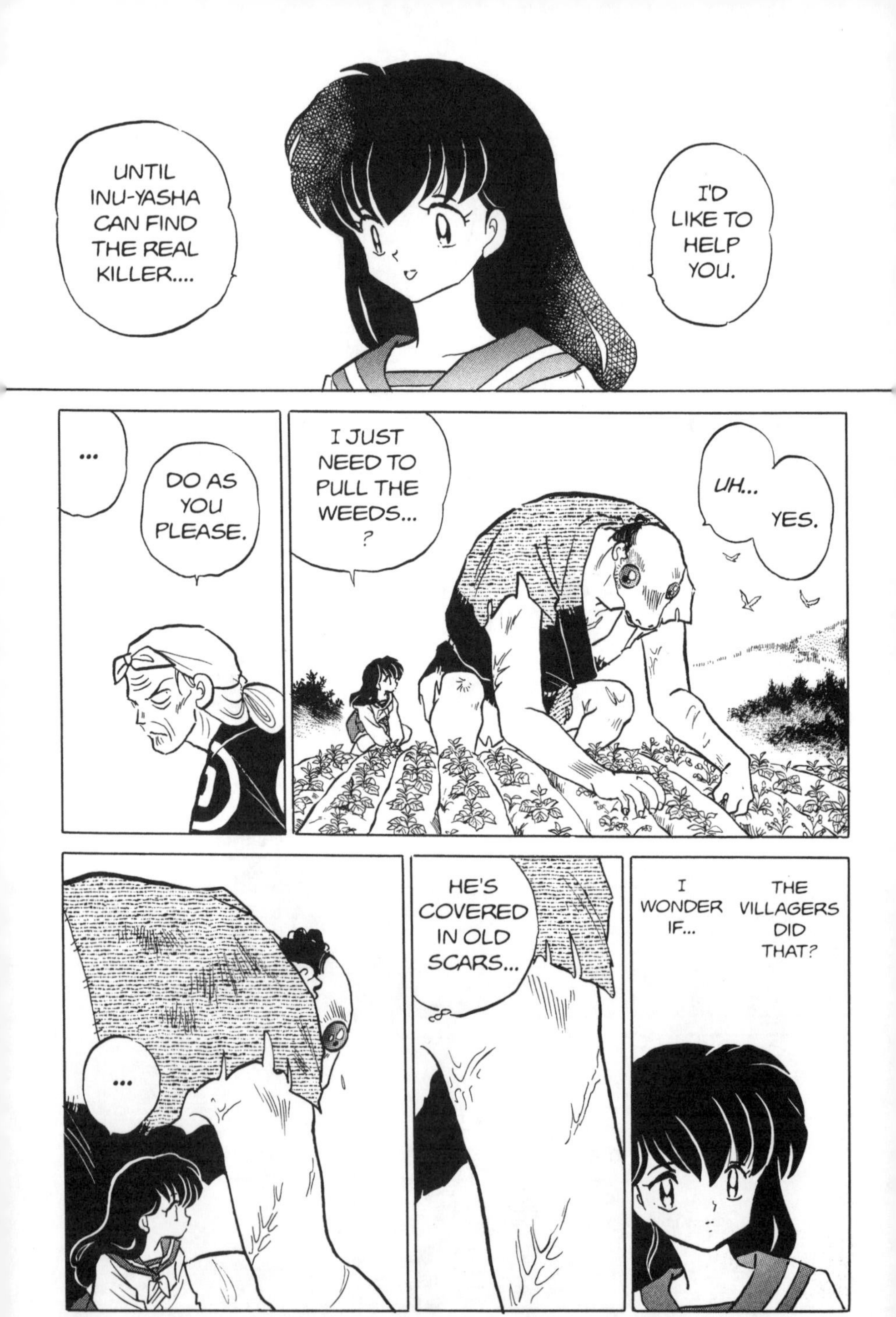
UNTIL INU-YASHA CAN FIND THE REAL KILLER....
I'D LIKE TO HELP YOU.
...
DO AS YOU PLEASE.
I JUST NEED TO PULL THE WEEDS...?
UH... YES.
...
HE'S COVERED IN OLD SCARS...
I WONDER IF...
THE VILLAGERS DID THAT?

HEY... DIDN'T YOU EVER THINK ABOUT LEAVING THIS PLACE?

I LIKE IT HERE.

MY FATHER LEFT THIS FIELD TO ME...

HHSSS

I SEE...

I-I'M TALKING... TO A *GIRL*...

FOR THE FIRST TIME IN MY LIFE... I'M HAVING A REAL CONVERSATION WITH A *GIRL*...!

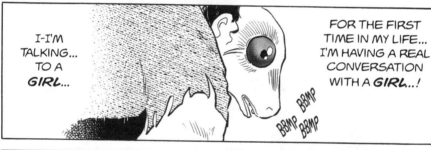

BBMP BBMP BBMP

YAAAA'!

FLINCH

IT'S A W-WORM--!

OH!

SHE'S SCARED OF *WORMS*... BUT SHE'S NOT SCARED OF JINENJI, EH...?

93

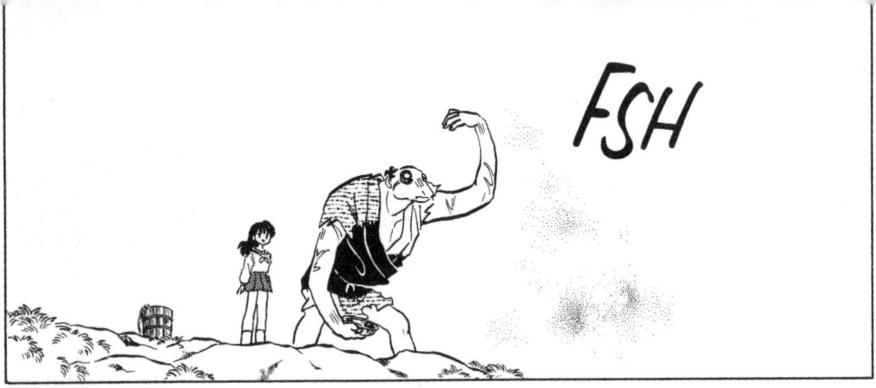
FSH

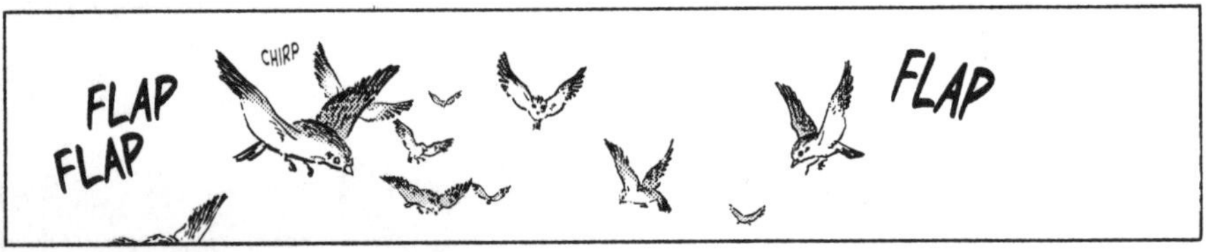
FLAP
FLAP
CHIRP
FLAP

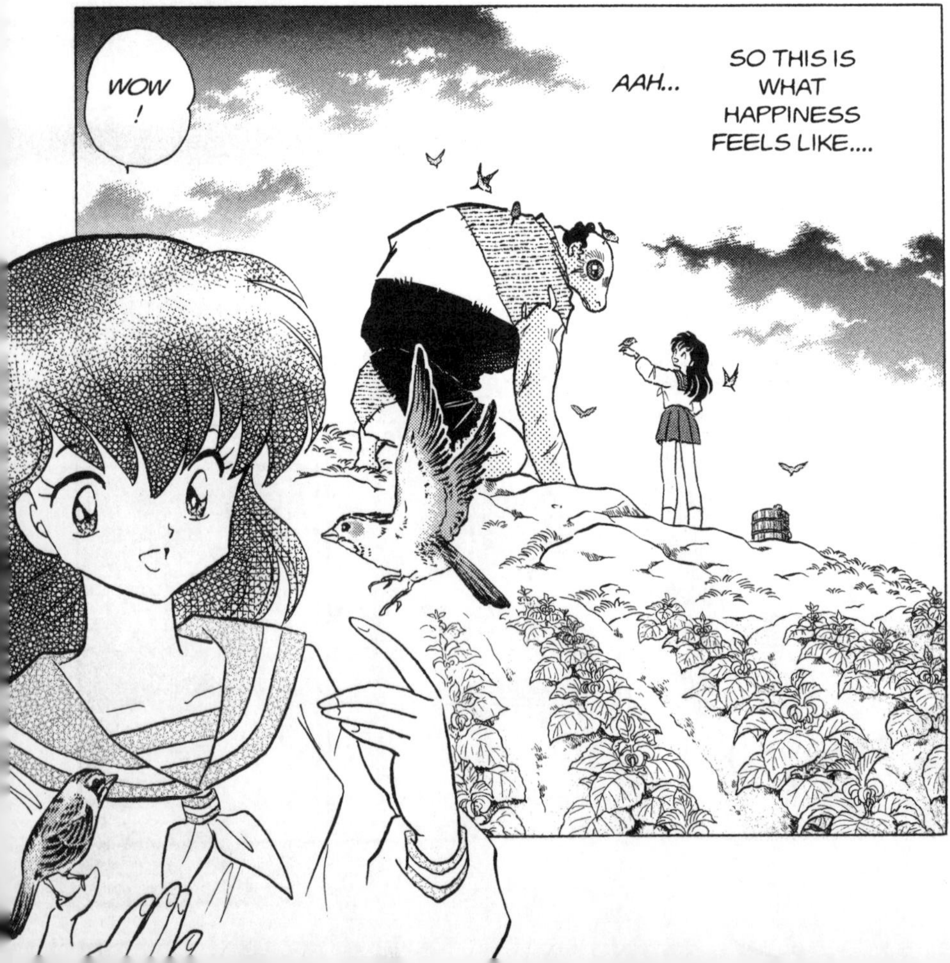
WOW!
AAH...
SO THIS IS WHAT HAPPINESS FEELS LIKE....

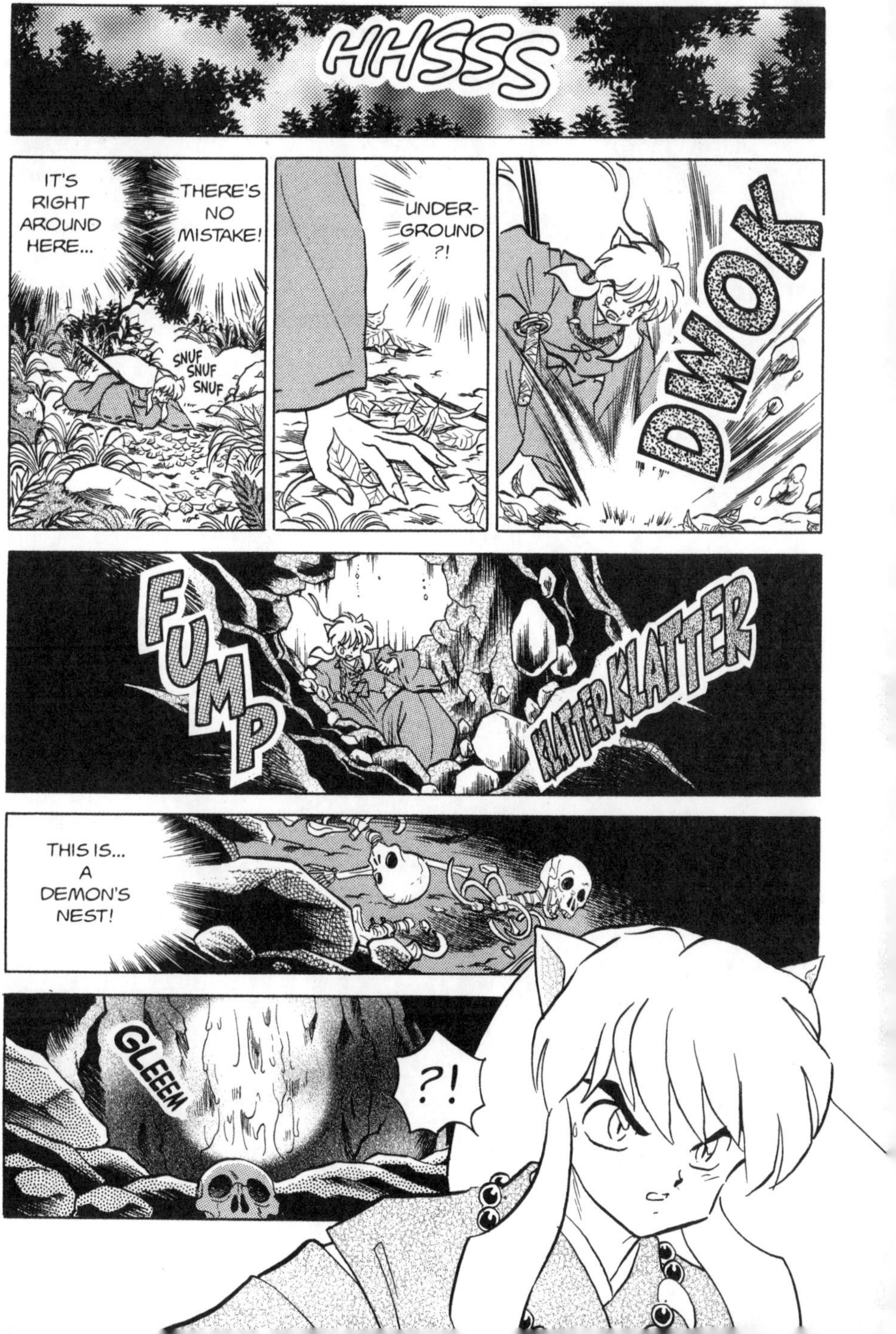
HHSSS
IT'S RIGHT AROUND HERE...
THERE'S NO MISTAKE!
SNUF SNUF SNUF
UNDER-GROUND ?!
DWOK
FUMP
KLATTER KLATTER
THIS IS... A DEMON'S NEST!
GLEEEM
?!

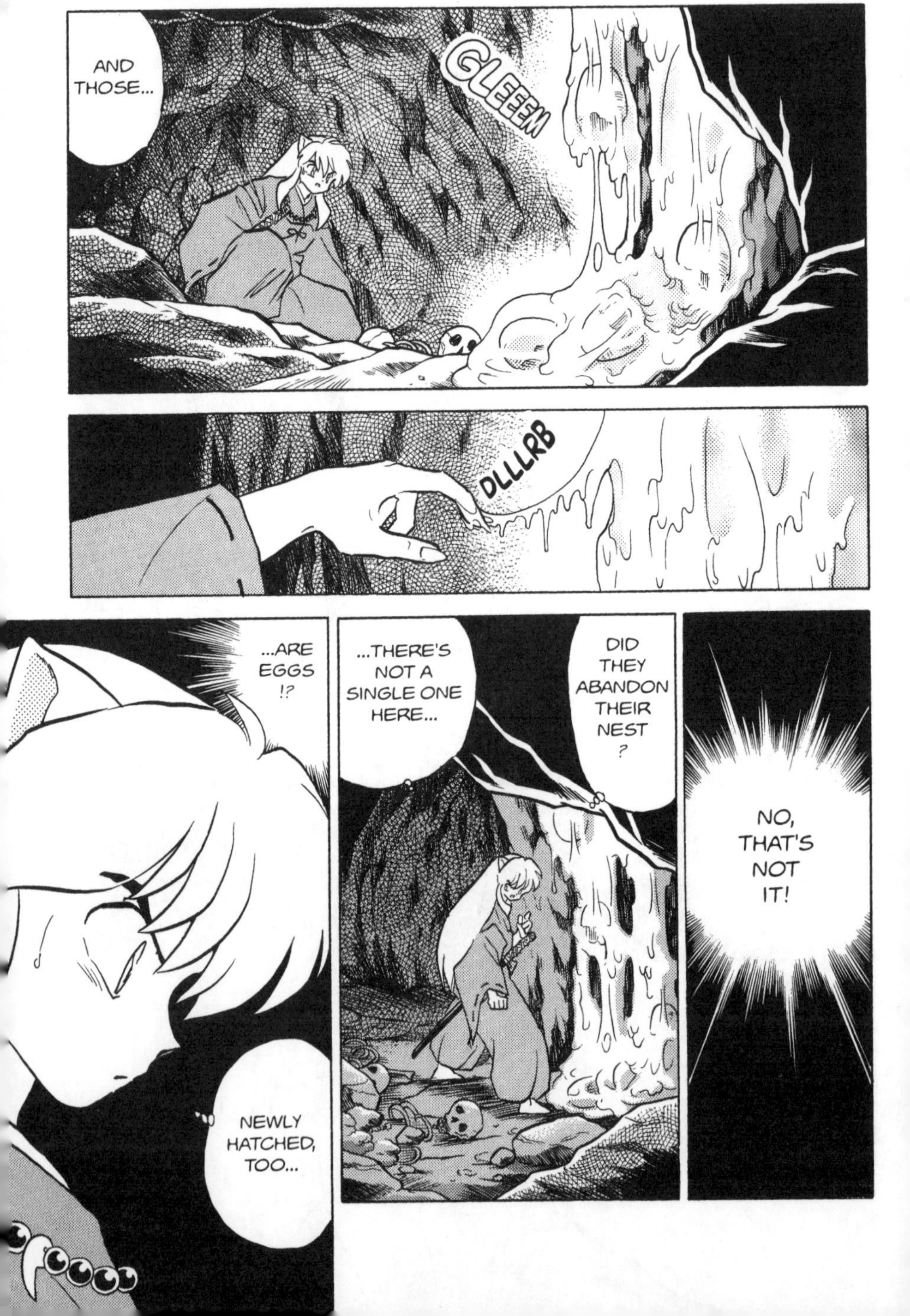
AND THOSE...
GLEEEM
DLLLRB
...ARE EGGS !?
NEWLY HATCHED, TOO...
...THERE'S NOT A SINGLE ONE HERE...
DID THEY ABANDON THEIR NEST ?
NO, THAT'S NOT IT!

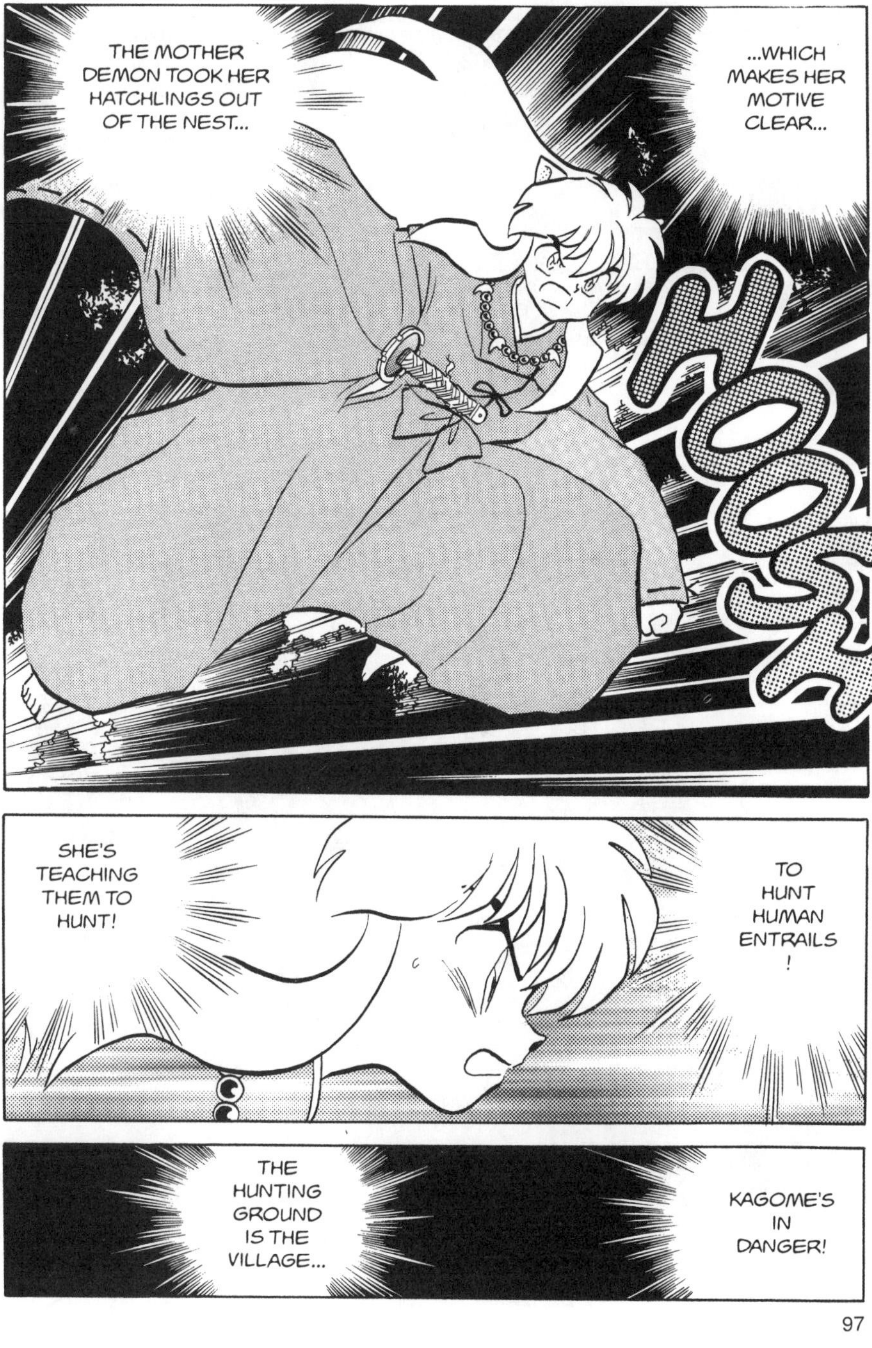
THE MOTHER DEMON TOOK HER HATCHLINGS OUT OF THE NEST...
...WHICH MAKES HER MOTIVE CLEAR...
WOOSH
SHE'S TEACHING THEM TO HUNT!
TO HUNT HUMAN ENTRAILS!
THE HUNTING GROUND IS THE VILLAGE...
KAGOME'S IN DANGER!

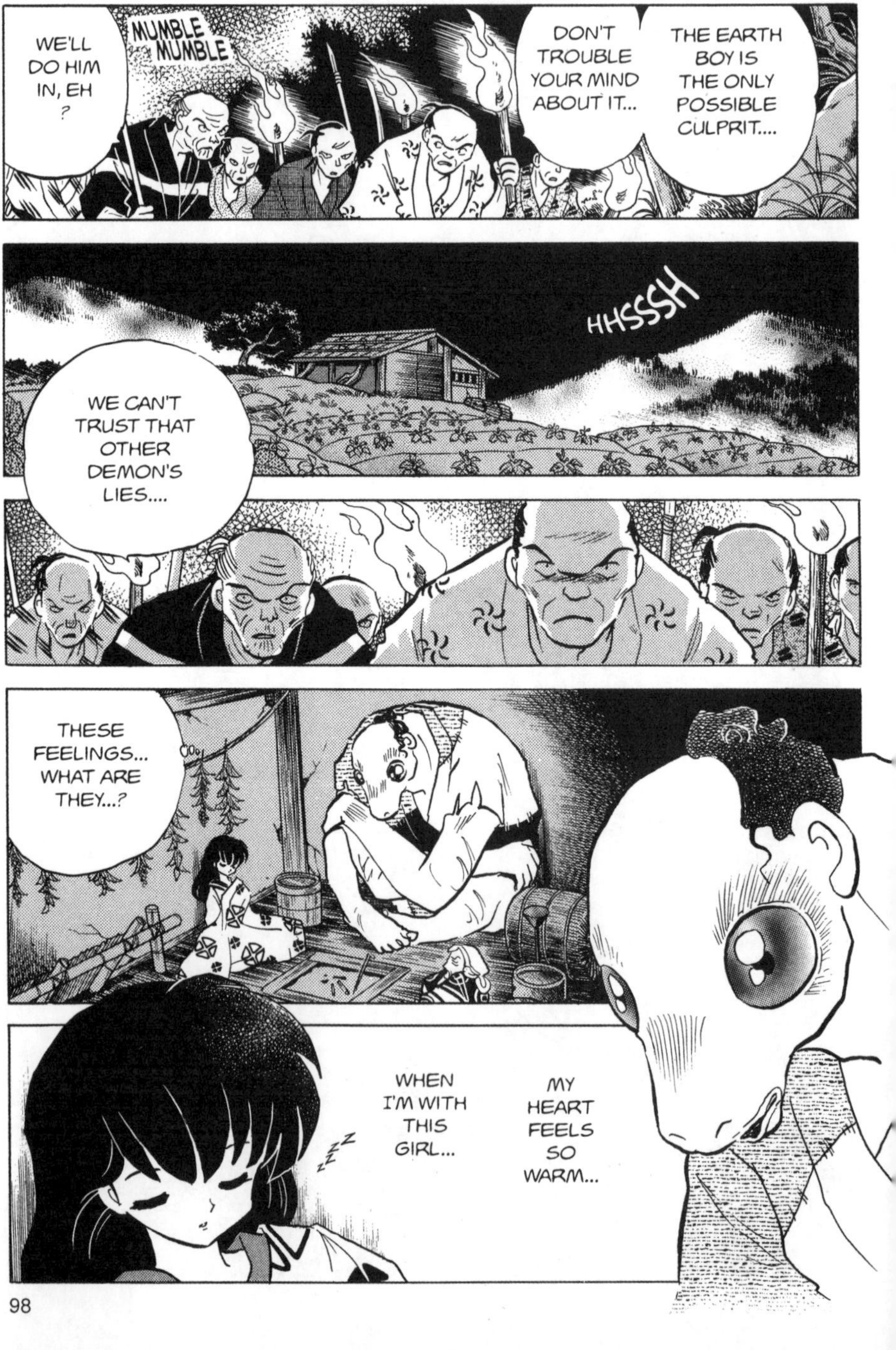
WE'LL DO HIM IN, EH ?
MUMBLE MUMBLE
DON'T TROUBLE YOUR MIND ABOUT IT...
THE EARTH BOY IS THE ONLY POSSIBLE CULPRIT....
HHSSSH
WE CAN'T TRUST THAT OTHER DEMON'S LIES....
THESE FEELINGS... WHAT ARE THEY...?
ZZZ
WHEN I'M WITH THIS GIRL...
MY HEART FEELS SO WARM...

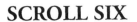

SCROLL SIX

THE HALF-BREED'S HEART

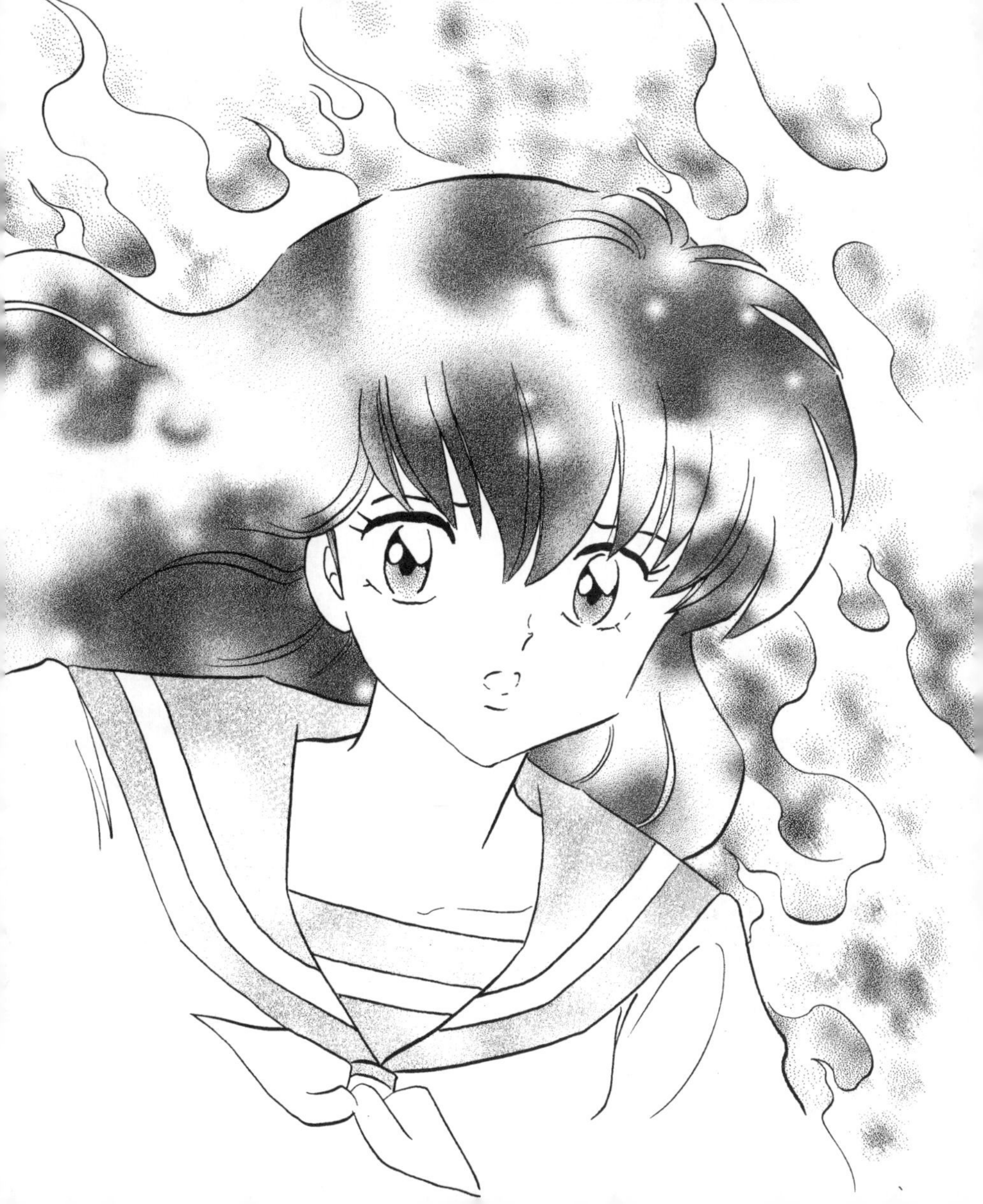

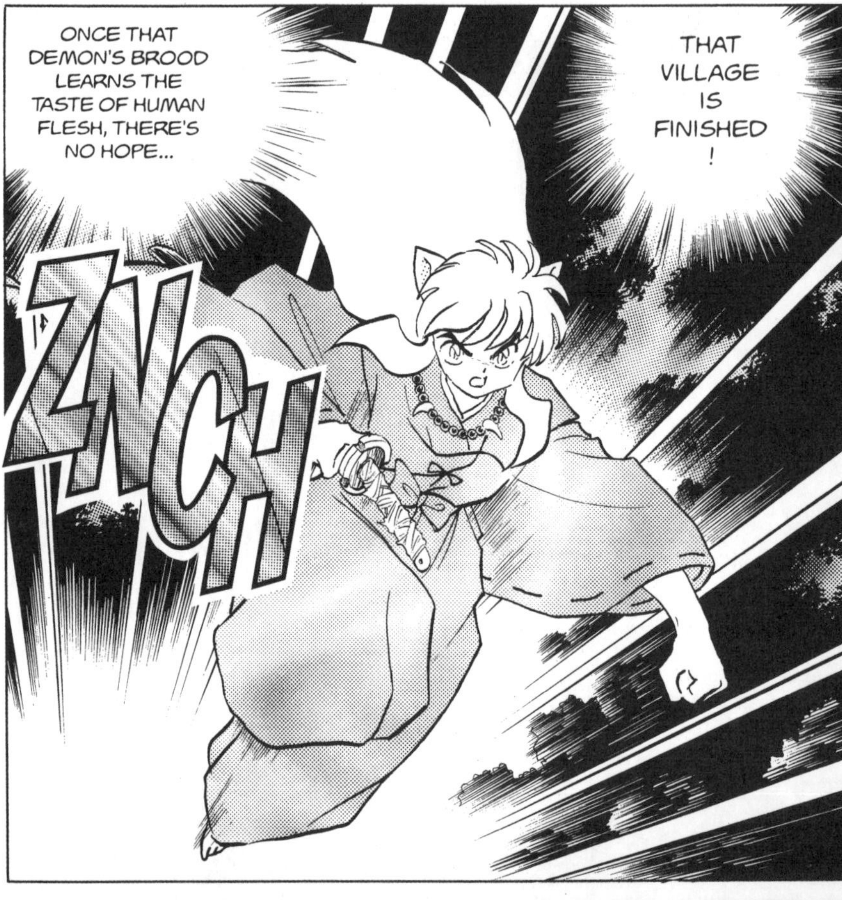
ONCE THAT DEMON'S BROOD LEARNS THE TASTE OF HUMAN FLESH, THERE'S NO HOPE...
THAT VILLAGE IS FINISHED!
ZNCH

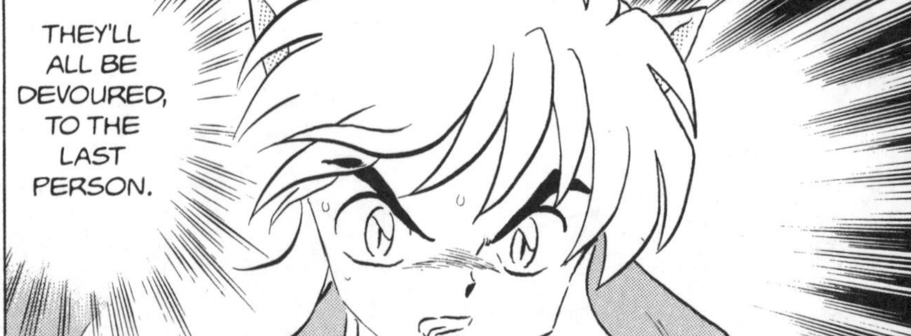
THEY'LL ALL BE DEVOURED, TO THE LAST PERSON.

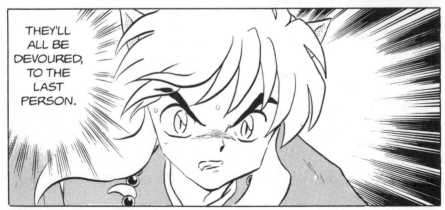

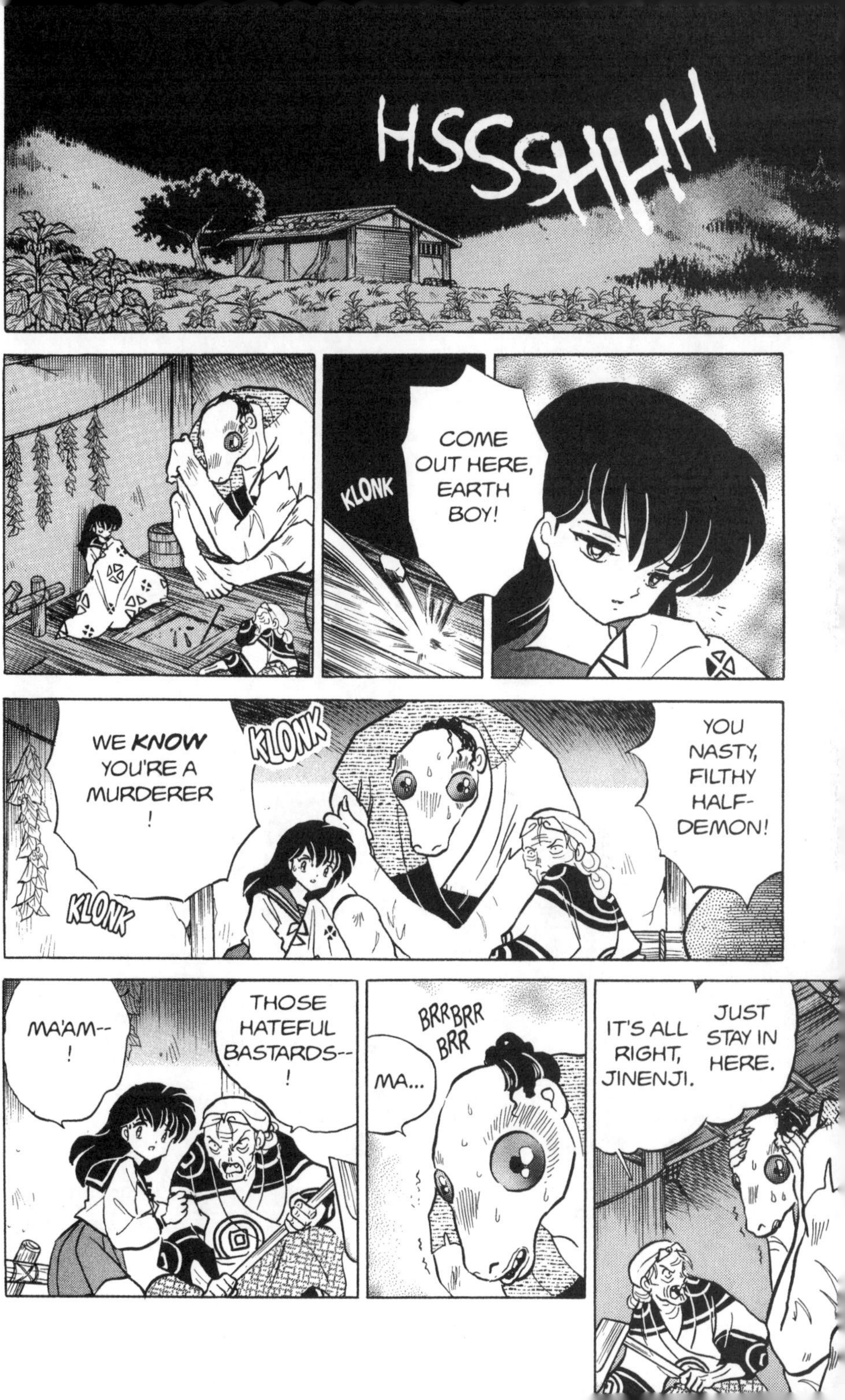
HSSSHHH
KLONK
COME OUT HERE, EARTH BOY!
WE KNOW YOU'RE A MURDERER!
KLONK
KLONK
YOU NASTY, FILTHY HALF-DEMON!
MA'AM--!
THOSE HATEFUL BASTARDS--!
BRRBRR BRR
MA...
IT'S ALL RIGHT, JINENJI.
JUST STAY IN HERE.

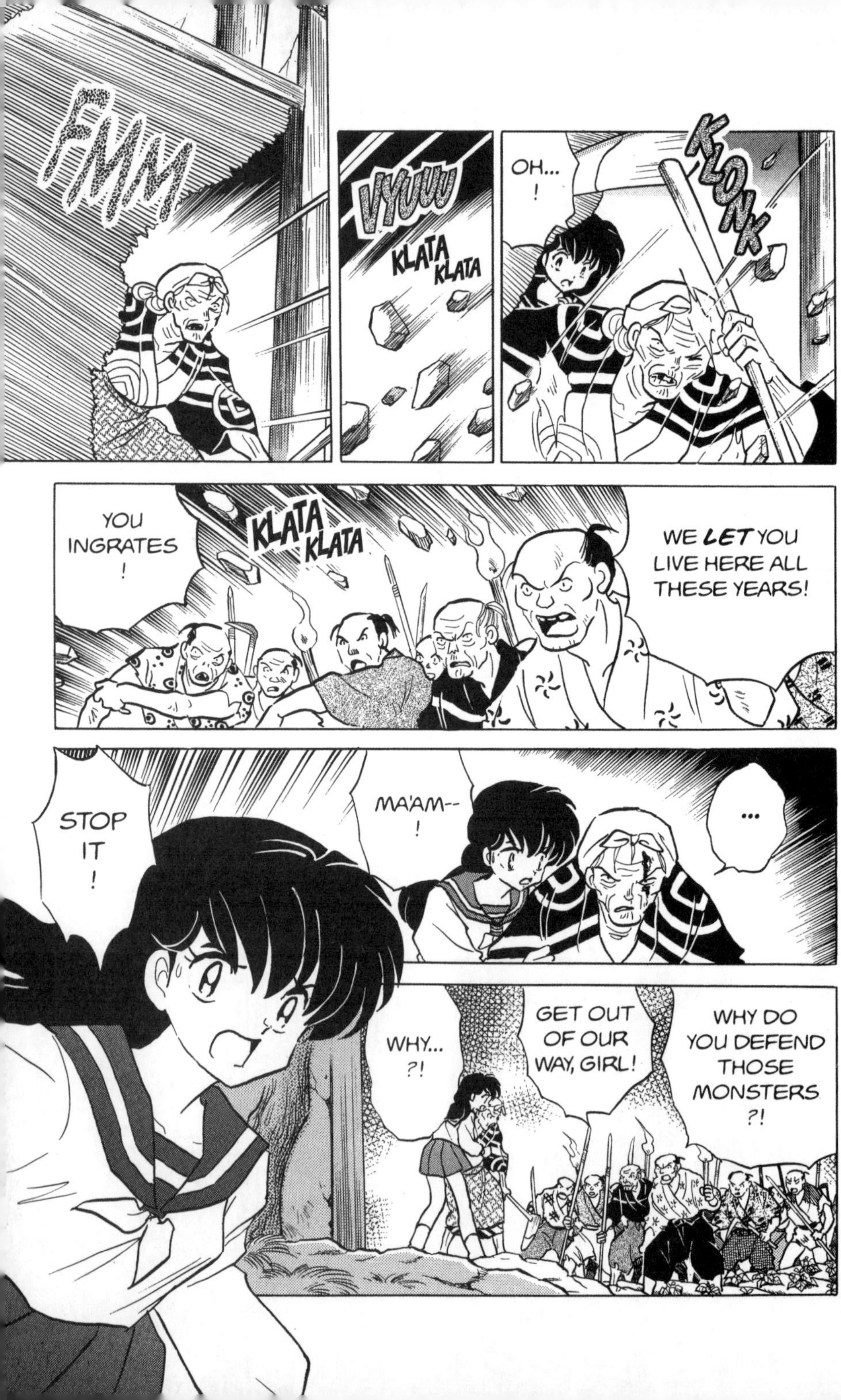
FMM
VYUUU
KLATA KLATA
OH... !
KLONK
YOU INGRATES !
KLATA KLATA
WE LET YOU LIVE HERE ALL THESE YEARS!
STOP IT !
MA'AM-- !
...
WHY... ?!
GET OUT OF OUR WAY, GIRL!
WHY DO YOU DEFEND THOSE MONSTERS ?!

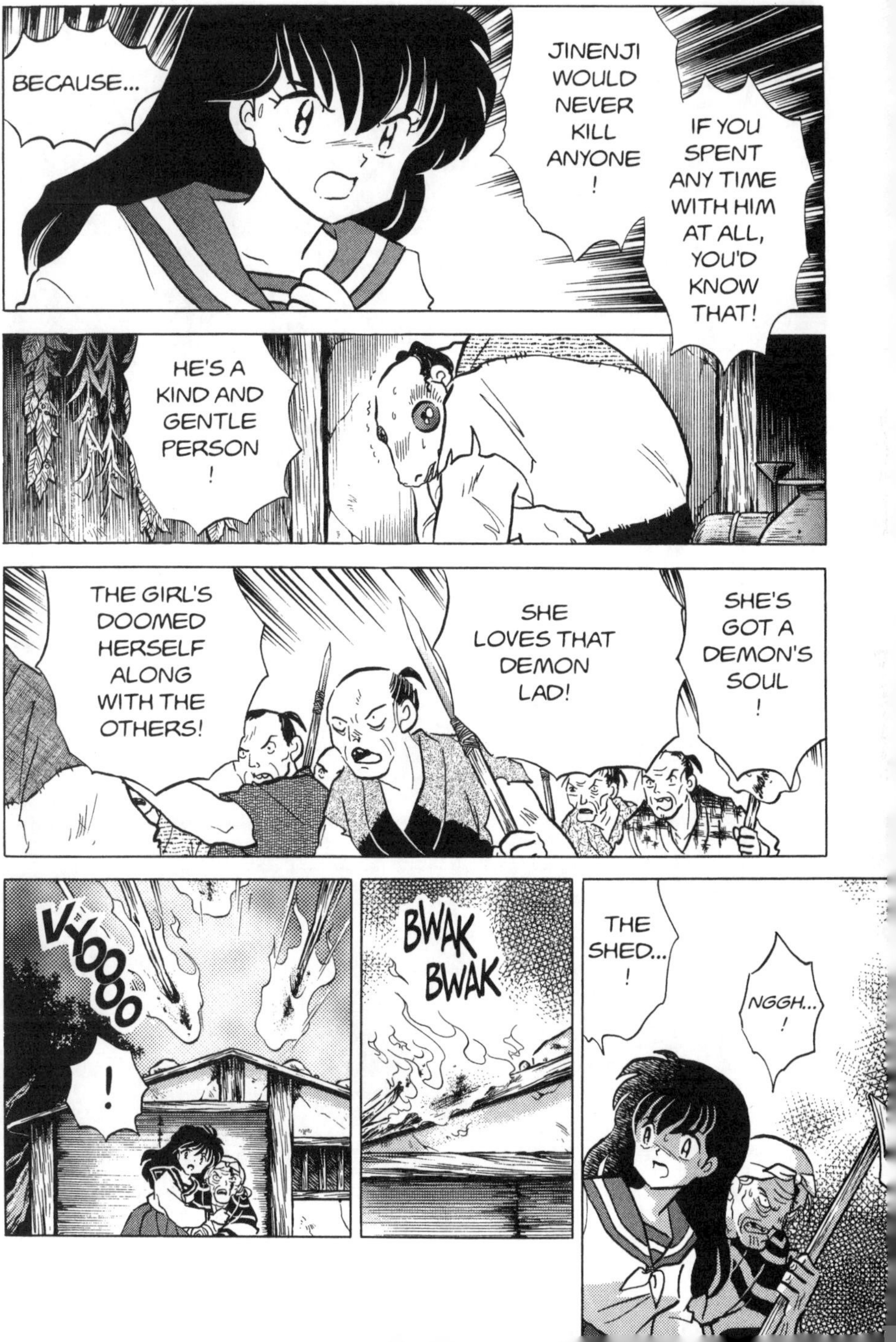
BECAUSE...
JINENJI WOULD NEVER KILL ANYONE!
IF YOU SPENT ANY TIME WITH HIM AT ALL, YOU'D KNOW THAT!
HE'S A KIND AND GENTLE PERSON!
THE GIRL'S DOOMED HERSELF ALONG WITH THE OTHERS!
SHE LOVES THAT DEMON LAD!
SHE'S GOT A DEMON'S SOUL!
V-YOOOO
!
BWAK BWAK
THE SHED...!
NGGH...!

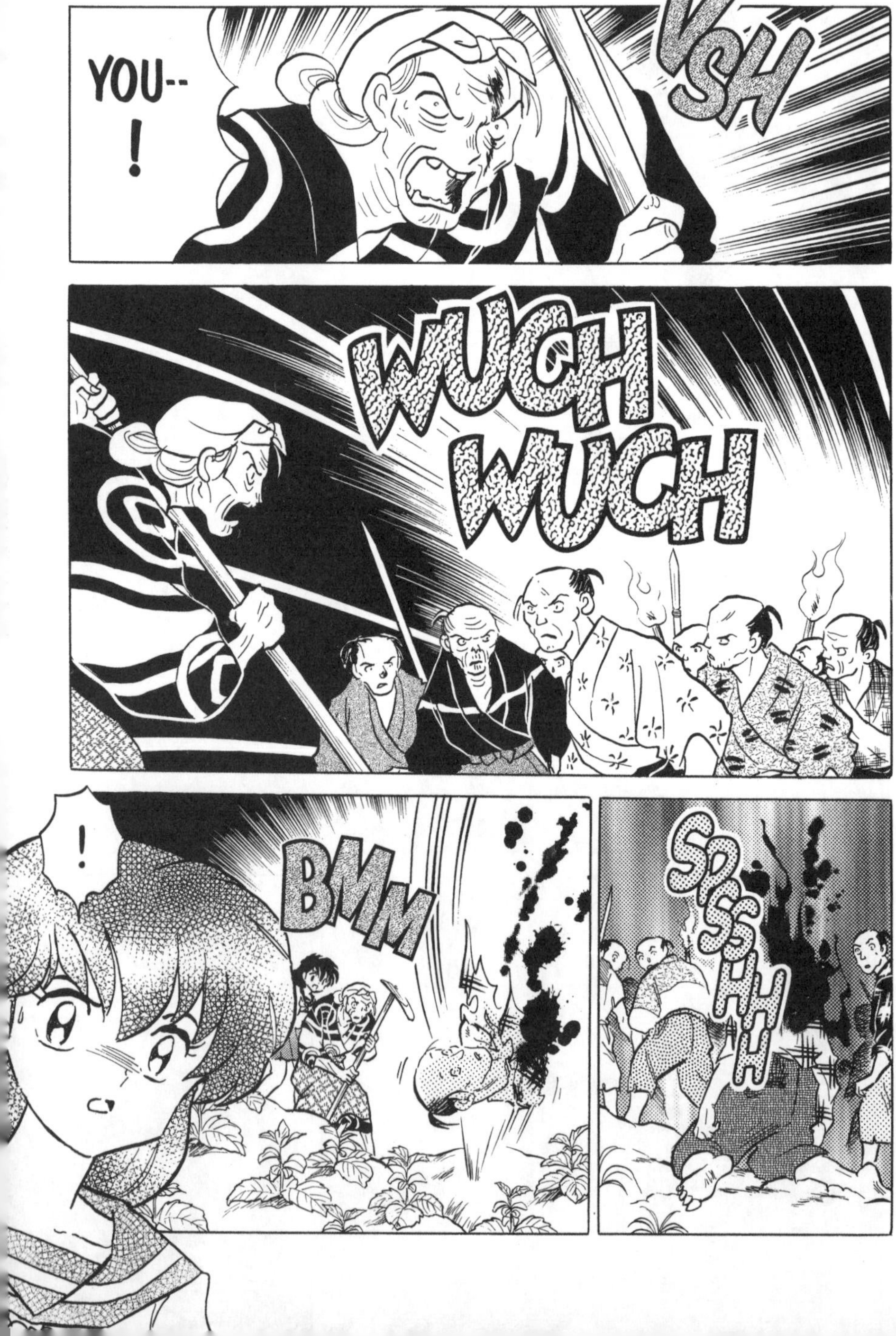
YOU-- !
VSH
WUGH WUGH
!
BMM
SPSSHHH

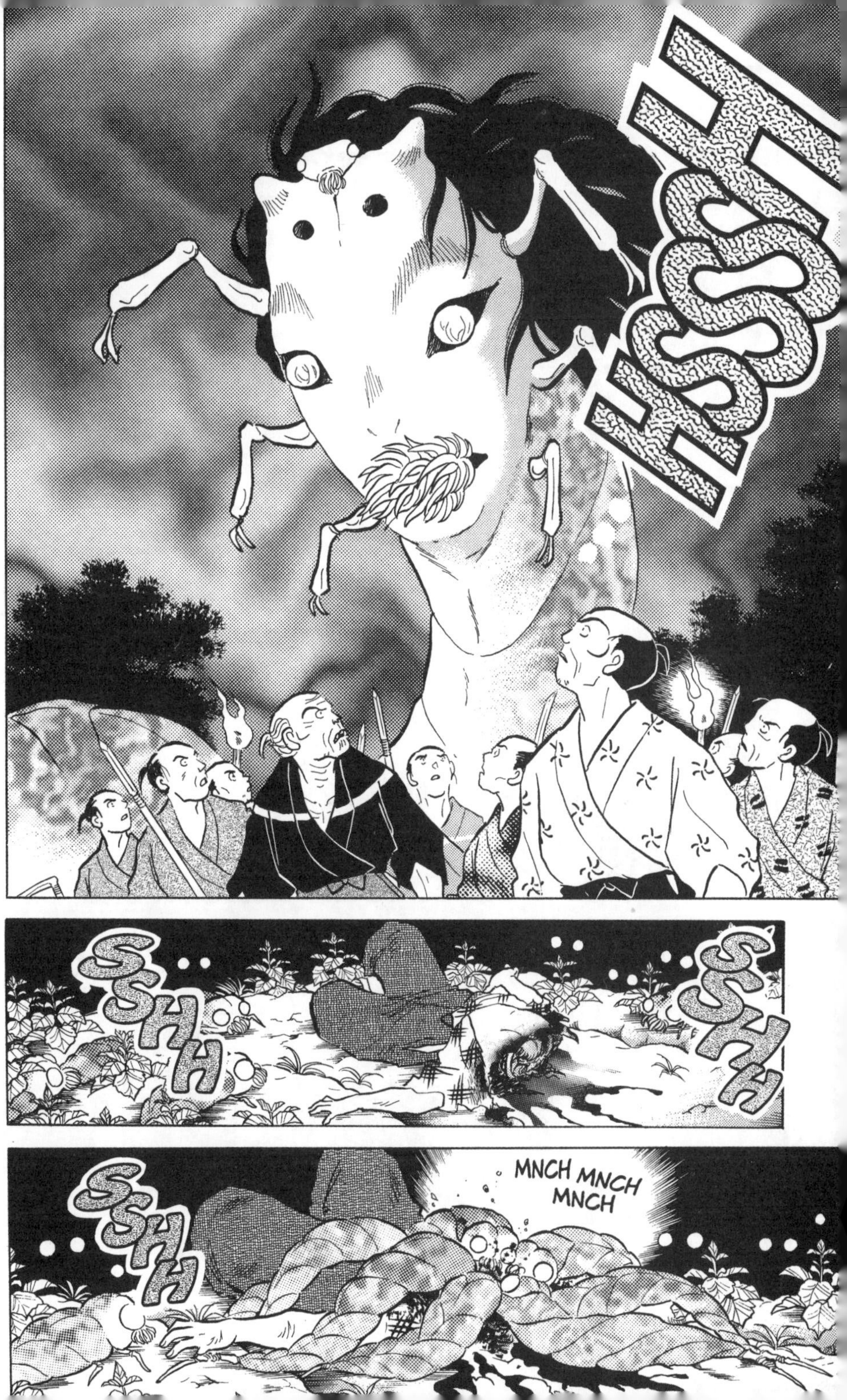
HISSSSH
SSHH...
SSHH
SSHH...
MNCH MNCH
MNCH

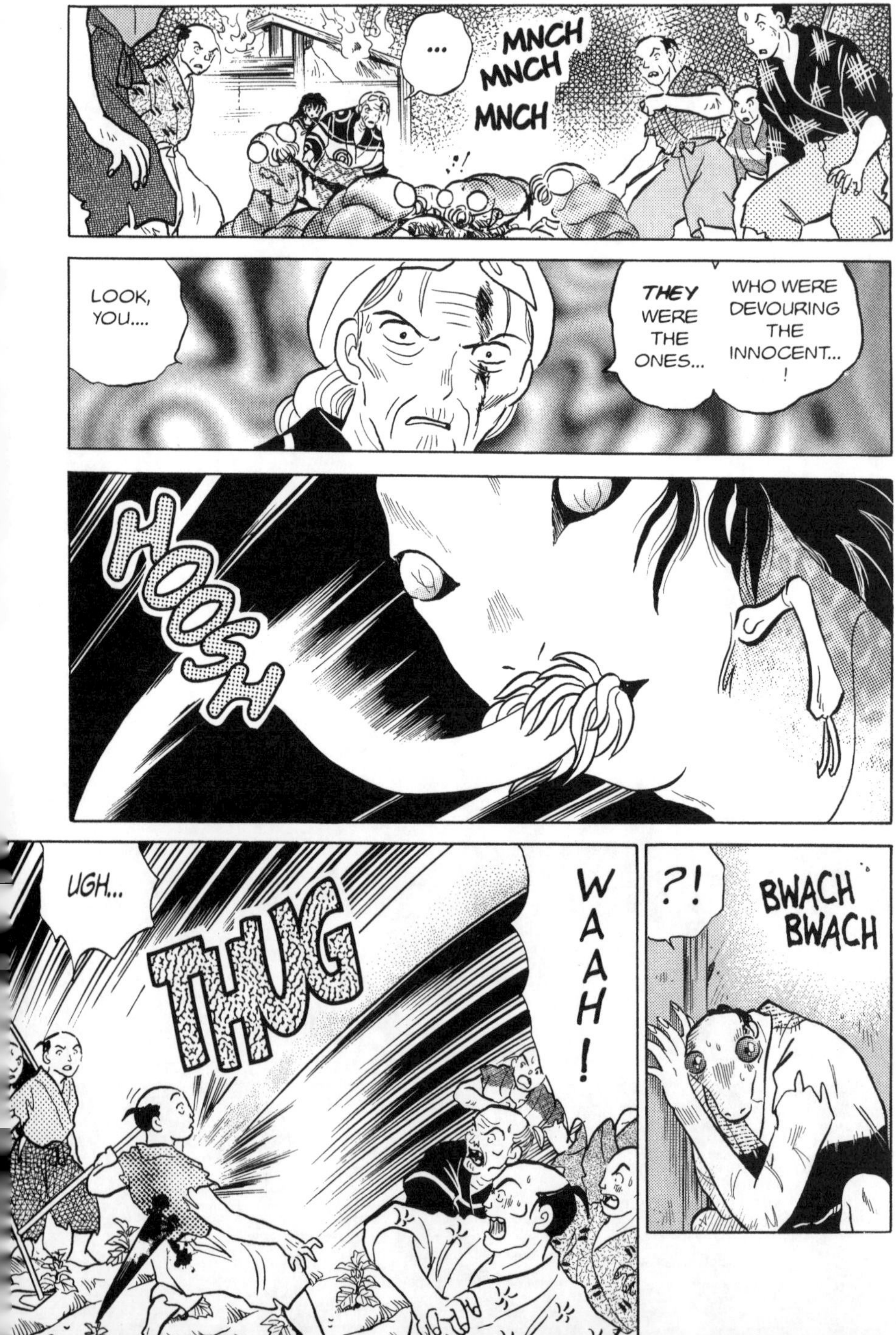
...
MNCH
MNCH
MNCH
LOOK, YOU....
THEY WERE THE ONES...
WHO WERE DEVOURING THE INNOCENT...!
WHOOSH
UGH...
THUG
WAAH!
?!
BWACH BWACH

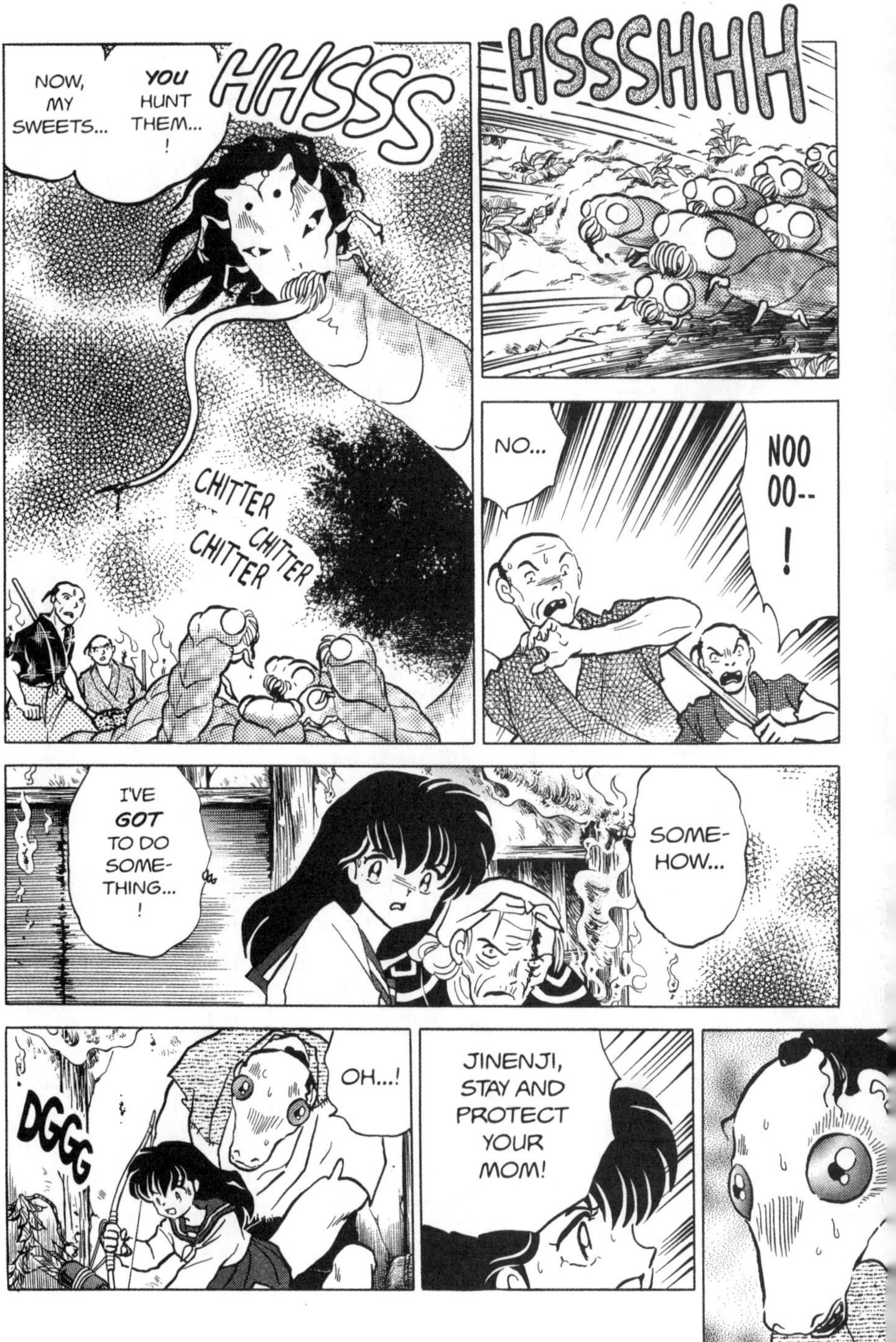

NOW, MY SWEETS...
YOU HUNT THEM...!
HHSSS
CHITTER CHITTER CHITTER
HSSSHHH
NO...
NOOOO--!
I'VE GOT TO DO SOMETHING...!
SOME-HOW...
DGGG
OH...!
JINENJI, STAY AND PROTECT YOUR MOM!

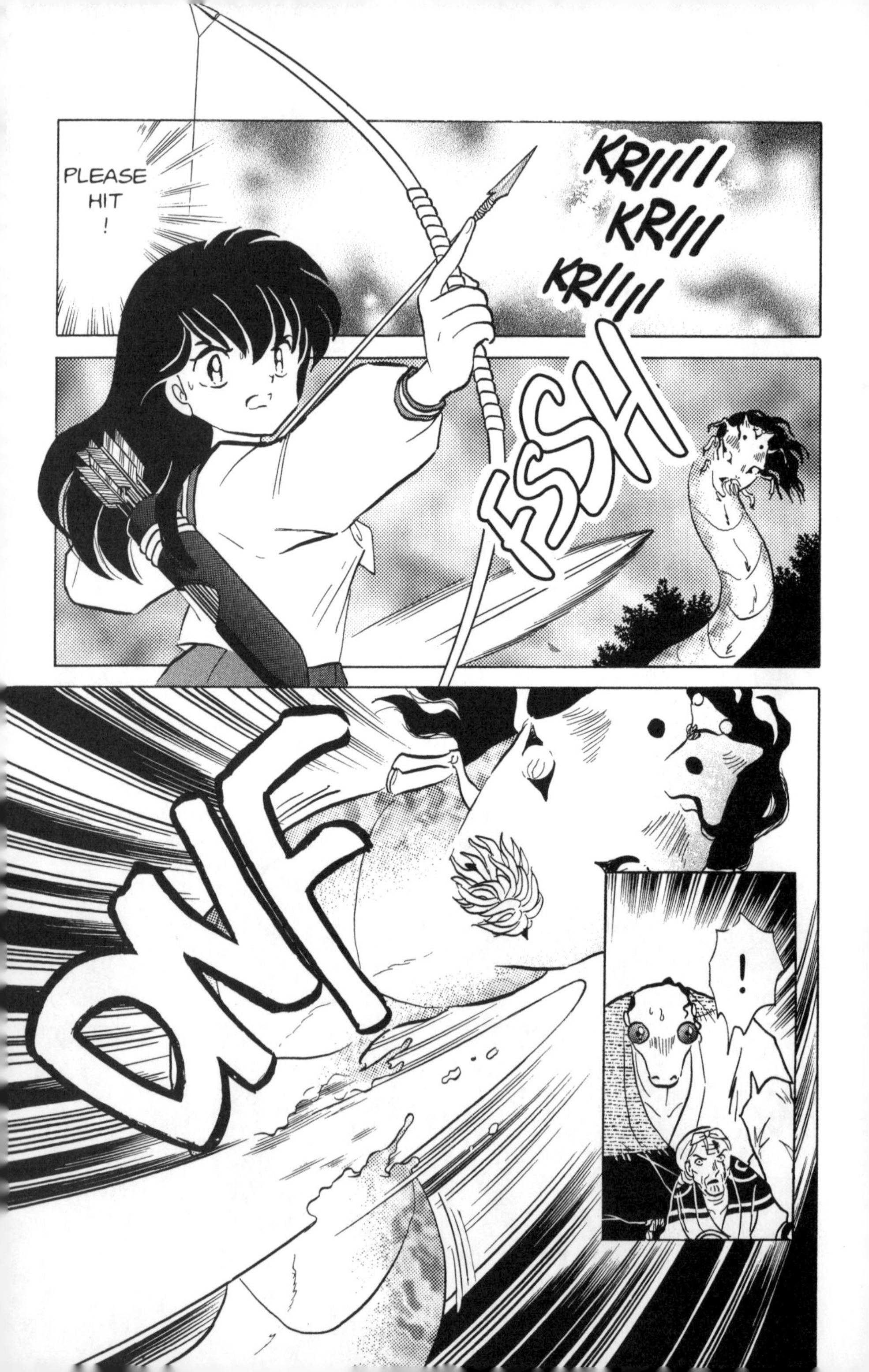

PLEASE HIT !
KRI!!!! KRI!!! KRI!!!!
FSSH
!

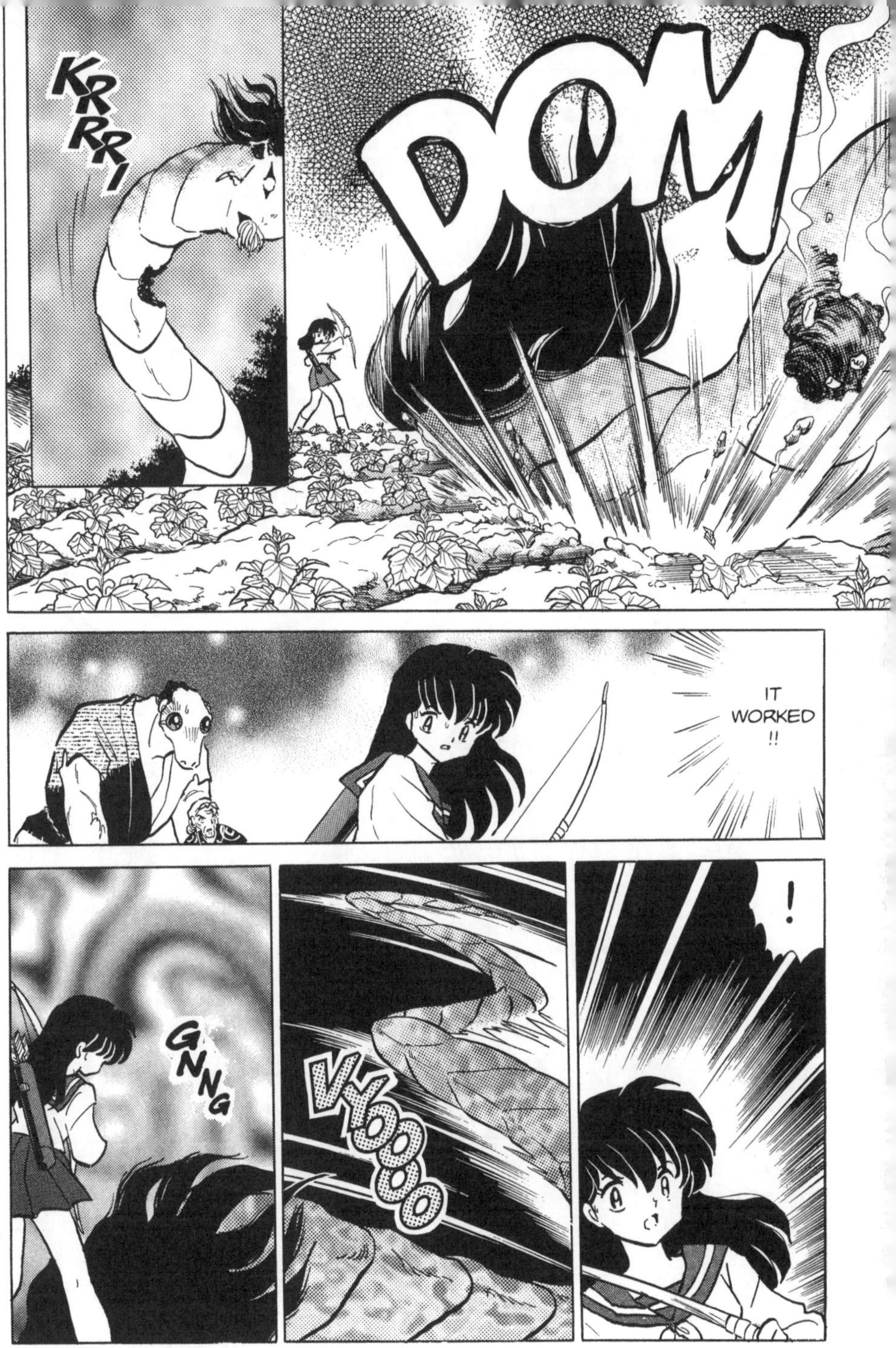
KRRRI
DOM
IT WORKED !!
GNNG
VYOOOO
!

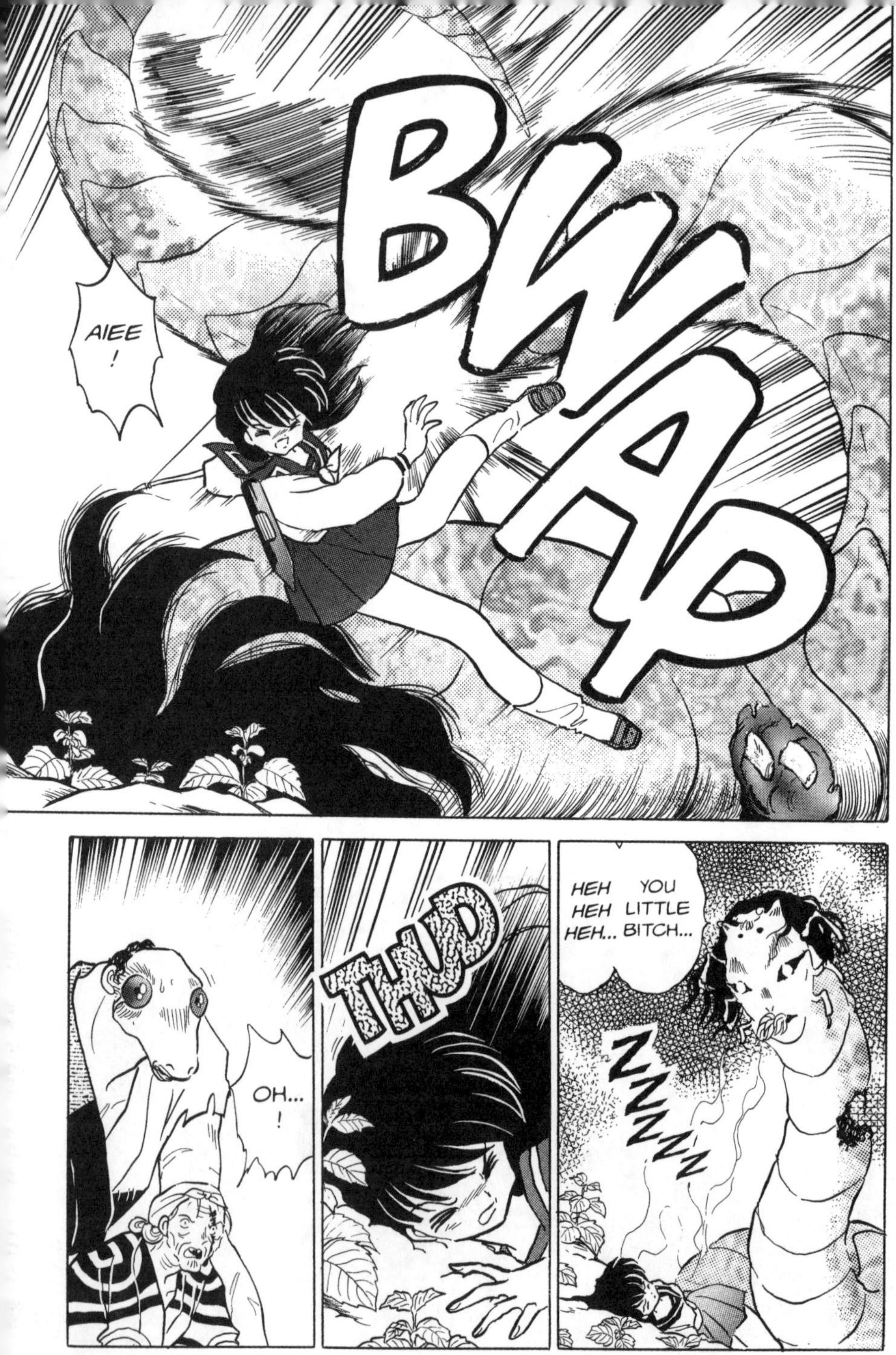
AIEE !
BWAP
OH... !
THUD
HEH HEH HEH... YOU LITTLE BITCH...

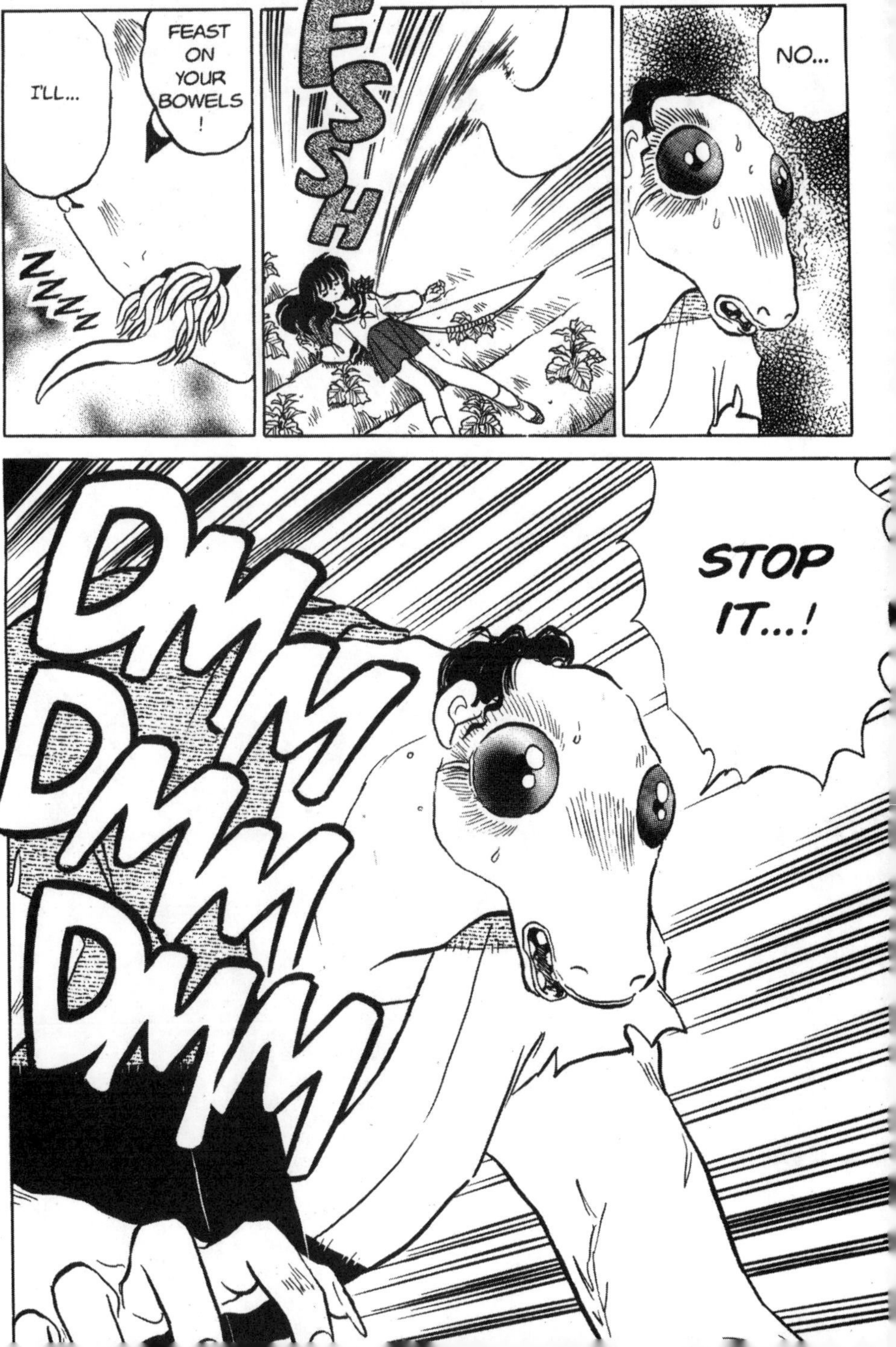
I'LL...
FEAST ON YOUR BOWELS!
ZZZZZ
FSSH
NO...
DMM DMM DMM
STOP IT...!

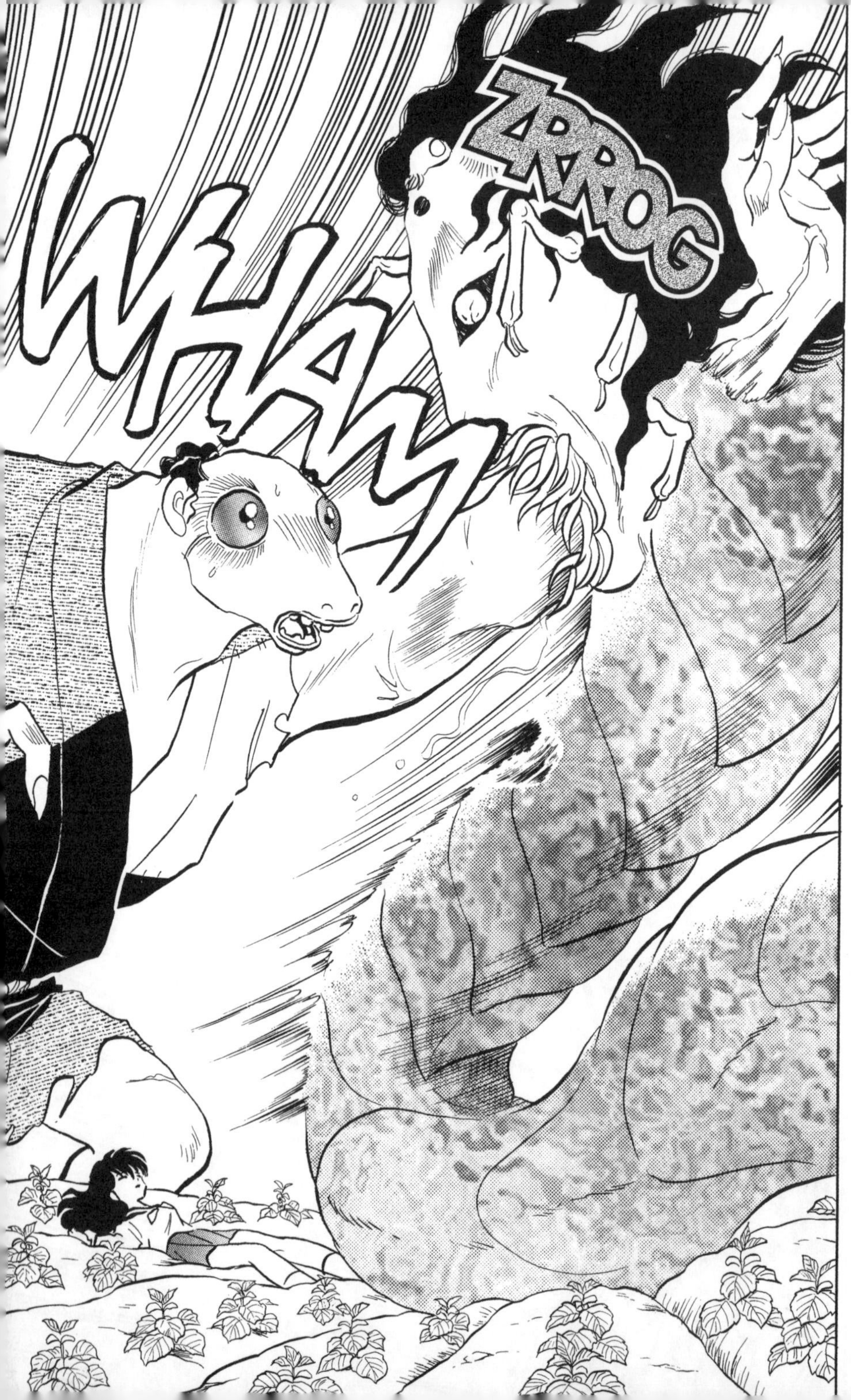
WHAM
ZRROG

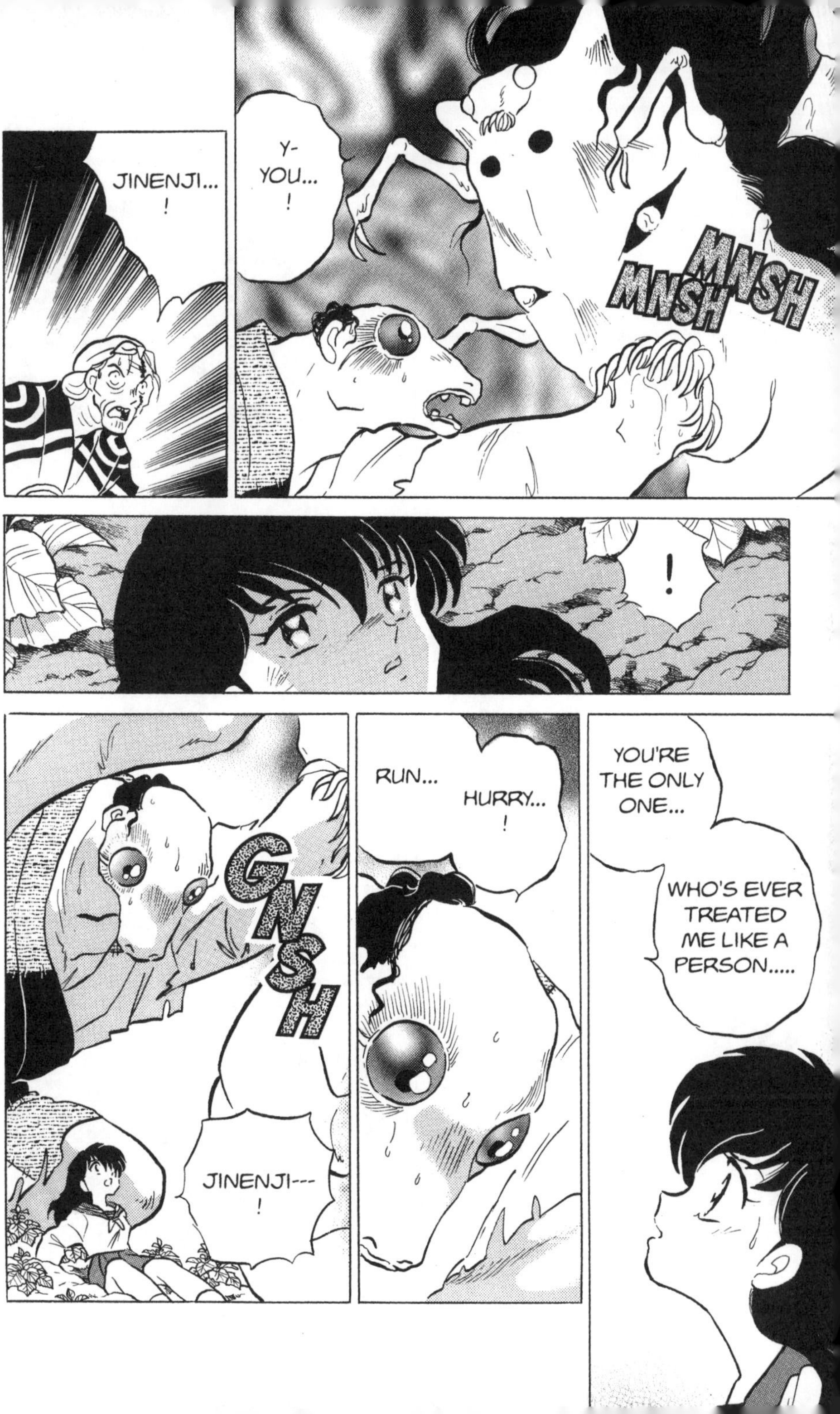
JINENJI... !
Y- YOU... !
MNSH MNSH
!
GNSH
JINENJI--- !
RUN...
HURRY... !
YOU'RE THE ONLY ONE...
WHO'S EVER TREATED ME LIKE A PERSON.....

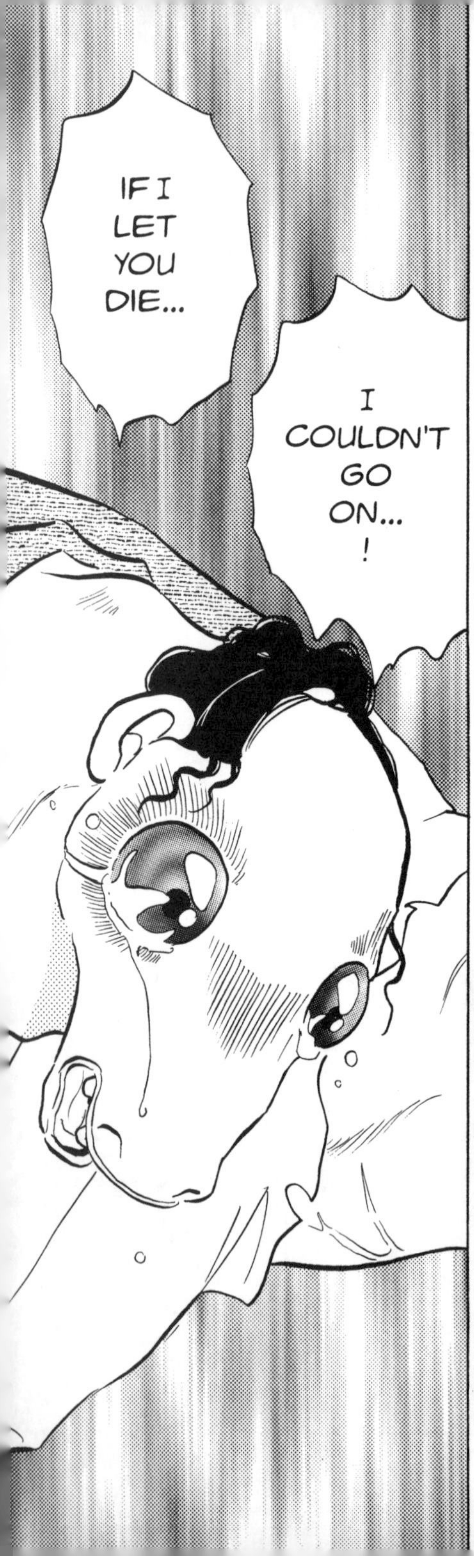
IF I LET YOU DIE...
I COULDN'T GO ON...!
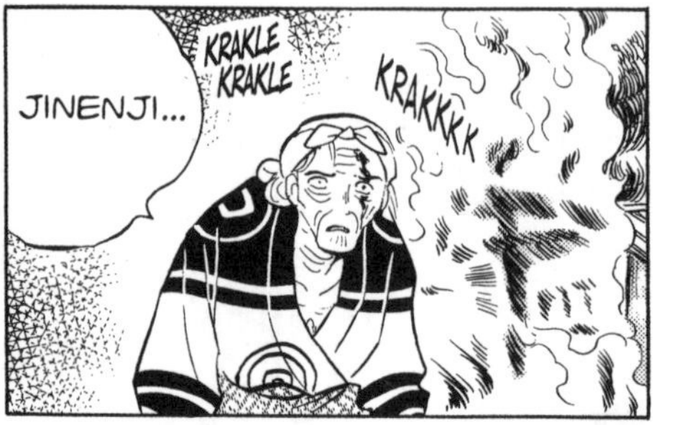
JINENJI...
KRAKLE KRAKLE
KRAKKKKK
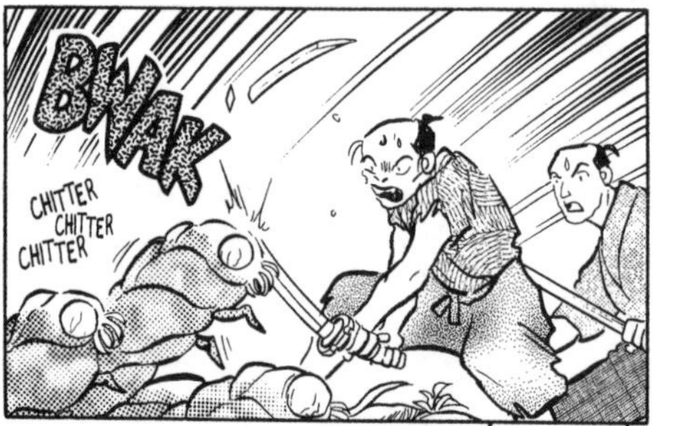
BWAK
CHITTER CHITTER CHITTER
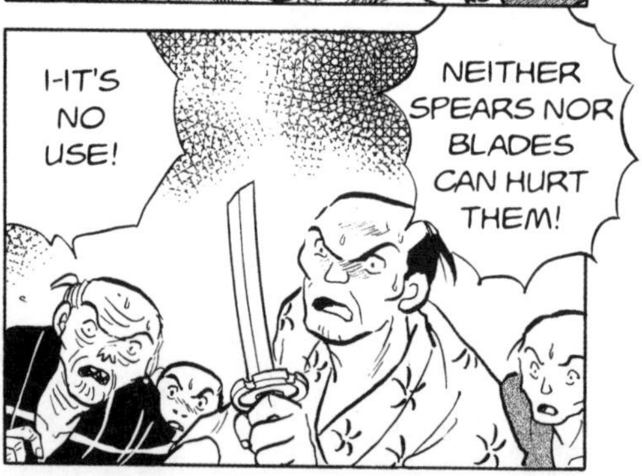
I-IT'S NO USE!
NEITHER SPEARS NOR BLADES CAN HURT THEM!
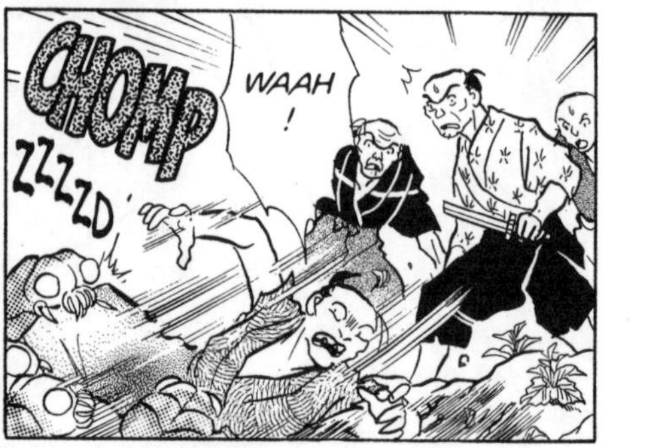
CHOMP
WAAH!
ZZZZD

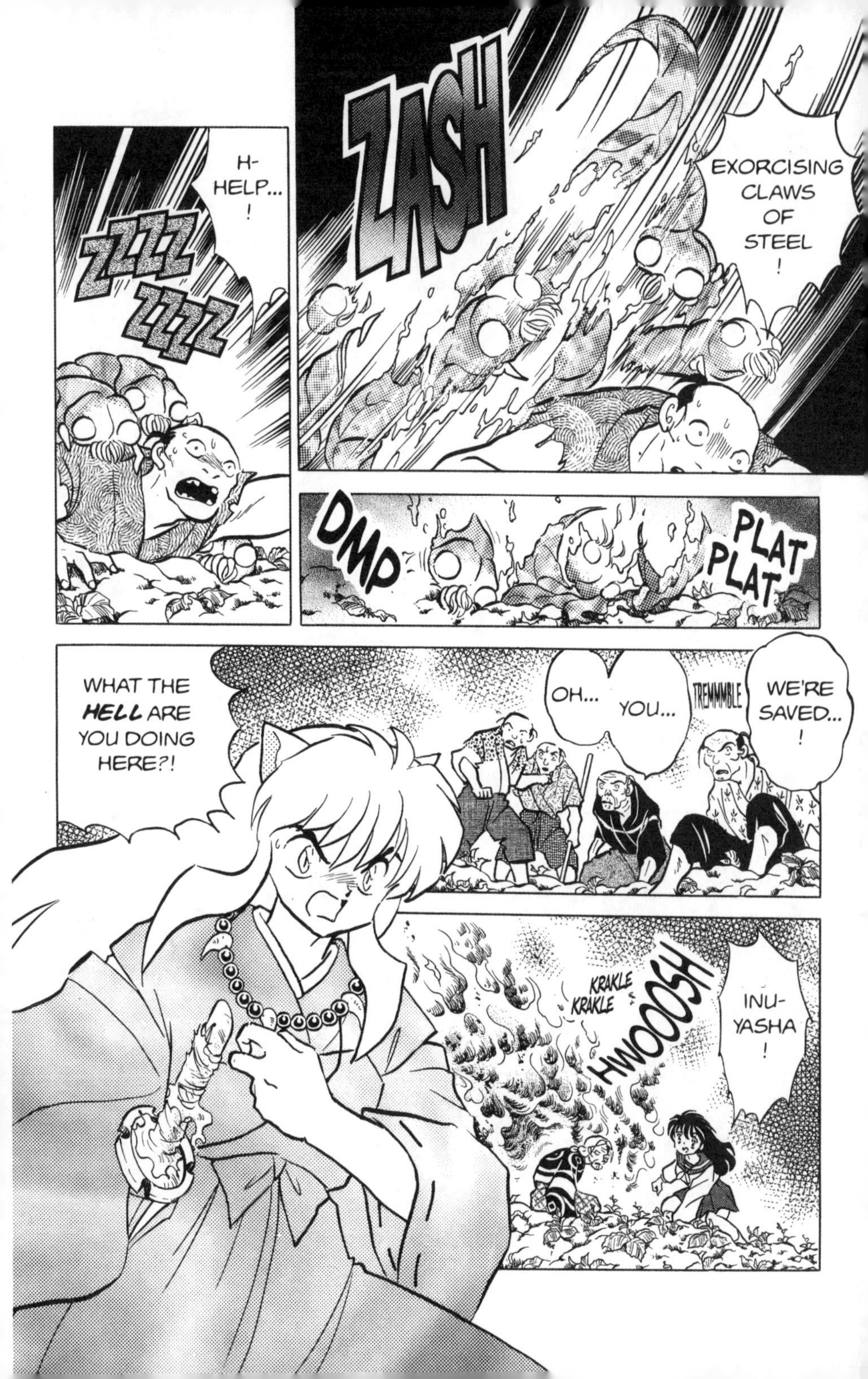
H-
HELP...
!
ZZZZZ ZZZZ
ZASH
EXORCISING
CLAWS
OF
STEEL
!
DMP
PLAT
PLAT
WHAT THE
HELL ARE
YOU DOING
HERE?!
OH...
YOU...
TREMMMBLE
WE'RE
SAVED...
!
KRAKLE
KRAKLE
HWOOOSH
INU-
YASHA
!

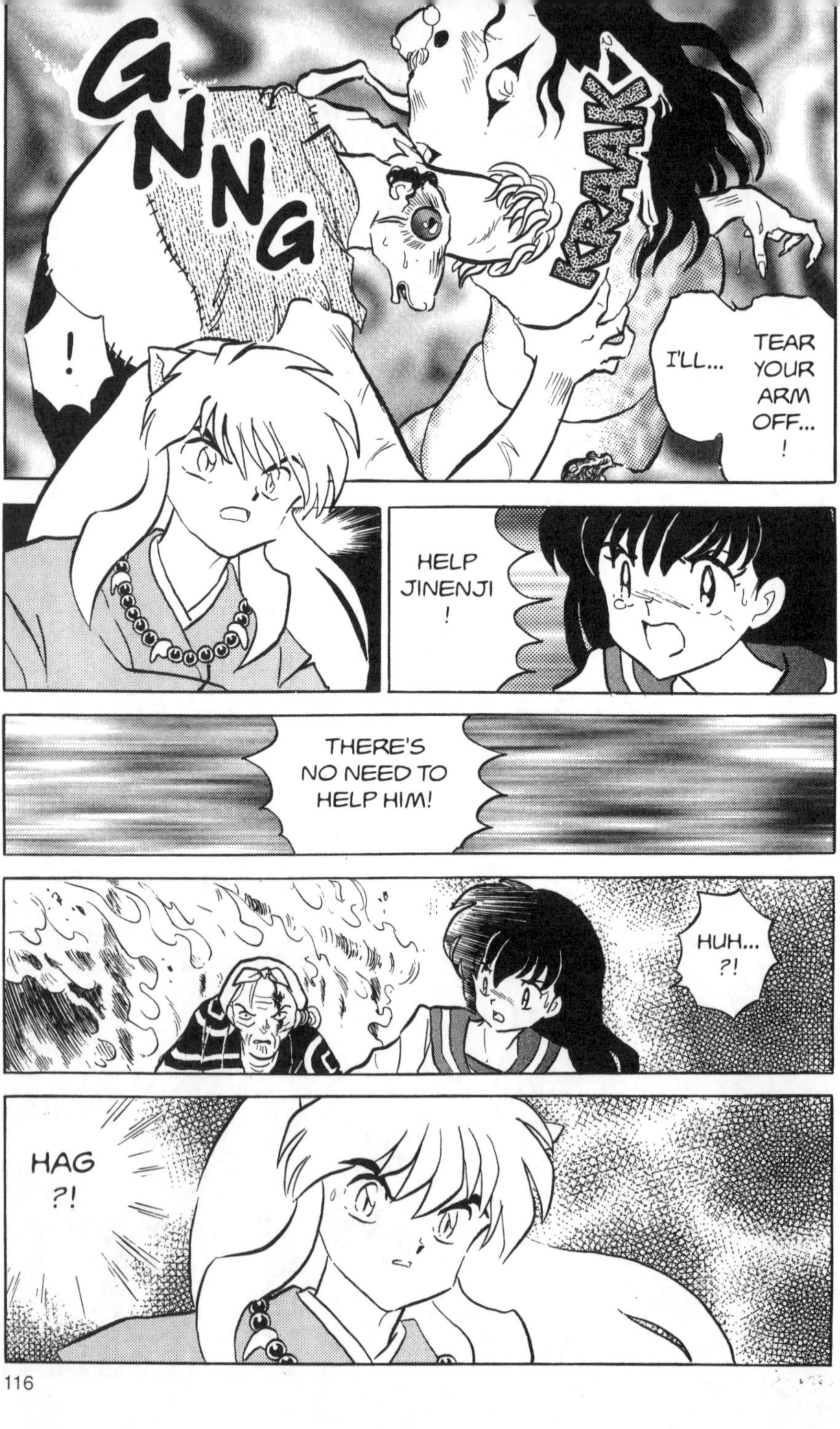
GNNG
KRAK
!
I'LL...
TEAR YOUR ARM OFF... !
HELP JINENJI !
THERE'S NO NEED TO HELP HIM!
HUH... ?!
HAG ?!

SCROLL SEVEN

THE BELONGING PLACE

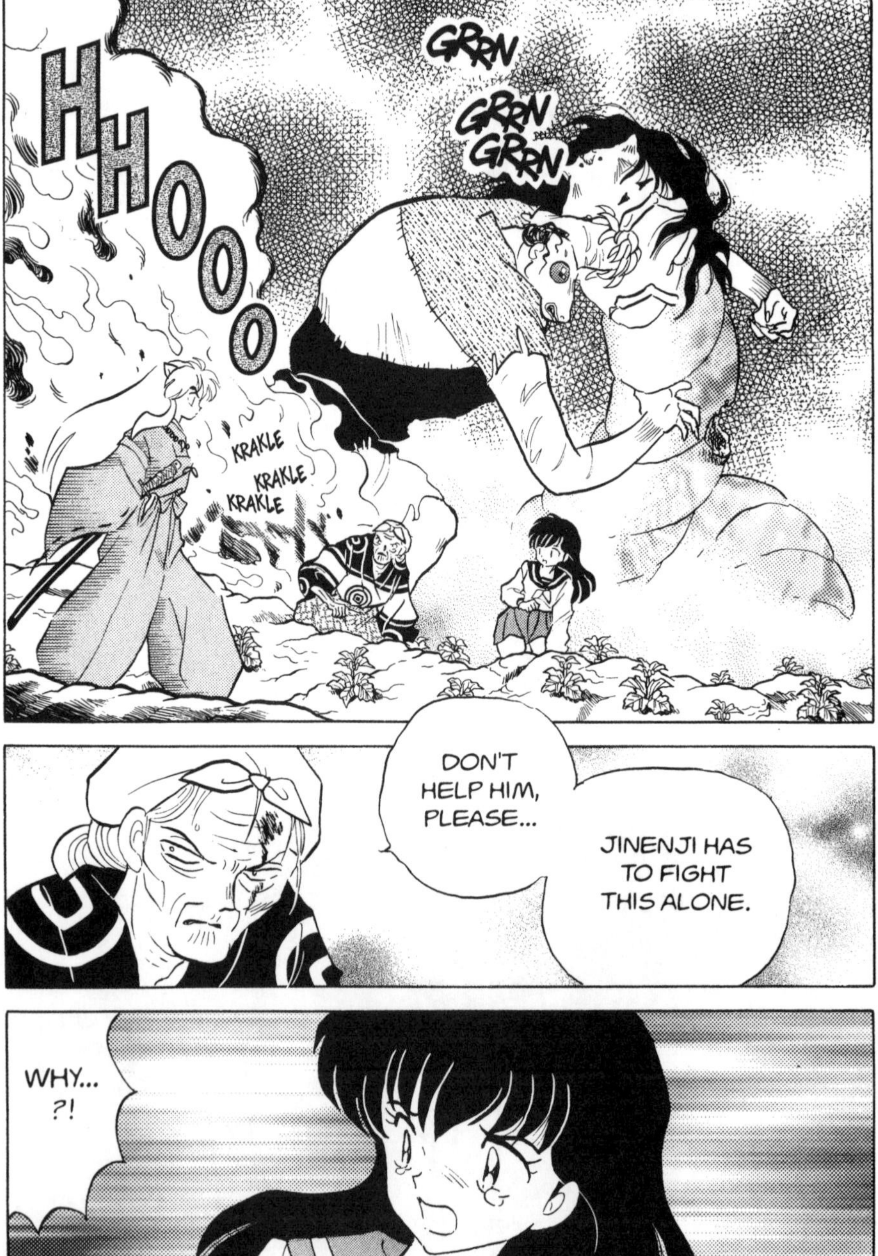
HHOOOO
GRRN
GRRN
GRRN
KRAKLE
KRAKLE
KRAKLE
DON'T HELP HIM, PLEASE...
JINENJI HAS TO FIGHT THIS ALONE.
WHY... ?!

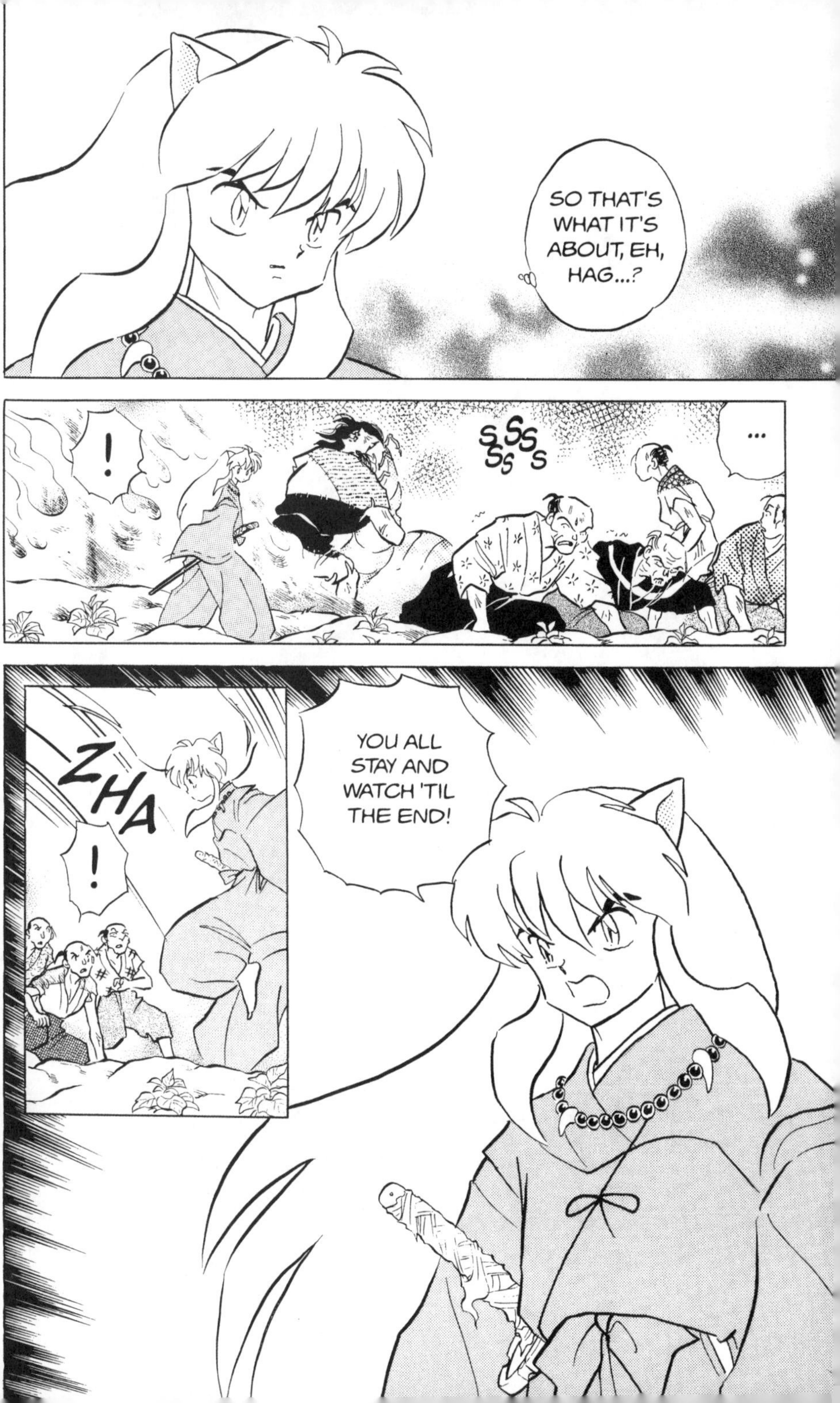
SO THAT'S WHAT IT'S ABOUT, EH, HAG...?
!
SSSSSS
...
ZHA
!
YOU ALL STAY AND WATCH 'TIL THE END!

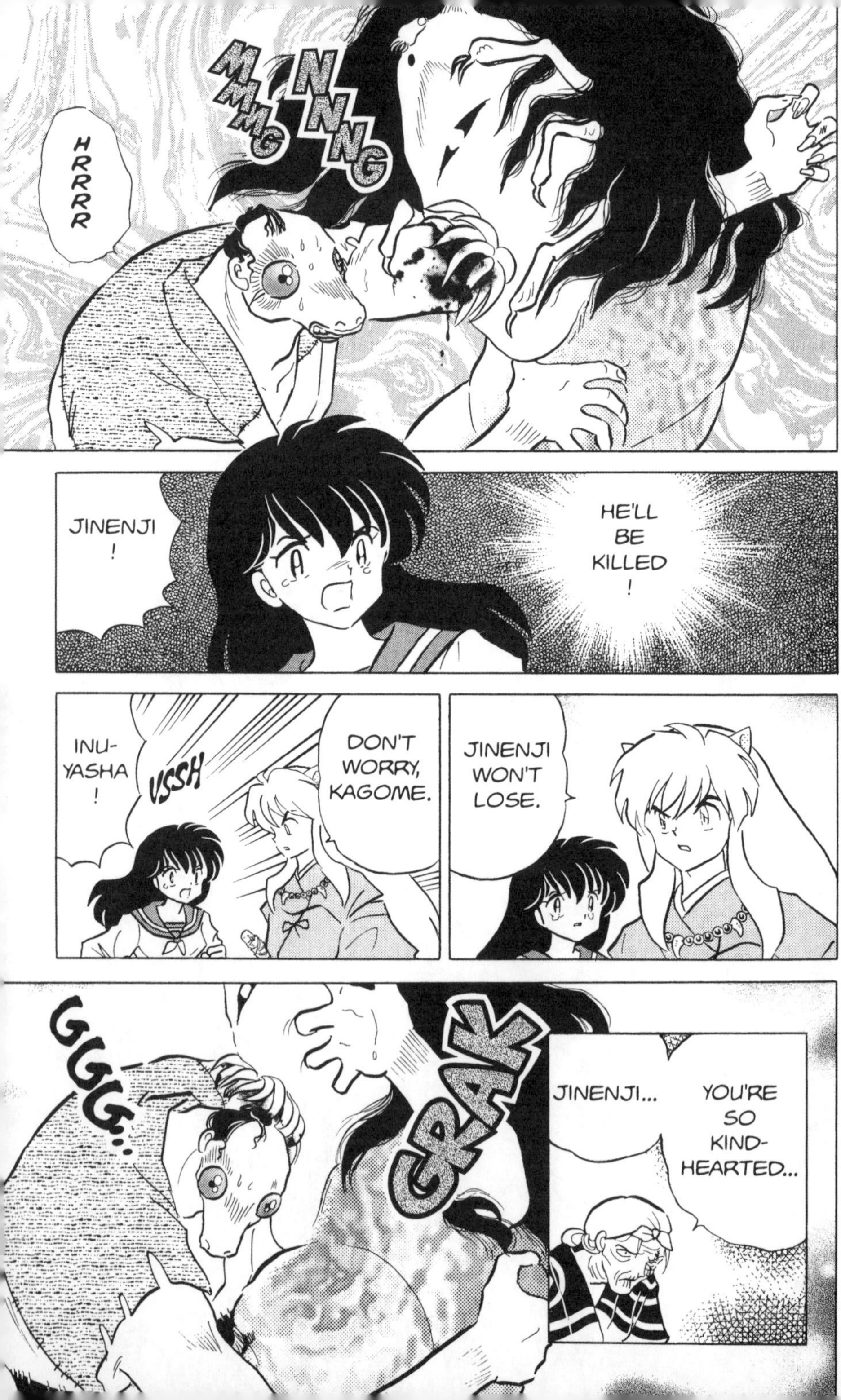
HRRRR
MMMMG
NNNNG
JINENJI!
HE'LL BE KILLED!
INU-YASHA!
VSSH
DON'T WORRY, KAGOME.
JINENJI WON'T LOSE.
GGG...
CRAK
JINENJI...
YOU'RE SO KIND-HEARTED...

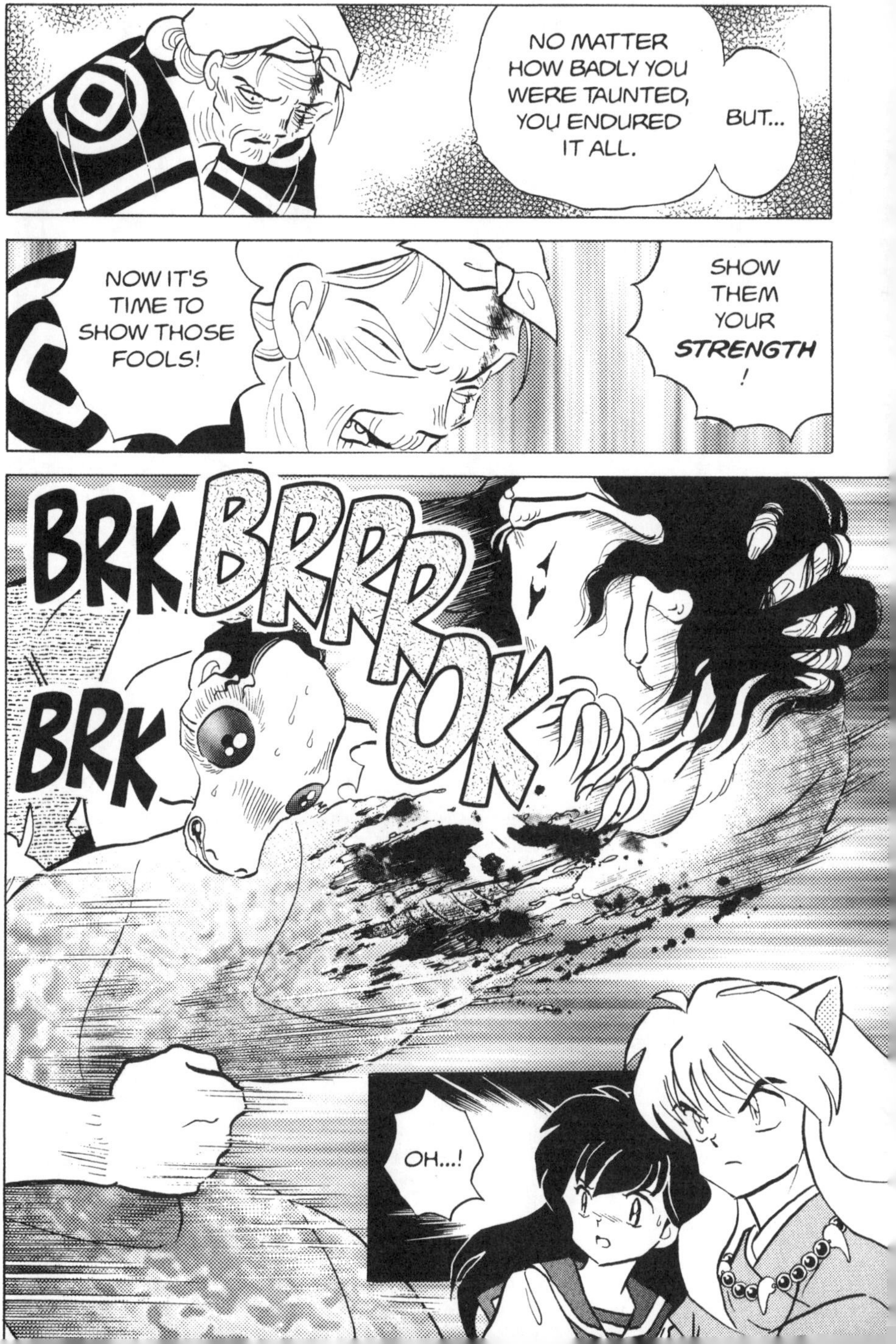
NO MATTER HOW BADLY YOU WERE TAUNTED, YOU ENDURED IT ALL.
BUT...
NOW IT'S TIME TO SHOW THOSE FOOLS!
SHOW THEM YOUR *STRENGTH*!
BRK BRK
BRRROK
OH...!

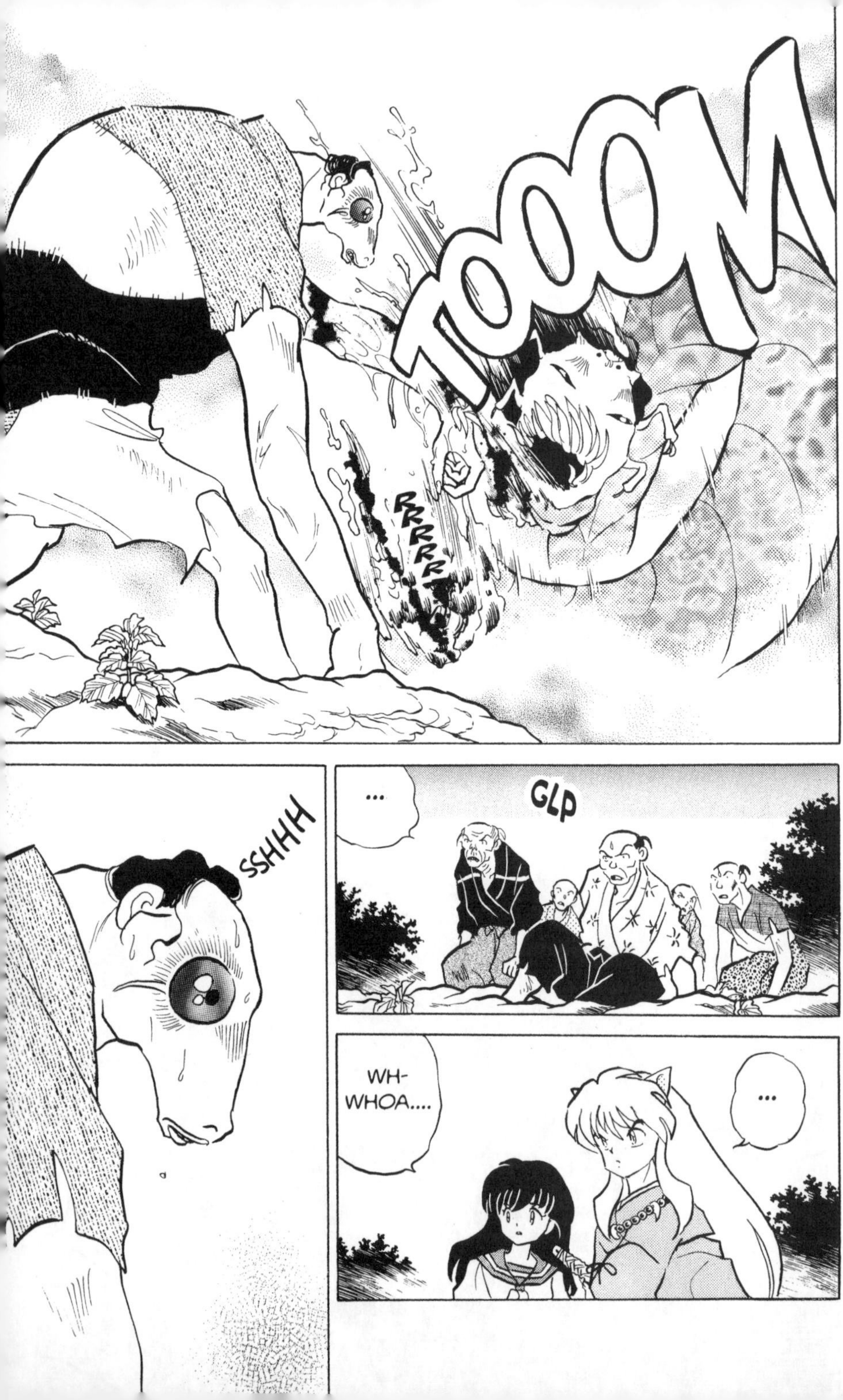
TOOOM
RRRRRT
SSHHH
...
GLP
WH-WHOA....
...

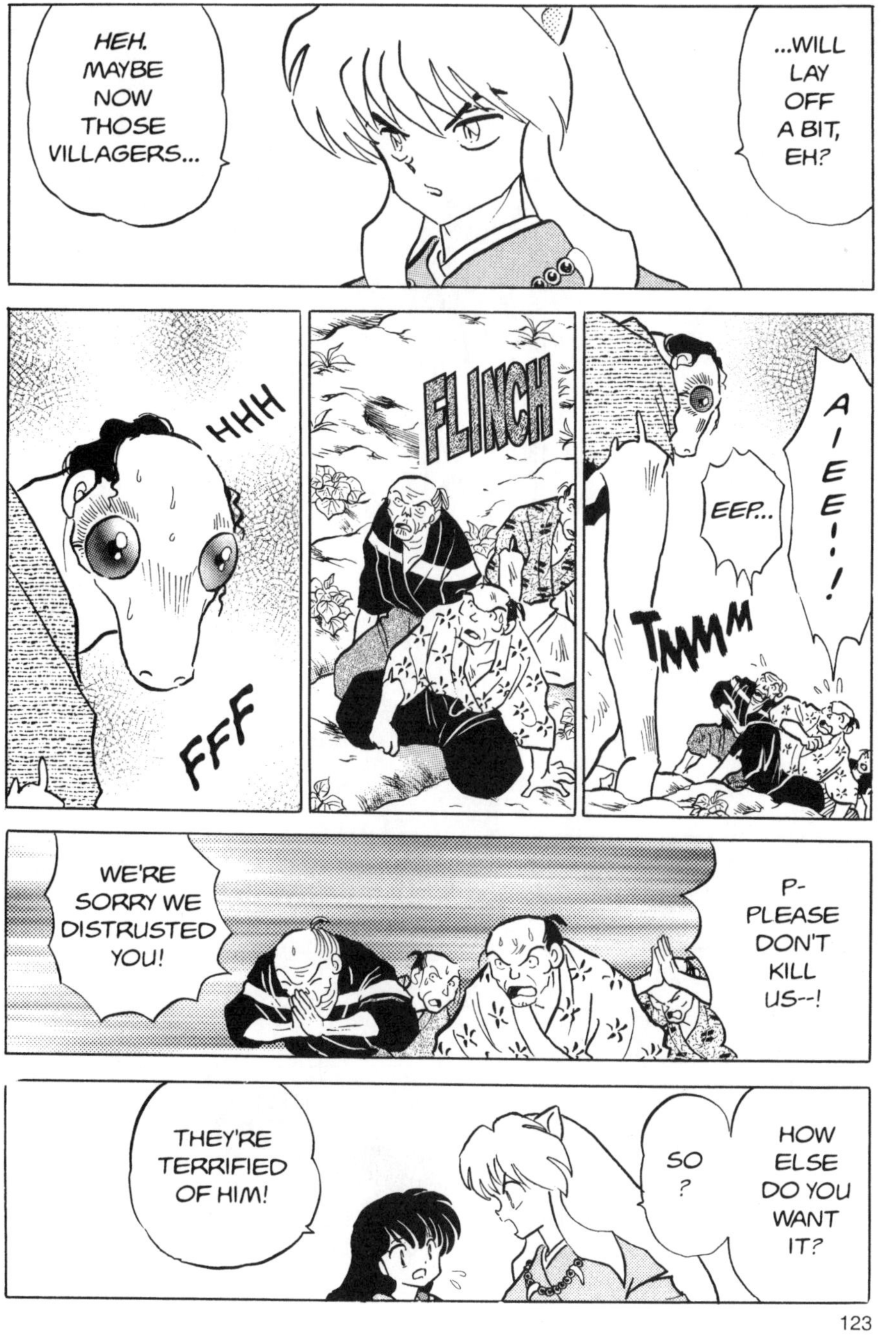
HEH. MAYBE NOW THOSE VILLAGERS...
...WILL LAY OFF A BIT, EH?
HHH
FFF
FLINCH
EEP...
AIEE!!
TMMM
WE'RE SORRY WE DISTRUSTED YOU!
P-PLEASE DON'T KILL US--!
THEY'RE TERRIFIED OF HIM!
SO?
HOW ELSE DO YOU WANT IT?

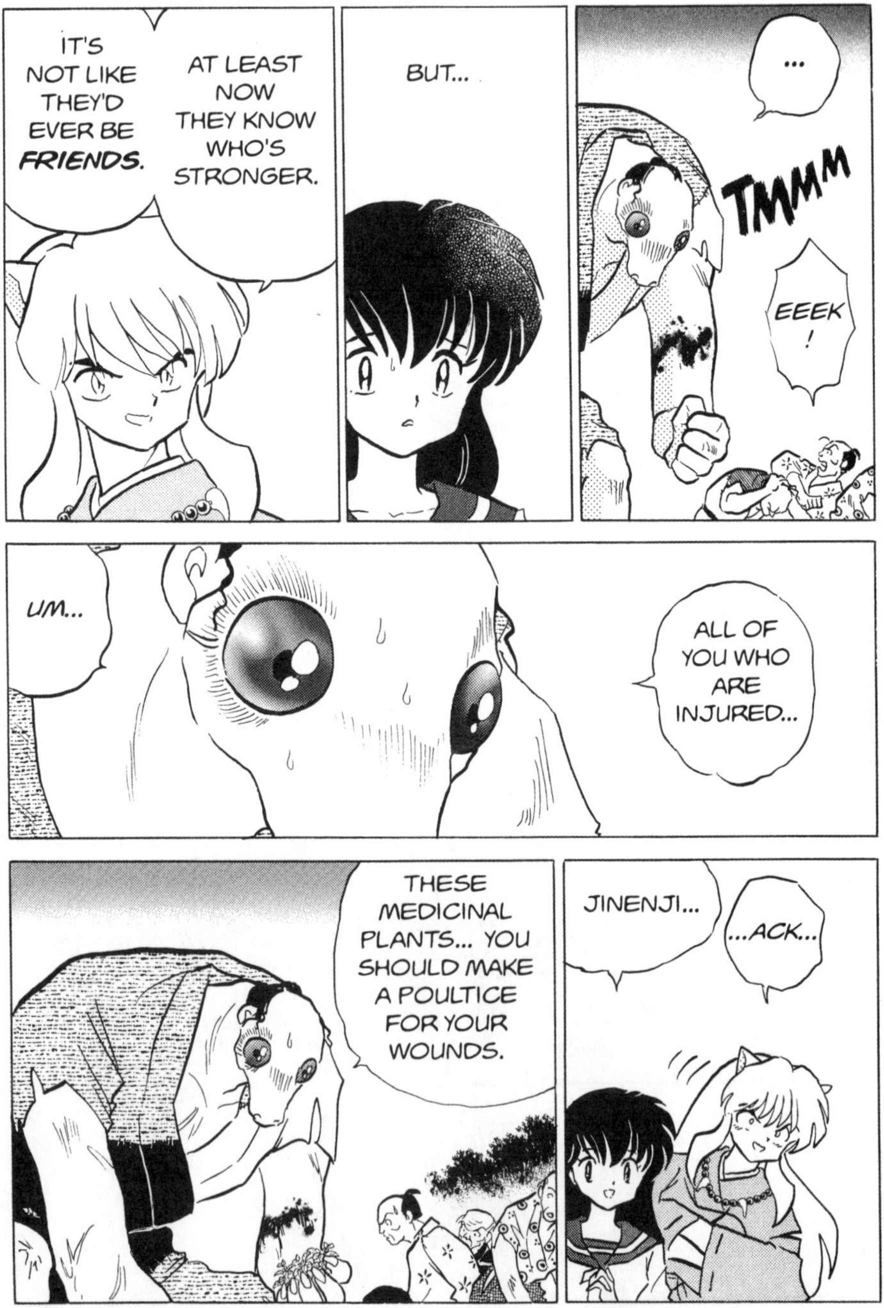
IT'S NOT LIKE THEY'D EVER BE **FRIENDS**.
AT LEAST NOW THEY KNOW WHO'S STRONGER.
BUT...
...
TMMM
EEEK!
UM...
ALL OF YOU WHO ARE INJURED...
THESE MEDICINAL PLANTS... YOU SHOULD MAKE A POULTICE FOR YOUR WOUNDS.
JINENJI...
...ACK...

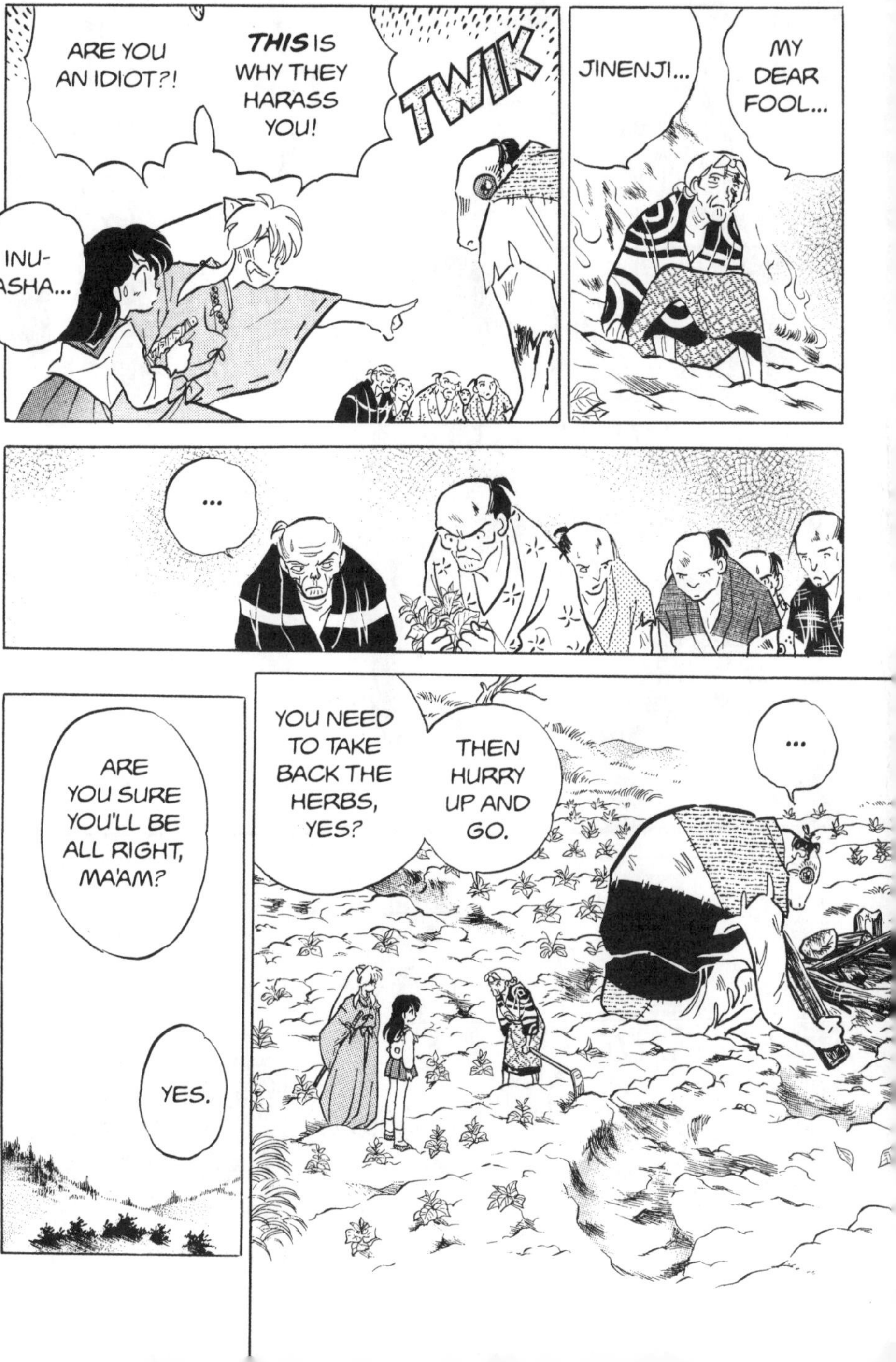
ARE YOU AN IDIOT?!
THIS IS WHY THEY HARASS YOU!
TWIK
INU-YASHA...
JINENJI...
MY DEAR FOOL...
...
ARE YOU SURE YOU'LL BE ALL RIGHT, MA'AM?
YES.
YOU NEED TO TAKE BACK THE HERBS, YES?
THEN HURRY UP AND GO.
...

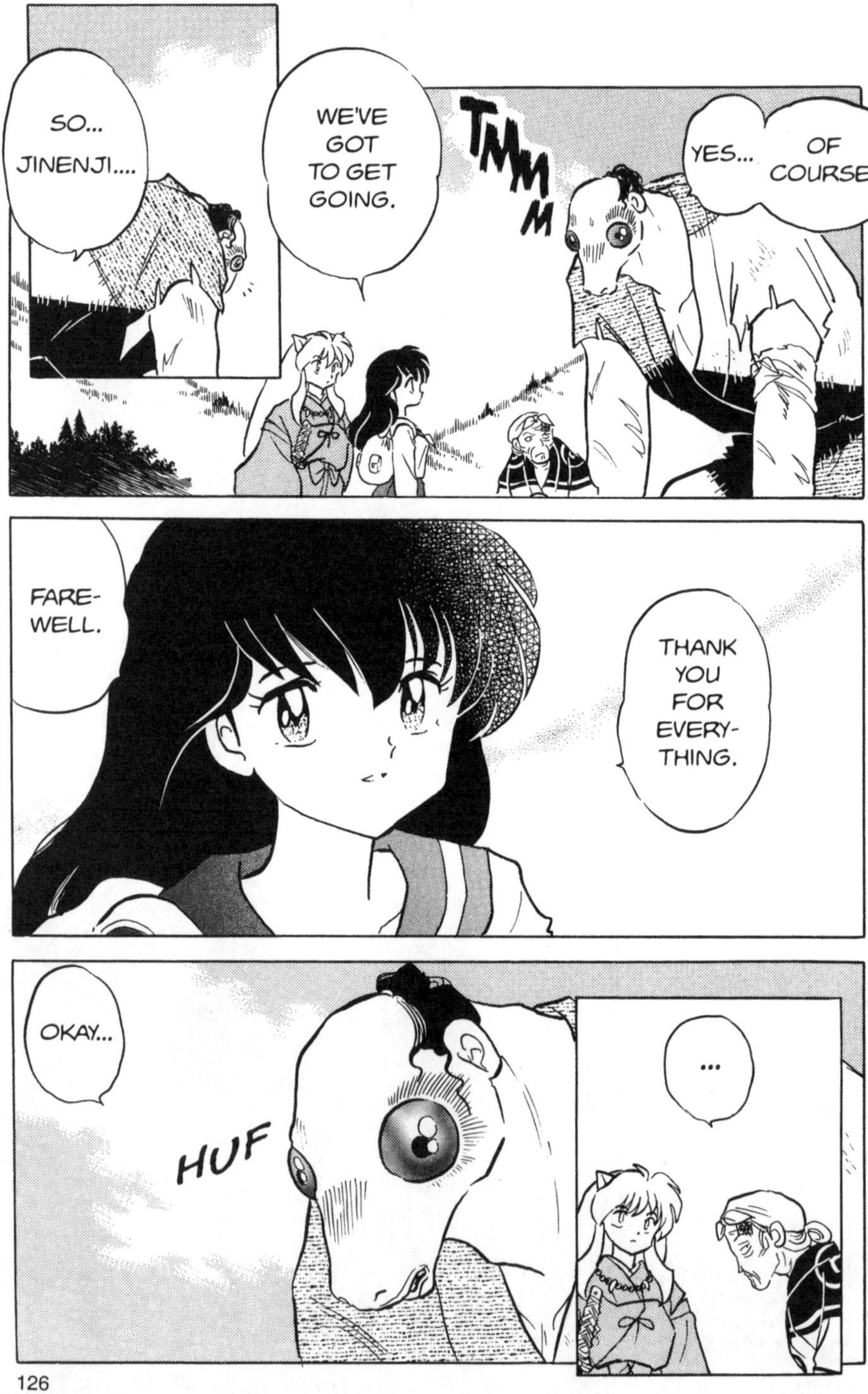
SO... JINENJI....
WE'VE GOT TO GET GOING.
TMMM
YES... OF COURSE.
THANK YOU FOR EVERYTHING.
FARE-WELL.
...
OKAY...
HUF

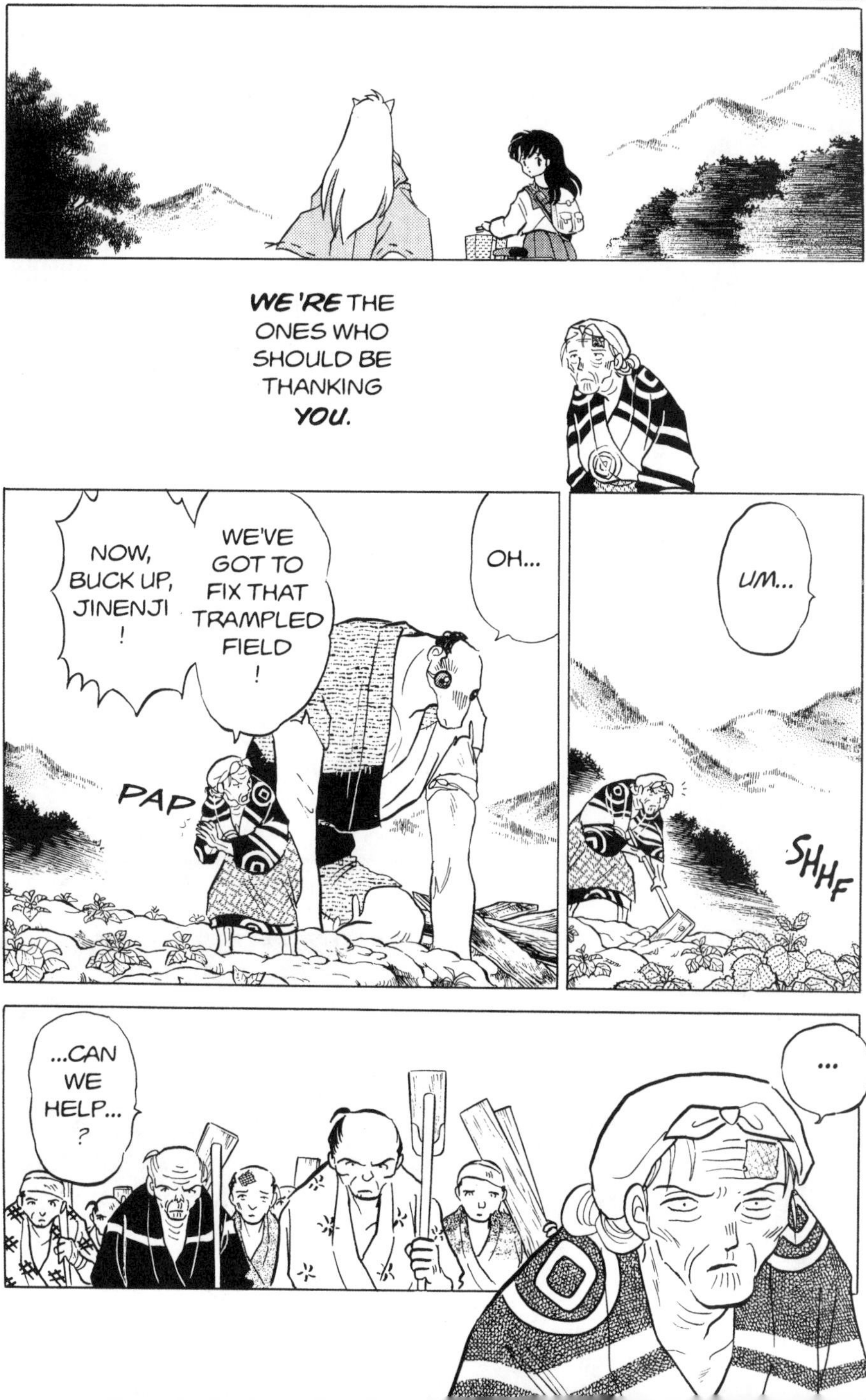
WE'RE THE ONES WHO SHOULD BE THANKING YOU.
NOW, BUCK UP, JINENJI!
WE'VE GOT TO FIX THAT TRAMPLED FIELD!
PAP
OH...
UM...
SHHF
...CAN WE HELP...?
...

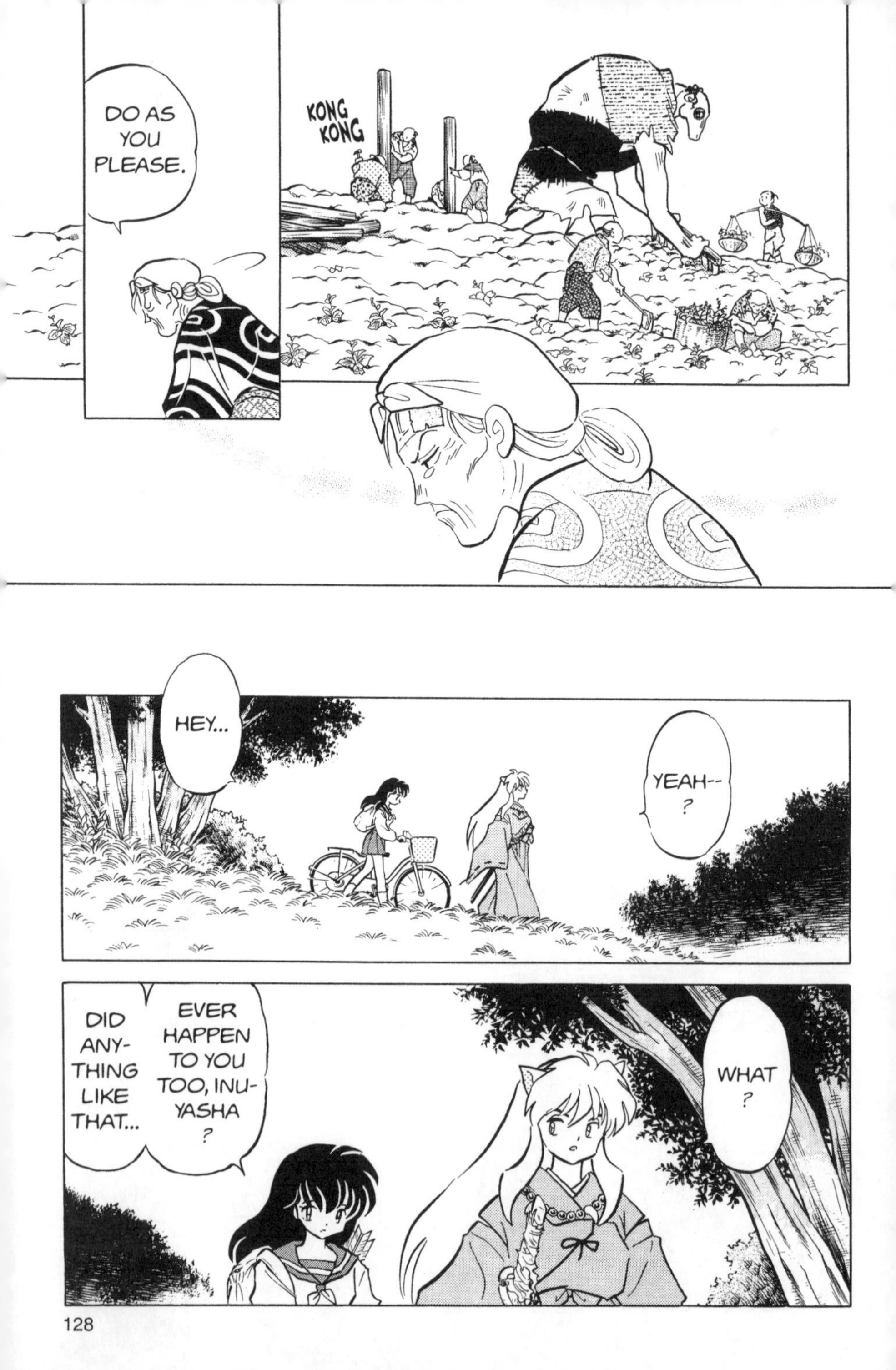
DO AS YOU PLEASE.
KONG KONG
HEY...
YEAH--?
DID ANYTHING LIKE THAT...
EVER HAPPEN TO YOU TOO, INU-YASHA?
WHAT?

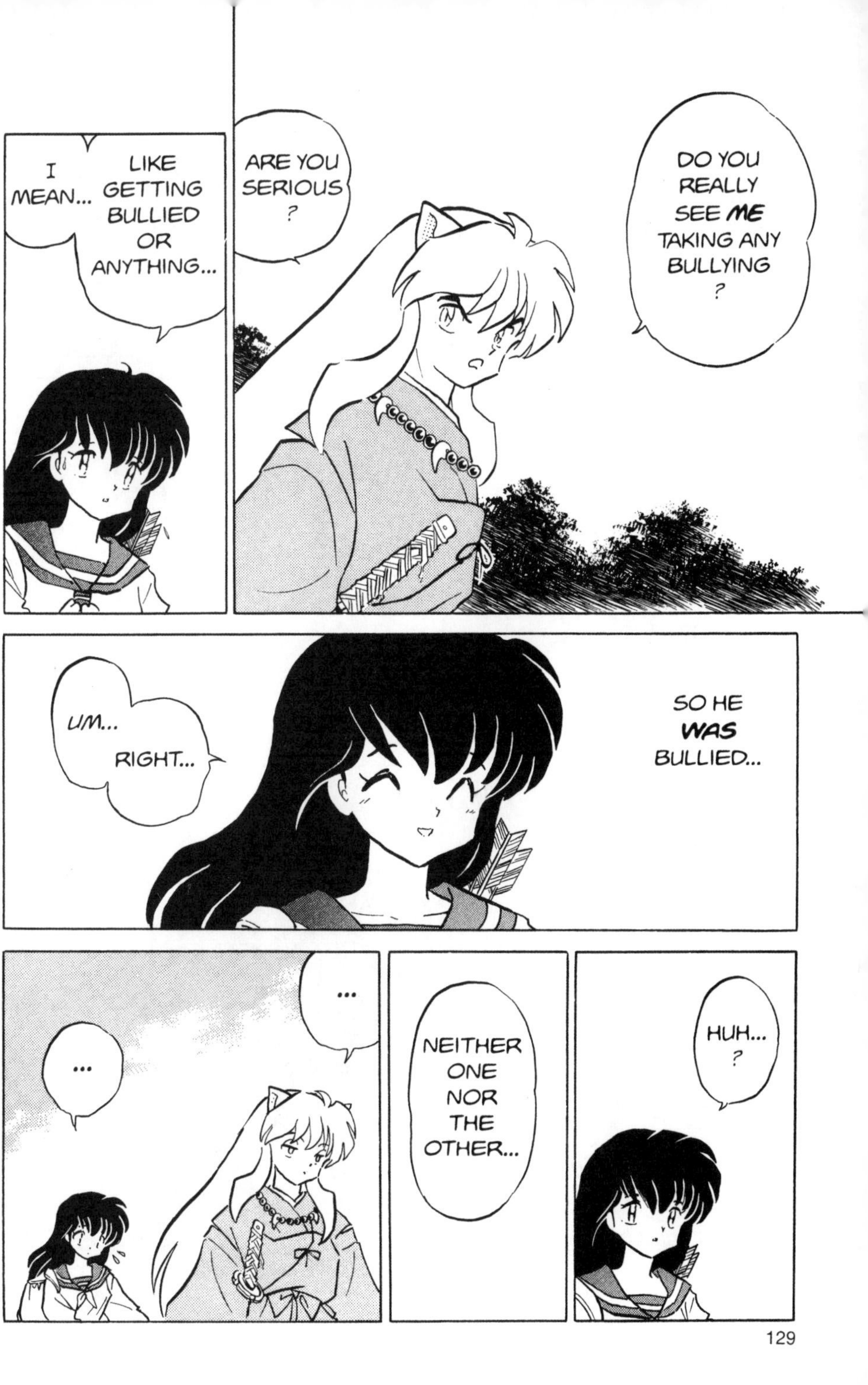
I MEAN... LIKE GETTING BULLIED OR ANYTHING...
ARE YOU SERIOUS?
DO YOU REALLY SEE **ME** TAKING ANY BULLYING?
UM... RIGHT...
SO HE **WAS** BULLIED...
...
...
NEITHER ONE NOR THE OTHER...
HUH...?

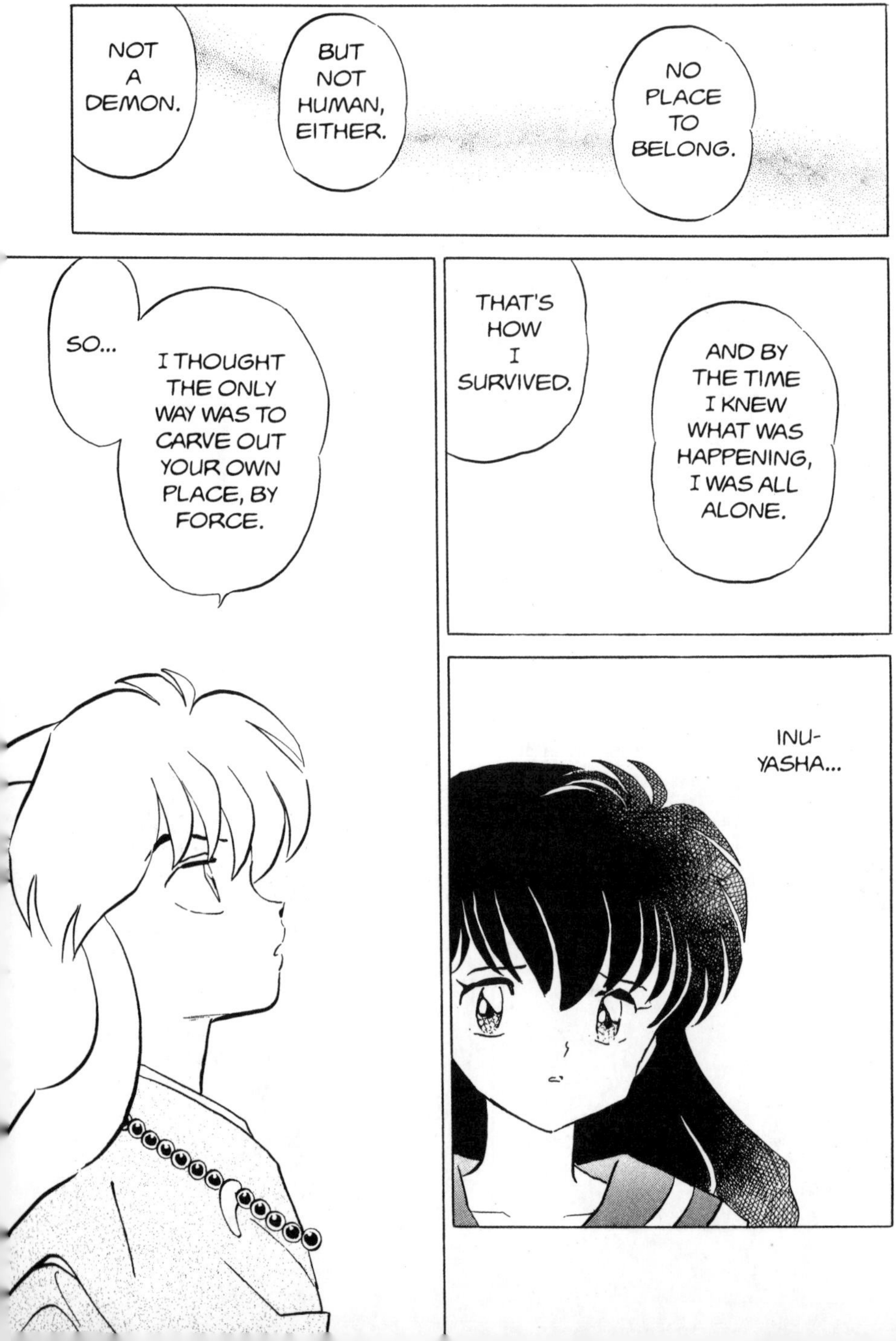
NOT A DEMON.
BUT NOT HUMAN, EITHER.
NO PLACE TO BELONG.
SO...
I THOUGHT THE ONLY WAY WAS TO CARVE OUT YOUR OWN PLACE, BY FORCE.
THAT'S HOW I SURVIVED.
AND BY THE TIME I KNEW WHAT WAS HAPPENING, I WAS ALL ALONE.
INU-YASHA...

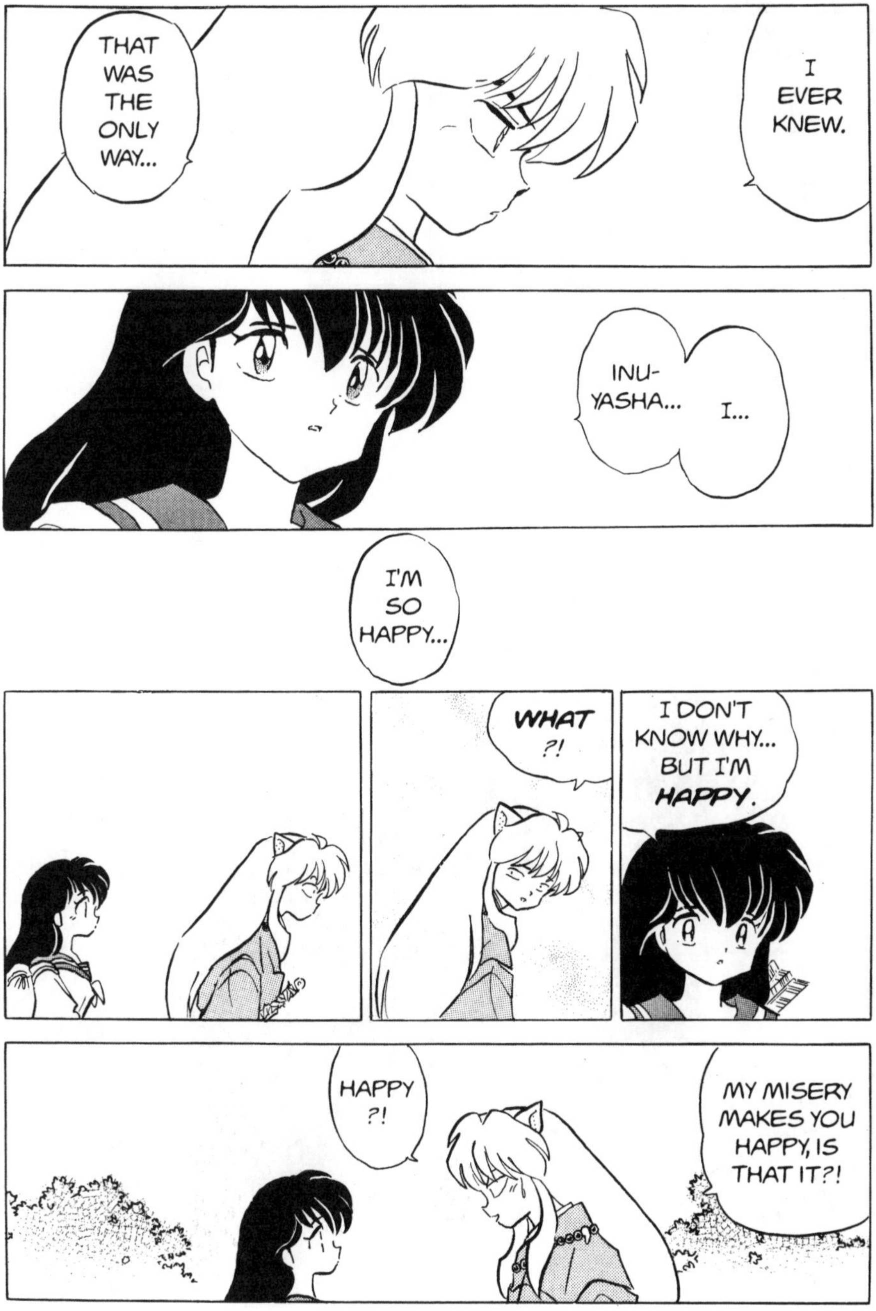
THAT WAS THE ONLY WAY...
I EVER KNEW.
INU-YASHA...
I...
I'M SO HAPPY...
WHAT ?!
I DON'T KNOW WHY... BUT I'M HAPPY.
HAPPY ?!
MY MISERY MAKES YOU HAPPY, IS THAT IT?!

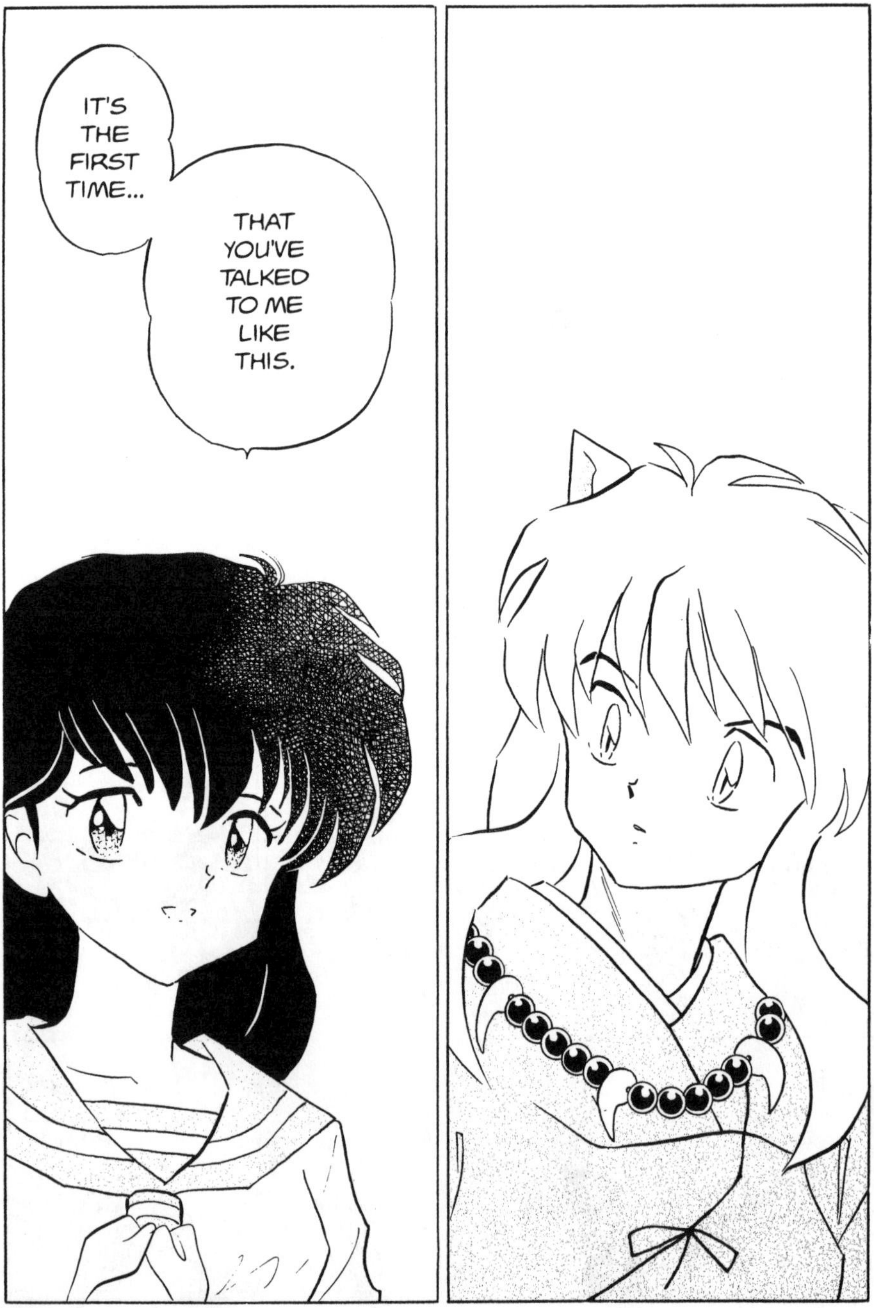
IT'S THE FIRST TIME...
THAT YOU'VE TALKED TO ME LIKE THIS.

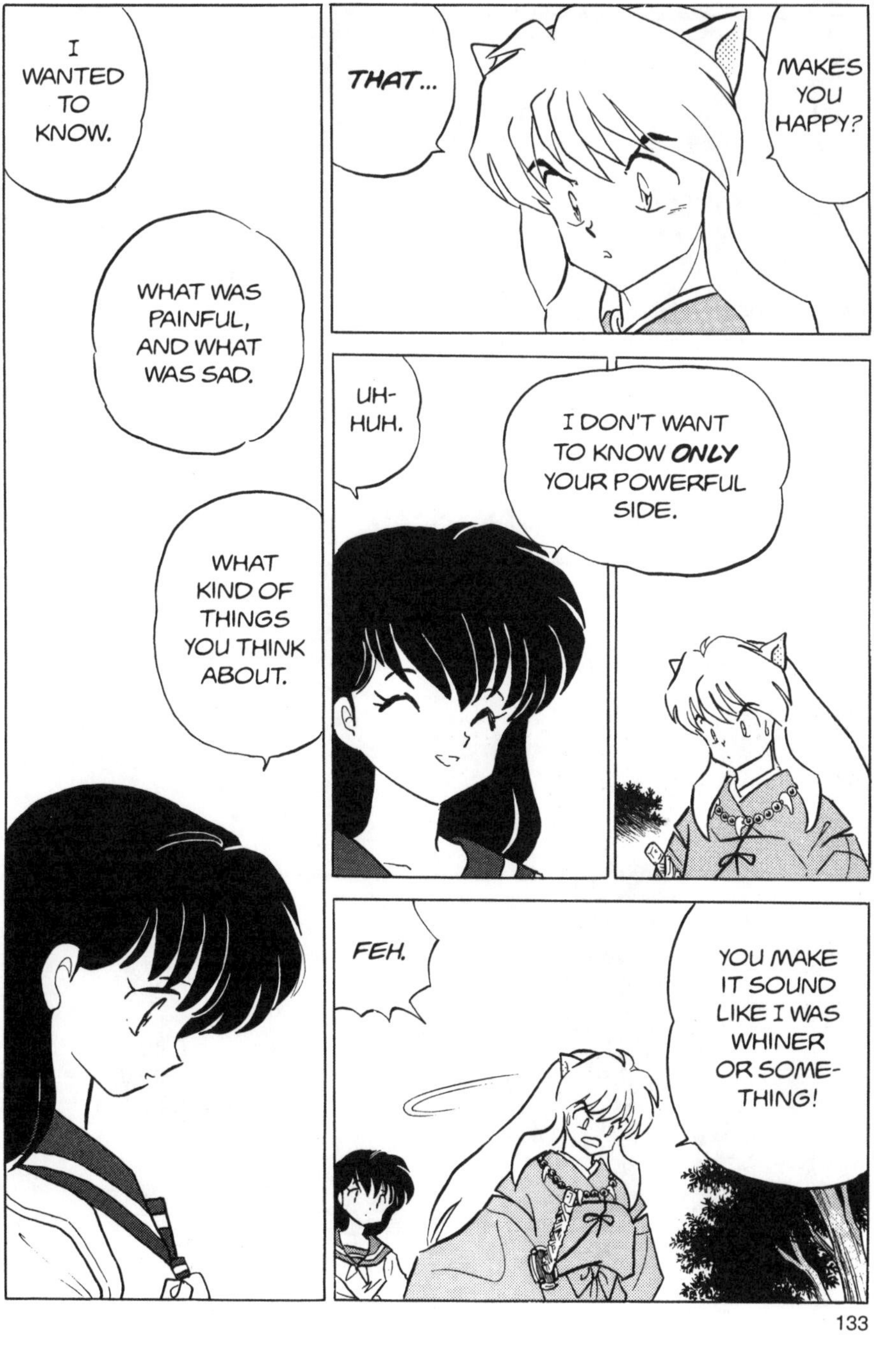
I WANTED TO KNOW.
WHAT WAS PAINFUL, AND WHAT WAS SAD.
WHAT KIND OF THINGS YOU THINK ABOUT.
THAT...
MAKES YOU HAPPY?
UH-HUH.
I DON'T WANT TO KNOW ONLY YOUR POWERFUL SIDE.
FEH.
YOU MAKE IT SOUND LIKE I WAS WHINER OR SOMETHING!

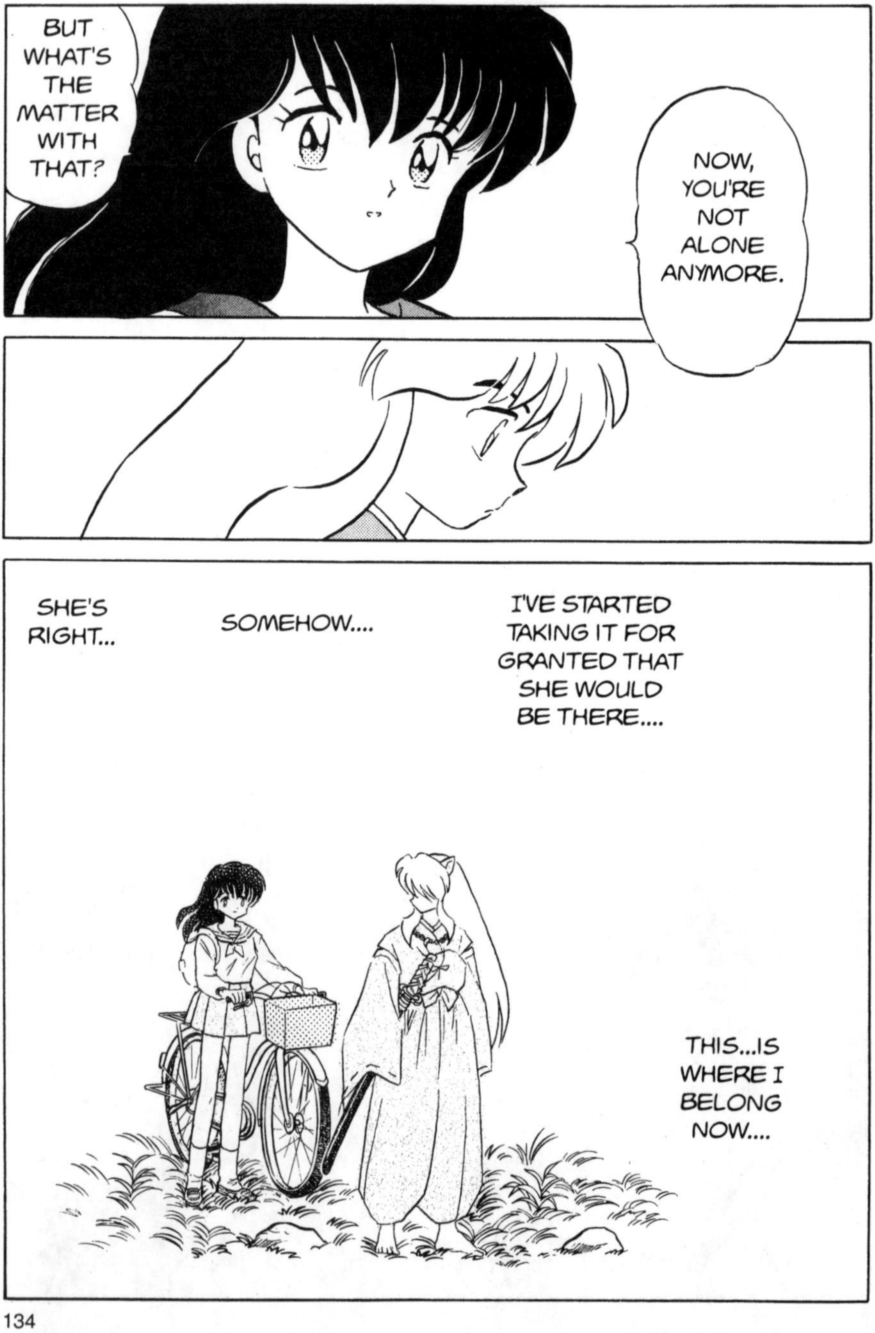
BUT WHAT'S THE MATTER WITH THAT?
NOW, YOU'RE NOT ALONE ANYMORE.
SHE'S RIGHT...
SOMEHOW....
I'VE STARTED TAKING IT FOR GRANTED THAT SHE WOULD BE THERE....
THIS...IS WHERE I BELONG NOW....

SCROLL EIGHT

THE CAVE OF EVIL

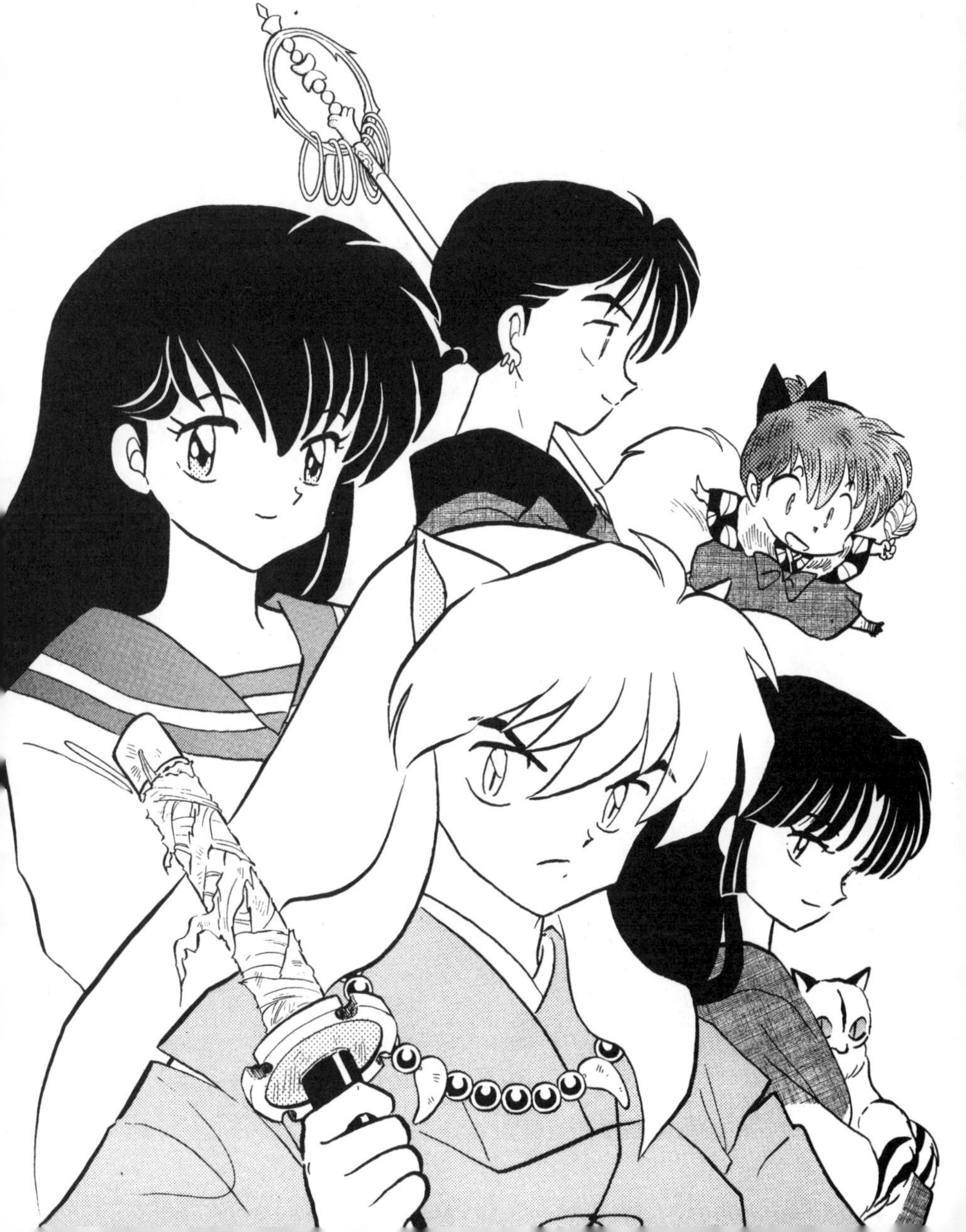

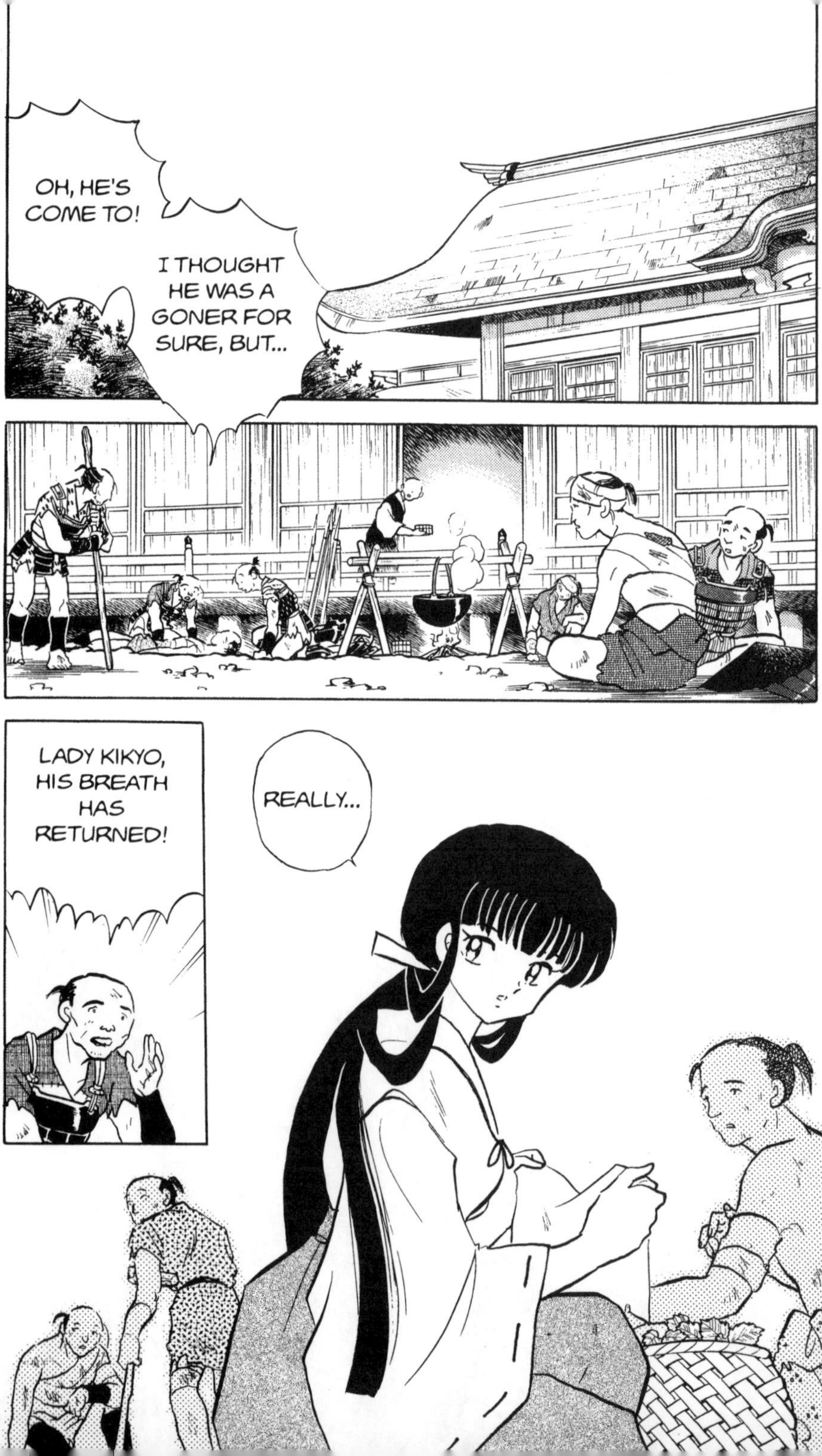
OH, HE'S COME TO!
I THOUGHT HE WAS A GONER FOR SURE, BUT...
LADY KIKYO, HIS BREATH HAS RETURNED!
REALLY...

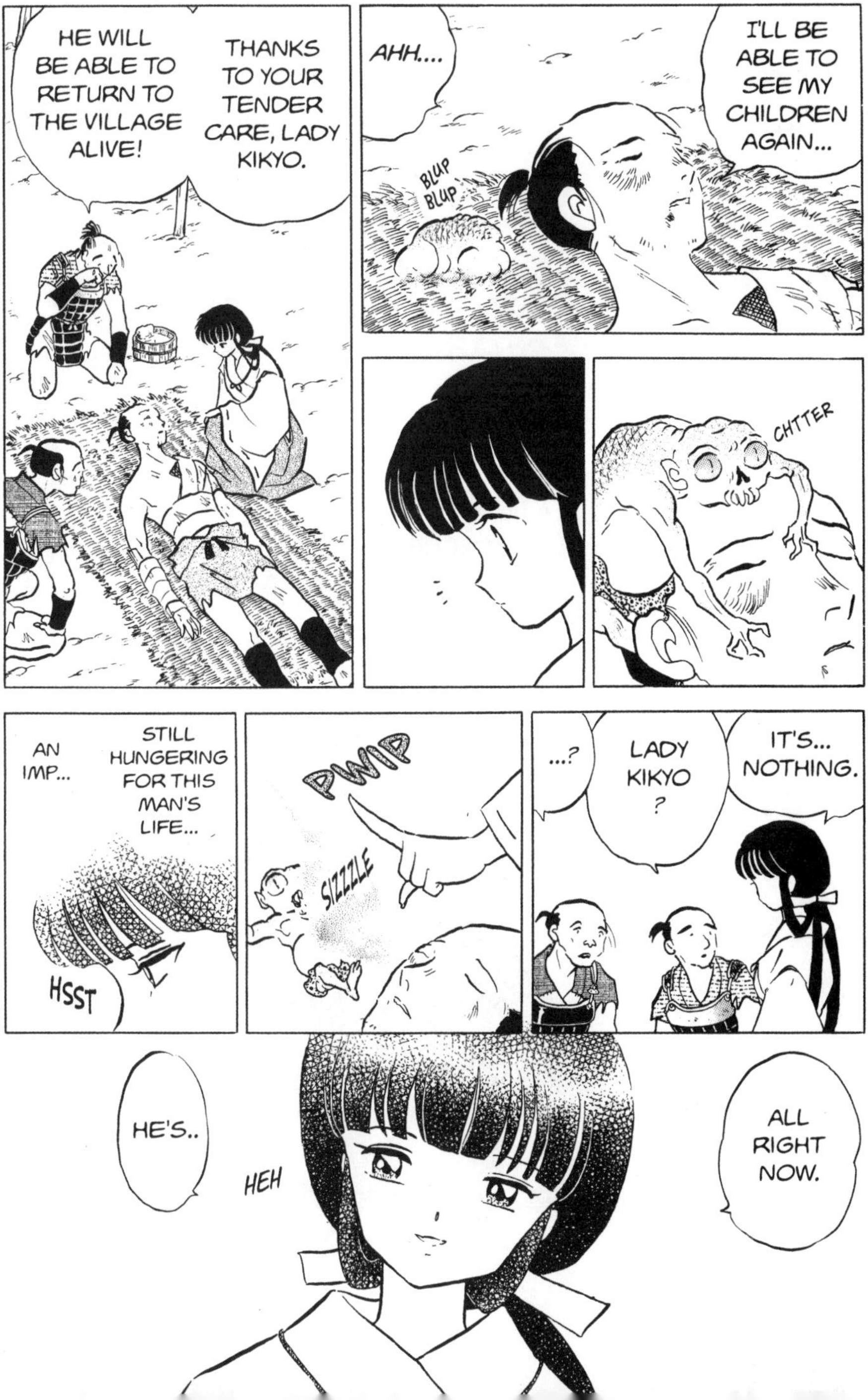
HE WILL BE ABLE TO RETURN TO THE VILLAGE ALIVE!
THANKS TO YOUR TENDER CARE, LADY KIKYO.
AHH....
BLUP BLUP
I'LL BE ABLE TO SEE MY CHILDREN AGAIN...
CHTTER
AN IMP...
STILL HUNGERING FOR THIS MAN'S LIFE...
HSST
PWIP
SIZZZLE
...?
LADY KIKYO ?
IT'S... NOTHING.
HE'S..
HEH
ALL RIGHT NOW.

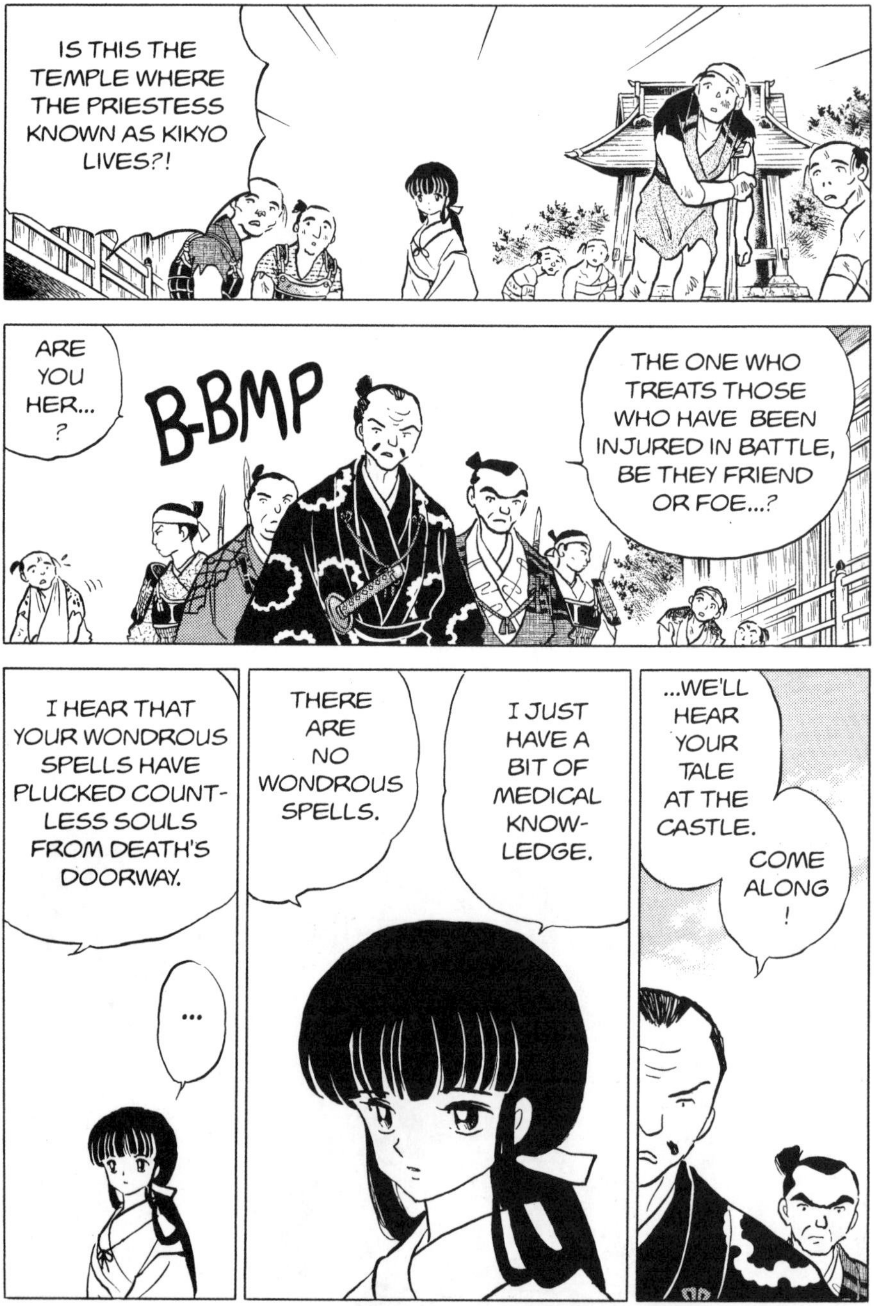
IS THIS THE TEMPLE WHERE THE PRIESTESS KNOWN AS KIKYO LIVES?!
ARE YOU HER...?
B-BMP
THE ONE WHO TREATS THOSE WHO HAVE BEEN INJURED IN BATTLE, BE THEY FRIEND OR FOE...?
I HEAR THAT YOUR WONDROUS SPELLS HAVE PLUCKED COUNT-LESS SOULS FROM DEATH'S DOORWAY.
...
THERE ARE NO WONDROUS SPELLS.
I JUST HAVE A BIT OF MEDICAL KNOW-LEDGE.
...WE'LL HEAR YOUR TALE AT THE CASTLE.
COME ALONG!

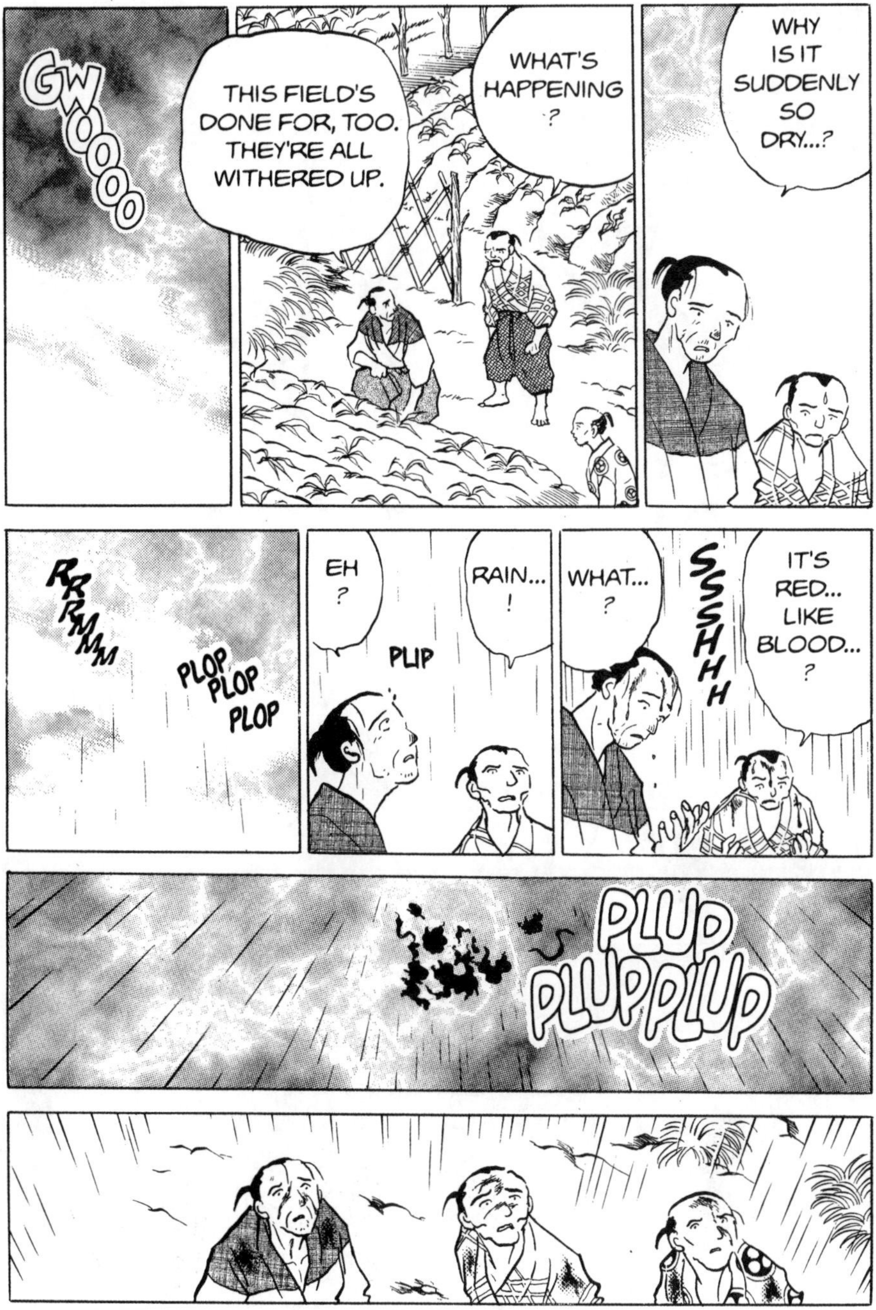
GWOOOO
THIS FIELD'S DONE FOR, TOO. THEY'RE ALL WITHERED UP.
WHAT'S HAPPENING ?
WHY IS IT SUDDENLY SO DRY...?
RRRMMM
PLOP PLOP PLOP
EH ?
PLIP
RAIN... !
WHAT... ?
SSSHHH
IT'S RED... LIKE BLOOD... ?
PLUP PLUP PLUP

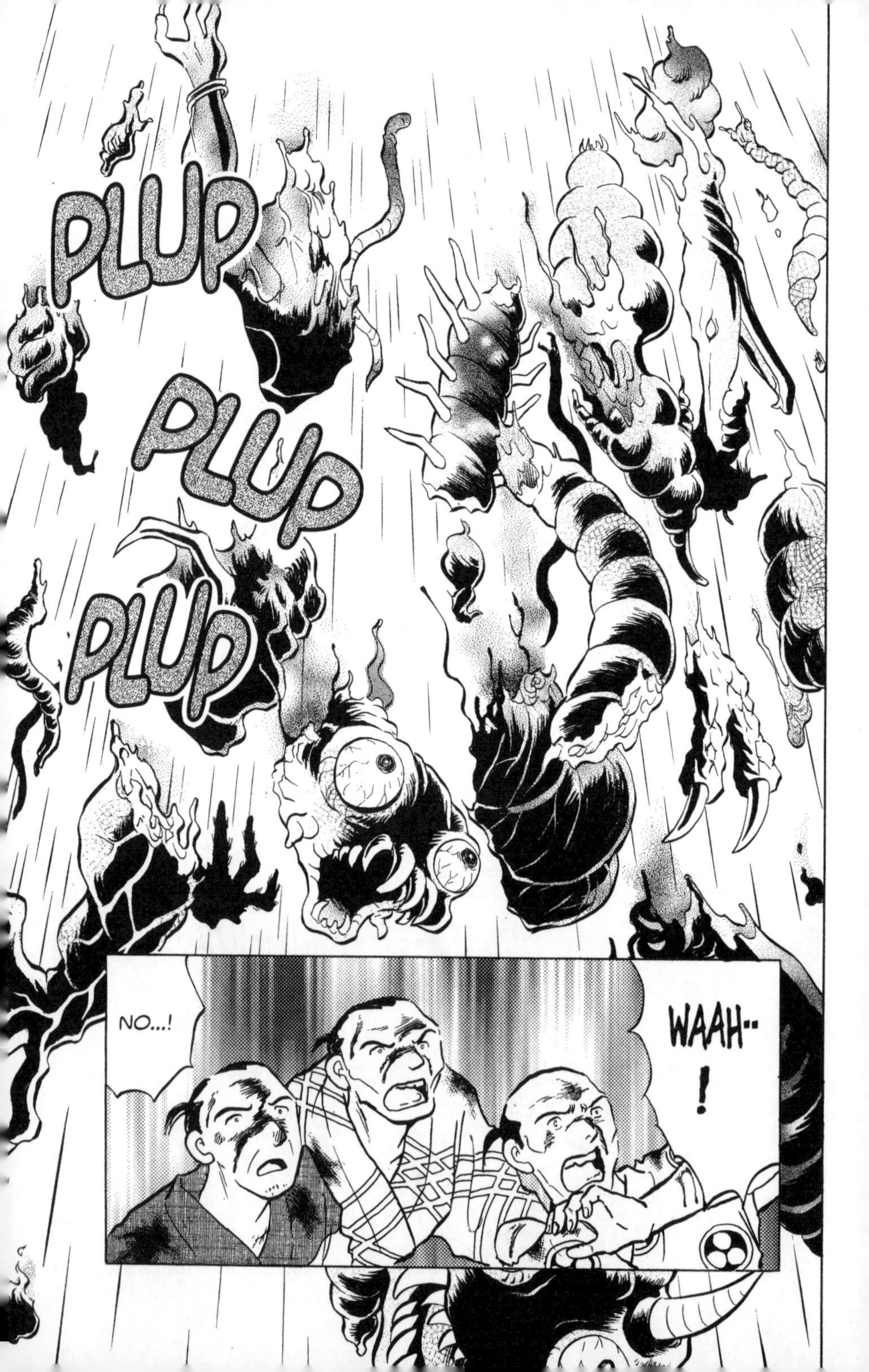
PLUP
PLUP
PLUP
NO...!
WAAH--
!

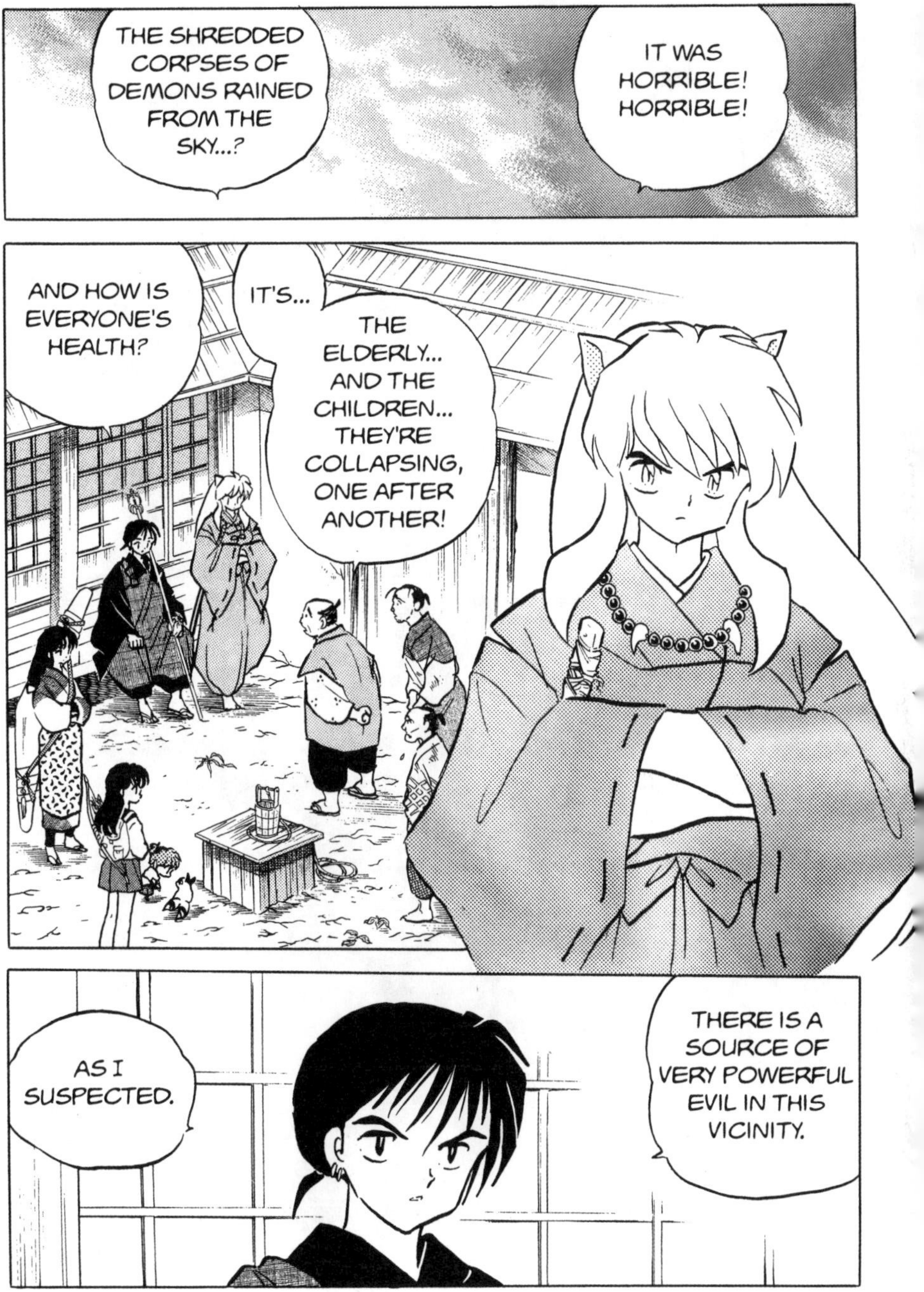
THE SHREDDED CORPSES OF DEMONS RAINED FROM THE SKY...?
IT WAS HORRIBLE! HORRIBLE!
AND HOW IS EVERYONE'S HEALTH?
IT'S...
THE ELDERLY... AND THE CHILDREN... THEY'RE COLLAPSING, ONE AFTER ANOTHER!
AS I SUSPECTED.
THERE IS A SOURCE OF VERY POWERFUL EVIL IN THIS VICINITY.

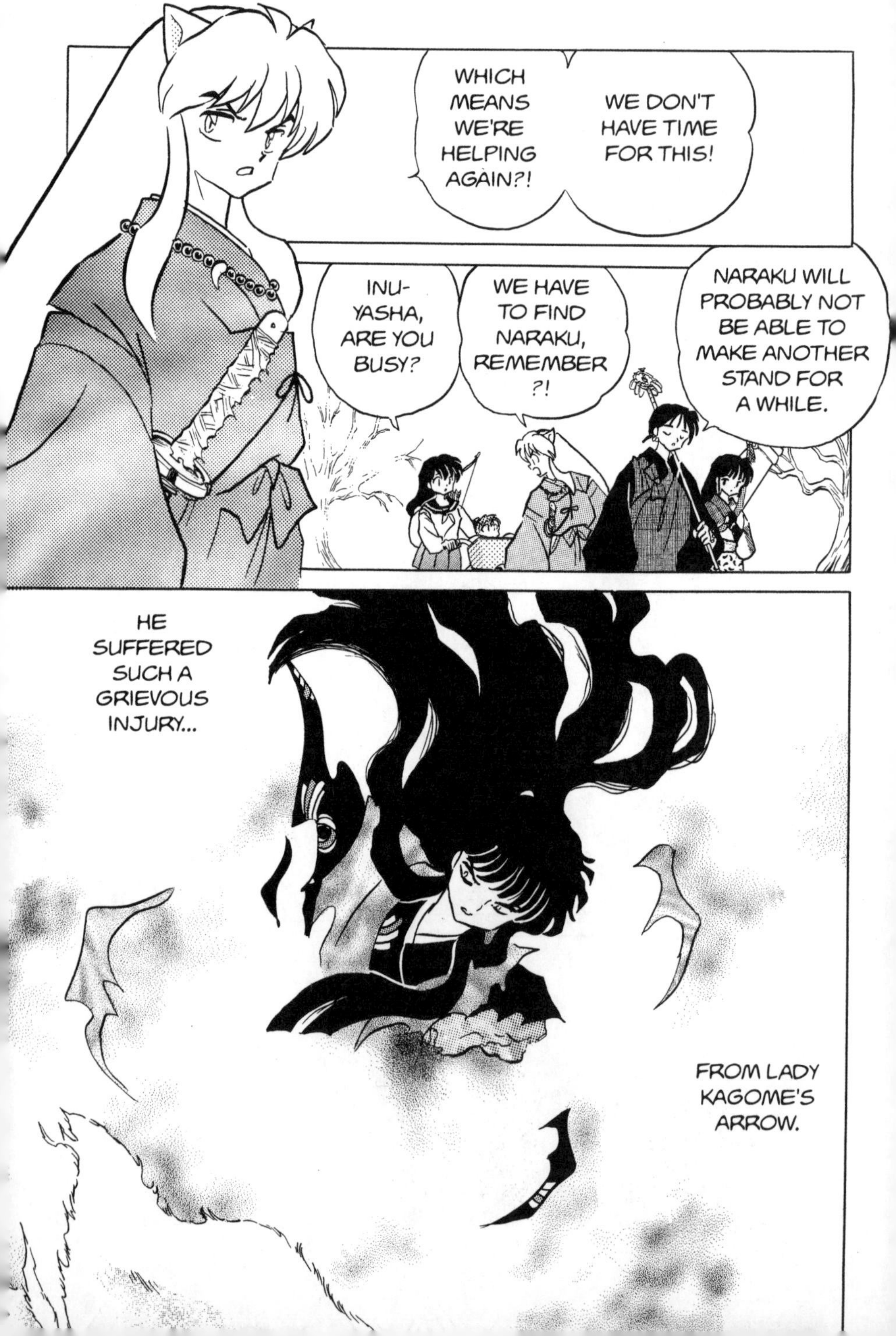
WHICH MEANS WE'RE HELPING AGAIN?!
WE DON'T HAVE TIME FOR THIS!
INU-YASHA, ARE YOU BUSY?
WE HAVE TO FIND NARAKU, REMEMBER?!
NARAKU WILL PROBABLY NOT BE ABLE TO MAKE ANOTHER STAND FOR A WHILE.
HE SUFFERED SUCH A GRIEVOUS INJURY...
FROM LADY KAGOME'S ARROW.

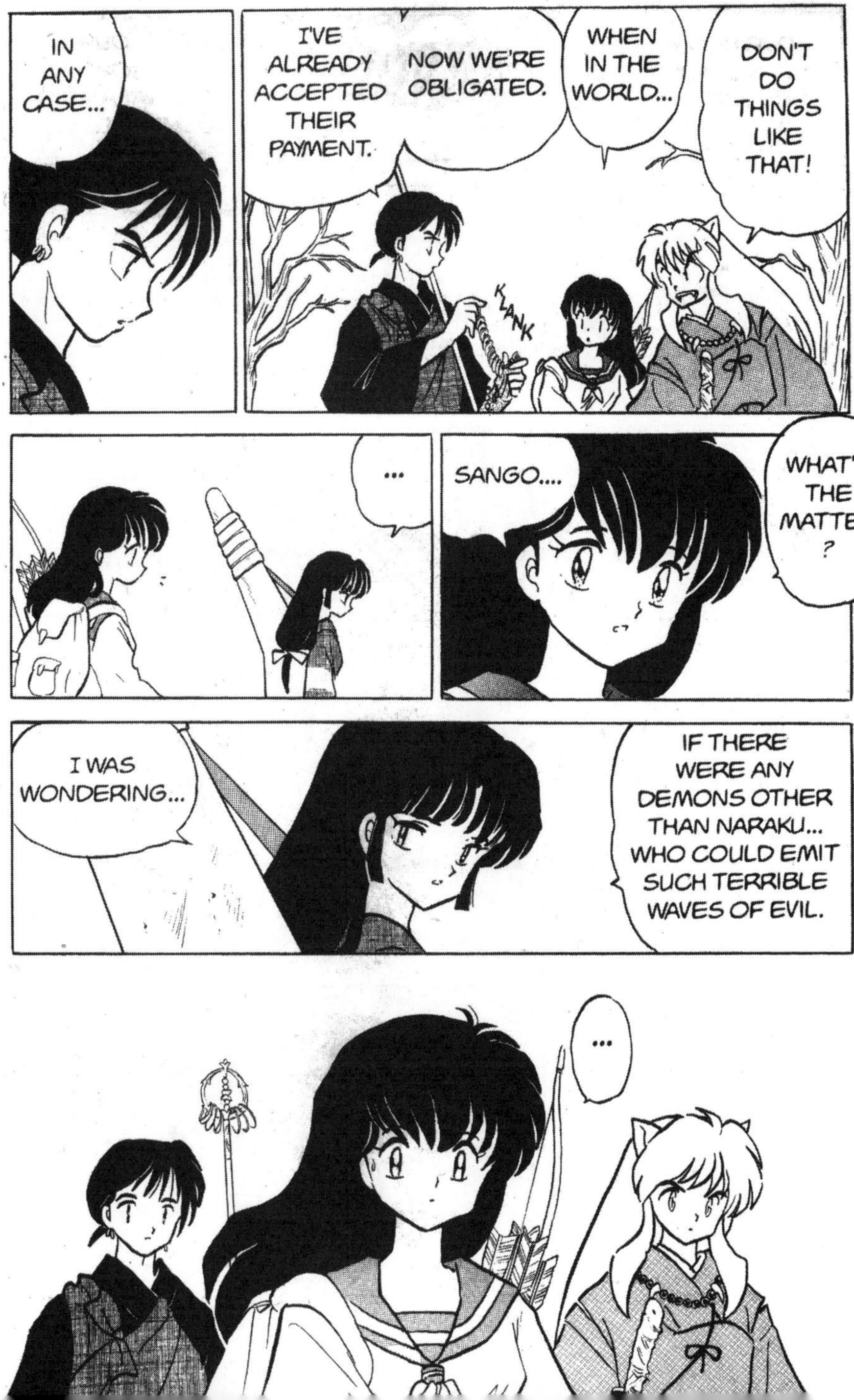
IN ANY CASE...
I'VE ALREADY ACCEPTED THEIR PAYMENT.
NOW WE'RE OBLIGATED.
KLANK
WHEN IN THE WORLD...
DON'T DO THINGS LIKE THAT!
...
SANGO....
WHAT'S THE MATTER?
I WAS WONDERING...
IF THERE WERE ANY DEMONS OTHER THAN NARAKU... WHO COULD EMIT SUCH TERRIBLE WAVES OF EVIL.
...

OUR HITOMI CLAN LEADER LORD KAGEWAKI WAS BORN WITH A WEAK CONSTITUTION.

YESTERDAY, OUR PREVIOUS LORD PASSED AWAY AND HE SUCCEEDED TO THE TITLE...

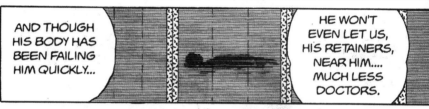

AND THOUGH HIS BODY HAS BEEN FAILING HIM QUICKLY...

HE WON'T EVEN LET US, HIS RETAINERS, NEAR HIM.... MUCH LESS DOCTORS.

NO, I CAN- NOT!

I WAS TOLD TO LET NO ONE PASS...!

STAND ASIDE! STAND ASIDE, I SAY!

I BROUGHT A PRIESTESS WHO CAN CURE LORD KAGEWAKI'S ILLNESS!

THE LORD WILL NOT SEE ANYONE!

EH? THIS CASTLE...

THE RETAINERS, ALL MERE MORTALS, BUT...

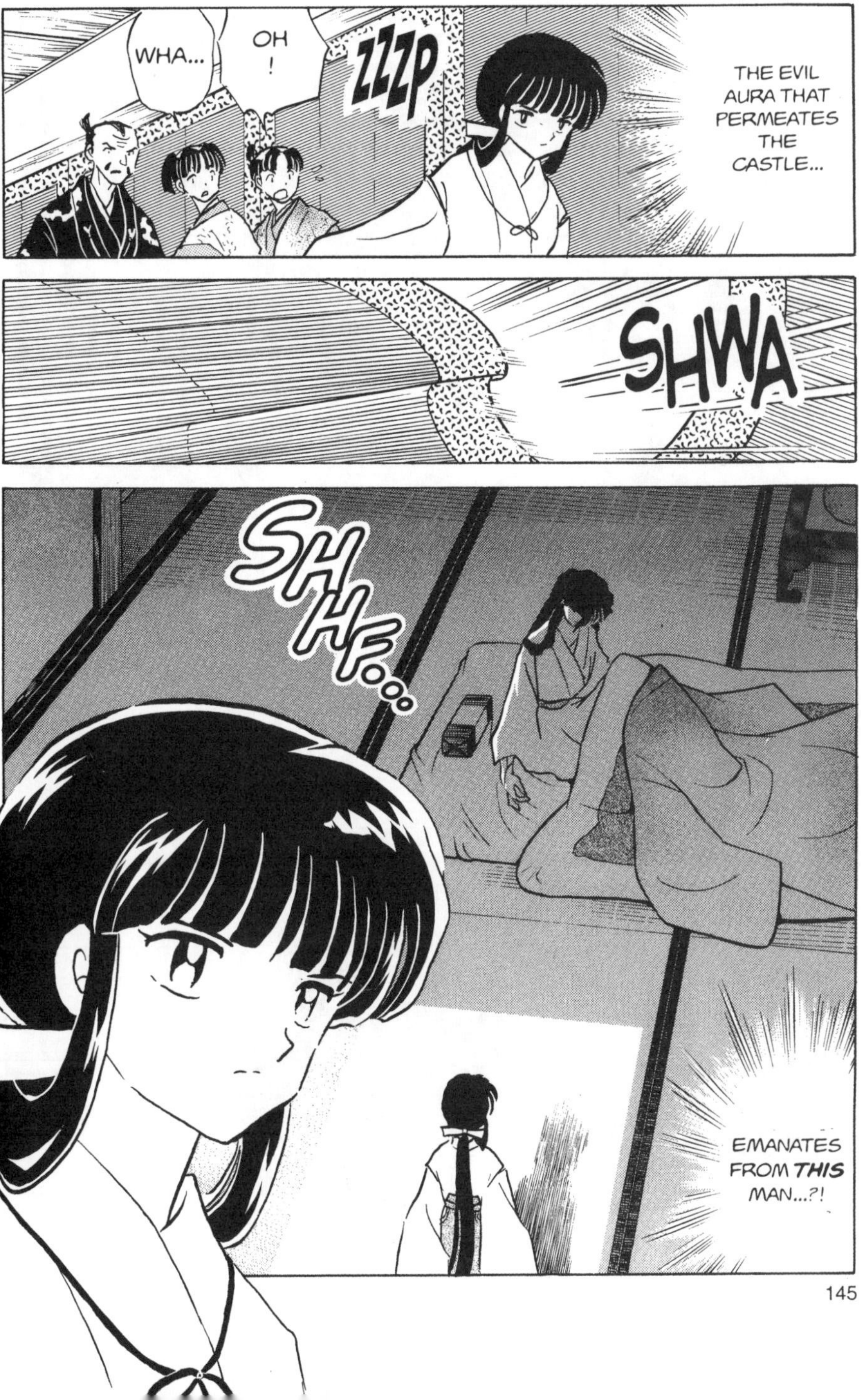
WHA...
OH!
ZZZP
THE EVIL AURA THAT PERMEATES THE CASTLE...
SHWA
SHHF...
EMANATES FROM THIS MAN...?!

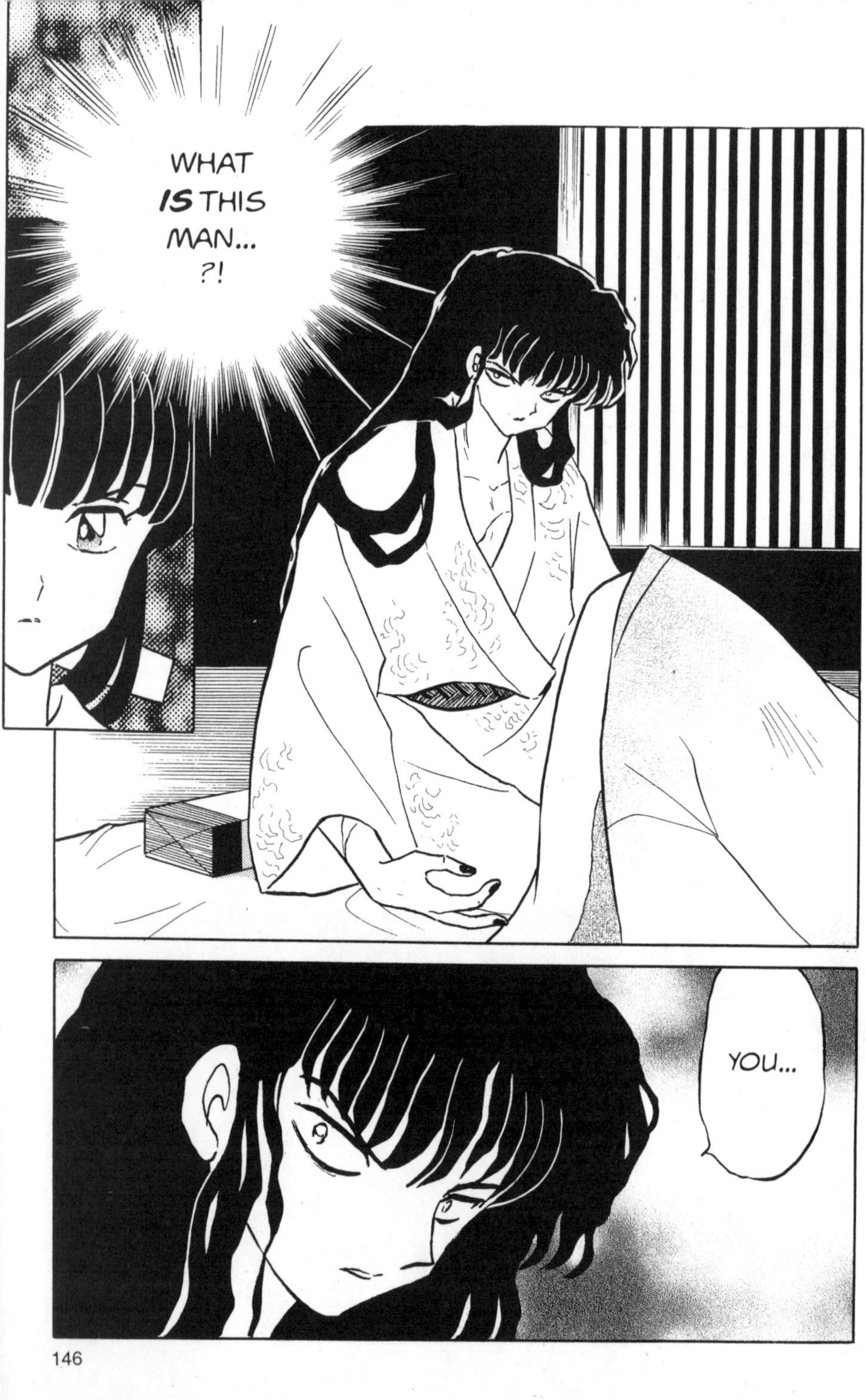
WHAT *IS* THIS MAN... ?!
YOU...

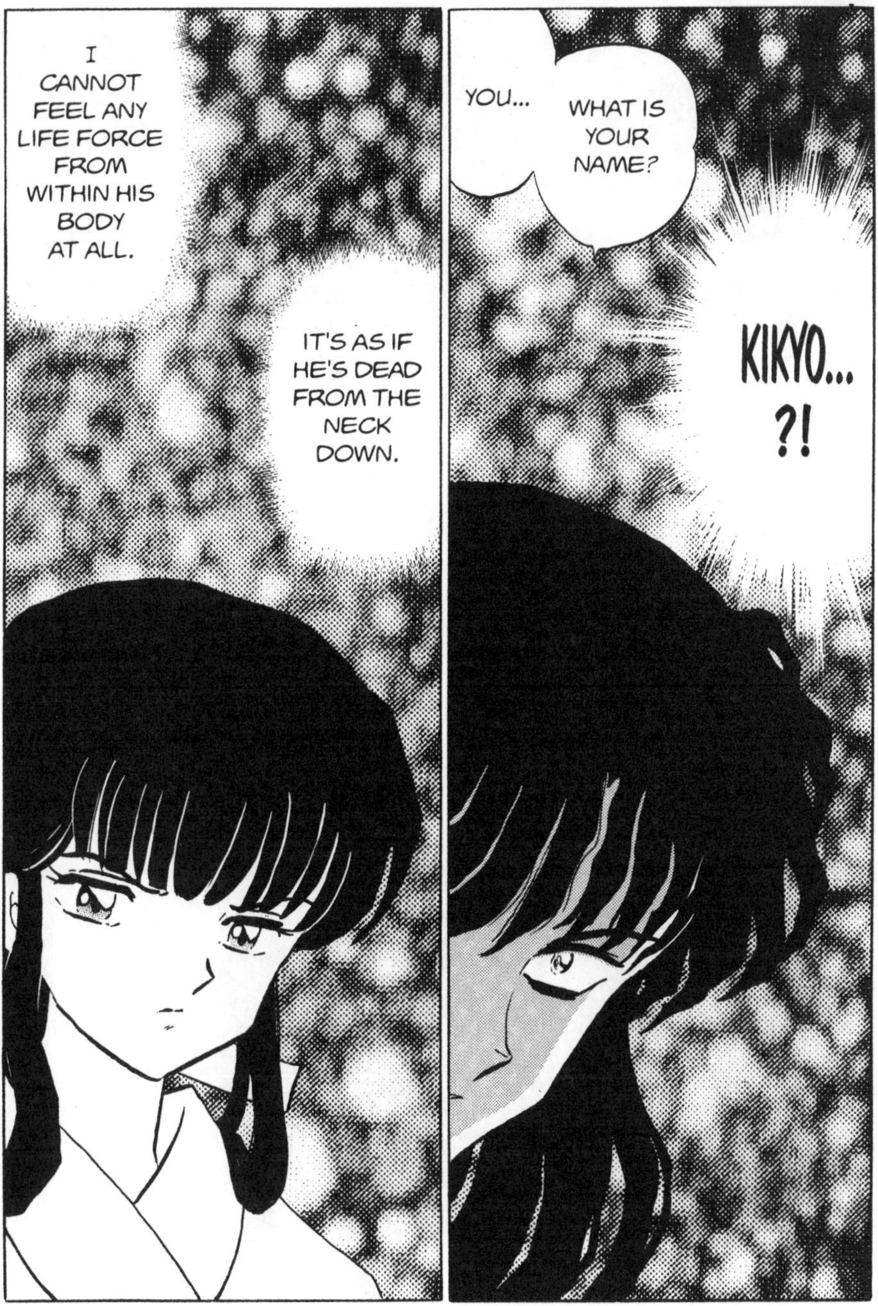
I CANNOT FEEL ANY LIFE FORCE FROM WITHIN HIS BODY AT ALL.
IT'S AS IF HE'S DEAD FROM THE NECK DOWN.
YOU...
WHAT IS YOUR NAME?
KIKYO... ?!

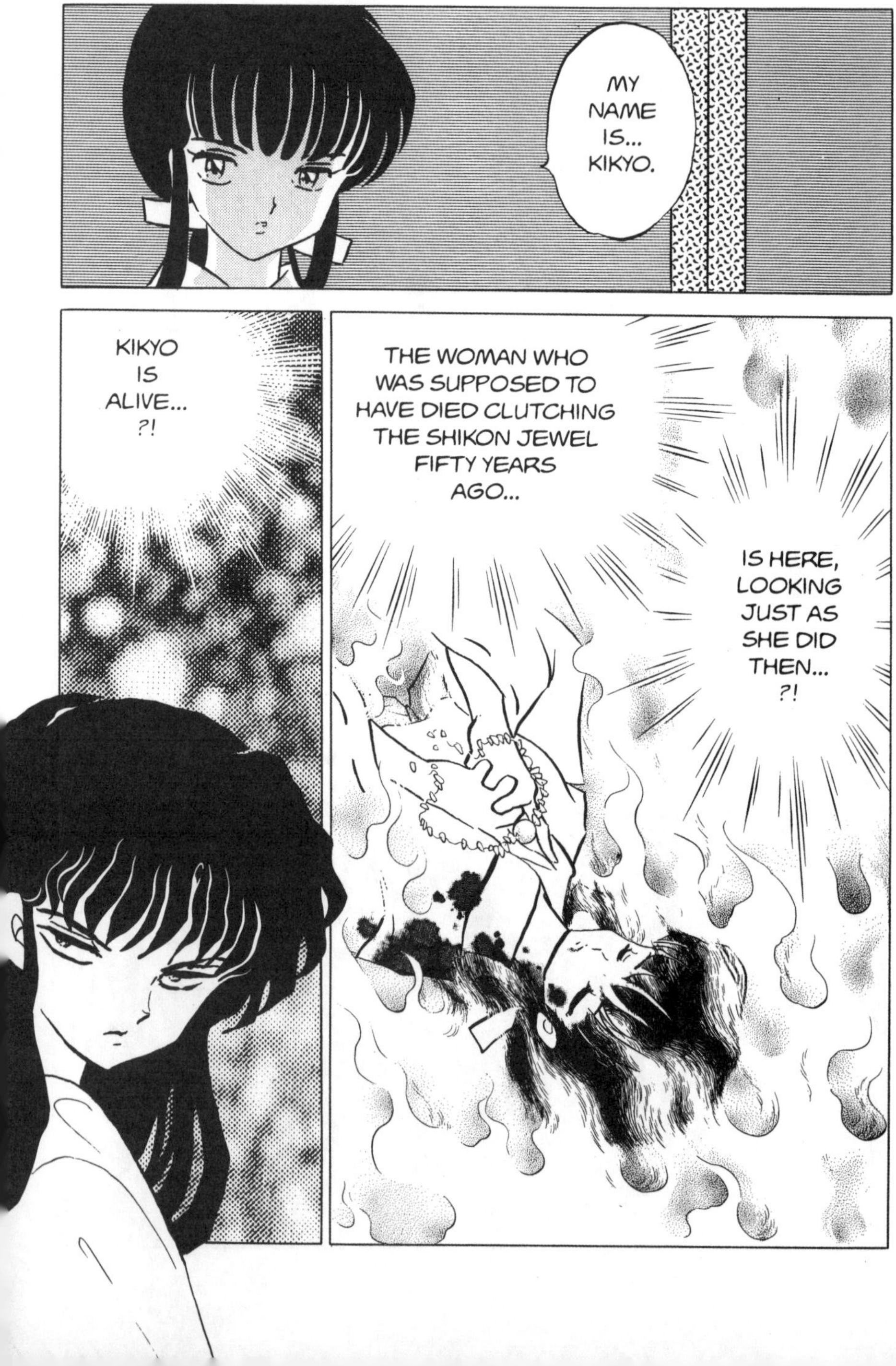
MY NAME IS... KIKYO.
KIKYO IS ALIVE... ?!
THE WOMAN WHO WAS SUPPOSED TO HAVE DIED CLUTCHING THE SHIKON JEWEL FIFTY YEARS AGO...
IS HERE, LOOKING JUST AS SHE DID THEN... ?!

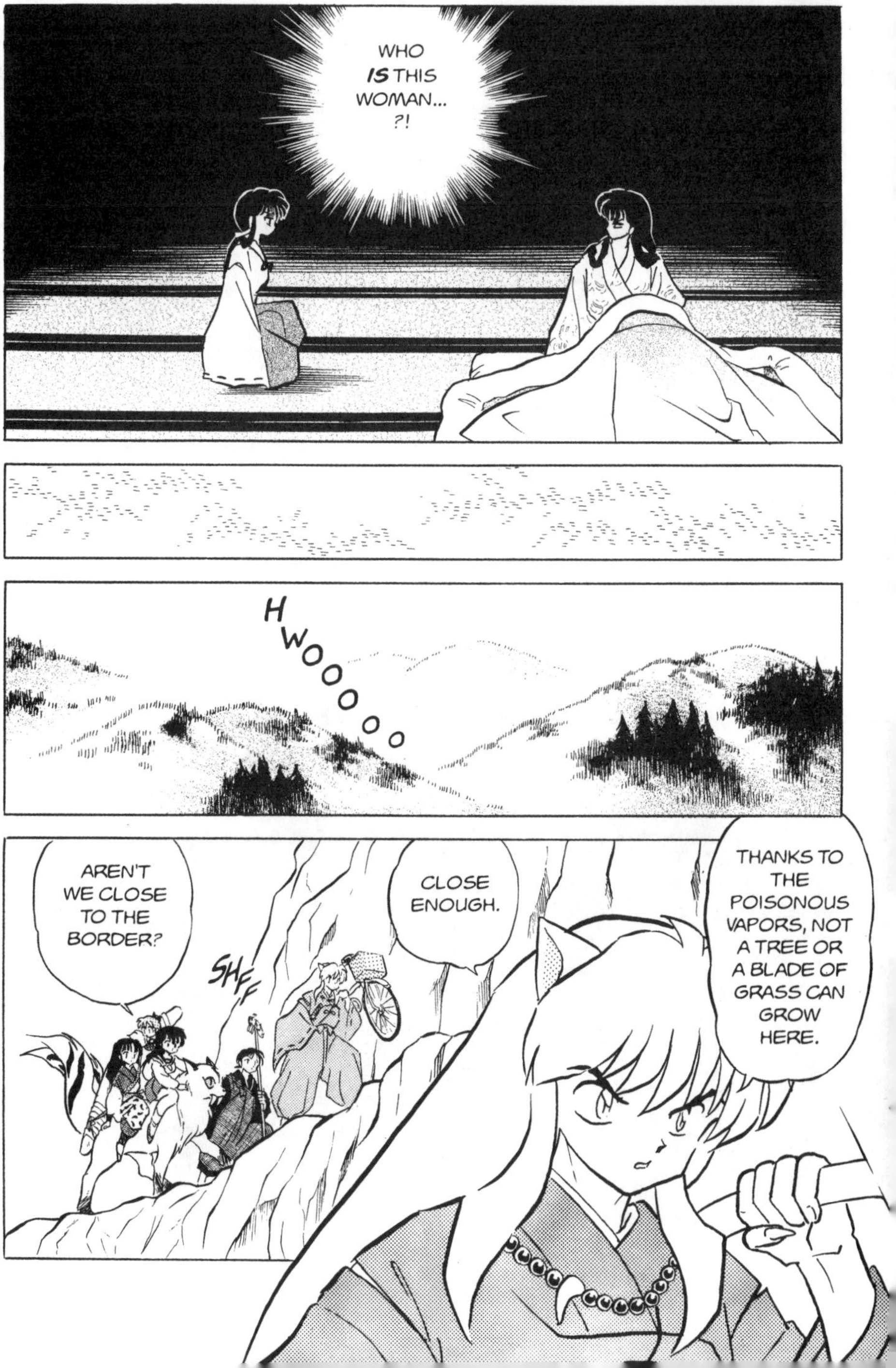
WHO *IS* THIS WOMAN... ?!
HWOOOOOO
AREN'T WE CLOSE TO THE BORDER?
SHFF
CLOSE ENOUGH.
THANKS TO THE POISONOUS VAPORS, NOT A TREE OR A BLADE OF GRASS CAN GROW HERE.

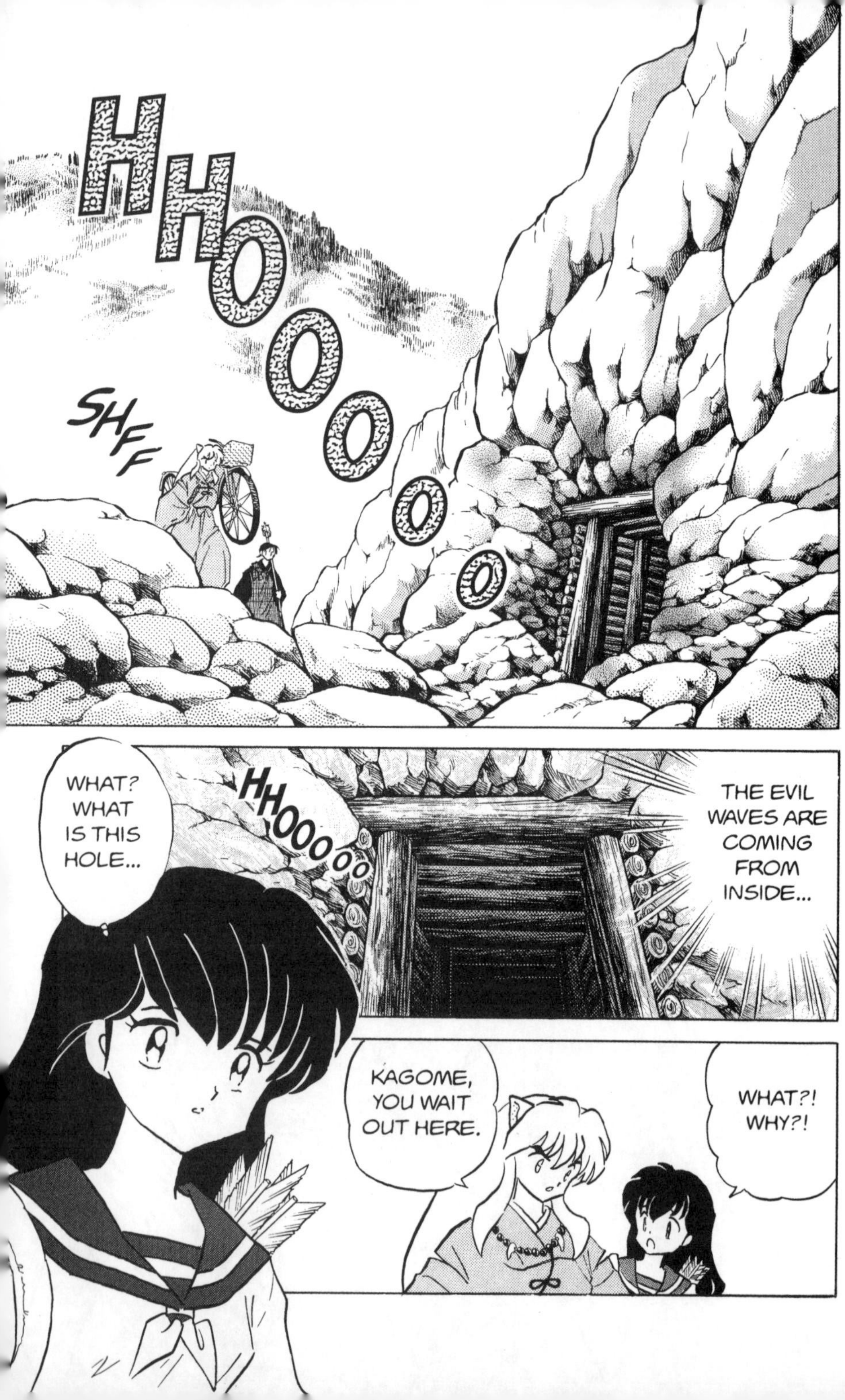
HHOOOOOOO
SHFF
WHAT? WHAT IS THIS HOLE...
HHOOOOOO
THE EVIL WAVES ARE COMING FROM INSIDE...
KAGOME, YOU WAIT OUT HERE.
WHAT?! WHY?!

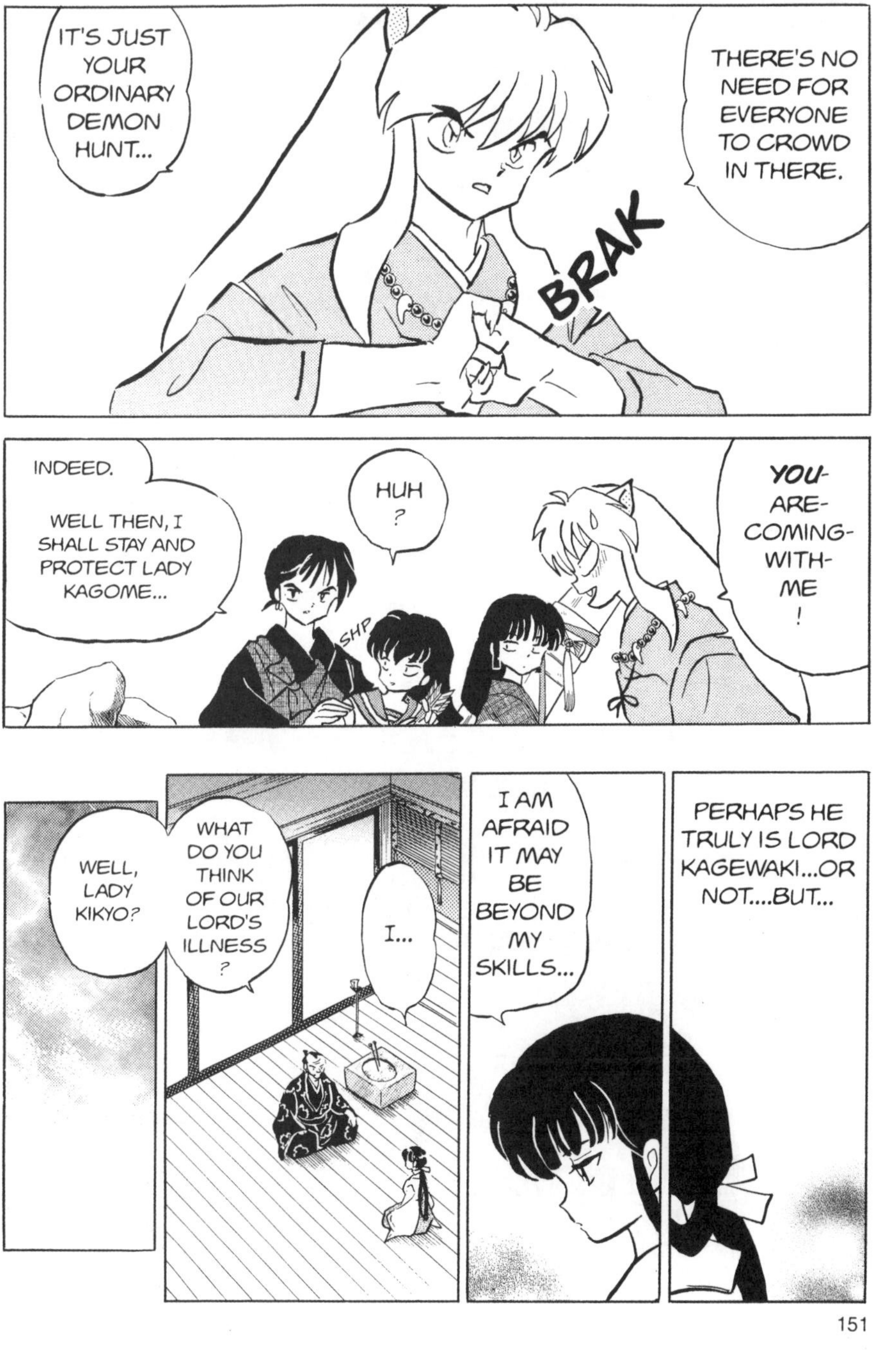
IT'S JUST YOUR ORDINARY DEMON HUNT...
THERE'S NO NEED FOR EVERYONE TO CROWD IN THERE.
BRAK
INDEED.
WELL THEN, I SHALL STAY AND PROTECT LADY KAGOME...
HUH?
SHP
YOU-ARE-COMING-WITH-ME!
WELL, LADY KIKYO?
WHAT DO YOU THINK OF OUR LORD'S ILLNESS?
I...
I AM AFRAID IT MAY BE BEYOND MY SKILLS...
PERHAPS HE TRULY IS LORD KAGEWAKI...OR NOT....BUT...

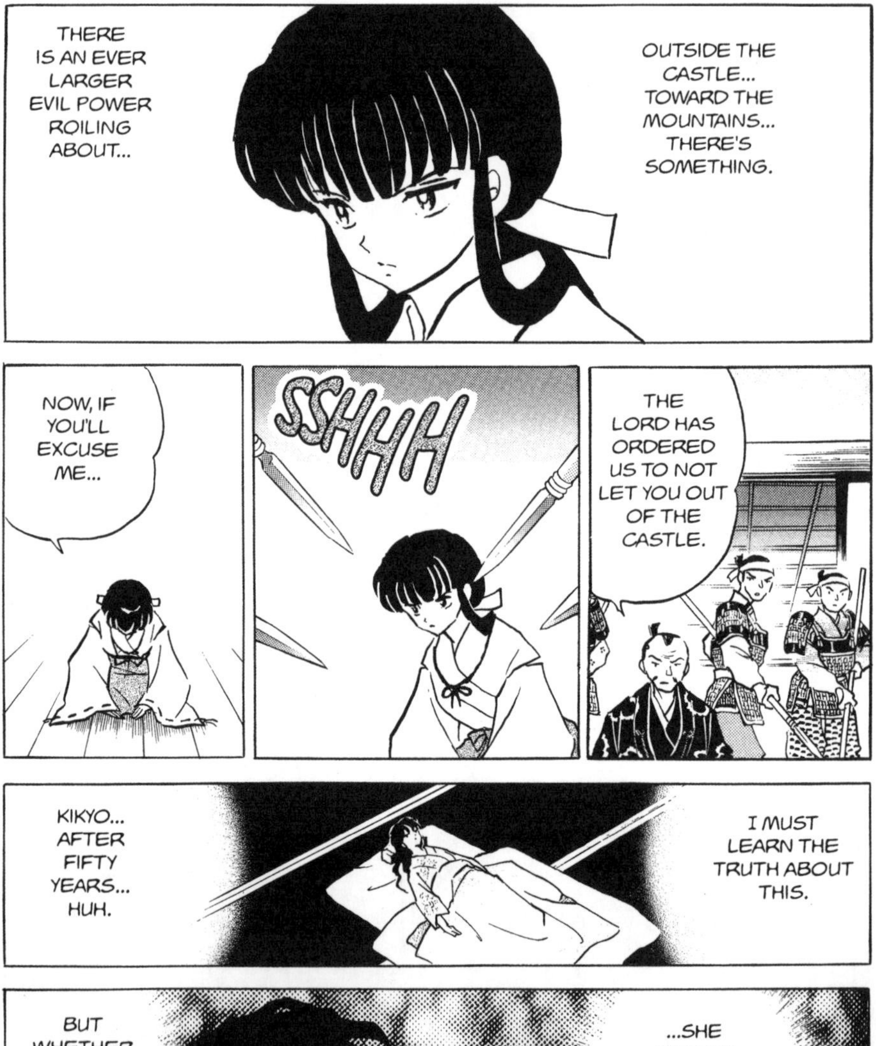
THERE IS AN EVER LARGER EVIL POWER ROILING ABOUT...
OUTSIDE THE CASTLE... TOWARD THE MOUNTAINS... THERE'S SOMETHING.
NOW, IF YOU'LL EXCUSE ME...
SSHHH
THE LORD HAS ORDERED US TO NOT LET YOU OUT OF THE CASTLE.
KIKYO... AFTER FIFTY YEARS... HUH.
I MUST LEARN THE TRUTH ABOUT THIS.
BUT WHETHER I LET HER LIVE OR KILL HER...
...SHE SHOULD PROVE TO BE A MOST USEFUL WOMAN...

SCROLL NINE

FULFILLMENT

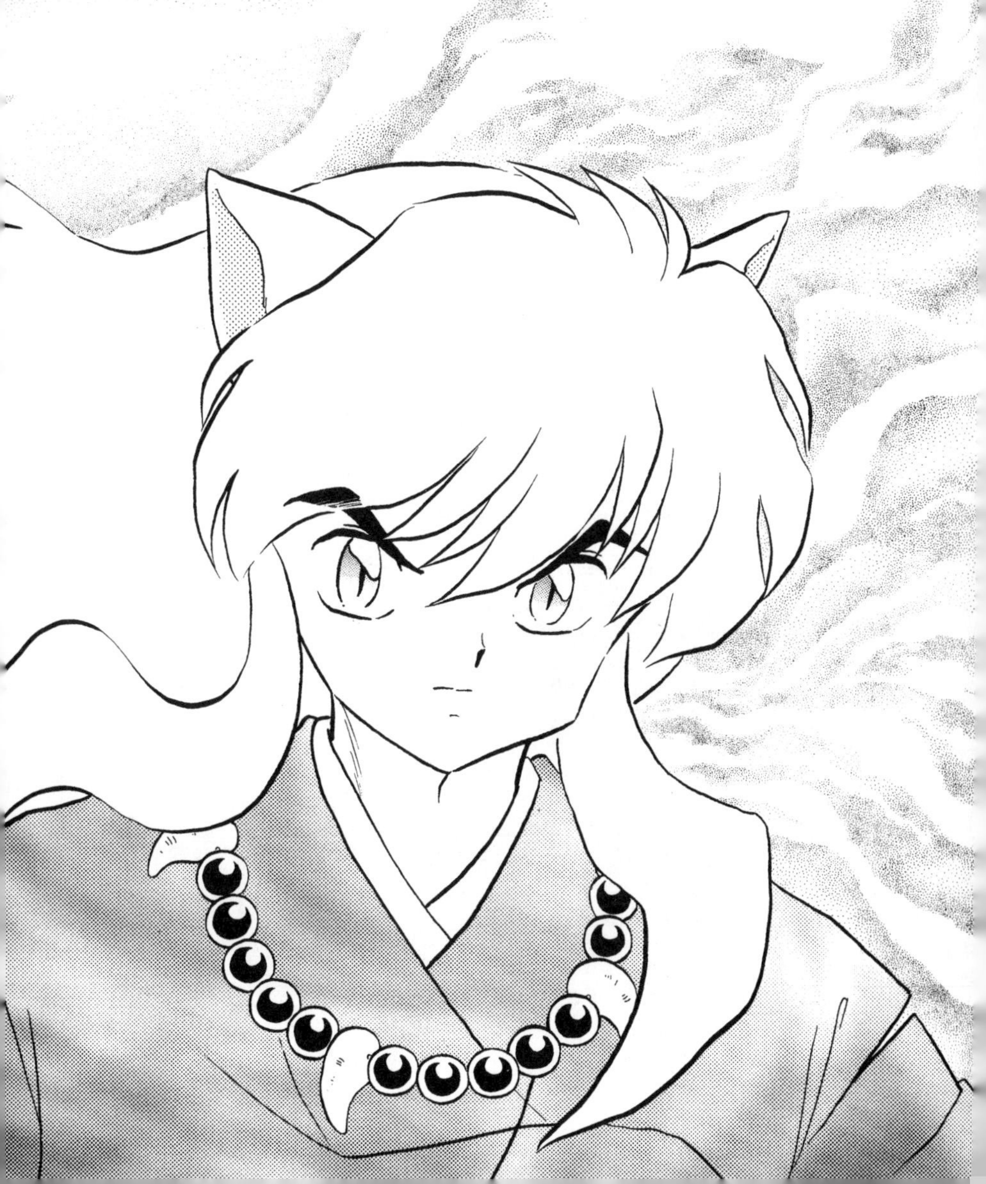

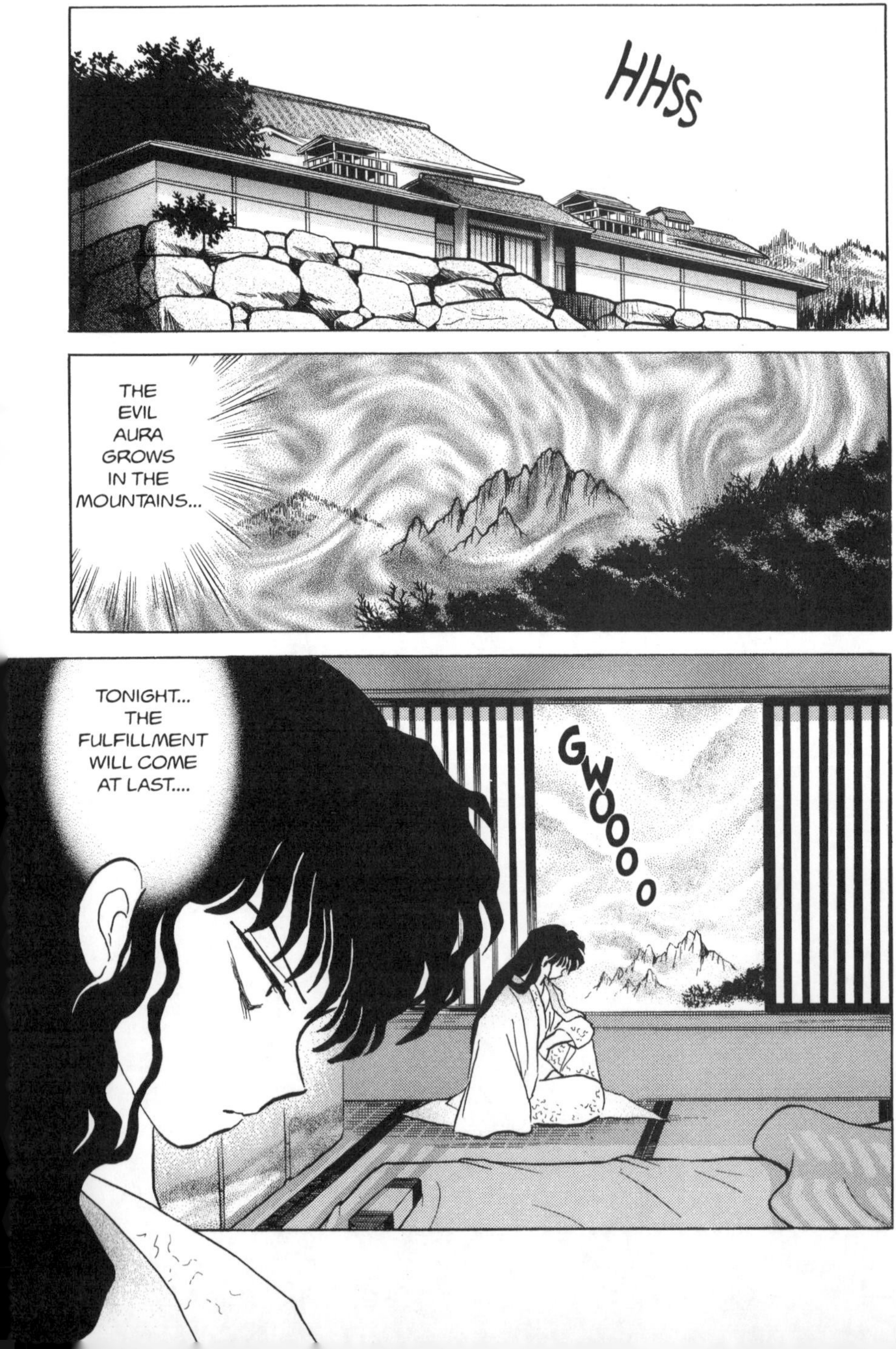
HHSS
THE EVIL AURA GROWS IN THE MOUNTAINS...
TONIGHT... THE FULFILLMENT WILL COME AT LAST....
GWOOOOO

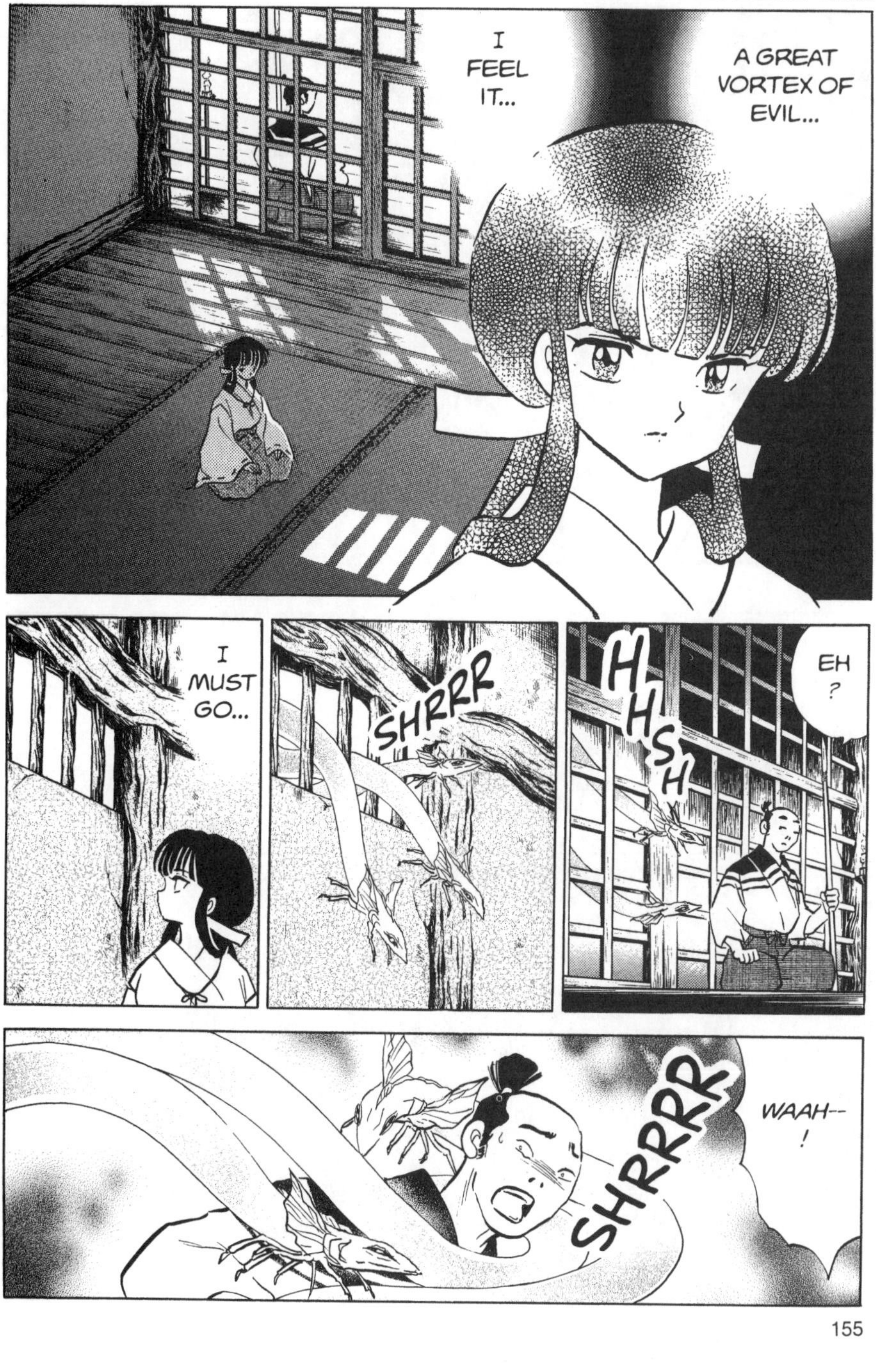
I FEEL IT...
A GREAT VORTEX OF EVIL...
I MUST GO...
SHRRR
HHSH
EH ?
SHRRRR
WAAH-- !

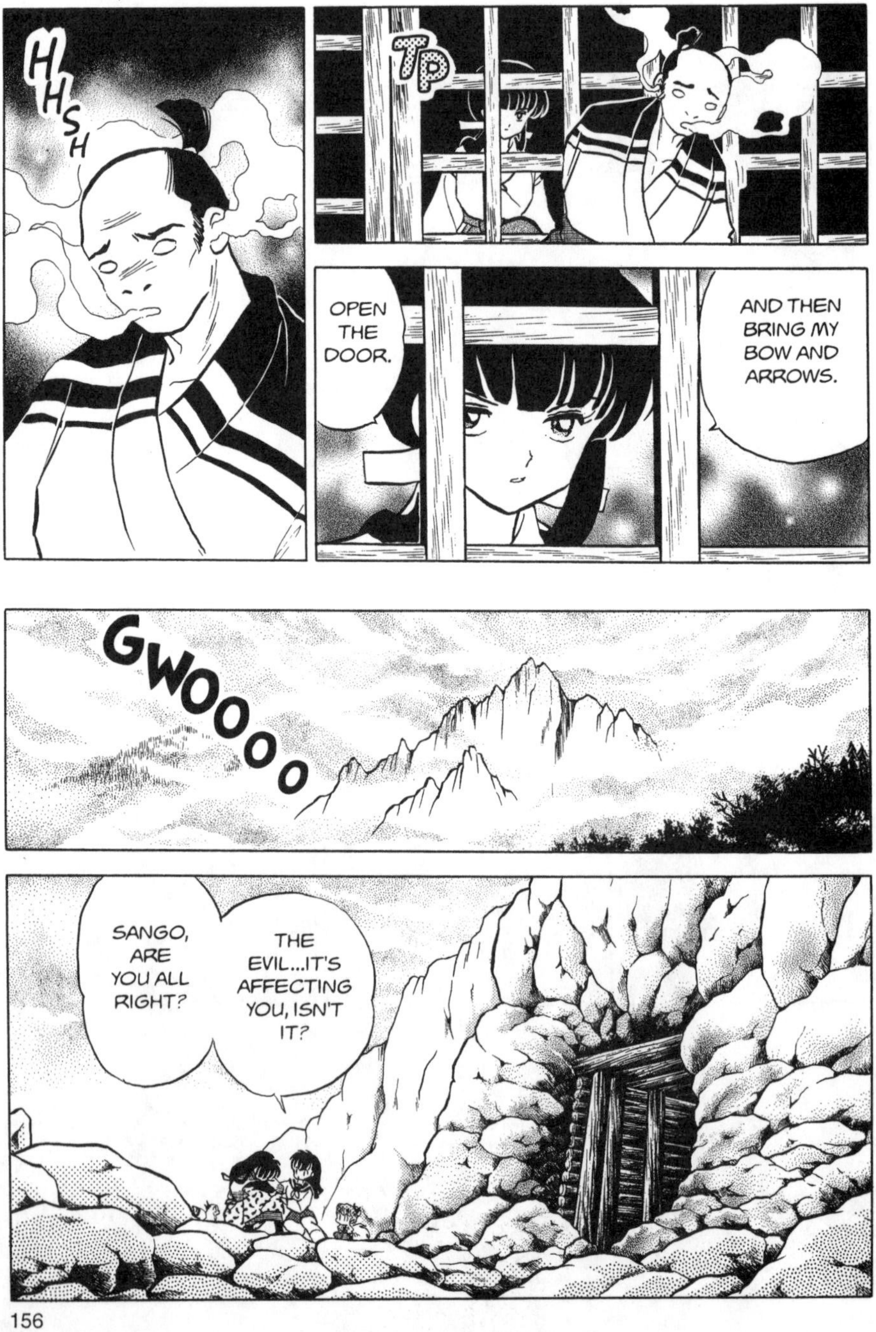
HHSH
TP
OPEN THE DOOR.
AND THEN BRING MY BOW AND ARROWS.
GWOOOOO
SANGO, ARE YOU ALL RIGHT?
THE EVIL...IT'S AFFECTING YOU, ISN'T IT?

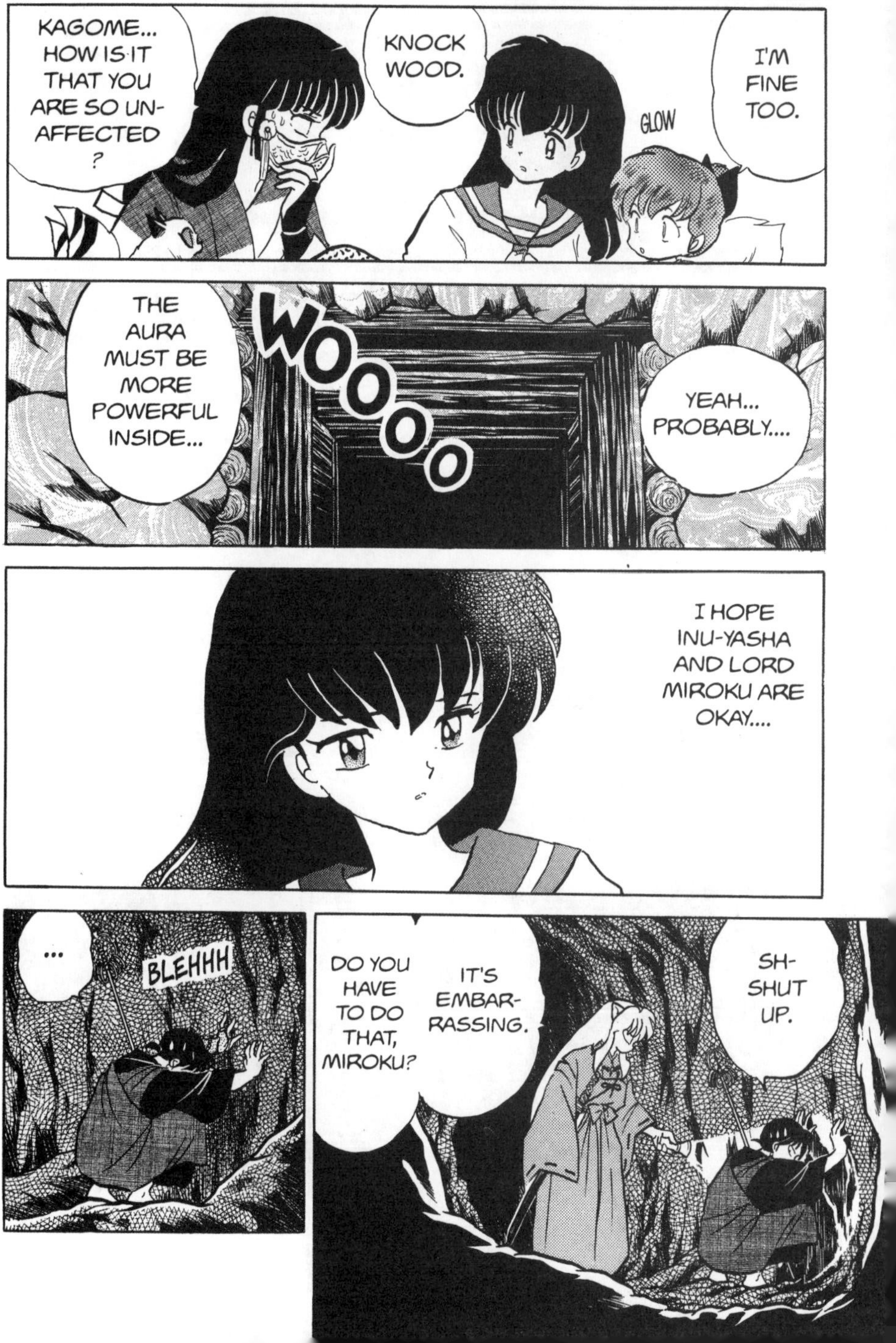
KAGOME... HOW IS IT THAT YOU ARE SO UN-AFFECTED?
KNOCK WOOD.
GLOW
I'M FINE TOO.
THE AURA MUST BE MORE POWERFUL INSIDE...
WOOOOO
YEAH... PROBABLY....
I HOPE INU-YASHA AND LORD MIROKU ARE OKAY....
...
BLEHHH
DO YOU HAVE TO DO THAT, MIROKU?
IT'S EMBARRASSING.
SH-SHUT UP.

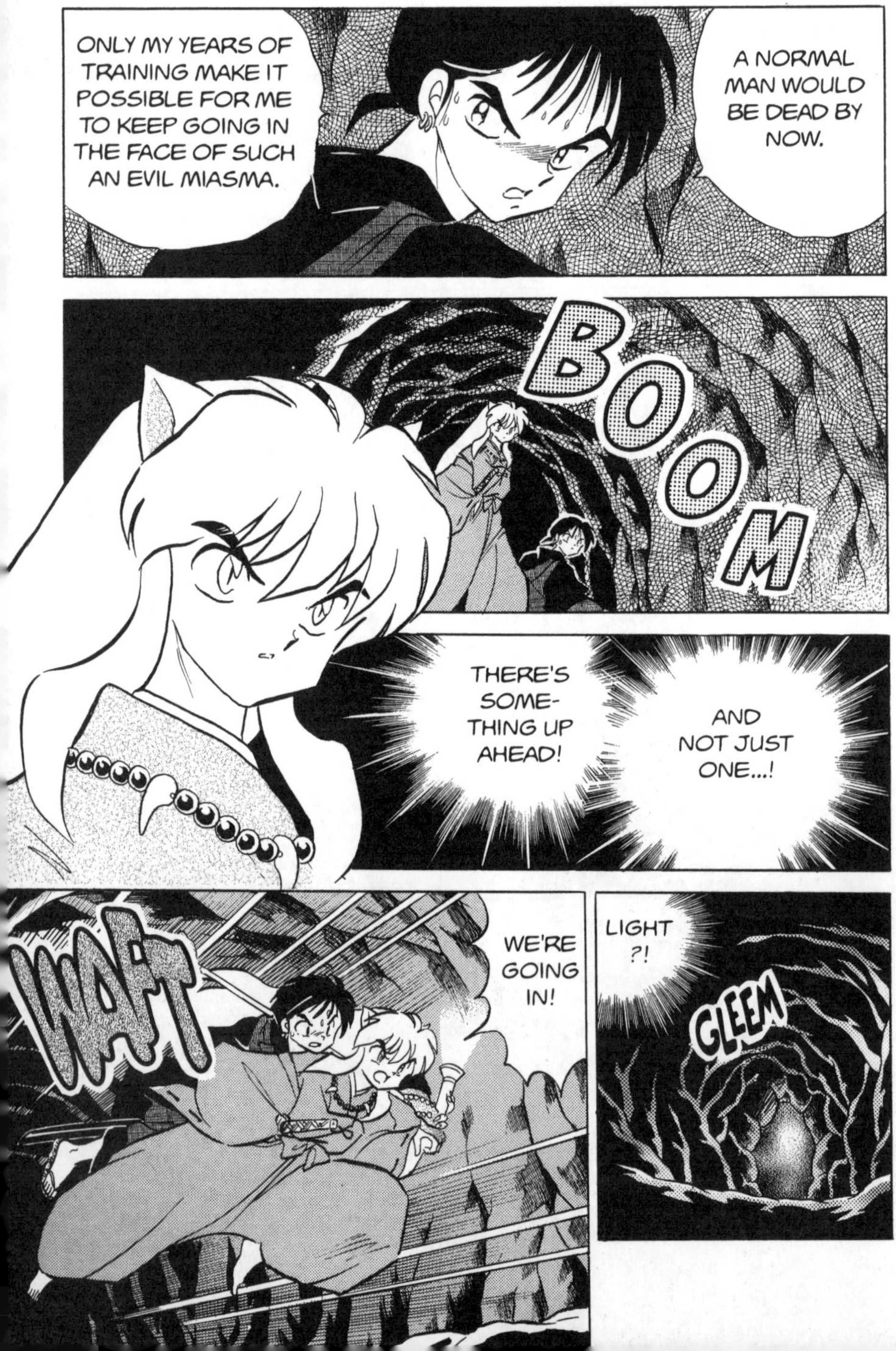
ONLY MY YEARS OF TRAINING MAKE IT POSSIBLE FOR ME TO KEEP GOING IN THE FACE OF SUCH AN EVIL MIASMA.
A NORMAL MAN WOULD BE DEAD BY NOW.
BOOOM
THERE'S SOME-THING UP AHEAD!
AND NOT JUST ONE...!
WAFT
WE'RE GOING IN!
LIGHT ?!
GLEEM

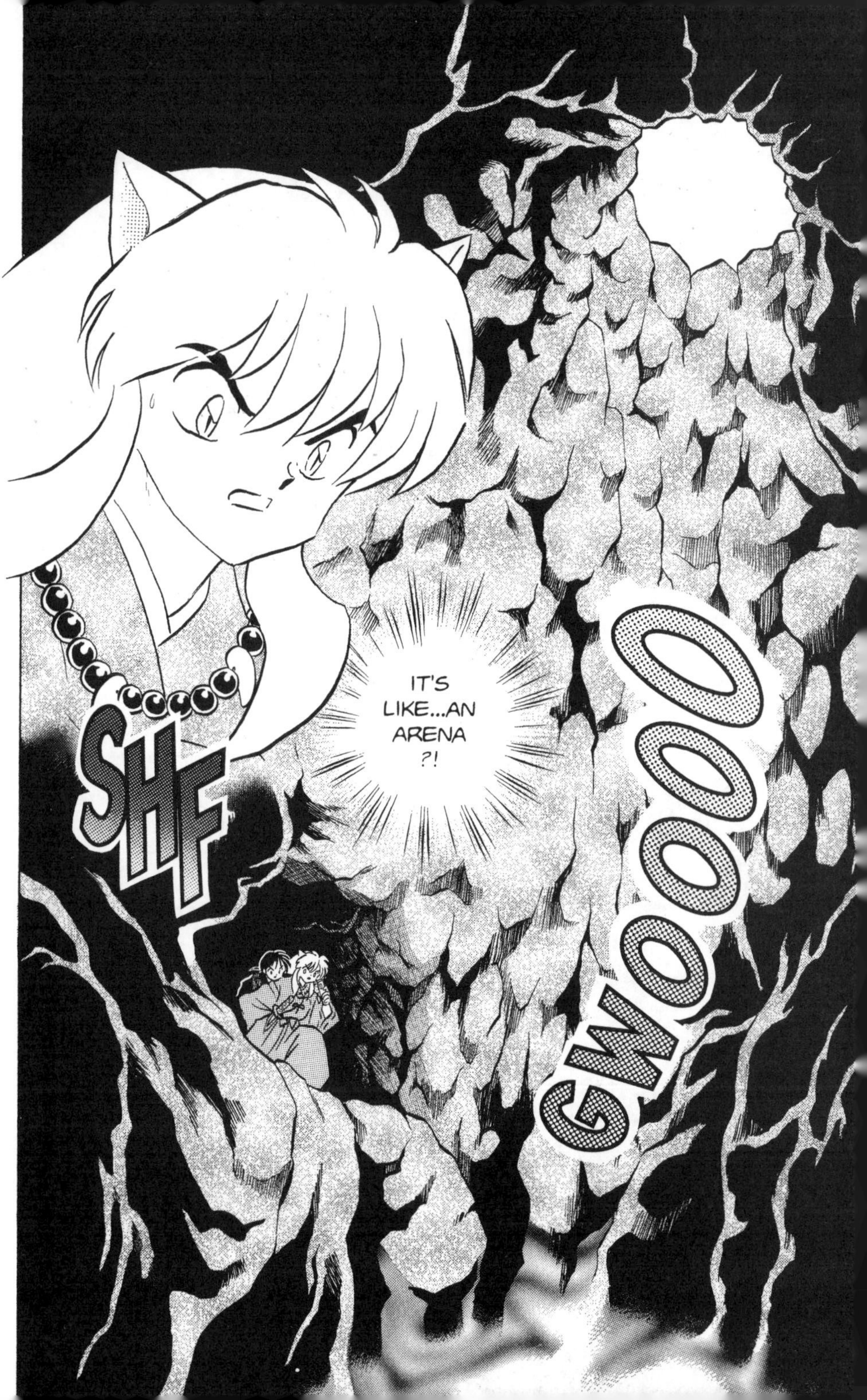

SHF
IT'S LIKE...AN ARENA ?!
GWOOOO

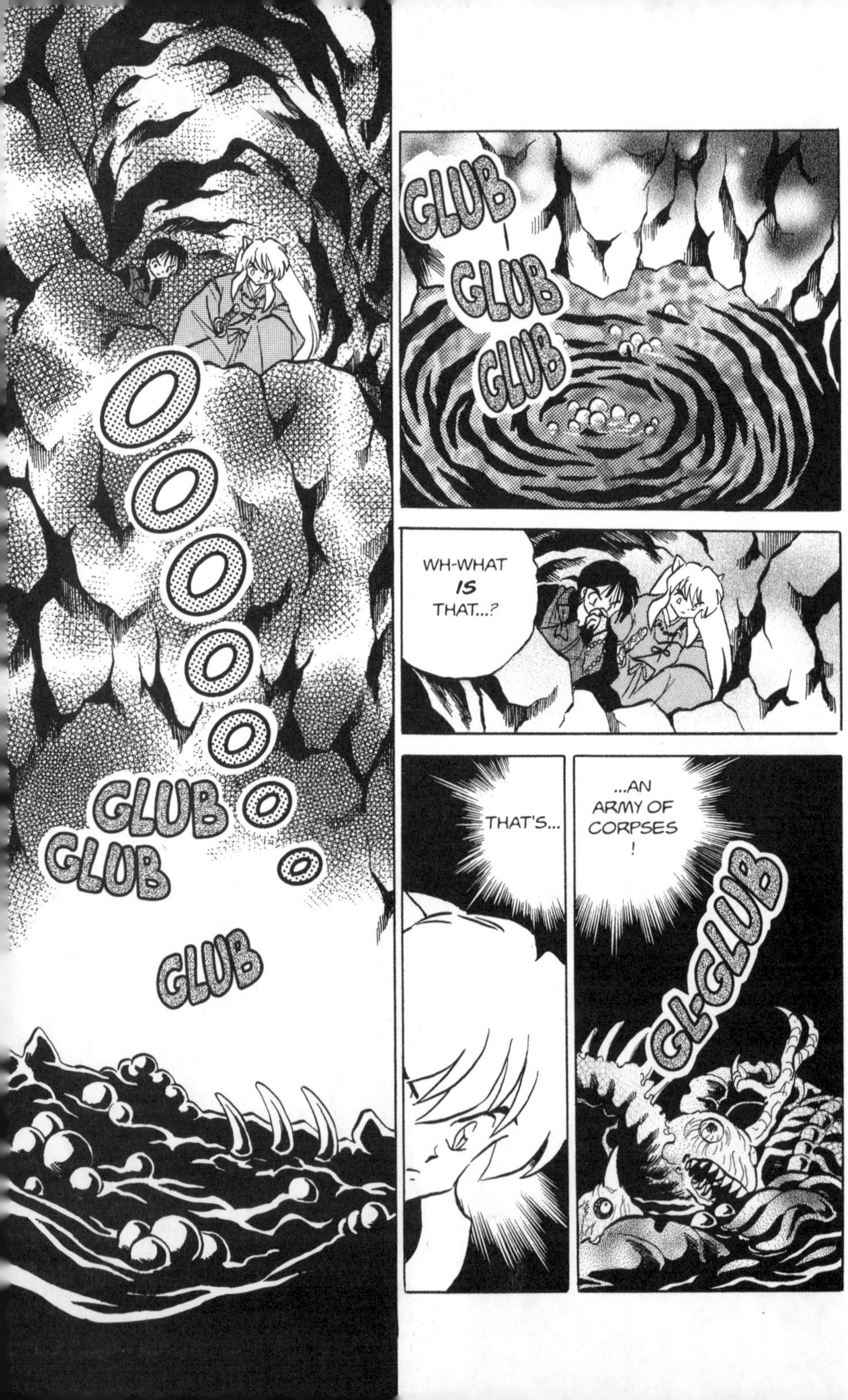
OOOOOOO
GLUB
GLUB
GLUB
GLUB GLUB GLUB
WH-WHAT IS THAT...?
THAT'S...
...AN ARMY OF CORPSES!
GL-GLUB

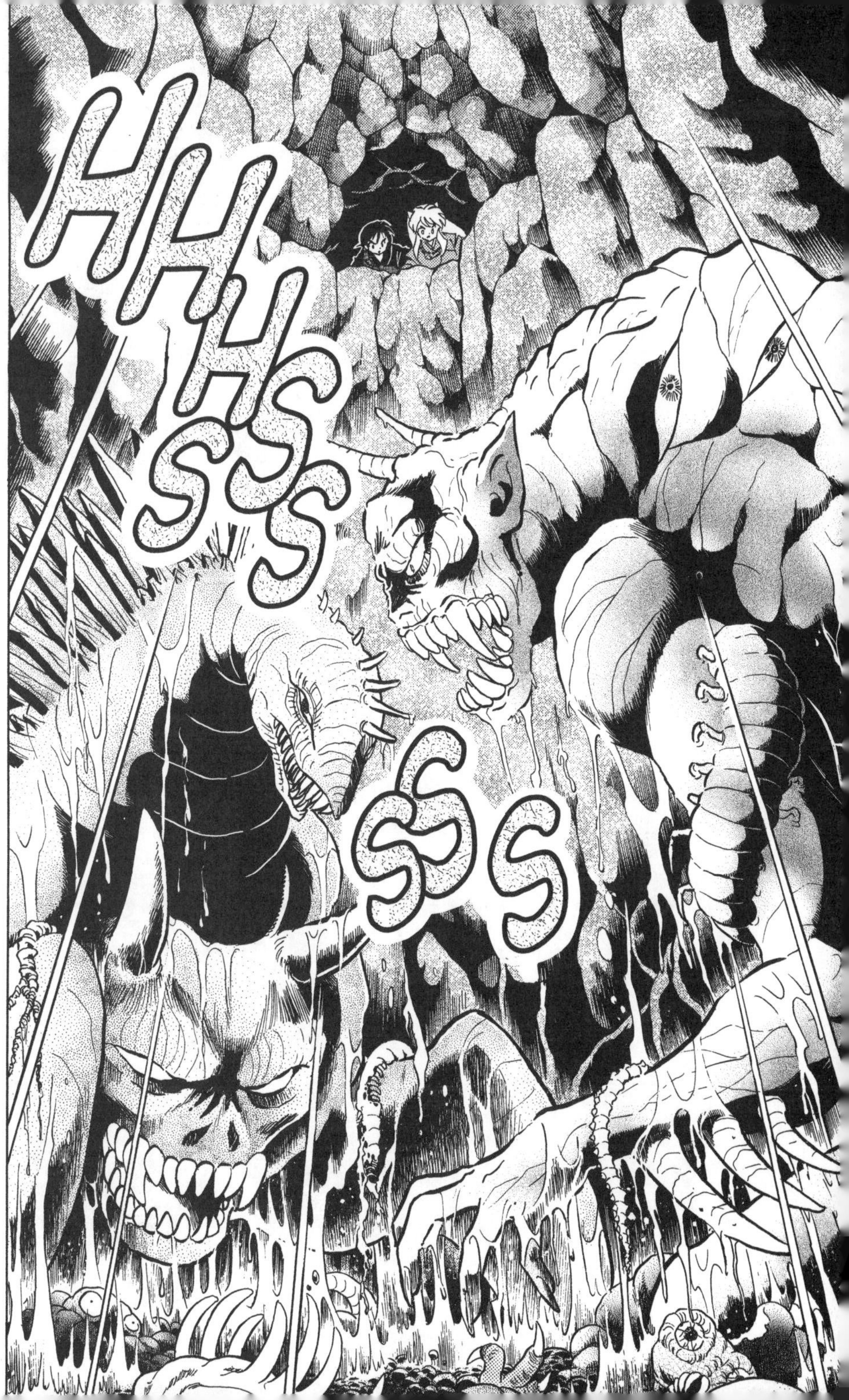
HHHHSSSS
SSSS

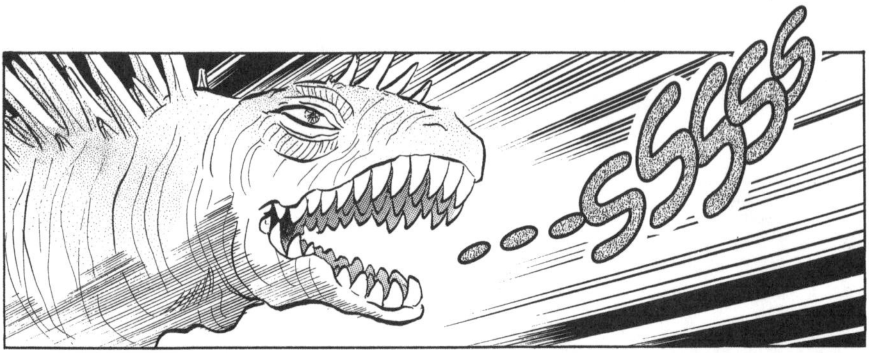
...SSSSS

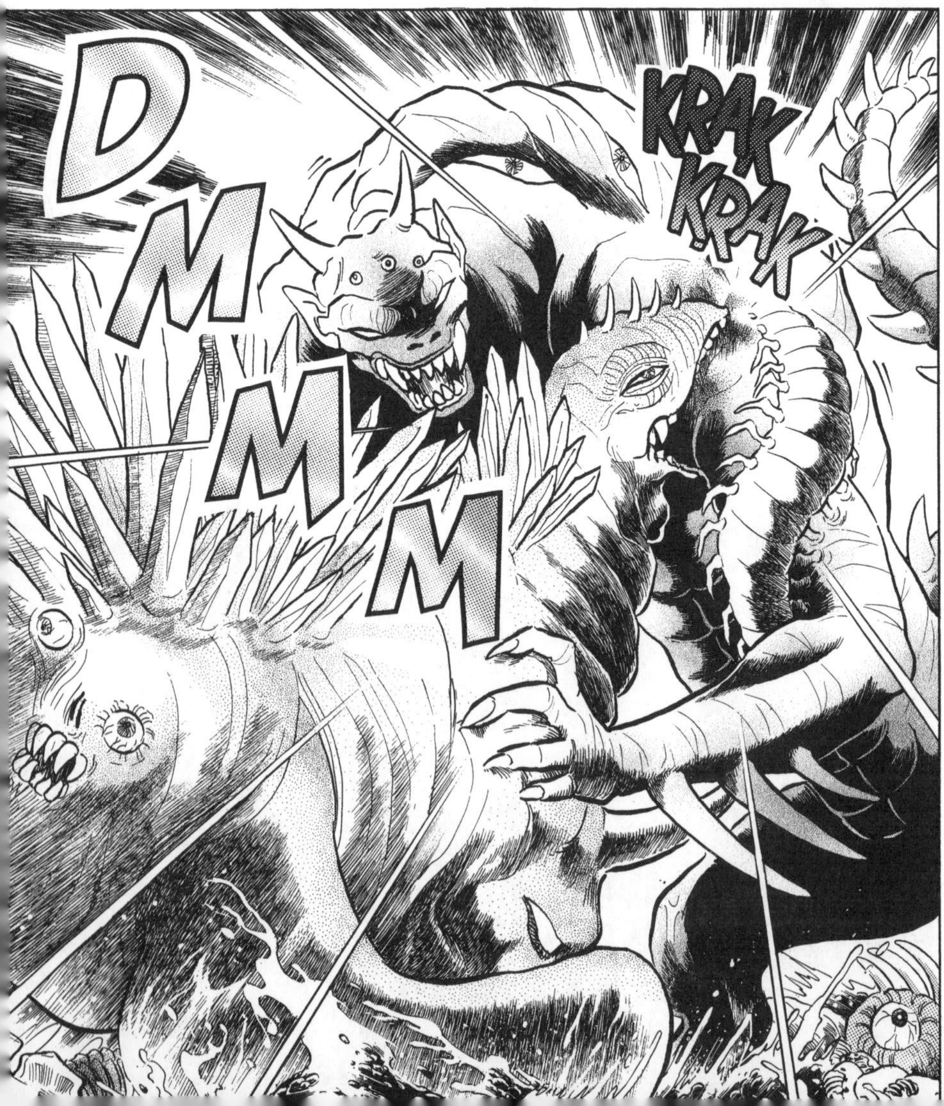
DMMMM
KRAK KRAK KRAK

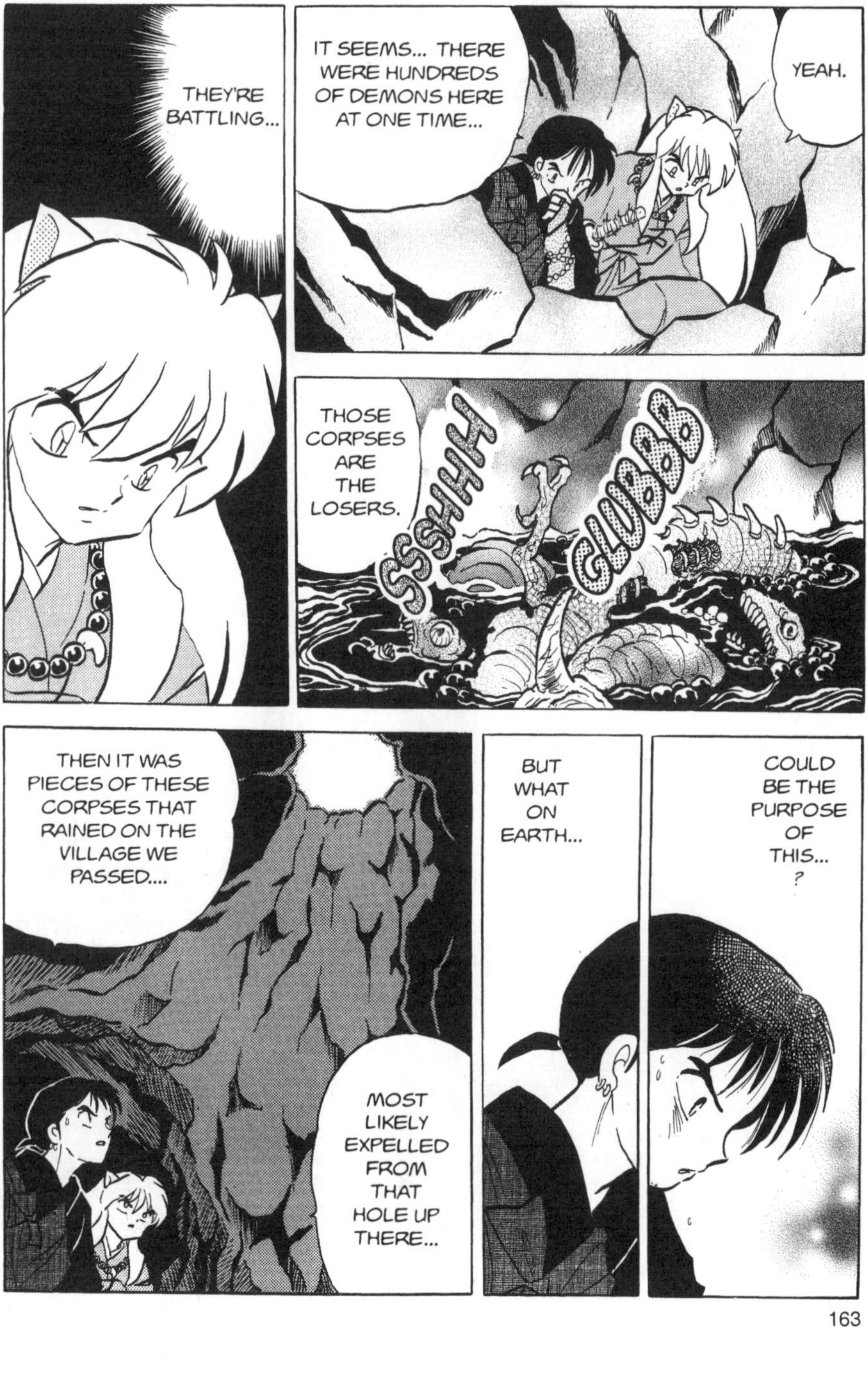
THEY'RE BATTLING...
IT SEEMS... THERE WERE HUNDREDS OF DEMONS HERE AT ONE TIME...
YEAH.
THOSE CORPSES ARE THE LOSERS.
SSSHHH
GLUBBB
THEN IT WAS PIECES OF THESE CORPSES THAT RAINED ON THE VILLAGE WE PASSED....
MOST LIKELY EXPELLED FROM THAT HOLE UP THERE...
BUT WHAT ON EARTH...
COULD BE THE PURPOSE OF THIS... ?

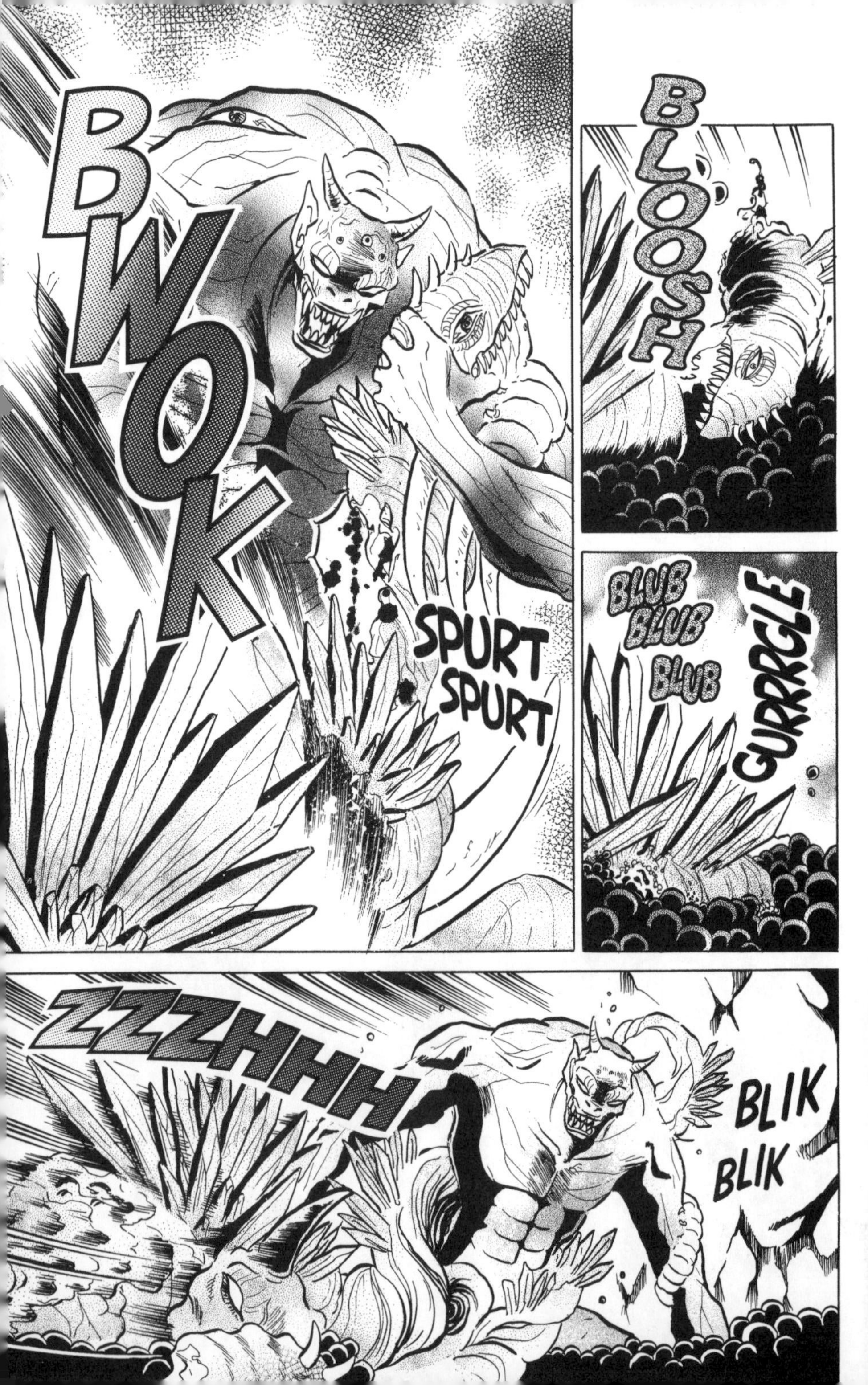
BWOK
SPURT SPURT
BLOOSH
BLUB BLUB BLUB
GURRRGLE
ZZZHHH
BLIK BLIK

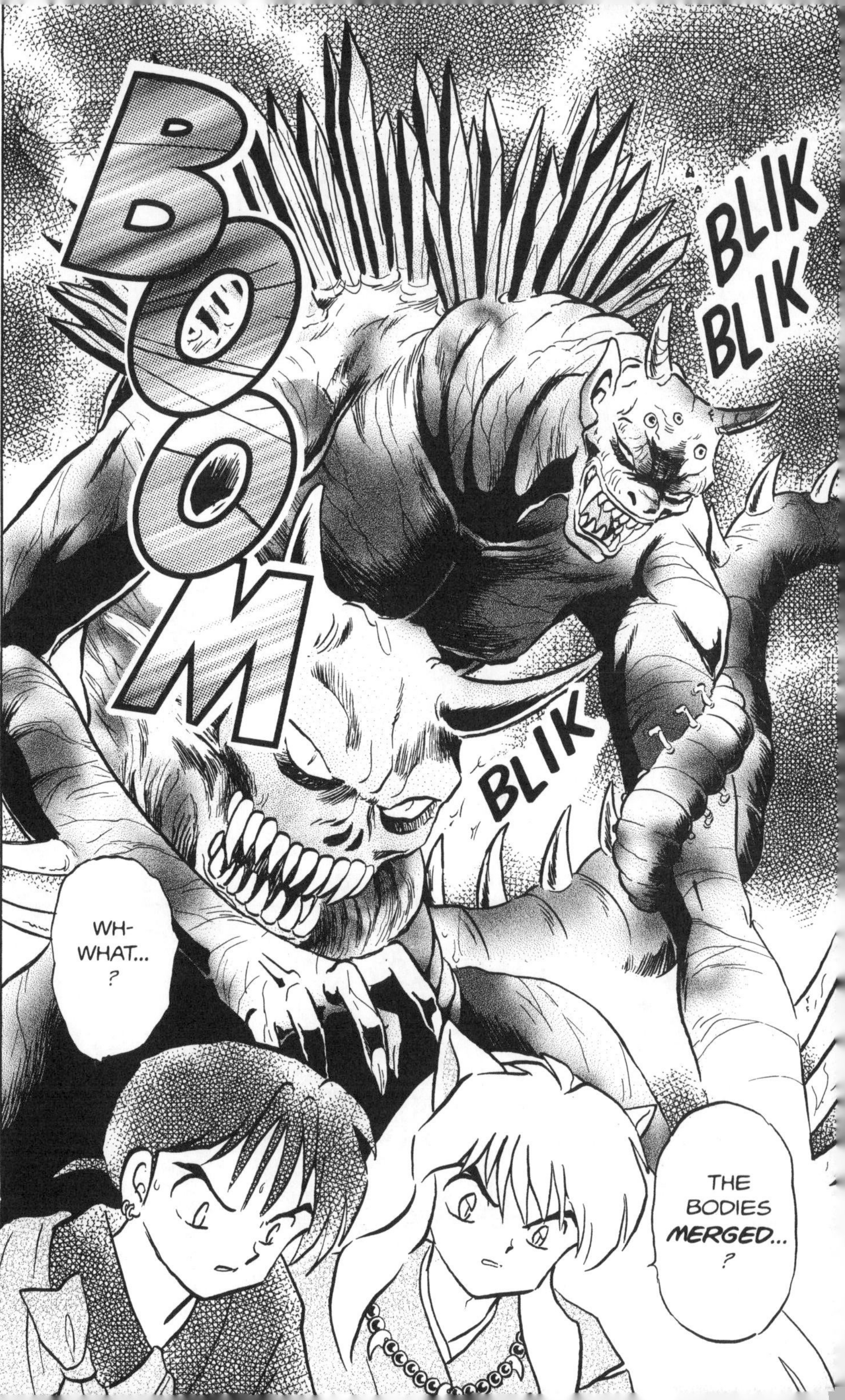
BOOM
BLIK BLIK
BLIK
WH- WHAT...?
THE BODIES MERGED...?

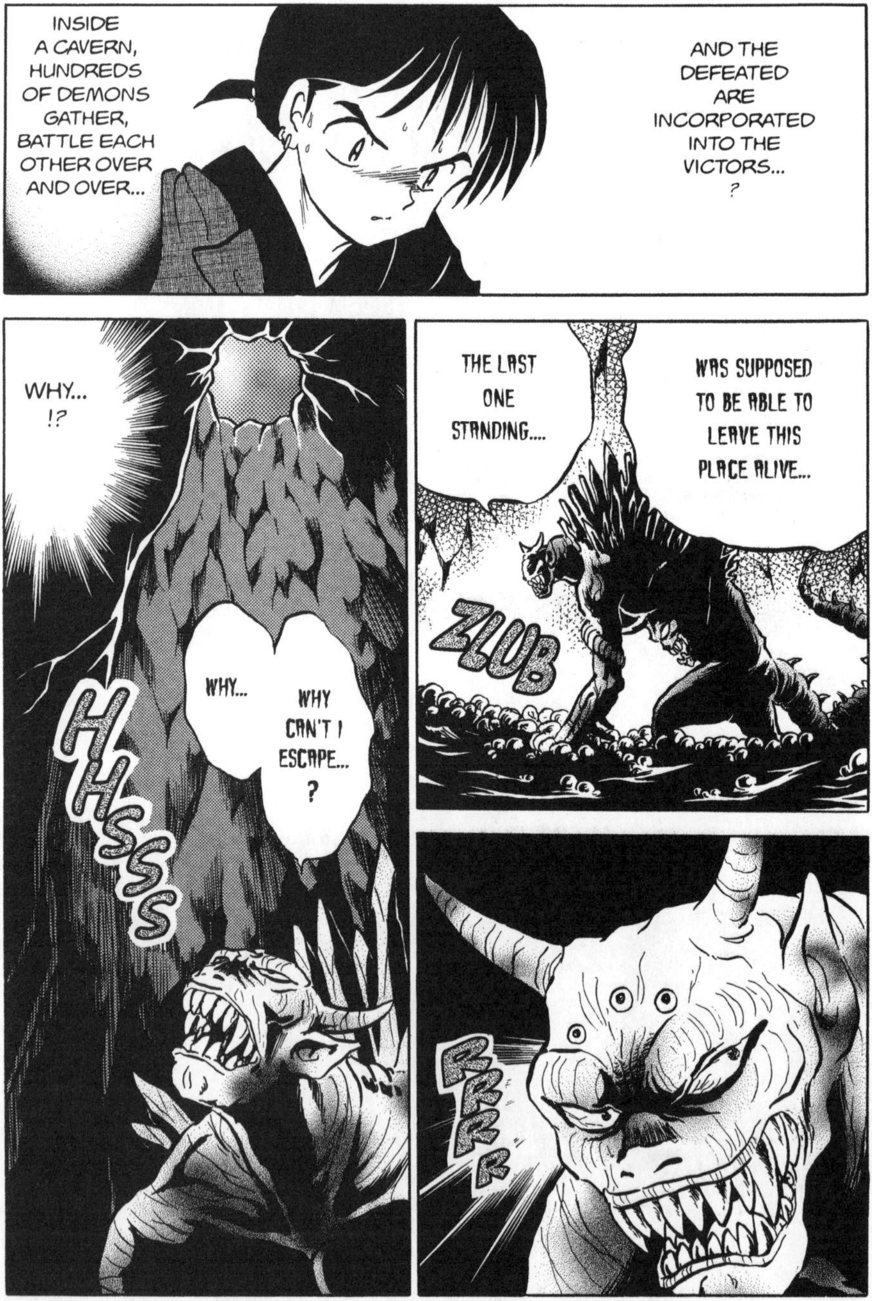
INSIDE A CAVERN, HUNDREDS OF DEMONS GATHER, BATTLE EACH OTHER OVER AND OVER...
AND THE DEFEATED ARE INCORPORATED INTO THE VICTORS...?
WHY...!?
WHY...
WHY CAN'T I ESCAPE...?
HHSSSS
THE LAST ONE STANDING....
WAS SUPPOSED TO BE ABLE TO LEAVE THIS PLACE ALIVE...
ZLUB
RRRRR

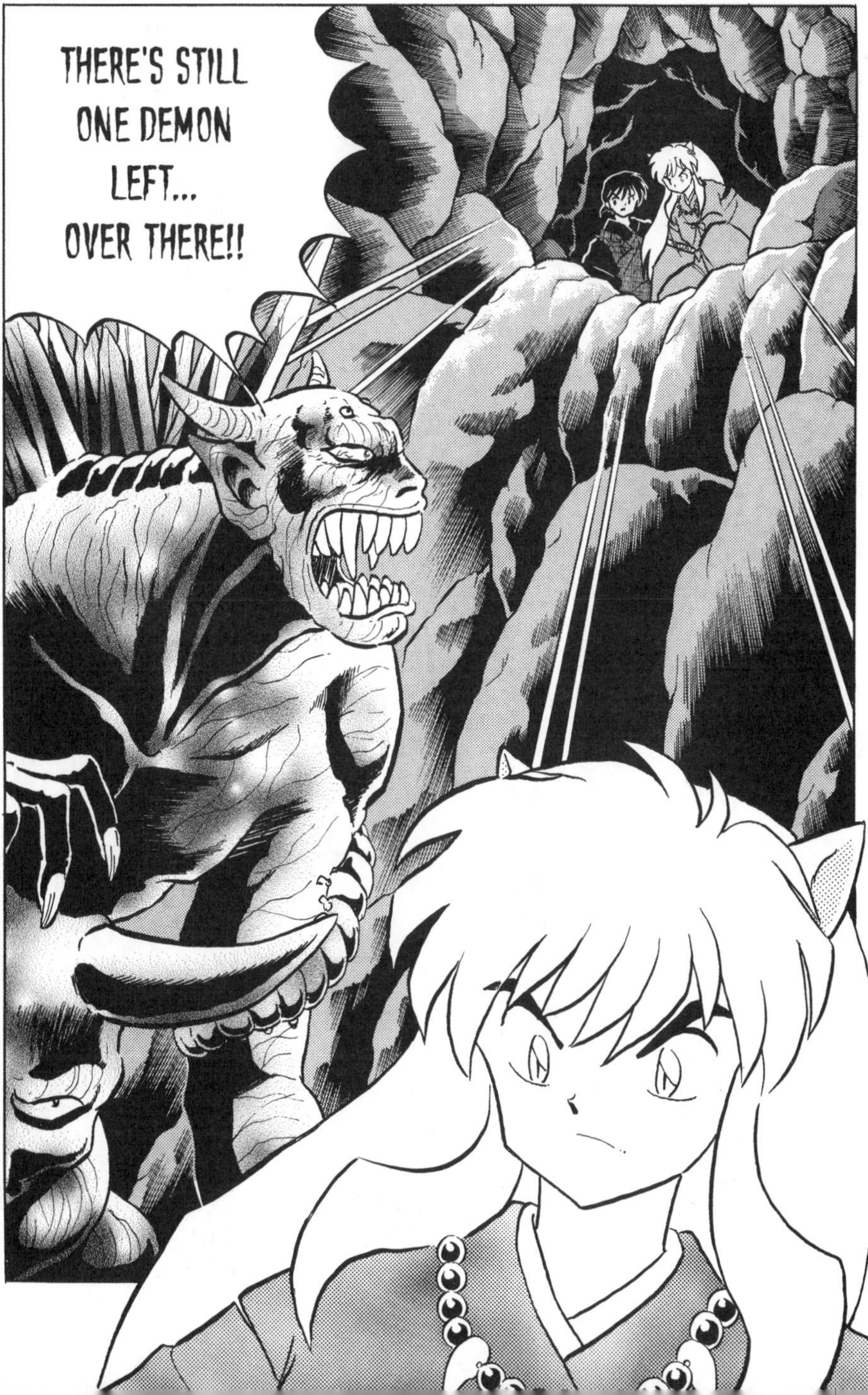
THERE'S STILL ONE DEMON LEFT... OVER THERE!!

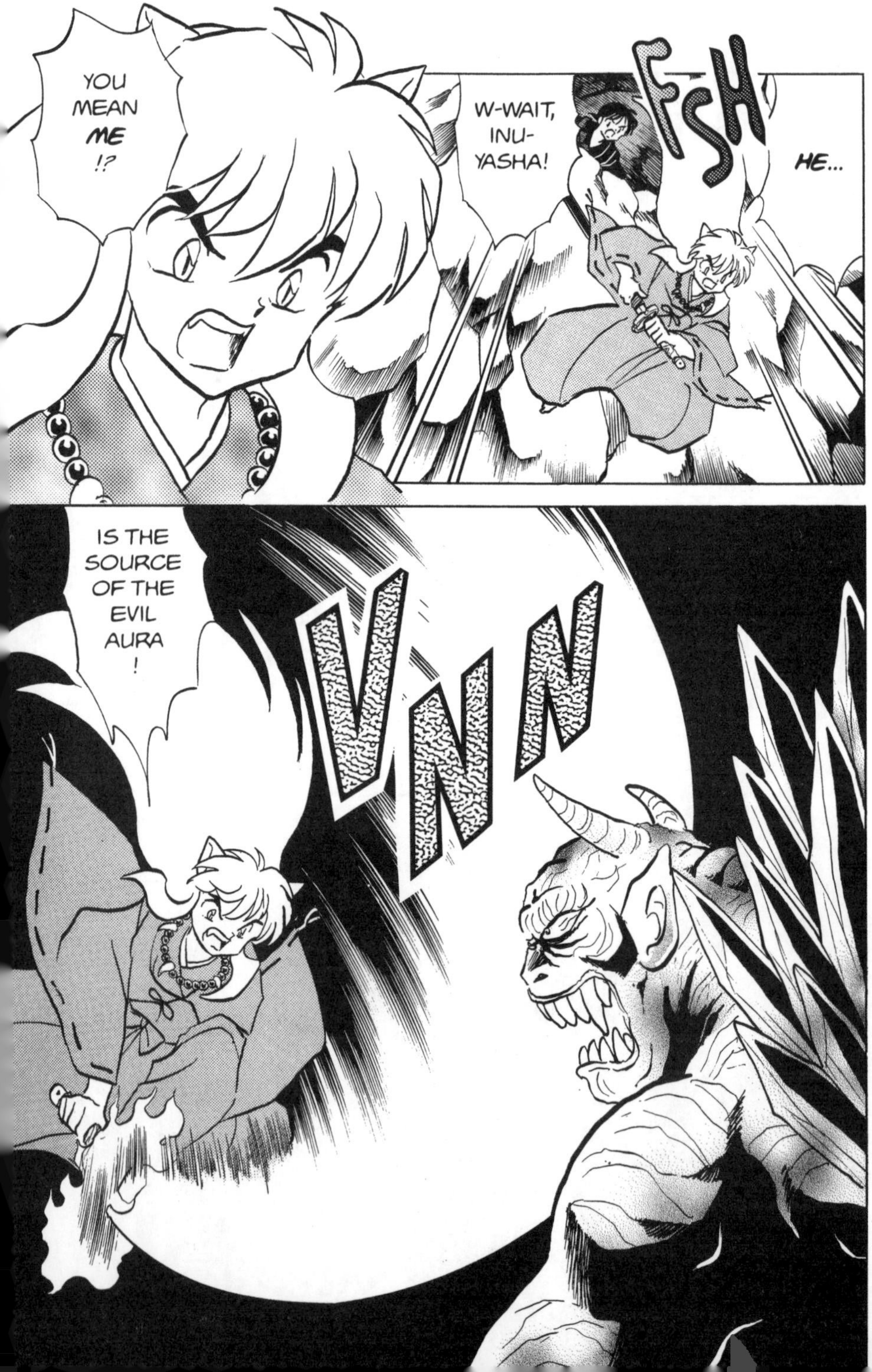
YOU MEAN ME !?
W-WAIT, INU-YASHA!
FSH
HE...
IS THE SOURCE OF THE EVIL AURA !
VNN

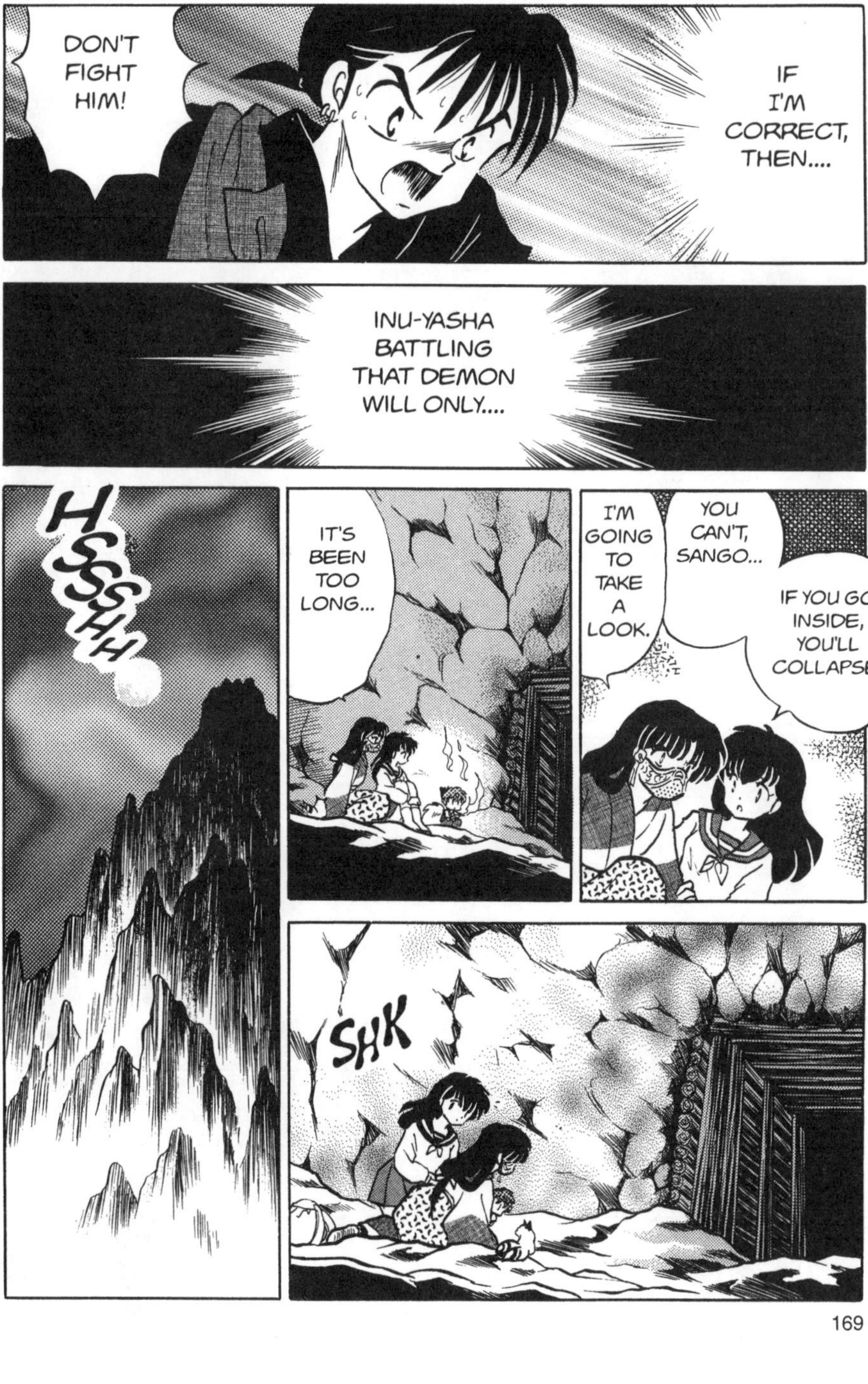
DON'T FIGHT HIM!
IF I'M CORRECT, THEN....
INU-YASHA BATTLING THAT DEMON WILL ONLY....
HSSSHH
IT'S BEEN TOO LONG...
I'M GOING TO TAKE A LOOK.
YOU CAN'T, SANGO...
IF YOU GO INSIDE, YOU'LL COLLAPSE.
SHK

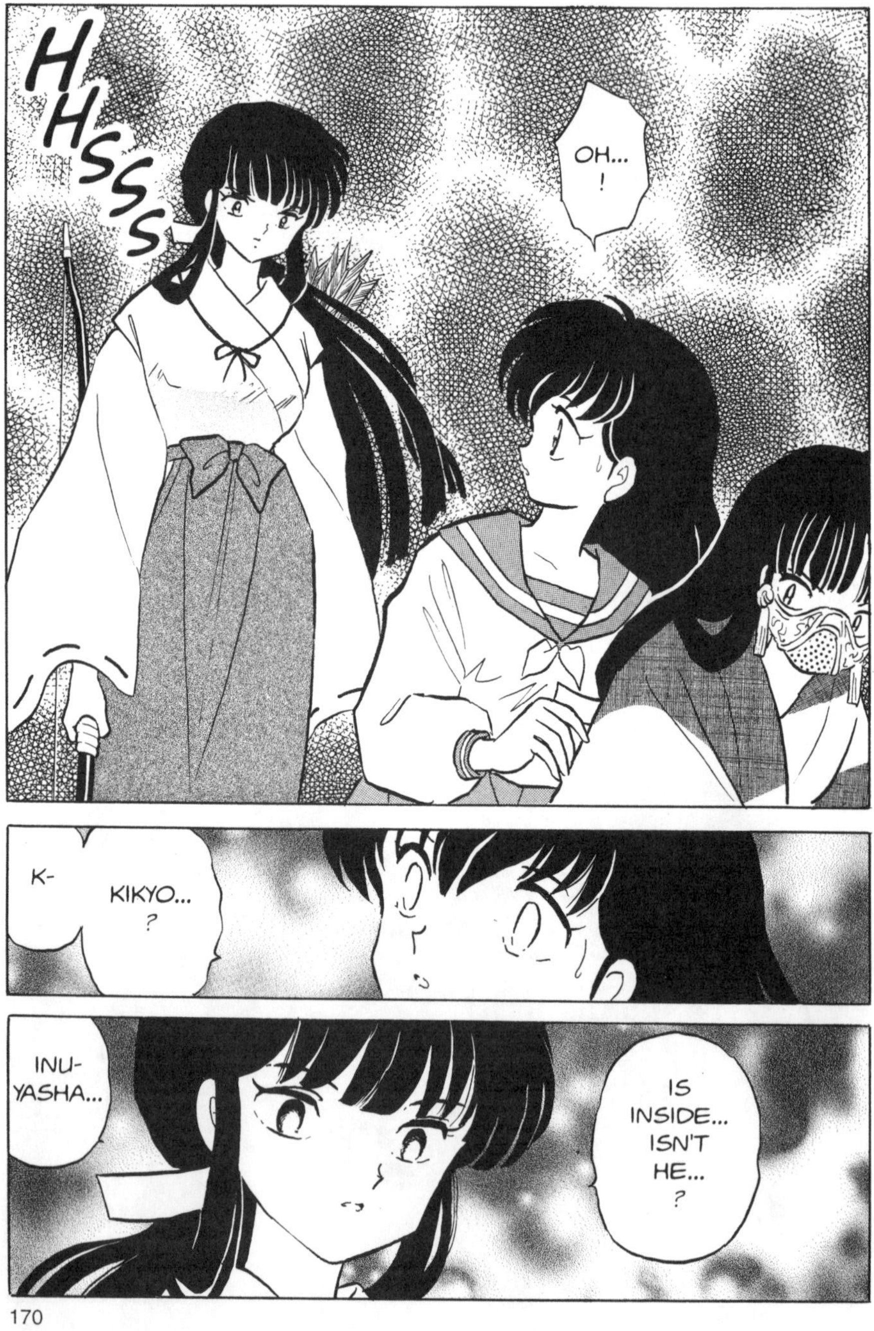
HHSSSS
OH... !
K-
KIKYO... ?
INU-YASHA...
IS INSIDE... ISN'T HE... ?

SCROLL TEN
POISON

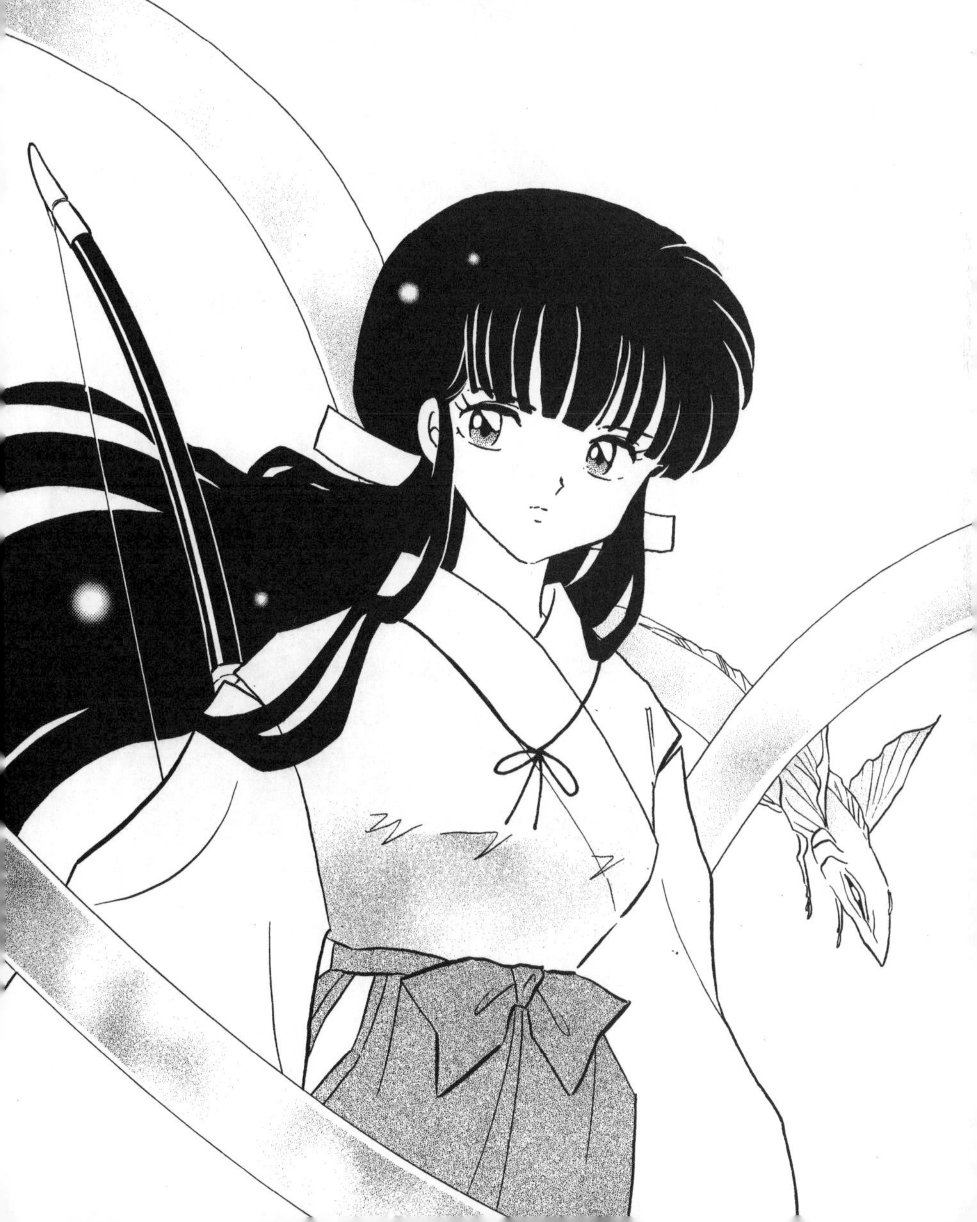

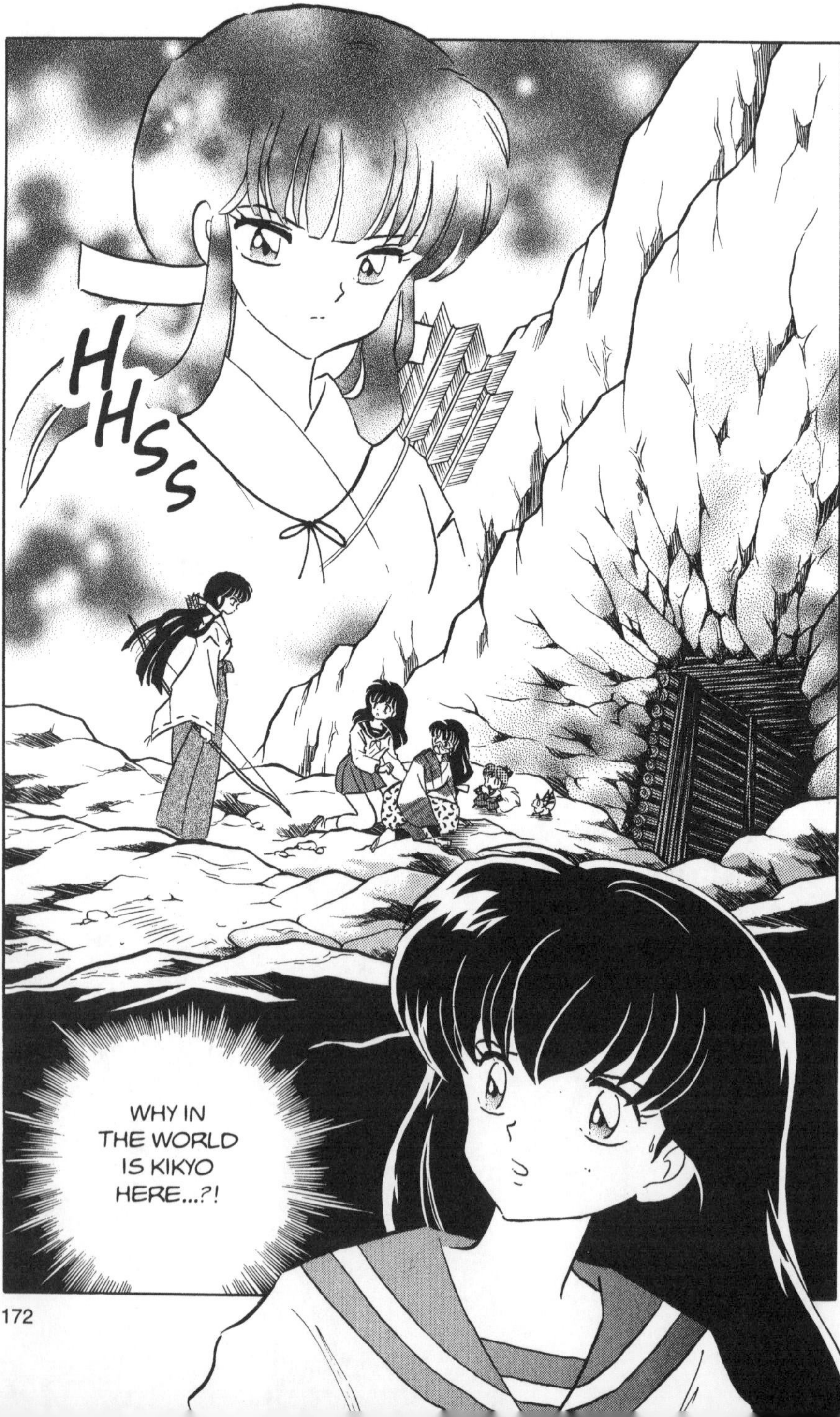
HHSS
WHY IN THE WORLD IS KIKYO HERE...?!

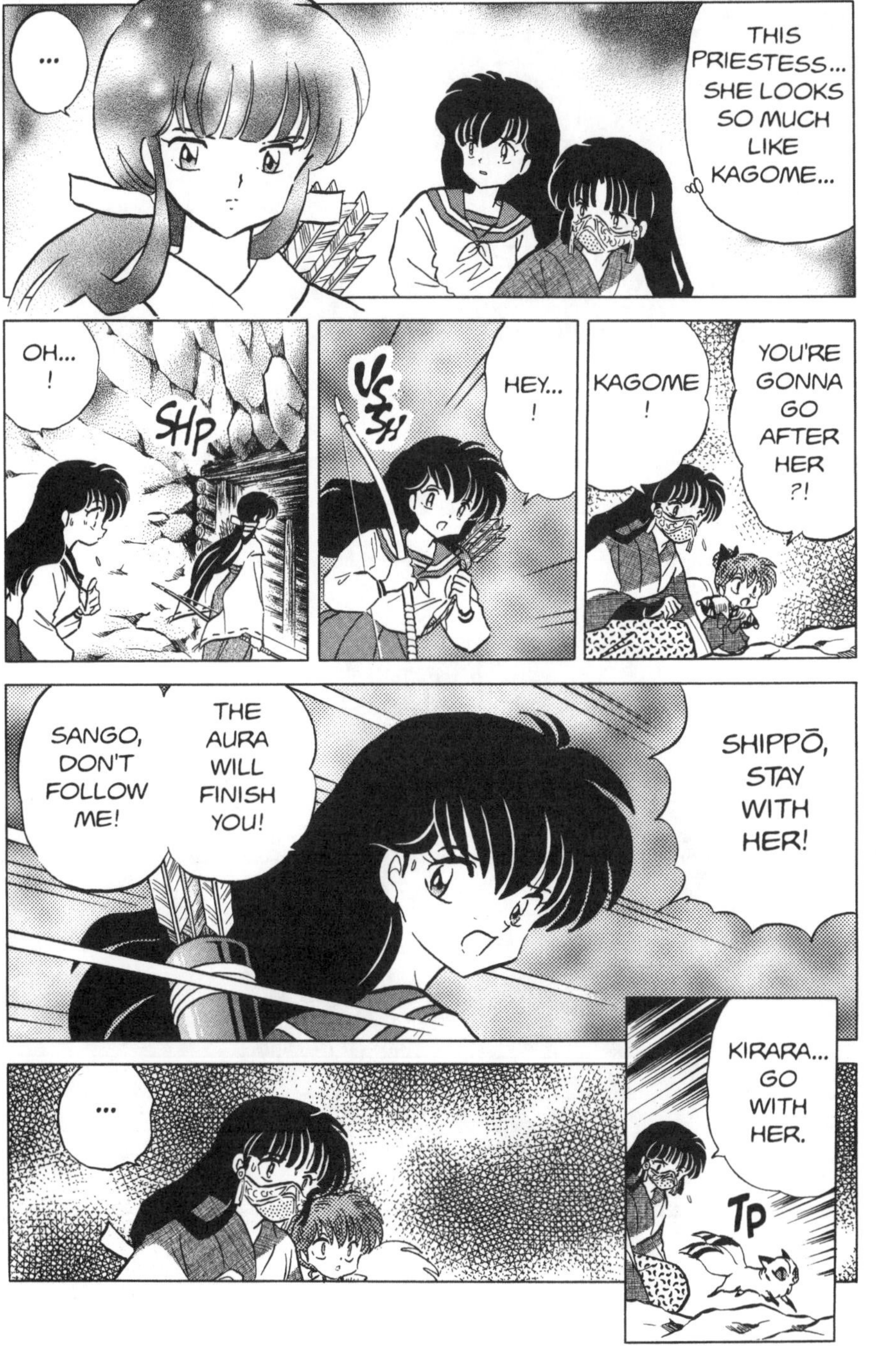
...
THIS PRIESTESS... SHE LOOKS SO MUCH LIKE KAGOME...
OH... !
SHP
VSSH
HEY... !
KAGOME !
YOU'RE GONNA GO AFTER HER ?!
SANGO, DON'T FOLLOW ME!
THE AURA WILL FINISH YOU!
SHIPPŌ, STAY WITH HER!
...
KIRARA... GO WITH HER.
TP

THAT PRIEST-ESS...

IS KIKYO.

THE WOMAN INU-YASHA USED TO LOVE... A LONG TIME AGO.

SHF

HWOOOO

THE DEAD SOULS INSIDE ME ARE TRYING TO GET OUT.

ARE THEY DRAWN TO THE EVIL AURA IN THIS CAVE...?

HHHSSSS

AND...IS INU-YASHA IN THERE... ?

HWOOOOO

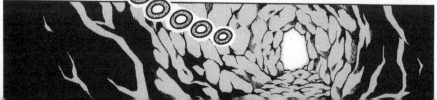

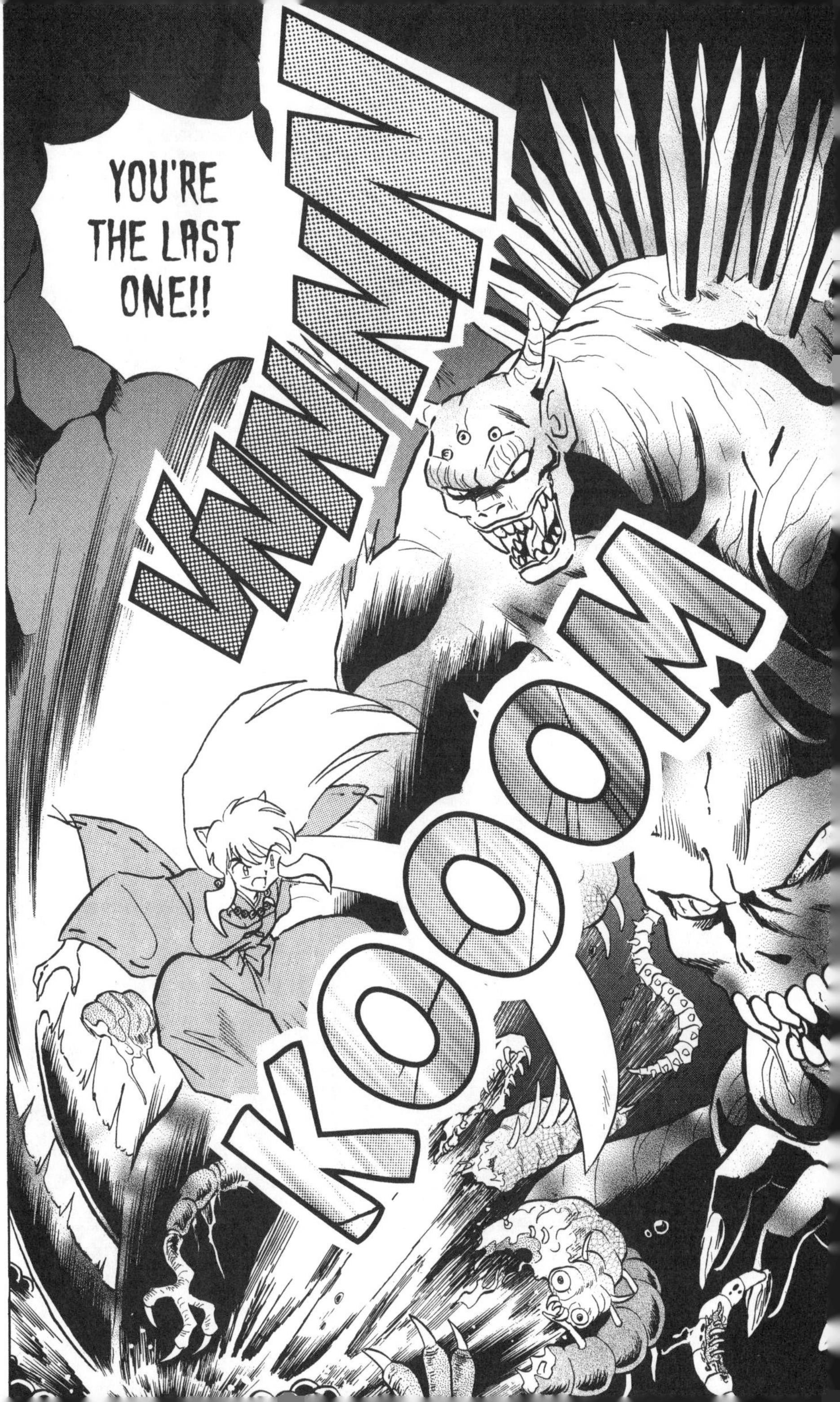
YOU'RE THE LAST ONE!!
VWWWWM
KOOOOM

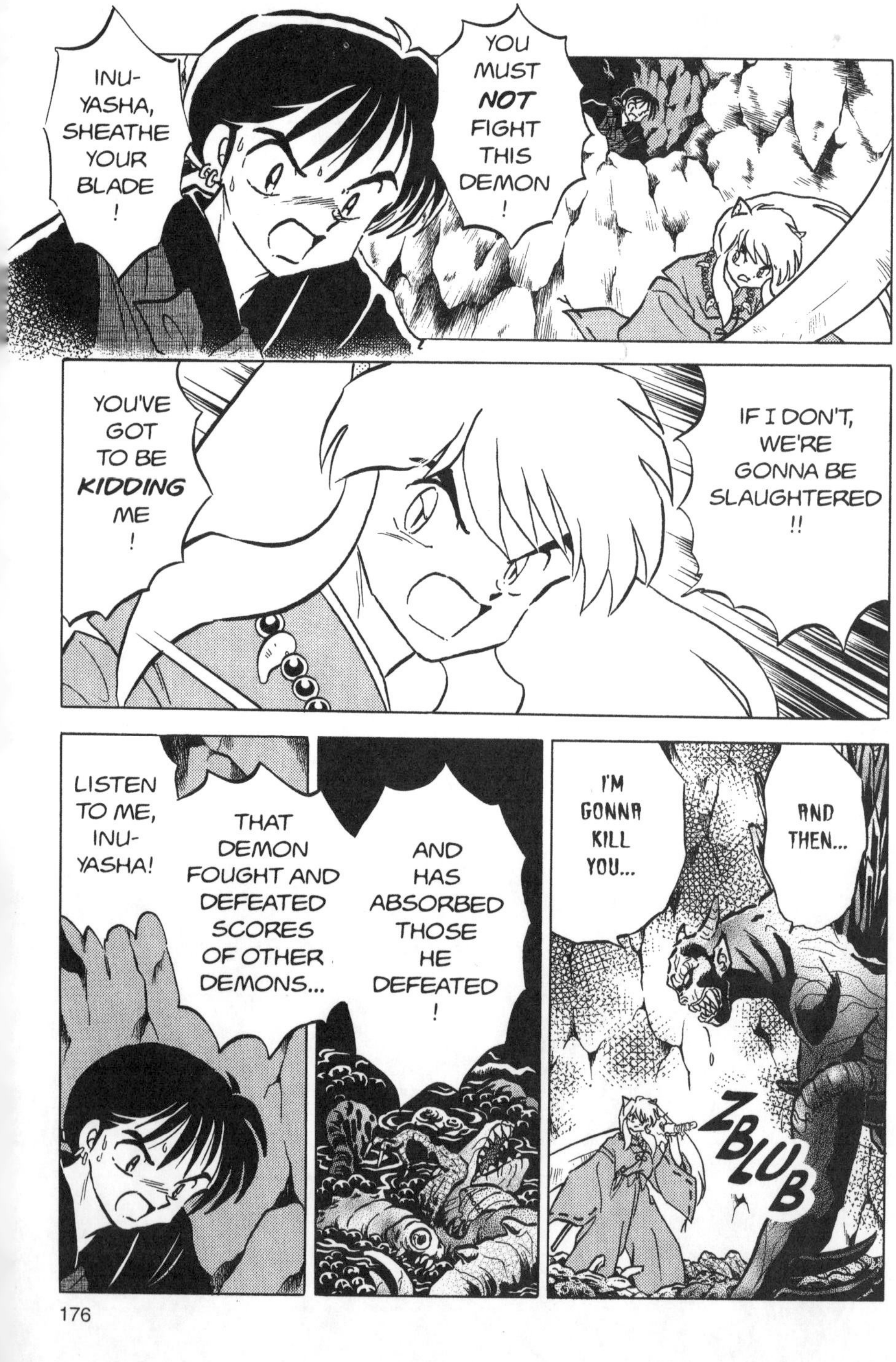
INU-YASHA, SHEATHE YOUR BLADE!
YOU MUST **NOT** FIGHT THIS DEMON!
YOU'VE GOT TO BE **KIDDING** ME!
IF I DON'T, WE'RE GONNA BE SLAUGHTERED!!
LISTEN TO ME, INU-YASHA!
THAT DEMON FOUGHT AND DEFEATED SCORES OF OTHER DEMONS...
AND HAS ABSORBED THOSE HE DEFEATED!
I'M GONNA KILL YOU...
AND THEN...
ZBLUB

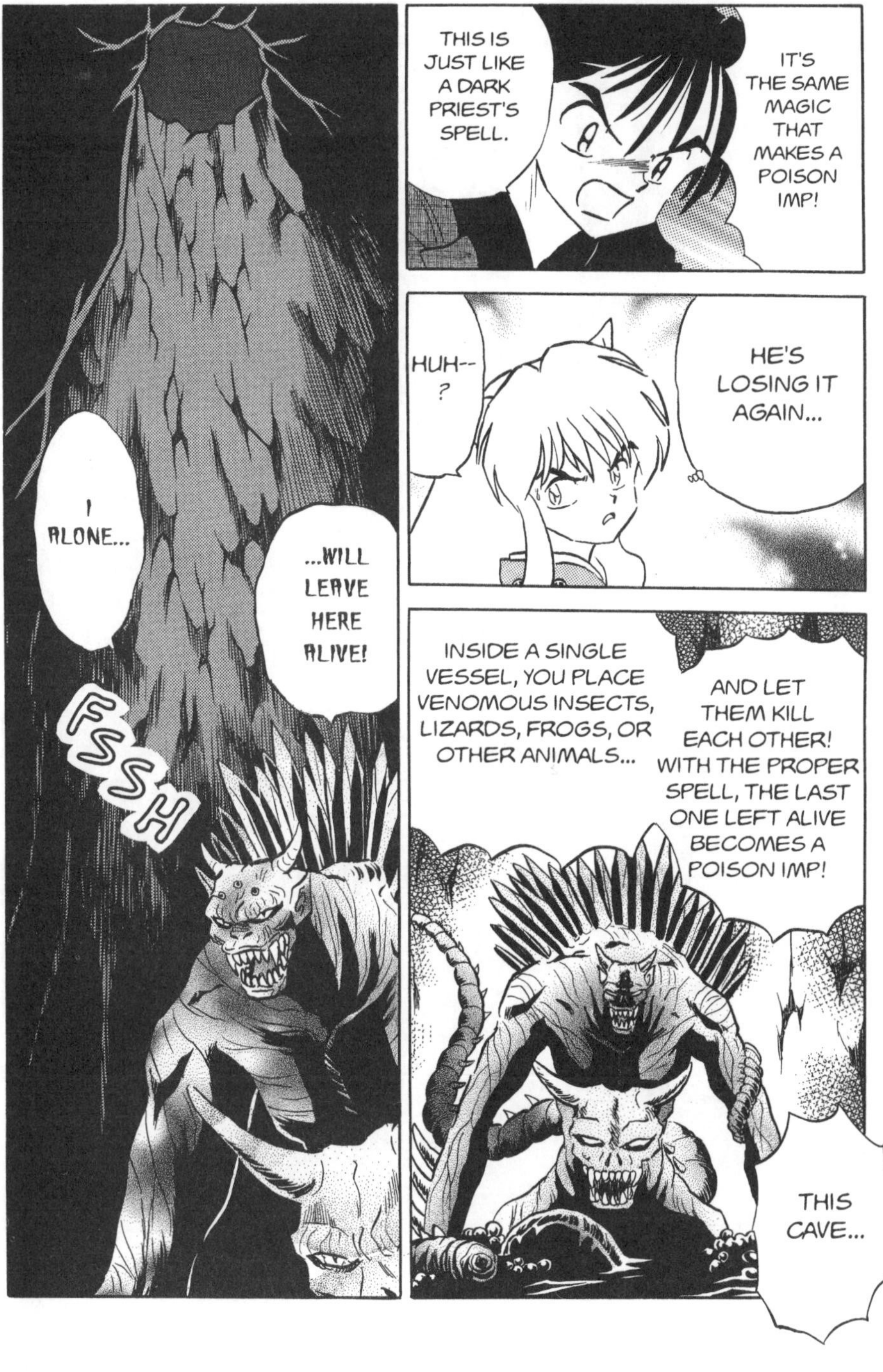
I ALONE...
...WILL LEAVE HERE ALIVE!
FSSH
THIS IS JUST LIKE A DARK PRIEST'S SPELL.
IT'S THE SAME MAGIC THAT MAKES A POISON IMP!
HUH--?
HE'S LOSING IT AGAIN...
INSIDE A SINGLE VESSEL, YOU PLACE VENOMOUS INSECTS, LIZARDS, FROGS, OR OTHER ANIMALS...
AND LET THEM KILL EACH OTHER! WITH THE PROPER SPELL, THE LAST ONE LEFT ALIVE BECOMES A POISON IMP!
THIS CAVE...

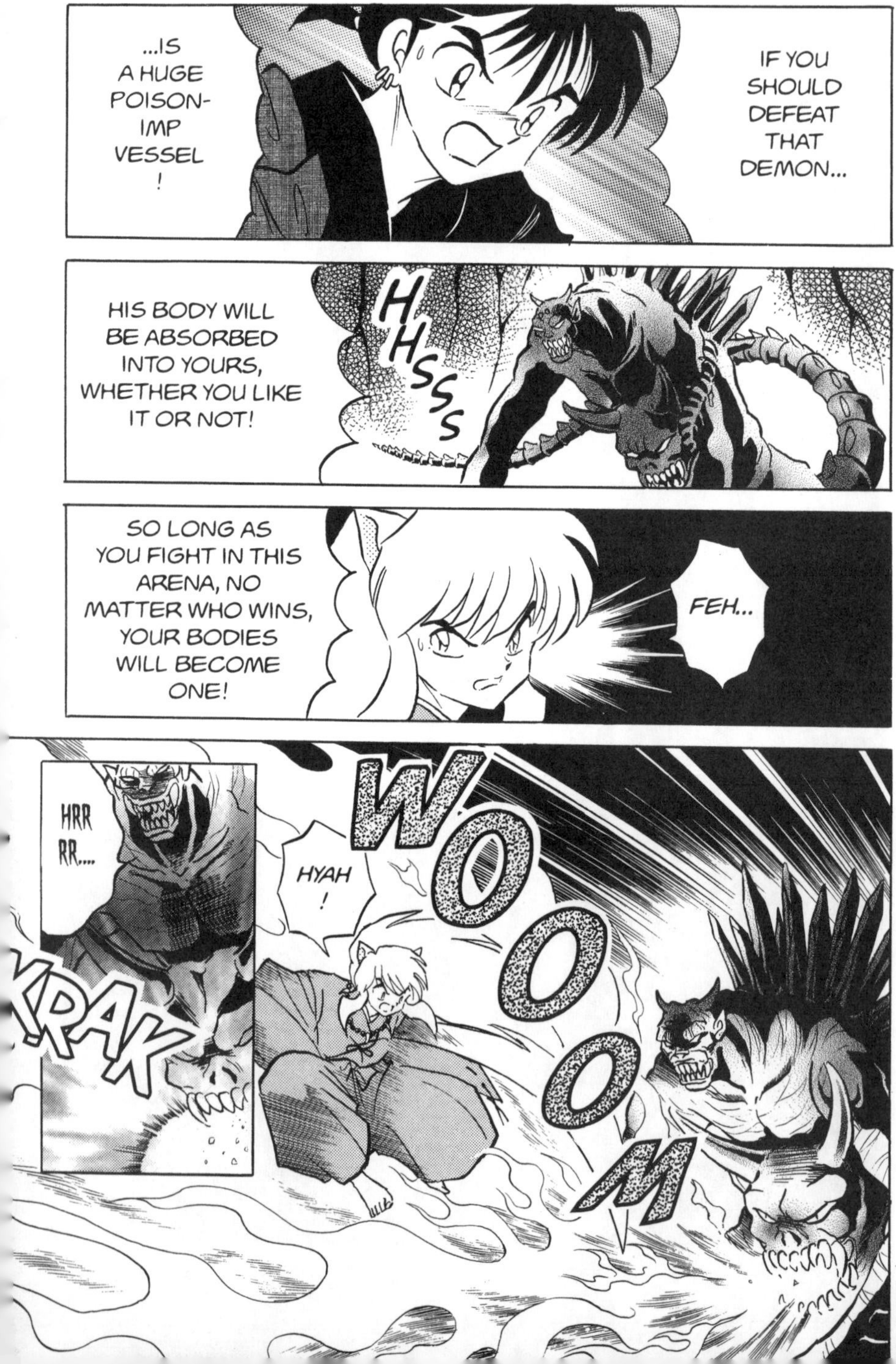
...IS A HUGE POISON-IMP VESSEL!
IF YOU SHOULD DEFEAT THAT DEMON...
HIS BODY WILL BE ABSORBED INTO YOURS, WHETHER YOU LIKE IT OR NOT!
HHSSS
SO LONG AS YOU FIGHT IN THIS ARENA, NO MATTER WHO WINS, YOUR BODIES WILL BECOME ONE!
FEH...
HRR RR....
KRAK
HYAH!
WOOOOM

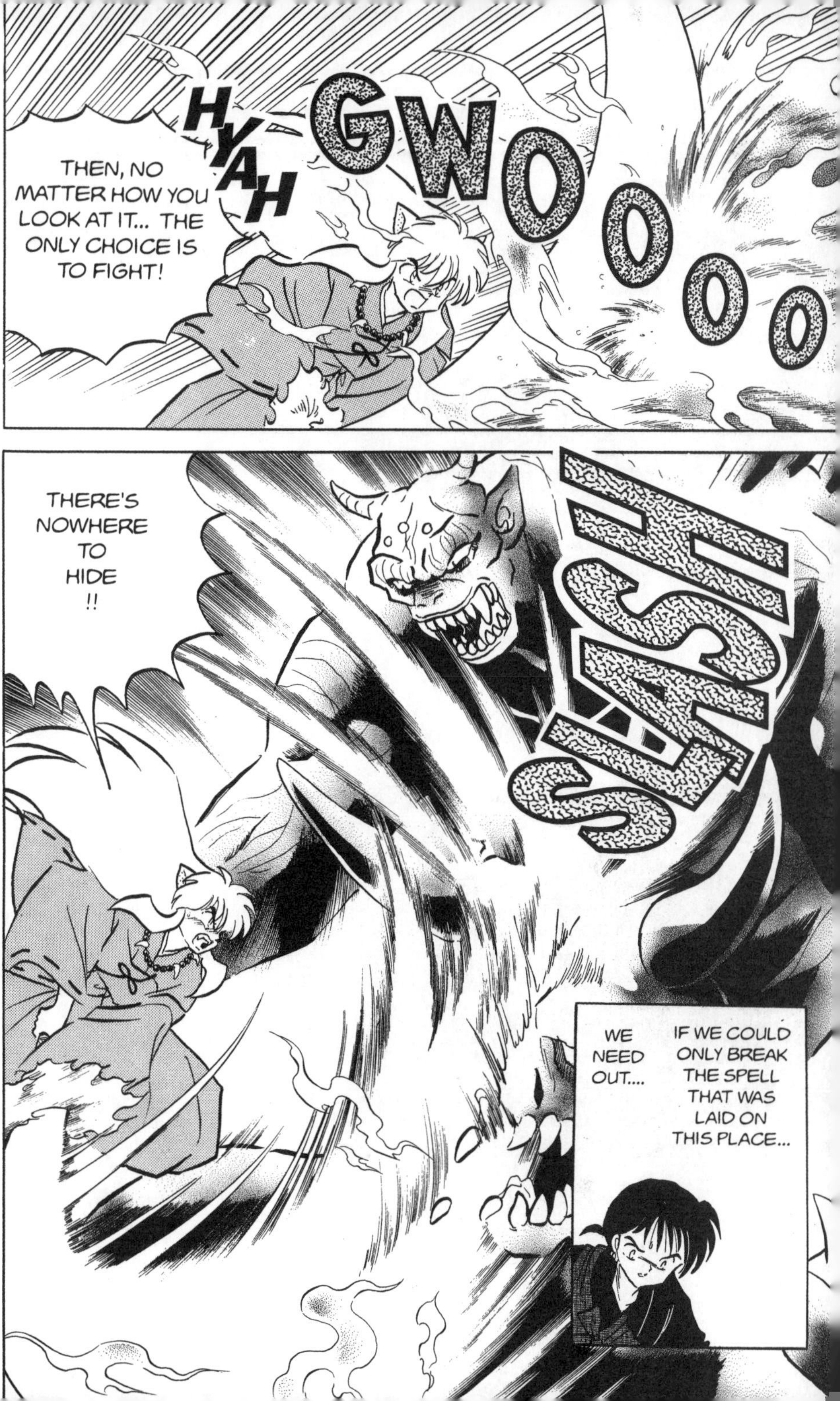
THEN, NO MATTER HOW YOU LOOK AT IT... THE ONLY CHOICE IS TO FIGHT!
HYAH
GWOOOOOO
THERE'S NOWHERE TO HIDE !!
SLASH
WE NEED OUT....
IF WE COULD ONLY BREAK THE SPELL THAT WAS LAID ON THIS PLACE...

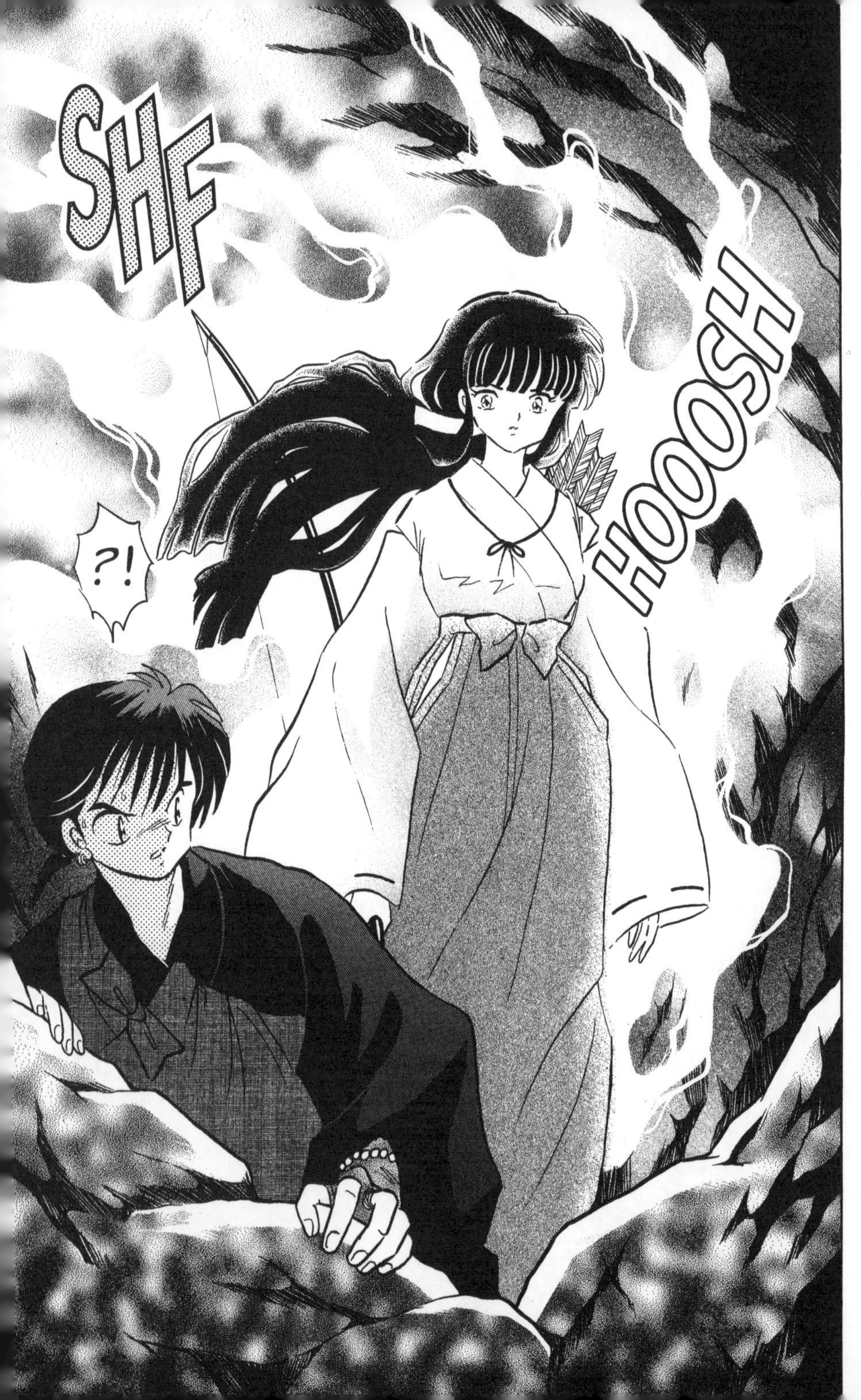
SHF
?!
HOOOSH

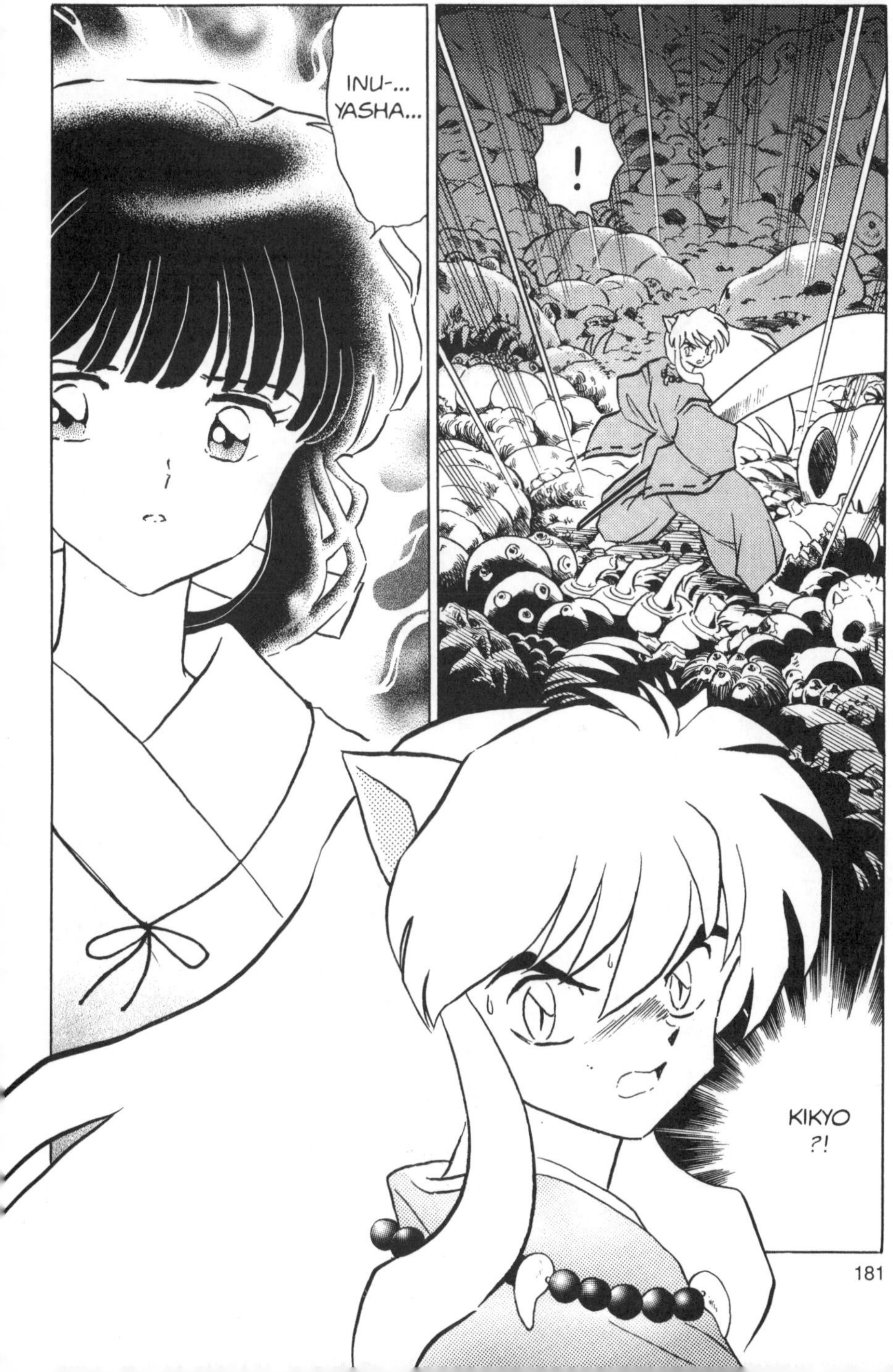
INU-...
YASHA...
!
KIKYO
?!

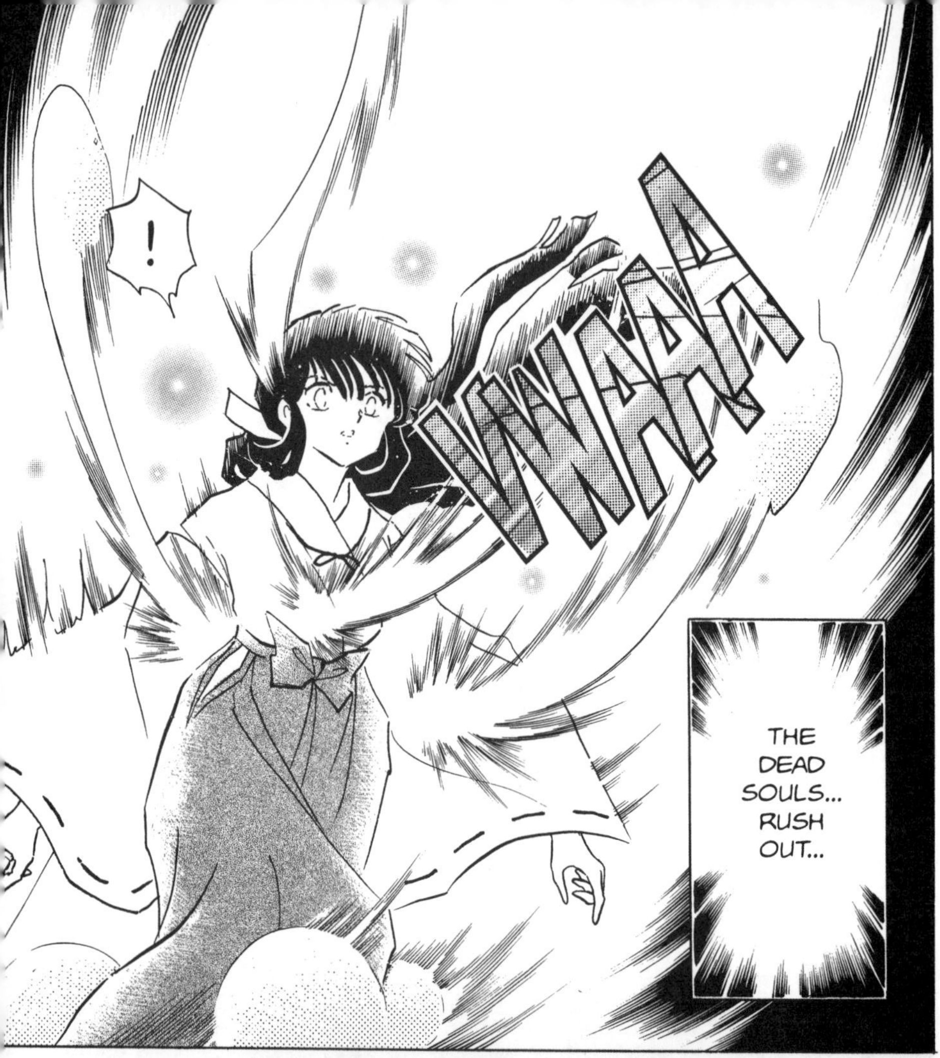
!
THE DEAD SOULS... RUSH OUT...

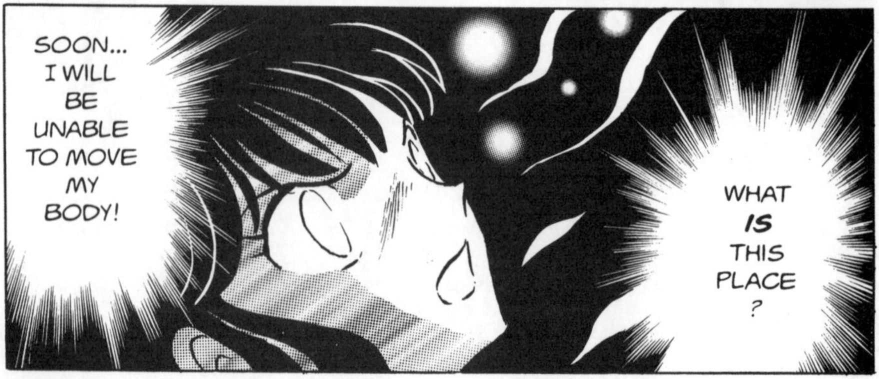
SOON... I WILL BE UNABLE TO MOVE MY BODY!
WHAT *IS* THIS PLACE?

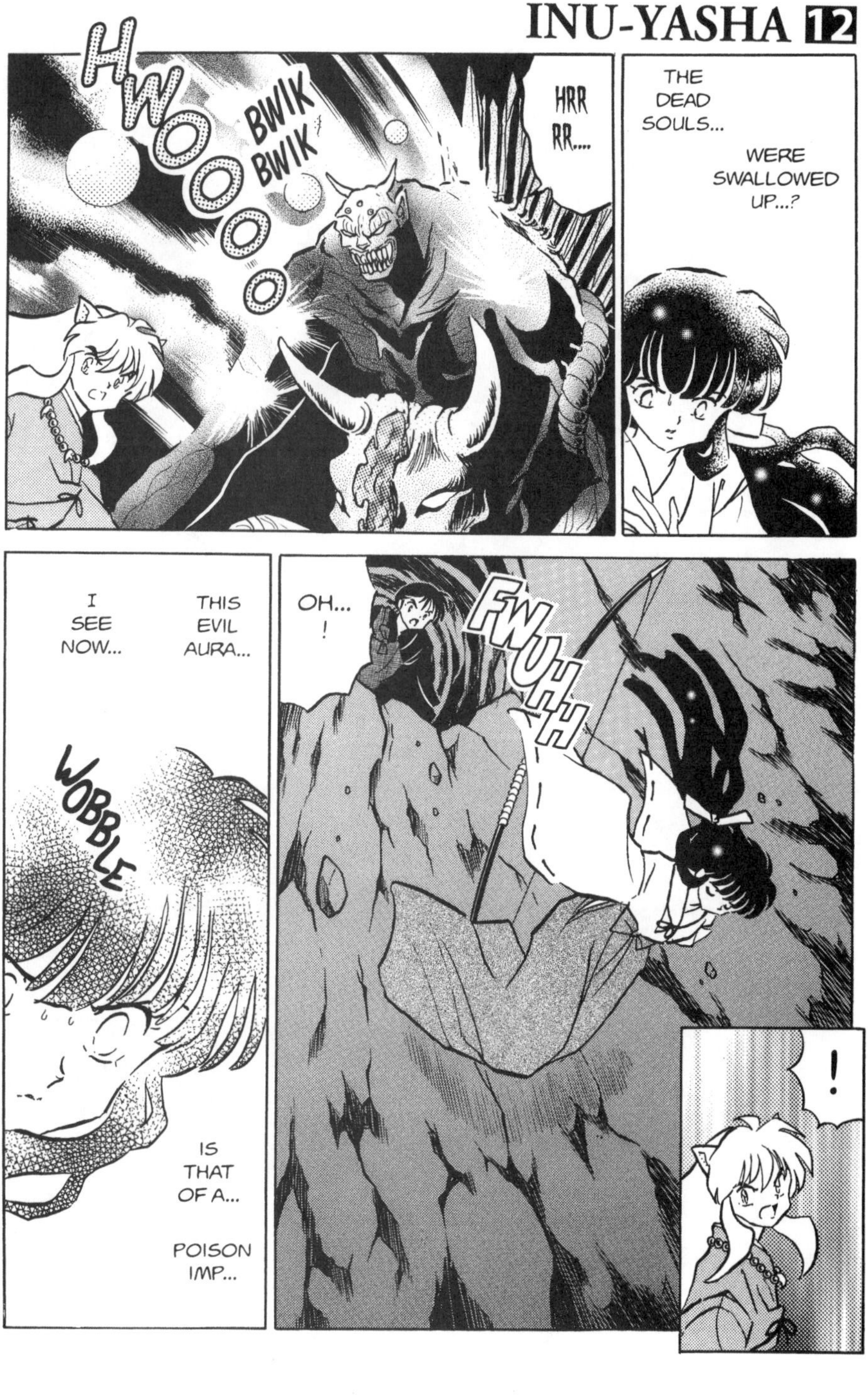
HWOOOOO
BWIK BWIK
HRR RR....
THE DEAD SOULS...
WERE SWALLOWED UP...?
I SEE NOW...
THIS EVIL AURA...
WOBBLE
IS THAT OF A...
POISON IMP...
OH... !
FWUHH
!

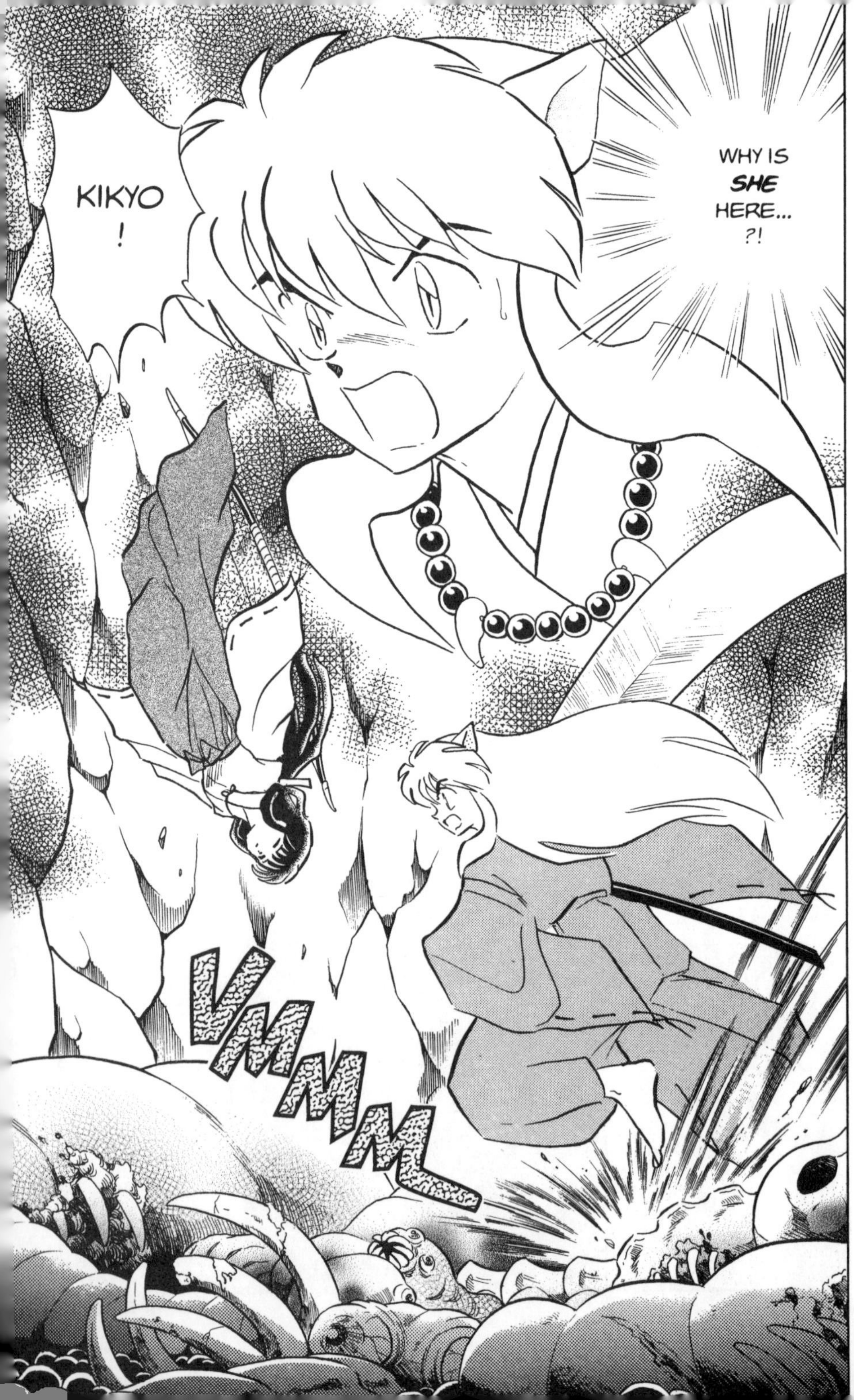
KIKYO
!
WHY IS *SHE* HERE...
?!
VMMMML

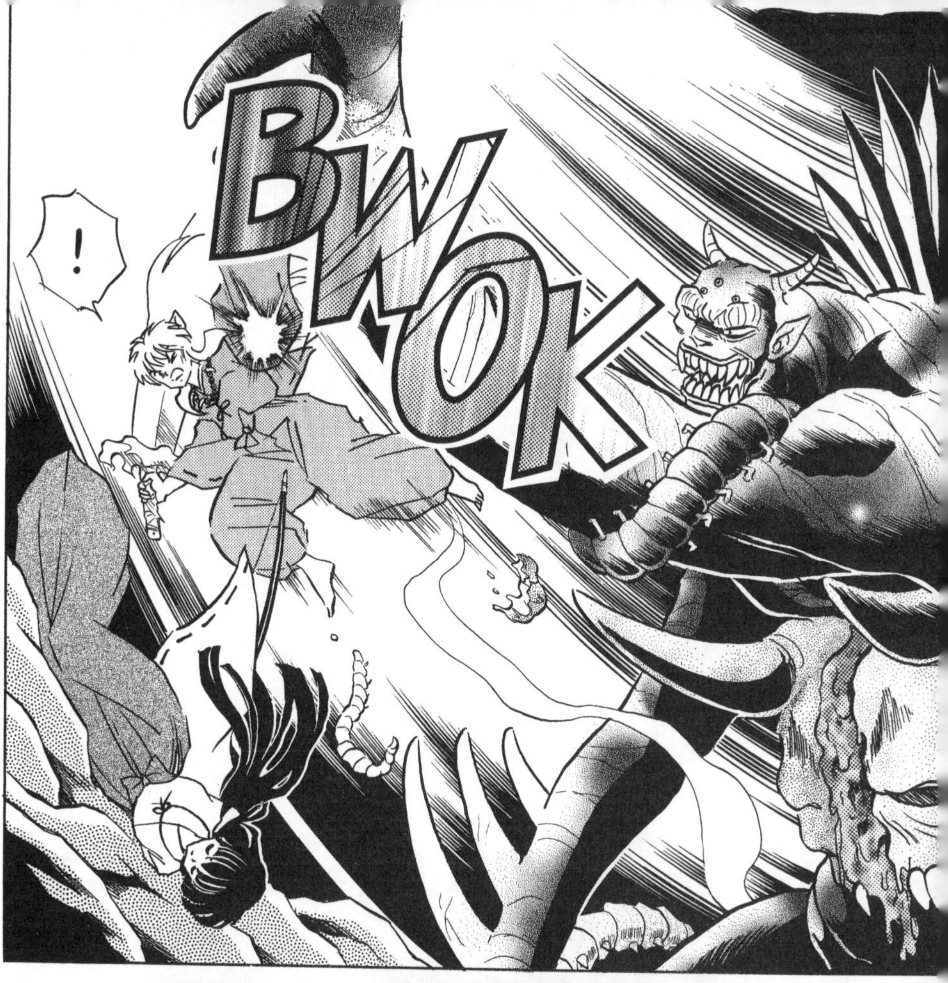
!
BWOK
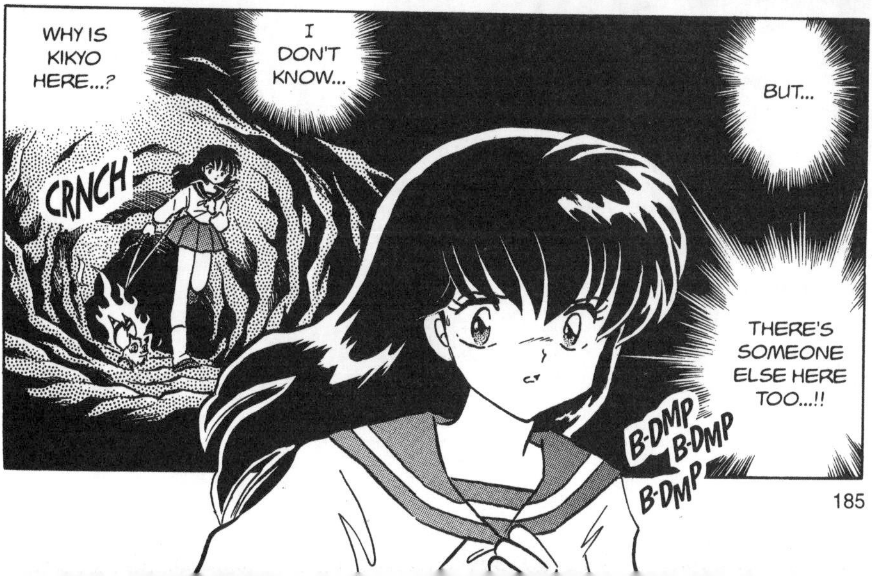
WHY IS KIKYO HERE...?
I DON'T KNOW...
BUT...
CRNCH
THERE'S SOMEONE ELSE HERE TOO...!!
B-DMP B-DMP B-DMP

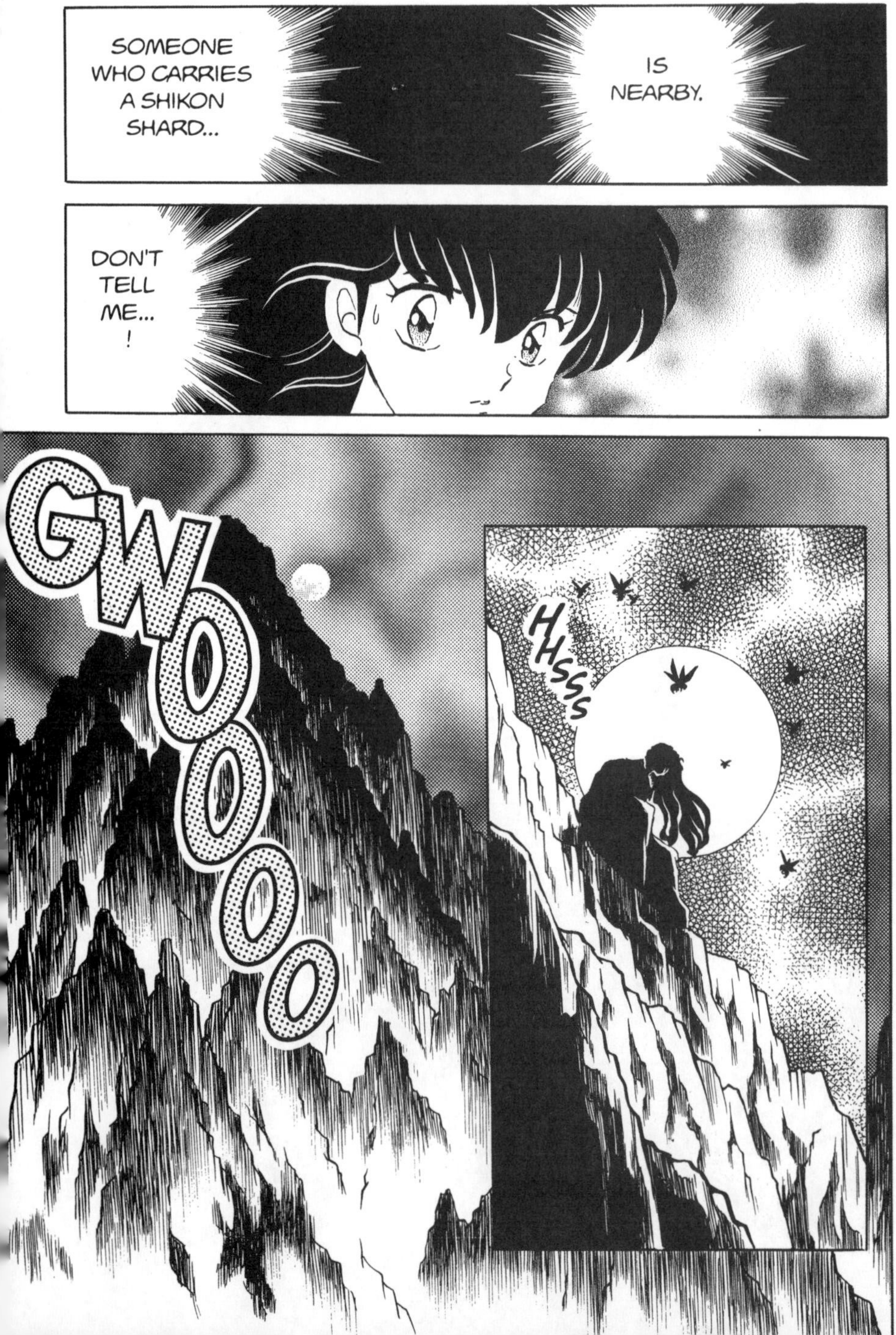
SOMEONE WHO CARRIES A SHIKON SHARD...
IS NEARBY.
DON'T TELL ME... !
GWOOOOO
HHSSS

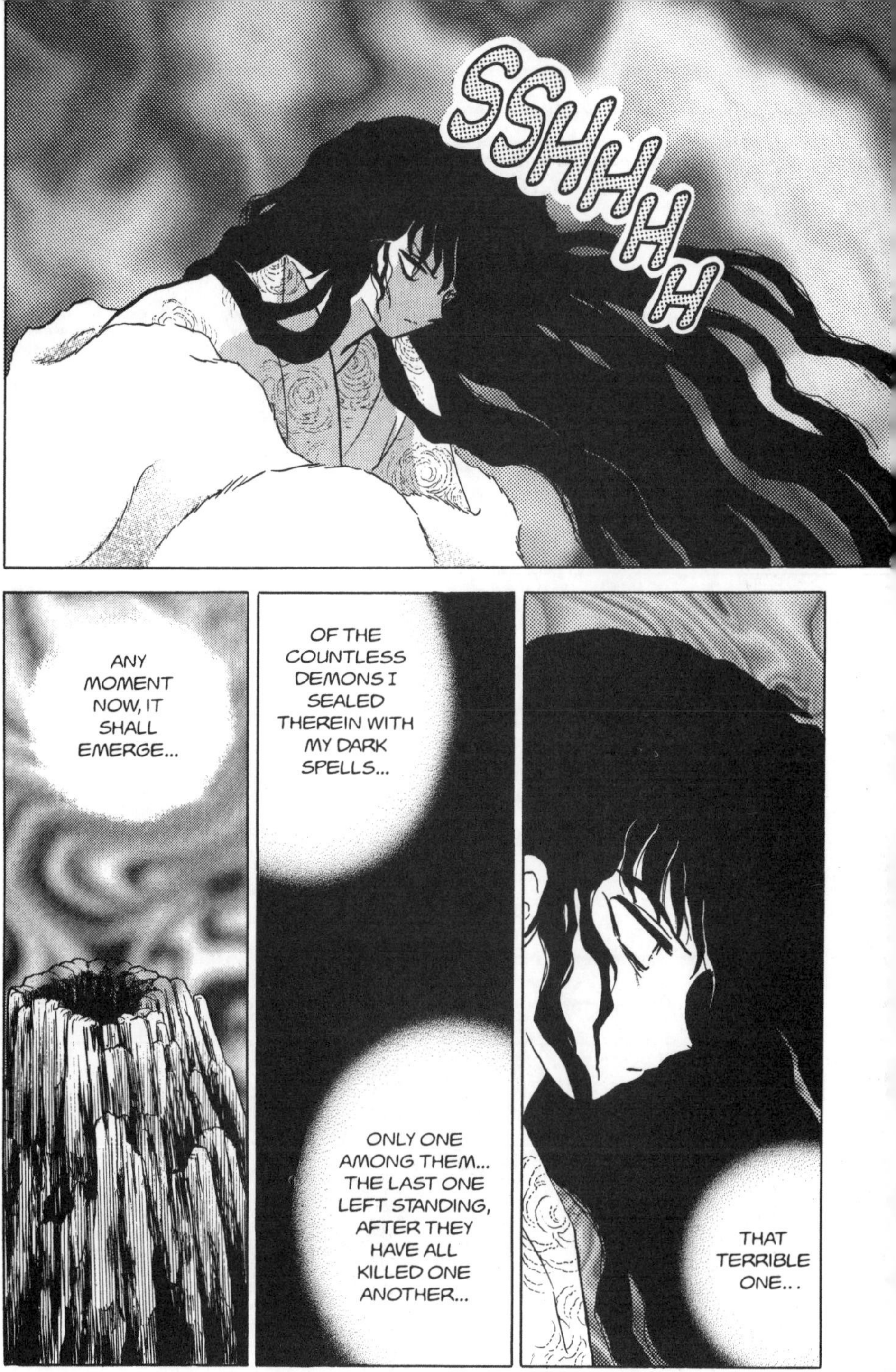
SSHHHH
ANY MOMENT NOW, IT SHALL EMERGE...
OF THE COUNTLESS DEMONS I SEALED THEREIN WITH MY DARK SPELLS...
ONLY ONE AMONG THEM... THE LAST ONE LEFT STANDING, AFTER THEY HAVE ALL KILLED ONE ANOTHER...
THAT TERRIBLE ONE...

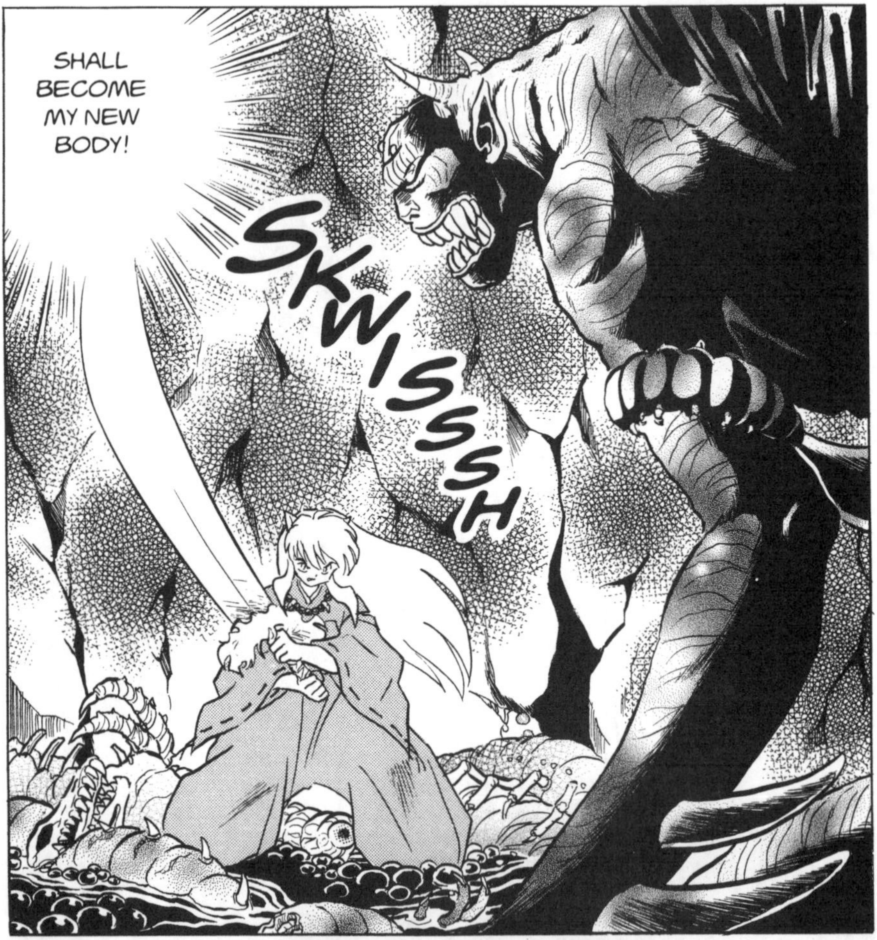
SHALL BECOME MY NEW BODY!
SKWISSSH
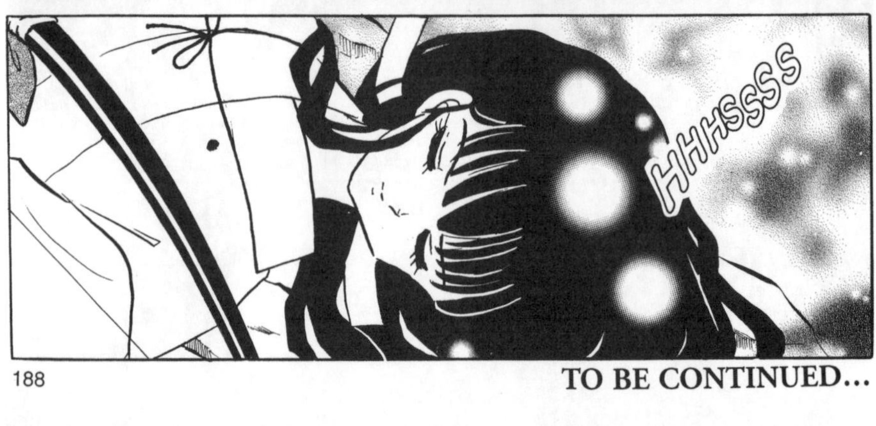
HHHSSSS

TO BE CONTINUED...

Rumiko Takahashi

Rumiko Takahashi was born in 1957 in Niigata, Japan. She attended women's college in Tokyo, where she began studying comics with Kazuo Koike, author of *Crying Freeman*. She later became an assistant to horror-manga artist Kazuo Umezu (*Orochi*). In 1978, she won a prize in Shogakukan's annual "New Comic Artist Contest," and in that same year her boy-meets-alien comedy series *Lum*Urusei Yatsura* began appearing in the weekly manga magazine *SHŌNEN SUNDAY*. This phenomenally successful series ran for nine years and sold over 22 million copies. Takahashi's later *Ranma 1/2* series enjoyed even greater popularity.

Takahashi is considered by many to be one of the world's most popular manga artists. With the publication of Volume 34 of her *Ranma 1/2* series in Japan, Takahashi's total sales passed *one hundred million* copies of her compiled works.

Takahashi's serial titles include *Lum*Urusei Yatsura*, *Ranma 1/2*, *One-Pound Gospel*, *Maison Ikkoku* and *Inu-Yasha*. Additionally, Takahashi has drawn many short stories which have been published in America under the title "Rumic Theater," and several installments of a saga known as her "Mermaid" series. Most of Takahashi's major stories have also been animated, and are widely available in translation worldwide. *Inu-Yasha* is her most recent serial story, first published in *SHŌNEN SUNDAY* in 1996.

"TAKAHASHI MAKES IT FRESH AND AMUSING, TIME AND TIME AGAIN."

—ANODYNE MAGAZINE

Ranma 1/2

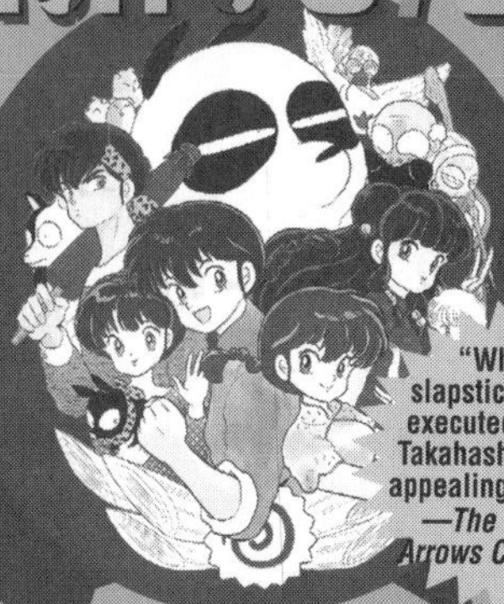

"Whimsical slapstick, elegantly executed by Rumiko Takahashi...solid and appealing characters."
—*The Slings and Arrows Comics Guide*

The *manga cum laude* of sex-changing, martial arts high school romantic comedies!

LUM
URUSEI YATSURA

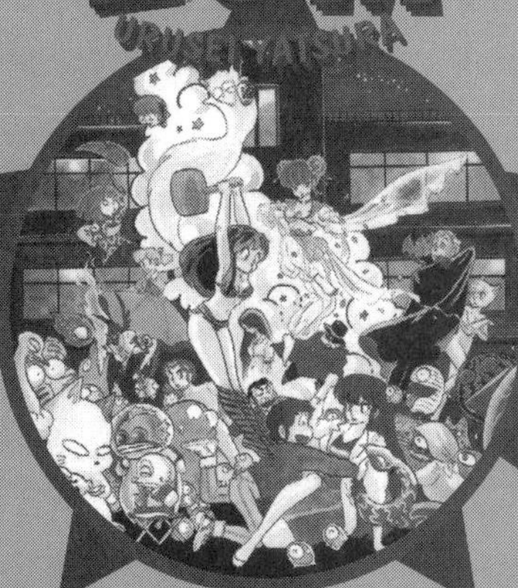

Sci-fi mayhem with an alien princess and the world's most lecherous teenage loser!

MAISON IKKOKU

"A fine achievement in comics storytelling... engaging, entertaining, and addictive."
—www.amazon.com

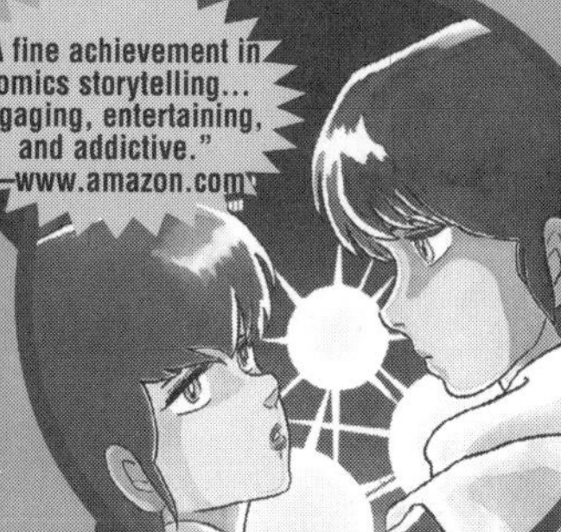

Bashful college student Yusaku is in love with his beautiful apartment manager Kyoko... but between romantic rivals and nosy neighbors, will their hearts ever meet?

INU-YASHA
A Feudal Fairy Tale

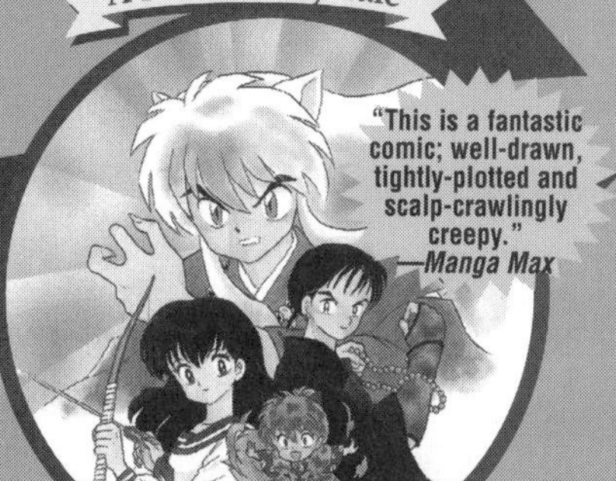

"This is a fantastic comic; well-drawn, tightly-plotted and scalp-crawlingly creepy."
—*Manga Max*

When Japanese schoolgirl Kagome stumbles back in time, she must join forces with half-demon Inu-Yasha to fight monsters of the present and past!

All available from VIZ COMICS

www.viz.com
www.j-pop.com
www.animerica-mag.com

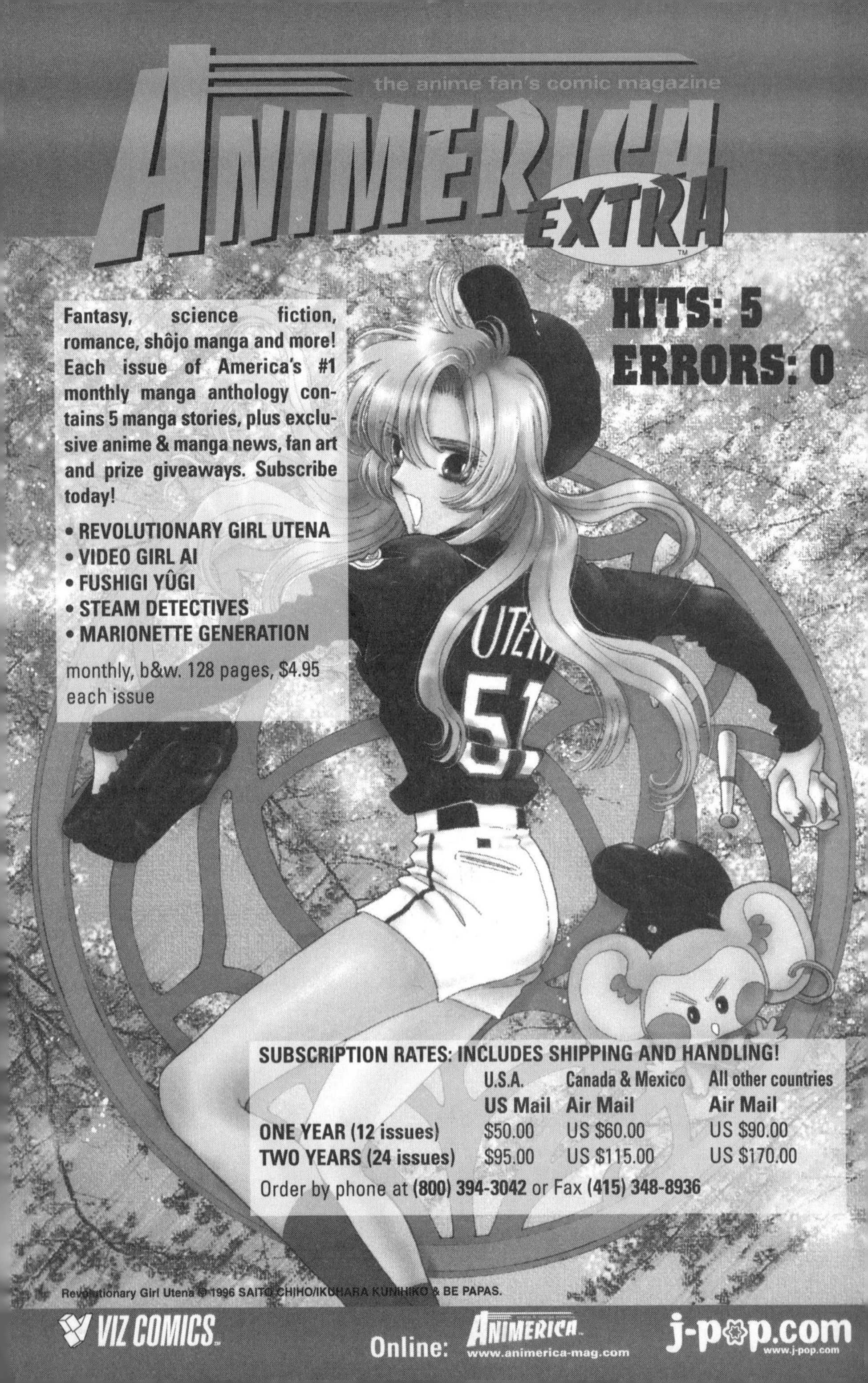
the anime fan's comic magazine
ANIMERICA EXTRA
HITS: 5
ERRORS: 0
Fantasy, science fiction, romance, shôjo manga and more! Each issue of America's #1 monthly manga anthology contains 5 manga stories, plus exclusive anime & manga news, fan art and prize giveaways. Subscribe today!
• REVOLUTIONARY GIRL UTENA
• VIDEO GIRL AI
• FUSHIGI YÛGI
• STEAM DETECTIVES
• MARIONETTE GENERATION
monthly, b&w. 128 pages, $4.95 each issue
UTENA 51
SUBSCRIPTION RATES: INCLUDES SHIPPING AND HANDLING!
U.S.A. US Mail
Canada & Mexico Air Mail
All other countries Air Mail
ONE YEAR (12 issues) $50.00 US $60.00 US $90.00
TWO YEARS (24 issues) $95.00 US $115.00 US $170.00
Order by phone at (800) 394-3042 or Fax (415) 348-8936
Revolutionary Girl Utena © 1996 SAITO CHIHO/IKUHARA KUNIHIKO & BE PAPAS.
VIZ COMICS
Online: ANIMERICA www.animerica-mag.com
j-pop.com www.j-pop.com